MOODY PHILBROOK TUFO

THE
BLEED
RUPTURE

DEVILDOG PRESS

SWANVILLE, MAINE

Rupture; The Bleed: Book One
Copyright © 2020 David Moody, Chris Philbrook, Mark Tufo

All rights reserved. No part of this book may be reproduced or transmitted in any form or by any means, electronic or mechanical, including photocopying, recording, or any information storage and retrieval system, without prior written permission of the author. Your support of author's rights is appreciated.

Published in the United States of America

First Publishing Date 2020

All characters in this work are fictitious. Any resemblance to actual persons, living or dead, is purely coincidental.

Cover by Dean Samed
Interior layout and illustrations by Alan MacRaffen

TABLE OF CONTENTS:

Prologue 9
1: London, Next Week 12
2: Base Station New Start,
   Sea of Crises, Earth's Moon Surface... 36
3: Filthy Halfsies 51
4: London 65
5: The Moon – Day 2 73
6: Don't You Want to be Something? ... 81
7: London 94
8: The Moon – Clive Barrow 113
9: The Red Tide 117
10: The Moon – Day Three 142
11: Coronation 155
12: London 165
13: The Moon – Day Three – 4:45 PM... 185
14: The Trade Road 197
15: London 208
16: The Moon – Day Three – 5:15 PM... 228
17: The Channel 235
18: The Moon – Day Three – 6:16 PM... 248

19: Walking Through Walls 274
20: London 289
21: The Moon – Day Three – 6:36 PM... 298
22: A Feast Fit for Three 319
23: London 334
24: The Moon – Day Three – 6:46 PM... 338
25: Divergent Paths 360
26: London 385
27: The Moon – Day Three – 6:56 PM... 430
28: The Clock Tower 453
29: London 468
30: The Moon – Day Three – 7:07 PM... 472
31: The Great Goodbye 479
Epilogue 1: Nowhere We Know 496
Epilogue 2: No One We Know............ 498

About David Moody......................... 502
About Chris Philbrook 504
About Mark Tufo 506

We would like to thank all of our readers and listeners across the globe for their support. Our careers exist because of your dedication to our writing, and the characters we've dreamed up, and stories we've told. We thank each and every one of you, and hope Rupture, and the other books of The Bleed bring you entertainment.

Prologue

The planet was so old that it didn't have a name. The people who lived there were nameless too. They had evolved and grown over countless generations and had become a strong and complex society. The needs of all individuals were considered; the collective was everything; the past, the present and the future were always in mind.

In this utopian society, the rule of law was sacred. People understood that, for them to remain strong and prosper, their friends, families, and neighbors needed to be strong and prosperous too. And for generation after generation, those principles held true and people worked with each other for collective reward. But the multiverse is a whirlwind of chaos, and sometimes no matter how hard people try to plan for it, chance and circumstance conspire to devastating effect.

An asteroid.

A massive spinning, rolling lump of rock hurtled through the void of space and hit the planet, and though the initial damage of the impact was limited, the long-term implications were stark. Clouds of noxious dust and ash were spewed into the atmosphere, plunging the planet into a brutal ice age. Oceans froze. Crops failed. Millions died. And the millions more who survived now faced the most uncertain of futures.

When there's not enough food to keep everyone alive, how do we decide who lives and who dies?

The ancient society collapsed with terrifying ease and speed.

With the world's equilibrium now out of balance, it became a fight for survival. The society was torn in two. On one side, those who still believed in the values of their elders and the past did all that they could to help as many people as possible. Those on the other side of the divide, however, said fuck you to the rest of their world. Base and carnal, they spilled the blood of their brothers and sisters without a second thought. The roads and rivers ran red.

This was the genesis of the Bleed.

Those who still believed in the values and structures of their ancient society used their collective wisdom to find a way of escaping the hell their planet had become. Able to travel between different worlds, universes, and dimensions, they became gods and sowed the seeds of all civilizations throughout the multiverse.

Those left behind, consumed by anger, jealously, and rage, became demons.

The abandoned people of the Bleed stole the technology of the gods and set out for revenge. And wherever they found the children of the gods, they attacked. They mutated and killed. They turned natural worlds against their indigenous inhabitants; insects became giant monsters, life-giving water turned to blood and was filled with disease....

Blinded by its anger, the Bleed won't rest until the gods and all other living things are dead and it is the only thing that remains.

1

London, Next Week

Somehow, everything in this complex sprawl of a city feels like it's interconnected. More than seven million people live here and work and play and learn here, and despite the fact most of them stay happily within their own little bubbles, doing all they can to avoid talking to anyone else, the day-to-day runs pretty much like clockwork. The masses are together, yet isolated. People weave around each other along the clogged pavements, side-stepping without even looking up from their phones, skillfully avoiding collisions. The traffic stops and starts along heavily congested roads in bad tempered order. Deep underground, tube trains race from station to station at speed, dumping hundreds of people at a time onto platforms already crowded with hundreds more waiting to get on and be whisked away elsewhere.

It's an incredibly complicated but largely well-oiled machine. It copes with occasional accidents and interruptions, compensating to keep everything moving. It would take something catastrophic to stop the whole damn thing in its tracks. Something way out of the control of Transport for London or the Metropolitan Police. Something bigger than anything ever seen here before. Something inexplicable and indisputably huge. Something mind-bending, world changing, even perception altering.

Something like what's going to happen next Thursday.

It began as a barely perceptible greenish glow illuminating the underbelly of a disconcertingly specific section of the overcast gray sky above the heart of the city. Hardly anyone noticed it at first, preoccupied as they were, as usual, with the Thursday morning commute. At just before seven o'clock, few people were in the mood to be interrupted or diverted. The daily race to their weekday destinations had begun.

But the glow remained and slowly increased in brightness, the bile-green hue growing brighter, more and more noticeable. There was something of the Northern Lights about it, but the possibility was so remote, and anyway...surely not with this much cloud overhead? In any case, whatever it was, it wasn't as important as the meeting at the offices near Westminster at nine sharp, or catching the connecting train to Milton Keynes at eight-twenty-three, or making that appointment with the casting director of that show and not looking like a complete hungover mess, or getting a decent place in the queue for tickets for the—

Everything changed when the cloud cover was breached.

It looked like a comet—a luminous nucleus with a sickly green-tinged tail—but its movement was all wrong. Instead of racing across the London skyline, it was instead bearing down. And actually, as crowds of people now gazing skyward began to realize, it wasn't racing at all. The impossible mass seemed to be drifting down with control, sinking slowly as if coming in to land. As the comet-thing descended, its speed almost so slow now as to be imperceptible, people began to react.

Most stopped dead in their tracks.

There were collisions on pavements and bumps in the road as people spotted it. Those who hadn't yet looked up followed fingers pointing skyward and all began to sense the early morning light changing. The subtle green tinge which had been barely noticeable now covered the city. It made everything and everyone look unwell.

Folks who normally completed their morning commute without saying a word to anyone they didn't know began to look to each other for explanations, though none were forthcoming. In an atmosphere of anxious uncertainty, strangers quickly became allies. Pointless questions were posed, pointless because even though no one had any answers, it didn't stop them asking. It was a nervous thing. As the bright mass continued its painfully slow descent towards the heart of the city, people nudged those next to them and cocked their heads in the vain hope this was just a publicity stunt they'd not heard about or a scheduled light display their fellow commuters might have seen mentioned on the TV news.

It wasn't long before panic set in. Despite the absolute lack of detail or information, one thing was clear as crystal: whatever it was up there, it was heading directly for the center of London on an unstoppable collision course. The true size of the comet—if that was what it really was—had been hard to discern, but when an Emirates Airbus 380 flew past and was dwarfed, and then a phalanx of military helicopters crawled in front of it like tiny but well-coordinated spiders, it became painfully apparent to everyone watching that this thing was huge. As in capable of wiping out the whole of London huge. As in...capable of ending all life on Earth.

Subdued British politeness turned to absolute fucking terror.

In contrast to the well-rehearsed order of just a few minutes ago, the pavements and streets were now chaotic in the extreme. And the faster people tried to walk or run or drive to safety, the slower everything became as one collision became two, two became four, and four became many more. It didn't take a genius to work out that if—*when*—the comet hit, the area for miles around this place would cease to exist in seconds. Of course, that didn't stop most people trying to get away.

Jennifer Allsopp wasn't like most people.

She knew that it probably wasn't worth running. She instead looked up at the glowing orb in the sky overhead, watching it tumbling over and over towards her. Although she'd have given anything to be somewhere—anywhere—else right now, she knew she was stuck. She could run at full speed for as long as she could manage, but it wouldn't make any difference. She could catch the fastest bullet train (if they even had them here), but she knew she wouldn't get far enough to escape the inevitable impact and blast wave.

Best not to bother trying, she decided. Save your energy. *None of us are going anywhere. We're all fucked.*

The street she'd been walking along was narrow; tall buildings hemmed her in on either side. It was a struggle to get along it at the best of times, but right now, inexplicably, this morning felt about as far from the best of times as it was possible to get. Normally, she'd take a sharp left here and follow an even narrower passage, just a strip of space between two buildings, which cut through to another main road...but that would have been a futile move today. The mouth of the alleyway was clogged with panicking people, all of them trying to get through a gap which wasn't there, no one prepared to give way to anyone else. The brief moment of camaraderie witnessed a couple minutes earlier was tossed aside. Now it was every man, woman and child for themselves.

Jenny felt unnaturally calm and disconnected from it all. She leant back against the glass frontage of a bank and watched the chaos continue to erupt around her. Doing a little impromptu people-watching provided a welcome distraction from her impending death. This city and its people, she thought, were made of the most impossible contrasts, and this part of the city in particular was where the *haves* were forced to co-exist alongside the *have-nots* in large numbers. This crowded capital, where multi-billionaires rubbed shoulders with street cleaners and garbage collectors, was where those who made the rules walked alongside those forced to follow them. *It's a snapshot of humanity*, she thought. Funny how everyone's imminent expiry had shifted the balance. No amount of cash in the bank, no designer wardrobe nor fancy tech gadget was going to protect anyone from what was tumbling down from the sky towards them. She saw one well-to-do gent on his knees with his hands clasped together, praying for salvation. *"If that's the best you can do,"* she whispered, *"you're fucked."*

Without warning, the brightness of the morning dimmed, leaving everything bathed in a subdued, sickly green glow. It took Jenny's eyes a few seconds to adjust, and when she looked up again she saw that the comet had simply stopped falling. It hung in silence over the heart of the city, no longer descending, but still spinning silently over and over above them. Its lack of noise seemed to amplify the panic in the streets. Jenny's stomach flipped with fear because she knew this could only mean one thing: the comet was being controlled by someone…or *something.*

The air pressure had changed; such was the size of the thing hovering overhead. It made her head hurt, and she pushed herself away from the bank and started to walk, fighting her way through the crisscrossing crowds. She felt her phone vibrate in her pocket and grabbed it because she knew who it would be.

"Dad?"

"Where are you, love?"

"On my way to work, but—"

"No time. Just listen to me. Are you

okay?"

"Yes. I just—"

"Don't talk, just listen. You need to stay away from—"

Gone.

Phone dead.

She could see other people looking at their phones too, shaking them and struggling with touch screens that had suddenly become unresponsive. She could see the reflection of the greenish orb overhead in her screen, as if it was saying *"Forget Dad; focus on me."*

She realized she was still walking to work. She'd been pushing her way through the panicking hordes for a couple of minutes longer when it occurred to her that she was still heading for the Thames and the tourist area around the London Eye. She'd graduated a few years back with a first-class degree but, much to Dad's annoyance, had so far done nothing towards getting a decent job. He just didn't understand. She might not have been earning big bucks, selling over-priced food to visitors (truth was she'd hardly earned any bucks at all last year), but she'd had experiences that couldn't be measured in pounds and pence. She'd met thousands of people from hundreds of different countries and from all walks of life. She'd told Dad she'd learnt more about the world than she ever would have sitting in a stuffy office somewhere. He just didn't get it, but what did she expect from a man whose lofty aspirations had taken him to the heady heights of being an assistant team leader in an insurance call center?

She was distracting herself with nonsense. None of that mattered anymore. Fact was, they were all about to die.

The growing confusion of the morning caused Jenny to take a wrong turn. It was hardly surprising, what with everyone running blindly in all directions, screaming, or breaking down crying at the sides of the road. The traffic was snarled and stationary; many drivers had abandoned their vehicles in the vain hope of finding some shelter from the inevitable storm. She took a shortcut through a momentary gap in the crowd and managed to get as far as a stretch of footpath running alongside the river.

Jesus, the water looks strange this morning. It was just another crazy sight among many, but it shocked Jenny enough to stop her in her tracks. The water was still, like a millpond. The river had stopped flowing.

When she turned back, all she could see was the comet hovering there.

It continued to tumble over and over

without dropping any lower; though the comet spun, its plumed tail of debris continued to stretch away from its rounded mass, shooting back up towards the heavens. A man walked into Jenny, and she caught hold of him, desperate to ask a question which had just struck her.

"What about gravity?" she said.

"Wh…what?" he grunted, barely able to keep himself together.

"How can the comet tail be moving away from the surface of the planet? Surely gravity should have the opposite effect."

"Are you crazy? WE'RE ALL GOING TO DIE!" And he squirmed free from her grip and ran off.

The longer the glowing orb remained stationary, the better were Jenny's chances of getting away from it. Except, she wasn't sure she wanted to go anywhere. She was witness to a monumental event, one that would change human history forever. That much was already clear. So did she really want to be anywhere else? Would anywhere be safe? Should she try and get to Dad? Try and get to work? Just try and get out of the center of London? Jenny had almost too many choices, and all of them seemed equally futile. She stepped out to cross the road and was taken out by a guy on a bike going at a furious speed. He was a courier, and he still carried an oversized box full of food strapped to his back like a cuboid rucksack. Jenny was sent flying, but the rider somehow managed to just about keep his balance, swerving around other people and shifting his weight from side to side to stop himself from going over. It looked like he'd had practice. He skidded to a halt and looked back.

She was out cold.

He dumped his bike and ran back to check on her. Countless people were still thundering past on either side, some so close that they scuffed her inert body, almost tripped over her. He crouched down and looked into her deceptively calm face, bathed in the unearthly green light from the comet. Had he killed her? He reached down to touch her neck and check for a pulse. The second his outstretched fingers made contact with her skin she sat up fast, grabbed his arm, and pulled him close.

"Whatthefuckhappened?" she demanded, she demanded and didn't wait for his explanation. "Bike. Someone hit me." She stopped and squinted at him, realized he had a cycle helmet on. "You! It was you, you stupid shit. You could have killed me!"

"I'm not entirely sure that matters this morning. If you ask me, we're all fucked."

She propped herself up onto her elbows, wincing with pain. "Well, I didn't."

"Didn't what?"

"Didn't ask you."

He helped her to her feet. She accepted his support at first but pushed him away as soon as she was upright and stable.

"Just trying to help," he said.

"Don't bother."

"You got any idea what's going on?" he asked.

"You haven't heard?"

"Heard what?"

She shoved him away. "Dumbass. Other than the fact it looks like the world's about to end, I don't know anything. I doubt anyone does. I need a drink."

"Seriously? At this time of morning?"

She answered without answering. Through the masses of people still streaming along the road, Jenny spotted a pub. The Shakespeare. Perfect. She wove through the crowds to get to it and breathed a sigh of relief when she found the door unlocked. She took a last glance up at the comet overhead, still hanging there, imperious, still tumbling over and over and over on itself but going nowhere. She went inside and shut the door on the rest of the world.

She'd barely poured herself a pint before

the door opened again and the bicycle courier followed her in. They were alone, the staff and any early morning drinkers having long gone.

"You still here?" she asked.

He didn't seem impressed. "Look, I'm thinking maybe you hit your head on the way down just now. We're in danger if we stay here."

"I reckon we're in danger wherever we go. And anyway, what's with all this we business?"

"I'm looking out for you."

"Says the guy who just knocked me over."

"Yeah, sorry about that."

"Want a beer?"

"I'd kill for a beer."

"Fine. One drink then we'll go our separate ways. I'm Jenny, by the way."

"Jayesh."

"Pleasure to meet you, Jayesh. What's that in your backpack?"

He realized he still had on his delivery pack. He swung it off and opened it on the table Jenny had claimed by the window. "There's all kinds of stuff in here. Breakfast for some rich kids in the city."

"Any bacon sandwiches?"

"There's sausage here."

"That'll do. Hand it over."

He did as she asked, and he watched as she took a massive mouthful and chewed like she hadn't eaten for a week. Beyond the window, the green-tinged chaos continued unabated. The sight of her tucking into breakfast as the world was ending felt more surreal than the notion itself that the world was ending.

There was a TV on the wall opposite. "Try and get that working, will you," she ordered as she dove into her second sandwich and sipped at her pint. Jayesh didn't argue; he just got up and did as he was told. He found the on/off button quick enough but was concerned he wouldn't be able to find the channel selector and get to the news. Turned out it didn't matter. Every station was broadcasting the news from London.

"Fucking hell," he said, staggering back from the screen.

The glowing green orb looked even more terrifying from above. The footage they were watching was being taken from a helicopter circling at a distance, and when it climbed and the camera panned down, for the first time they were able to appreciate the scale of the inexplicable object. The Houses of Parliament, the Shard, Tower Bridge, the London Eye, Big Ben...the familiar sights of London looked like miniature models in the shadow of the comet.

Jayesh picked up his beer and sank several large gulps. "This is real, isn't it?" he said. "I mean, I know what I saw out there, but when you see it on TV like this… it looks crazy. Unbelievable, like something out of a film."

"Go out there and check, if you like."

He was contemplating whether to do just that when the light outside changed again. The green disappeared as if it had been switched off, and a typical early Thursday morning gray was restored. The air pressure changed too, as a barely perceptible, storm-like heaviness was suddenly lifted.

"What the hell?" Jayesh said, and he was about to go back out when Jenny shot out an arm and stopped him.

"Don't. Stay here."

"But we need to know what's happening."

"Then keep watching TV."

"Are you serious?"

"Deadly."

With another sandwich in one hand and her beer in the other, Jenny walked towards the screen. The TV news was on a few seconds' delay, and as she watched, she saw the green light change, as it had outside.

Then the comet appeared to collapse in on itself, reducing until it was about a tenth of its original size.

"I don't like this," she started to say, "it makes me think that it's going to—"

Another unfinished sentence. The air was abruptly fractured by a deafening noise the likes of which neither of them had heard before. And then a shockwave like a sudden earthquake rocked the foundations of the pub and shattered the windows. Jayesh clung on to Jenny for support. She finished her sandwich and clung on to her beer.

"—drop," she said, eventually finishing her thought.

She pushed Jayesh out of the way so she could see the TV and confirm her suspicions. The comet had made a crash landing. It had dropped like a stone. The footage on the screen was a single steady shot from a distance: a circular wave of dust and debris spreading out from the point of impact.

"Aliens?" Jayesh asked.

"Could be."

"Or Russians?"

"Why Russians?"

"I don't know. Chinese, then? North Korea?"

"You think? I reckon you were probably

closer with aliens."

Jenny moved back towards the door. She pushed herself flat against a wall and gestured for Jayesh to do the same, keen for them both to stay hidden in the shadows.

"What's wrong?" he hissed at her.

"Look at the crowds."

"What about them?"

"They're...*herding*."

She was right. No longer running frantically in all directions, the terrified population of this part of London were now moving away *en masse*.

"We should go," Jayesh said.

"Go where? I'm not moving. I've got food and beer and all my options are still open. Go out there, and you don't know what you'll be dealing with."

She had a point. He stayed put.

Jenny helped herself to a final sandwich and ate it as she watched the chaos on the streets reduce. Jayesh gestured at the TV. On the screen he could see tanks and columns of soldiers. "Looks like the army," he said, sounding relieved. "Thank God. I wondered when they'd get here."

"That makes me even more nervous. How'd they get here so quick? I'm staying put until I know what's what."

Jenny held her position for a while longer, standing perfectly still, shifting only her eyes as she tracked the movements of the stragglers out front. She felt unexpectedly calm, but Jayesh was feeling the pressure. He talked incessantly, his voice a hushed but urgent-sounding whisper.

"I knew something bad was going to happen today. It always does when I'm delivering in this part of town. I mean, nothing like that thing that's landed, but things are never straightforward when you come out this way. You know what I mean? People here have got a bob on themselves. Think they're something special just because they earn megabucks and they know people who know people who know people...makes you sick. Makes me sick, anyway."

"Stop talking, Jayesh."

"I can't. I'm nervous. I talk a lot when I'm nervous."

"Put a sock in it."

"Sorry. I just—"

"I'm serious. Look!"

The appearance of a squad of heavily armed soldiers was enough to completely silence Jayesh at last. They marched in formation along the street, marshalling the crowds away from the general area where the comet-thing had come down.

Jayesh kept his mouth shut for almost a

minute after the last of the soldiers had passed the pub, but the pressure to speak was too much to bear.

"Is the army being here a good thing or not?"

"Good, I think. They're evacuating. Getting people to safety."

"Then shouldn't we go with them?"

"Maybe."

"Where exactly did that thing land? Do you think it was near here?"

"Very near."

"That's what I thought. Hard to tell, though, from what we can see on TV."

"It's not all about what you can see. Try listening."

He did as he was told. Now that the civilian masses and the marching military boots had gone, just one obvious noise remained.

"Helicopter."

"Exactly."

"Right overhead, it sounds like."

"That's what I think."

"Big and heavy. Probably one of those Chinooks. You know the ones? Two sets of rotor blades."

"I know the ones."

Jenny checked it was clear then stuck her head out the door. She could see the Chinook circling above them. Back inside, the TV screen confirmed her suspicions. She estimated the helicopter's position in relation to the downed comet, and from that she worked out roughly where it had landed.

"I think it was somewhere near Trafalgar Square."

"I really think we should get out of here," Jayesh said.

"Yeah. I think you're right."

They left the pub together and stepped out onto the street. The city had become eerily quiet now the rest of the population had done the sensible thing and disappeared under armed escort. They'd not been out long when dust began to come down like fine snow. At times, great swirling clouds of the stuff billowed around them, a grit-filled blizzard. Jayesh covered his mouth and nose and followed her into the spiteful haze.

"Wait," he shouted after her. "You're going the wrong way. You're going towards it."

"I know exactly where I'm going."

"Is this the beer talking? You sank a pint in about two minutes just now, and it's not even eight o'clock."

She ignored his protestations. Jayesh looked around and when he realized Jenny was the only other thing he could see moving, he ran after her.

She was looking at her phone again. "Weird."

"What is?"

She showed him the screen then gestured at the grubby-looking cityscape around them. The dust clouds were settling, but everything looked otherwise normal.

"All the landmarks are where they should be. You'd have thought if whoever was controlling that thing had serious intent or wanted to make a statement then they'd have done more damage. You could take your pick of iconic sights around this place and flatten the lot of them, yet it looks like they're all untouched. Buckingham Palace, St Paul's Cathedral...they're all close, but they look undamaged."

"You think they're friendly then?"

"I wouldn't go that far. It's not quite what you'd expect from an all-powerful invader, though." She stopped and wiped dust from her phone, then tried to work out exactly where she was in relation to the city and the Thames. "This makes no sense."

"*Nothing* makes sense right now."

"If I'm looking at this right, it looks like it landed on a half-built hotel."

"Seriously?"

"Yes. Not even a hotel that was open. One that was still under construction."

"Crazy."

"This isn't right. I think I'd be less concerned if they'd kicked off like something out of *War of the Worlds*. This is far too quiet, too controlled."

"It might be a good sign. They've deliberately chosen an unoccupied building."

"True, but they could have had their pick of the whole planet. If that thing was being flown with that level of control, they could have brought it down in the middle of a desert and not caused any damage at all. There's something we're not being told here."

"I've got news for you—we're the general public. No one ever tells us anything. We're just expected to—"

"And another thing," she continued, cutting across him, "how did the army get here so fast?"

"They must have seen it heading towards us."

"Fair enough, but wouldn't they have tried to evacuate the city sooner if they'd known? It's early in the morning. If they'd started clearing out even an hour earlier there'd have been thousands fewer people on the streets. They could have stopped people coming in."

"You're overthinking this."

"No, you're under-thinking it. We need to know what's happening. I need to know, anyway."

"But there's no one else left around here, Jenny. I think we should leave and get as far away from here as we can. If we can't head out, head up. Otherwise we're sitting ducks."

Jenny wasn't having any of it. She turned her back on him, conversation over. Feet crunching through the layer of dirty grit which now covered everything, she followed the directions on her phone, deeper into the unnaturally silent metropolis.

2

Base Station New Start, Sea of Crises, Earth's Moon Surface

It was 2035, the year the earth came to a tipping point it could not recover from. Deforestation, pollution, melting of the polar ice caps, overpopulation, and an inability to provide enough food had pushed the world into a war that dwarfed the two great wars combined. Nearly every country that had a standing military had joined the fray, battling for scraps of an ever-diminishing supply of resources. Alliances were tested, broken and reformed on a continual basis. It got to the point that most didn't even know which side, or who exactly, they were fighting with anymore. Humanity was on the brink of extinction, and somehow killing each other seemed the best solution. For twelve years, unbridled savagery was released upon the planet. Billions died in the conflict, and there seemed no end to the misery. War and the wretchedness of it were all anybody knew.

It was a French woman, Esmee Marchand, who had covertly approached what remained of the governments with a plan to save what was left. Esmee had been an ecologist; she'd studied at Harvard and Cambridge University before the war started. She bore witness to the destruction of her planet and had switched her field of focus to terra-forming. She'd devised an original method of rejuvenating environments; creating safe zones for human life, and with this knowledge in hand, she had offered an escape, a fresh start. So, even as countries tore themselves and each other apart, scientists and technicians worked in secret to create rockets and gather the materials, people and animals that would inhabit the moon, always with hope that someday they could return to the earth, once peace had been restored and the threats facing our survival had been removed. What they did not know, what they could not know, was that the Bleed had found their oasis among the stars, and it was doing what it had always done: destroy.

2070 / DAY 1 / 8:02 AM

"Woohoo!" Samantha Morrison screamed as Tyler sent the M.O.W.E.R., the Moon Octagon Wheeled Express Rover, into a tight donut. She was standing up in her seat, holding on to the turbulence bar mounted on the dashboard.

"Sam, sit your ass down!" her brother, Derrick, said from the back seat.

"Just drink more of Maddie's hot water and stop being a prude!" She smiled and twisted around, making sure Tyler got a good view of her backside.

"This beats the shit out of calculus!" Juan said, grabbing the illegal bottle of alcohol from Derrick's hands.

"Speaking of which, don't you think they're going to know something is up when half the kids are missing?" Derrick asked.

"Moon flu," Tyler said as he got the mower out of its slide and was now racing forward. At sixteen, he was the oldest of the four by three months. He stood nearly six feet tall and was the object of desire to almost every girl in his class, though there were only five. It didn't matter to him, as he only had eyes for Sam. He yearned for her. The only downside was her twin brother Derrick, whom she insisted come along on whatever adventure they leapt upon.

To Tyler, Sam was the perfect woman. She had dark hair, piercing blue eyes, and a smile that made him want to lasso the earth and give it to her on a charm bracelet. Then there was Juan, Tyler's oldest and dearest friend. Their parents were molecular scientists and had been working closely together since they'd landed on the moon some twenty years ago. They'd known each other since their first remembered thoughts. They were as different as two people could be; where Tyler was tall and wiry, Juan was short and stocky. Their only similarity was that they both loved a Morrison. Tyler often smiled when he imagined what Derrick would think if he knew Juan had a thing for him.

"Don't hog that!" Sam had to shout over the music blaring from the mower's speaker system. She reached her hand back for the hot water. She took a hefty swig and sat down hard. "I think I might be... ebriated."

"Ebriated?" Tyler laughed, looking over at her.

She laughed and then hiccupped. Tyler could not take his eyes from the heavenly sight.

"Dude! Tyler, man, look out!" Juan shouted from the back.

"Oh shit!" Tyler turned and was looking at one of the massive support pillars of a Terraforming Transfer Tower, a big one—a T3. The structure itself was over two hundred feet tall; the support pillar was ten feet across by ten feet high made of steel-reinforced concrete and it filled his windshield view. The mower wouldn't so much as scratch it if it struck. Tyler pulled the wheel hard to his right; the internal gyroscopes did not have enough time to compensate for the sudden maneuver. The wheels on the left came up off the ground just as the front passenger quarter panel squealed in protest and collided with the tower. The force tipped the vehicle completely over and sent it skidding and twirling for close to five hundred feet before it came to a teetering stop on its roof. Dust swirled around outside and inside the vehicle. Electrical circuits began shorting, leaving a smell of burnt ozone in the air.

"Fuck! Everyone all right?!" Tyler fell to the ceiling as he undid his seat restraint. He looked over in panic to Sam, who was in a curled-up heap, blood flowing from her head.

"Good," Juan said as he sat up and tried to help Derrick, who angrily shoved him away.

"Sam?" He was scurrying to move to the front and help his sister.

She sat up. "What a rush!" She was laughing.

"You scared us to death!" Derrick shouted.

"So dramatic, this one," Juan said. "Uh, guys, better suit up," he said as he watched a small crack in the window closest to him sucking out the all-important life-giving oxygen and replacing it with choking moon dust. "We've got a leak."

The mirth at having survived the accident quickly gave way to alarm as Derrick moved to the rear of the vehicle to grab the pressurized suits.

"How far are we from the base?" Juan asked as he began to dress.

"I...I don't know...." Tyler was quickly putting his feet through the legs as more oxygen seeped out. An alarm had sounded, warning of the loss of air, but promptly ceased as all electrical functions on the mower died.

Derrick again rooted around in the trunk, grabbing some liquid sealant. He squeezed the end of the tube; the semi-liquid moved toward the hole and before it could slip through, it spread out and sealed the breach.

"Good move, dork," Sam said. He stuck his tongue out at her.

Once Sam had her suit on, she looked to the tower and up. "That's number thirty-four, so we've got to be close to ten miles out."

"You know the layout of the towers?" Tyler asked as he pulled up the front of his jacket.

"Our dad helped put them there and is responsible for the maintenance. He takes us out all the time to show us, as eventually this is supposed to be our job. Of course, we'll be lucky if we don't end up in jail over this," Derrick replied, looking sourly at Tyler.

"There's no jail on the moon," Juan said. "That's only in the books and movies from Earth."

"Yeah, well, they might make one now just for us. We need to get moving; we've got two hours of air and a lot of miles to travel. Dumbasses," Derrick muttered that last part.

"What about the winch? Can't we use that to turn us over?" Sam asked.

"I think the damage is too severe to drive, and besides..." Derrick pointed to a spot some hundred feet away where the spiraled winch cable sat in its housing.

"Um, we have another problem," Juan said as he held up the broken faceplate of his suit.

"Shit, take mine," Tyler offered. "I'm the one that got us into this mess."

"Okay. Sam and I can go and get help; Tyler, you stay here with Juan. When the oxygen inside the vehicle is finally tapped out, you'll have to share what's in the suits. Should have plenty."

"Look at Take Charge Derrick, my hero!" Tyler went in to give the other a kiss.

"This is serious!" Derrick pushed him away.

"So was I." Tyler put on a mock countenance of hurt.

"Come on, sis."

"Shouldn't she stay here? It would be safer," Juan said.

"Not sure about that," Derrick answered, moving toward the airlock. "And you know we're always supposed to go out in pairs in case something happens."

"Not sure if the rules apply anymore,"

Tyler said. "We already drank something we weren't supposed to have and stole a mower."

"That's on Maddie for even making it," Juan said, trying to make light of the situation.

"I didn't drink any, and I didn't steal this truck." Derrick was next to the manual override. "Sam, come on."

"Why'd you even come?" Tyler could not hide the hostility in his voice.

"To save your asses when you invariably did something like this." His sister came up beside him. He turned the crank quickly; the inner door to the airlock opened with a hiss. He and Sam walked into the small anti-chamber before he shut and locked the door behind him. Then he went for the outer door. It took the combined effort of both of them to turn the wheel, the door having suffered damage from the collision.

"You should take it easy on him," Sam said through the comm device built into the suits.

"And maybe you should reevaluate what you see in him. He could have killed us all and we're still in a lot of trouble out here. It's not recommended to be more than a mile away from a facility, and here we are, ten times that."

"It's so boring here, Der! You know that. You must. You're always reading; don't the people in those stories ever have fun?"

"Most of what I read is on science."

"Maybe that's your problem."

"I hate to tell you this, sis, but Tyler isn't going to be riding a white stallion to your rescue any time soon."

Sam pushed him. "Shut up. I'm sixteen—almost seventeen—and besides playing board games with our parents, I barely have any fun."

"And I'm the dramatic one," Derrick sighed. "You should talk less and walk more. This is going to be close."

"Shouldn't we run? Jog, maybe?"

"We'll use up our air faster."

"What about the oxygen level outside? Haven't the towers made enough yet?"

"I realize Tyler is dreamy and all, but don't you pay any attention in school?"

"Why should I? You always fill me in."

"The oxygen around us is a little over sixteen percent."

"That's not enough?"

Derrick let his head sag.

"I'm kidding, okay? I know twenty-one percent is the optimal zone for human life, but won't sixteen point-two-five be enough?"

"The only thing that can survive in that

is fire. It's going to be five more years before we can live outside."

"Oh, can you imagine? To be free of these suits…to lie out on grass and stare up at the stars?"

"We can do all of that in the solarium."

"You mean that domed building with the glass ceiling? Not the same, baby brother."

"By four minutes. My guess is you probably tripped me on the way out so you could be first."

They walked the next few miles in silence, doing their best to conserve oxygen. Sam tapped the base of Tower 12 then looked over to her brother; his eyebrows furrowed.

"Five miles out," he said.

"I'm at a third of a tank," Sam replied.

Derrick said nothing.

"Derrick."

"I'm at less than that," was all he offered as he plodded on. After a few hundred yards, he stopped. "Sam, I'm not going to make it. If I give you my tank, you should have just enough."

"You'd sacrifice yourself for little old me? That means so much! Okay, take it off, I've got to get going."

"I'm serious!"

"Not a chance in hell I'm leaving you

out here. We're both going to make it."

Derrick didn't think so, but he didn't want to waste oxygen arguing with his sister. He couldn't remember the last time that had worked out in his favor. His visor began to flash red just as they saw the facility on the horizon. *So damn close*, he thought. His head began to swim as he took in more carbon dioxide than air.

He didn't remember falling to the ground.

"What...what happened?" Derrick asked as he sat up, banging his forehead off the top of the hyperbolic chamber he found himself in.

Dr. Perkins was on the far side of the room, going over some lab work. "Oh good...you're awake," she said, turning to the noise. "You realize if it weren't for the kids on this base I'd actually be able to get some real work done." She wore a scowl, doing her best to hide the smile underneath. "What were you thinking, taking a mower out like that?"

"Sam?"

"Oh, I would imagine she's receiving

the scolding of her young life right now — something you still have to look forward to."

"Tyler, Derrick?" he asked.

"They had to send a team from the Sea of Tranquility base to retrieve them. You dunderheads destroyed the only working mower we have here. I wouldn't be surprised if the four of you are swabbing decks for the next five years. If they had a plank, you'd be walking it."

Derrick's head sagged back down; he remembered his father saying something about the other vehicle's rear axle mysteriously rotting away. They were waiting for a replacement from Earth. Something that, given the volatility of their home planet, may or may not ever come.

"How did I get here?"

"Your sister dragged you for a ways before you were spotted by a search party. It was touch and go for a while."

"How long do I have to stay in here?"

"You in a rush to feel your parents' wrath?"

"No, not really."

"Then shut it so I can get some work done."

Derrick awoke a few hours later to a tapping on the glass above him. He opened an eye wide enough to see his sister's smiling face. His relief that she was here, safe and sound, was palpable.

"Gawd, can you milk it anymore? While you're sleeping away in there, I'm taking all the heat."

"You don't seem so distraught."

"You're welcome, by the way."

"For what, almost getting me killed?"

"For saving your life." She ignored his barb. "What are you so sour-pussed about? I'm the one that's been getting grilled for the last six hours. I'm grounded for, I think, the next thirty-seven years, by the way. I'm not too concerned, though. I think Dad will cave in fifteen or twenty at the most."

"Ah, there you two little shits are." Maddie's frame stood at the entryway to the hospital room. A shock of bright red hair stood out at odd angles under her grease-stained blue cap. "It doesn't often happen that karma comes around so quickly, but we three are going to have so much fun."

"What's she talking about?" Derrick asked his sister, alarm in his voice. At the best of times, Maddie was known for her fiery temper and her open contempt for others. Most steered clear of the woman, only dealing with her when necessary, which tended to be a lot, as she was by far the best mechanic on the planet.

"I own you for the next six months. I lobbied for a year, considering that's how long it's going to take to get the inept asses on Earth to get me the parts I need to fix the mower you trashed, but okay, I got half that. That's not even the worst of it. That bourbon you stole and drank had been aging for three years."

"Hard alcohol is illegal on base," Derrick said weakly.

"So is stealing government property. Don't think you can take the high road on this one, smarty pants." Maddie turned and looked down the hallway she was half standing in, then placed two fingers in her mouth and whistled loudly. "Yo Doc! His vitals are fine; can you let him go? I've got some septic issues that need checking out and by the size of him, he should be able to wriggle his way to the problem areas."

Derrick groaned.

3

Filthy Halfsies

When the grandfathers to the grandfathers were young, the race of gods stepped through time and space, appearing in the North. Fleeing an ancient, world-eating evil they called the Bleed, they came to build anew, in peace. Other than strange hair and eye colors, they appeared similar to normal human beings—but they were taller, stronger, and smarter, and were ripe with powers from their home world. They brought unheard of learning and experience with them; they built their Endless City from one edge of the North to the other, with its mile-high walls and towers of stone, steel and wood soaring above that. They ruled the world from afar, without war, or even effort, ever watchful for the signs of the Bleed, their unending, ever-hungry foe.

They took husbands and wives and left thousands of half-breed children behind when the enemy they fled bled through the fabric of the worlds. Deep in their city, servants of the evil ate at their new home, one bloody soul at a time. They made their stand at the edge of the world, almost a score ago, and not one god has been seen since.

Without their vibrant presence, the gods' city crumbles. The common folk wander through the world, aimless, as the world at the city's feet awaits their victory, or defeat, at the edge, where the seas turn to ice and fall into night's oblivion, where only gods dared tread.

"Why are there no more fish?" Arridon Gray muttered as he threw the nets down on Mercy Point's last remaining rickety pier which jutted out over the sea's edge. The sea's agitated waves rolled in, foamy and cold, and smashed against the shrinking village's stony shore wall.

Fishing under the summer sun off the docks with his father's old nets had yielded Arridon no fish for the third day running. The young man wasn't the only person with empty nets either; none of the other men standing on the shores of the Dawn Sea had catches that would fill a belly come dinnertime. After sitting on the pier's end, boots dangling over the brackish waters below, lamenting the fortune he'd received over his twenty short years and the fortunes of all the other people struggling to feed themselves in the village of Mercy Point, he got to his feet. He packaged the old net back into his father's large canvas bag and began the trudge inland to the home he shared with his father and younger sister. He walked carefully on the aged planks, using the golden eyes his mother had passed down to him to watch for rotted boards, perishing from disuse. The weight of the bag over his shoulder cut into his skin, but the calluses fought back.

He walked past the old fishery warehouses that no longer smelled of the day's catch—and hadn't for years—and then past the almost abandoned inns that used to cater to merchants coming and going on boats that no longer came or went on the Eastern Sea.

They were too close to the gods' war at the world's edge, or so the traders claimed.

Arridon believed in the war at the edge of the world, even though he couldn't see it and didn't know anyone who had. He believed in the gods fighting that war, including his mother, though she'd been gone for over a decade now. Worrying about his drunken father and protecting his little sister occupied all the anxiety he could work up in a day's time. The gods' war against the Bleed would come to them, or it wouldn't. He had no say either way.

He passed through the village's central courtyard, with its long-unused guillotine and trio of freshwater wells, and took the slight turn towards the street he and his family lived on. Several buildings ahead, he saw his sister leaning against the side of an abandoned home, surrounded by several of the local boys. Her eyes were narrowed into dagger slits of anger as she looked from one boy to the next.

"Shit," he whispered, and picked up speed to get to her before one of the boys did something they'd regret.

They were arguing with her when he arrived.

"Why won't ya?" one of them asked her, taunting. "You don't think he's good enough for ya, ya golden-eyed freak?"

"No, actually, he isn't good enough for me," Thistle shot back as she put her long brown hair up in a ponytail. "Not a soul in this godless village is worth so much as my freakish kiss, and at the bottom of that wretched, worthless pile is all of you and your friend Sebastian especially. Now kindly, you can all go walk off the edge."

"Come on now," the one Arridon knew to be Sebastian said. "No harm meant. Just one kiss. A plump, wet one, and I'll be off."

"Seb, you heard her," Arridon said, approaching the four teenage boys harassing his sister. "Her lips are hers to decide what to do with. Now be off or I'll drag each of you to the pier and throw you in, one by one. Let you float to the war and right over the edge of the world."

"Oh, we was just having fun with Thistle, Arridon. You both get your halfsie panties twisted over nothing," Sebastian shot back.

Halfsie.

It wasn't the first time he'd been called a halfsie, but it stung just as bad every time. Arridon's blood boiled. He dropped the heavy bag filled with netting on the cobblestone street and shot a hand out at the throat of the kid who'd called his sister and him such a terrible name.

"Say that again," Arridon dared him. "Call my sister and me a halfsie one more time."

One of the boys stepped forward to intervene, to rescue his friend from the older, stronger Arridon, but the "halfsie" man stared at him with his golden god's eyes, and the bully froze in his footsteps.

"But that's what you are," Sebastian choked out. "Dirty half-people. You think the two of you would add up to one worthless person but you don't. Your two good halves are gone and the halves you got left don't add up to nothing."

"We are both more than half a person, thank you," Thistle shot back. "Our mother was a god from the Endless City, and at least we know what man mounted her in the dark, you fatherless bastard."

Sebastian slipped into rage and struggled, but the deceptively strong grip skinny and tall Arridon had on his neck held him from attacking Thistle. He resorted to grunting in anger at her, and foaming at the mouth like the angry surf, or the mouth of a rabid dog held barely at bay. After several seconds of that, Sebastian gave up the struggle, and stood, arms limp at his sides.

"Listen to me," Arridon said, leaning down into the bully's face. "All of you listen to me. I won't say this again; next time I'll save my breath and just punch you in the face." He looked to each of their scared faces, and when he knew they were paying attention, he continued. "My sister and I are good people. Whole people. We didn't choose that our mother was one of the god-kind, and I'll be honest: I'm glad she was, no matter what the haters say. Now you say what you will about the other gods, and where they went when they left, but our mother was a good person, and so are we. Now pay close attention. I'll stop being a nice person if you keep harassing my sister and me, you understand? I'll use the part of me that came from her, and I'll shrivel your little dicks so small they'll turn inside out. And then, I'll lay a curse upon your fields and your harvests, and your children — if anyone ever willingly touches your shriveled cocks. None of you will ever be happy again if you cross my family, and none you know will be either."

Arridon felt Sebastian start to tremble with fear in his grip, and he let the dirty, smelly, scared kid go with a gentle push. The four boys backed away and then turned and ran towards the town's central courtyard. Just before disappearing out of view, Sebastian stopped.

"Halfsie pieces of filth!" he hollered, then ran from sight.

Arridon thought about chasing him down and breaking his nose, but dismissed the notion. He had to worry about his father's state when he and Thistle got home.

"One of these days, they're going to fight you. They're getting bigger, and you're full grown. They'll test you."

"I look forward to that day. Maybe by then any powers from Mom's side of the family will have surfaced."

"When did you add shriveling dicks and cursing farmland to your as-yet unmanifested godly repertoire?" his sister asked him as she rested a hand on his shoulder. Her touch soothed his nerves. Calmed his anger.

"I needed to diversify. Threatening to make them piss themselves was losing its impact."

"Especially when you aren't making anyone piss themselves in the streets," she said. "You should've just punched him and broken his nose. Threats only work when they're followed through on from time to time. Not like a flattened beak would ruin his chances with a pretty girl; Mercy Point doesn't have any pretty girls left."

"Well, there's you."

"Big brother, did you just insinuate that I'm pretty?" Thistle said, feigning shock. "What's next? Will gold coins rain from the sky? Will the fall harvest of crops yield us medicines and salvation from the absence of the gods?"

"It's a real war."

"I'm sure you think it is."

"Dad said Mom left to go do her part. To fight against the creatures turned by the Bleed. Demons from the void over the edge. I believe him."

"Bleed schmeed. Demons schmeemons. I'm not part of that believing troupe of clowns."

"You're such a cynic. You may not remember Mom, but I do. She didn't just leave us. She went to fight for us. I remember the day she left. She cried. She had her sword, and that thing Dad called a gods' rifle." He sighed. "Forget it. Come on, let's get moving," he said, picking up the heavy bag and its empty, damp contents.

"Nothing again?" Thistle asked him. "You certainly aren't a professional at this. How many days since you brought food home from the shore?"

They walked towards their home, Thistle slipping an arm into her brother's as they went. The summer afternoon was warm, and the seaside air rich. With their eyes closed, it was easy to imagine they were in paradise.

Much harder with their eyes open.

"Three days. Not one fish for anyone."

"Why do you think?"

"I'm not a fisherman, sister. Nor am I sailor. The sea keeps her mysteries from me."

"What about the other fishermen? Are any of the boats coming back with a catch? Do the sailors have any ideas about what's happening?" she asked him.

"Not many real sailors coming to port here anymore. Most have headed south for good. The old sailors, too stubborn to leave, have ideas, but it's all…doom related."

"I love a good story about doom. Does it involve gloom as well? Those are my *favorite*," she said, swooning.

"Ha, yes. Plenty of doom and gloom," Arridon said. "The prevailing theory is that the gods are losing the war at the horizon, and that means the Bleed is spreading deeper towards the mainland here. They fear that the demons are walking along the sea floor, headed to the mainland, and they worry that the taint of demon blood has sent all the fish away."

"That's an awful lot of doom," she said as they stopped at the doorstep to their single-story cottage on the edge of the downtown area of Mercy Point. "Do you think they're right?"

"I've no idea, but I believe that the gods are fighting demons at the world's edge, and I believe our mother is there, fighting alongside the other gods to protect us and our world."

"You mean to say 'all the gods,' because all of them up and left us to rot," Thistle said. "The Endless City is empty, and so is our little village."

"They had to," Arridon said. "You have to believe that they're fighting for us. They didn't just abandon the world."

"I wish I had the faith you do," his little sister whispered so low Arridon thought she meant for him to not hear it.

"One day, you will. Mom will come back."

"And Dad will stop drinking too, then? Because it'll take the first for the second to happen."

"You're so damned bitter," Arridon said. "As salty as the sea."

"Truth. Have faith in that. What are we going to eat tonight? No fish to fry and our larder is as empty as Sebastian's racist soul. Pity Dad couldn't be bothered to sober up long enough to head to the city markets for us once in a while to get some food."

"You know Dad hates the city."

"I wish he loved us more than he hated the city. At least then we'd have supper on the table and the strength to fight the sea demons allegedly clawing their way here right now."

Arridon's hand went still on the knob to the front door of their house. It wasn't really a home; hadn't been in a long time. This was just the place they lived, and what their dad did with his life was barely living. Might as well have been part of the shed attached to the side near the garden.

"Come on," Thistle said with a sigh. "Let's get it over with. Make sure he eats something and gets put into bed before he decides to wander out and pick a fight with the Eastern Sea for being too damned wet again."

"I'm sorry," he said to her.

"For what?"

"For how this is. How our lives are."

She stepped back, removing her arm from his. "What?"

"We're outcasts. The only half-gods in this village. No one really trusts us, no one really likes us, and we have no friends. Our dad is a drunk, our mother is gone. We scrape by, wearing old clothes and eating old food, crying tears with golden eyes that make everyone think we're freaks. I'm sorry for it all. I wish I could do better for us. I *will* do better for us."

"Arridon," she said, putting that soothing hand on his shoulder again, "none of this is your fault. You need not apologize for anything."

"Still."

"I see. You think you've wronged me somehow? Fine. Let that guilt stand. I challenge you then; make it up to me by bringing me to the Citadel of the Temples, or Ranmyr. The Channel between the tower-cities at the very least."

"You want to go to the city? Whatever for? You know it's at least a full day's walk to the entrance between the two great citadels."

"I've been walking around Mercy Point for no good reason for a lot more than a day. And why do I want to go? Oh I don't know. Food. Culture? A lack of idiots who hate us for having a parent from an unpopular race of supposed demigods? Arridon…I hate this town. I hate it with a passion and have no future worth having here. If only for a day, or two, or five, I'd like to see crowds of people. Markets filled with vegetables and fruits. Artists painting and singing and playing songs. I'd like to see what a thriving world looks like. I'd like to see a damned smile."

"And maybe you'll stay there. Leave dad and I here."

"And maybe you'll stay there too. And maybe we'll leave our dad here to die the way he clearly wants to, all alone, with us somewhere he's never been. Now, open the damned door, and let's take care of our drunkard father like the good children we are, in spite of him."

"I love you."

"And I love you too."

4

London

Jenny knew these streets like the back of her hand. Usually. This morning they looked very different. Frozen lines of traffic blocked the roads, cars, buses and trucks having been hastily abandoned. Buildings were empty, and the layer of dust gave everything a feel of utter desolation. It had been less than an hour since the area had been evacuated, but it felt as if there had never been people here at all.

"You still here?" Jenny said to Jayesh as he caught up with her again. She'd stopped at a usually busy intersection, standing in the middle of roads which would normally have been teeming with bad-tempered traffic at this time.

"Didn't want to leave you on your own," he said, whispering because his voice suddenly seemed so loud against the oppressive silence of everything else.

"My hero. This is the twenty-first century, not the sixties. I don't need a man to watch over me, thanks. I am capable of looking after myself."

"I don't doubt that for a second."

"And don't forget, you did knock me over with your bike. That's not really the kind of help I need."

"I really think we should be heading the other way. We need to get far from whatever that thing is."

Trafalgar Square looked like it had been frozen in time. Nothing moved save for the two of them and the flickering advertising hoardings which still burned brightly through the oppressive grayness. The statue of Admiral Nelson was barely visible at the top of his column. They worked their way through the chaotic tangle of vehicles. Midway, Jenny paused to check her phone again.

"I reckon it's somewhere over there," she said, gesturing wildly with one hand while still focusing her attention on the screen.

"Yeah, I think you might be right," Jayesh said, and something about the tone of his voice made her look up. The sky over to their right had suddenly lit up, the base of the clouds bathed in an unnatural looking yet immediately familiar greenish hue. Jenny started to move with more pace now that she was certain of where she was heading. They crossed between the fountains and the statues of lions, able to move more freely across the pedestrian part of the square. They were only half-way when they heard a voice that made them both freeze in their tracks.

"You two, stop where you are or we'll shoot!"

"What the fuck?" Jayesh said under his breath. They'd both frozen straight away. He stood completely still and held his hands up in surrender.

"Why would they shoot us?"

"Does it matter?"

"Yes. We're not doing anything wrong."

"They've got guns. I don't think we should argue."

"Where are they, anyway?" Jenny asked, looking around.

The voice was being amplified via a loudhailer. The distortion, combined with the way the woman's tinny voice echoed off the buildings, bouncing all around the square, made it almost impossible to locate the source.

"Keep moving," Jenny said.

"You're kidding me?"

"Not at all. Run!"

Jenny started to sprint, and Jayesh instinctively followed. They zigzagged across the open part of the square then abruptly changed direction when whoever it was who was watching them carried out their threat and opened fire.

"Oh god!" Jayesh cried.

"They're either really bad shots or they missed us intentionally," Jenny said, out of breath as she watched bullets tear chunks out of the stone plinth the nearest lion rested on. "At least we know where they are now…."

The shooter's wayward aim had given away their approximate location. Jenny disappeared back into the motionless traffic, crouching down behind a taxi so she couldn't be seen. She gestured for Jayesh to do the same, then dashed from the back of the taxi over to the far side of a bright red London bus: Number 172.

"This'll do," she said. "My lucky

number."

"What?"

"172."

"Bit of a random lucky number."

"It's the number of my flat. I've been lucky there. So far."

The door of the bus had been left open. She slipped inside then ran upstairs to get a better view. Jayesh crouched down on the seat in front of her.

"You'd think they'd have bigger things on their mind than us, wouldn't you?" she said. "It's potentially the end of the world, yet they're more interested in chasing a couple of random nobodies. Makes you wonder why, doesn't it?"

"You're not wrong. And to open fire like that...."

"Exactly. It's a bit over the top."

"Are we in trouble here, Jenny?"

"Most definitely."

"Who the hell are these people anyway? They don't look like regular military to me."

He was right. A steady stream of black-suited figures rushed through the freeze-frame traffic jam, looking everywhere for Jenny and Jayesh—except up. The two of them held position, afraid to move until the immediate danger had passed.

"Special Forces?" she suggested. "SAS

or whatever they're called?"

"Maybe. There's a heck of a lot of them though. I thought Special Forces worked in small groups, not squads."

From where she was sitting midway along the floor of the top deck of the bus, Jenny could see out through the window and towards the part of town where the comet had struck. The sky's green tinge was strangely calming, not concerning. She wanted—no, she *needed*—to get closer, but didn't know why. Logic said to stay away, but what did logic have to do with anything this morning? Logic also said that, judging by the size of that thing, this part of London should have ceased to exist when it hit. The whole of the capital should have been a crater by now.

Nothing was making sense, so why bother holding back? She was about to tell Jayesh as much when her phone started to vibrate. "Dad?"

"Tell me you're on your way home, love."

"Listen, don't worry about me. I'm fine. It's all kinds of crazy out here, but I'm safe. I've found somewhere I can—"

"Come home, Jenny," he shouted, interrupting her. "There are things happening that you don't understand. You're in real danger."

"Don't waste the macho bullshit on me, Dad. I know the score. I'll be fine."

"But that's exactly my point. You don't know the score at all. There are things about today you could never have known."

"No one could have known about this."

"I knew."

"What?"

"You need to get home quick, love. Wherever you are, you're not safe. None of us are."

"Hang on. Rewind. What do you mean, *you knew*?"

"I couldn't tell you before, but now that it's begun you need to know that you were always meant to—"

Gone.

Phone dead.

"Dad? Dad, are you still there? Don't do this to me...*Dad*? What do you know about all this?"

"He was probably just going to tell you that he loves you very much and he wants you home," Jayesh suggested unhelpfully. "Smart guy."

"He tells me he loves me every day," Jenny said, staring into the phone's lifeless screen and trying every combination of button press and finger swipe to bring it back to life again. Nothing worked. "This is different. He said he knew this was going to happen."

"What, so your old man is some kind of mystic?"

"No, he's an assistant team leader in an insurance contact center."

"Who just happens to be crazy?"

"Fuck you. Dad is the most sensible bloke you could meet. Bordering on boring as hell. How could he know anything about this?"

She returned her attention to her phone again, desperate to continue the conversation with her father. Jayesh put a hand on her arm.

"It's not just your phone," he told her. "Look out there."

Blackout.

The power was down. For the first time in forever the Trafalgar Square advertising hoardings were dull and unlit. The only light now was the invasive green, dimming out the murky early morning sun.

"We clear?" Jenny asked. Jayesh peered down. The last of the soldiers were on the other side of the square.

"Yeah. We're clear. They're gone."

"I have to keep going. I need to find out what's going on."

5

The Moon

DAY TWO / 5:15 PM

Derrick sat down slowly on the living room couch. "I think she's actively trying to kill us." He was rubbing his legs; they had gone numb. He'd spent the majority of the morning in an electrical conduit, chasing down a short.

"Better than where I was." Sam had just dressed after her shower. "I'm never going to get that smell out of my hair, and Tyler's going to be back tomorrow." She sighed.

"Can't wait to see the next mortal peril he's going to get us in."

Sam chucked the towel she'd used to dry her hair at her brother. He spun it up and was about to crack it at her when the door to their apartment chimed.

"Think he's back early?" Sam almost floated to the opening.

"Surprise, sweetie!" Maddie said, seeing the disappointment upon the girl's face.

"Oh, come on, we worked all day!" Derrick moaned.

"You call that work? I did more in the bathroom this morning."

"Gawd Maddie, how are you ever going to get a guy, talking like that?" Sam said, walking away from the open door.

"I came to this dust bucket to get away from men. They're nothing but trouble wrapped up in nice packaging. Where are your parents?"

"Should be back soon." Derrick looked at the clock on the wall.

"Aren't you going to invite me in and offer me a beer? I might be easier on you two if you do."

Derrick got up and went into the kitchen. When he came back, his parents were walking through the door. His father scowled at him when he saw the beer in his hand.

"It's not mine! It's for Maddie."

"Never touch the stuff, gives me gas." She thumped a fist against her chest and burped. "But since he's not old enough, I should probably take it from him; resources are much too precious here to waste a cold one." She walked over to Derrick and winked as she snatched the can from his hand. "You two should go get some rest. Tomorrow's going to be a doozy!" Derrick rolled his eyes. "Now scoot. I need to talk to your parents."

"Whatever she says, it's a lie!" Sam beseeched as Maddie pushed her down the hallway. "She's a tyrant!" she managed to say over her shoulder. "What do you think she's saying?" she asked Derrick as their father shut the door to her room.

"Easy enough to find out." Derrick went through their shared bathroom and into his room. He grabbed a tiny translucent device, no bigger than the tip of his pinkie. He attached a wristband to his arm.

"A drone? You still play with children's toys?"

"Far from a toy, and do you want to know or not?"

"Of course," his sister responded.

Derrick fumbled with a few buttons on

the wrist device, shutting off the drone's running lights. Then he pushed it under the door and hit another button to send a projection of what the drone's camera saw onto the wall.

"It's facing the wrong way, dummy," his sister chided.

Derrick got the drone to hover a few feet from the ground before spinning it in the appropriate direction. He slowly moved it down the hallway and took a hard left to the kitchen, where the three adults were sitting at the table. Maddie had her back to the drone. They watched as her head tilted back and she swallowed what remained in the can.

"Got another?" she asked, handing the can to their father, Dean.

"Oh, Mom looks pissed," Sam said as she watched Sandra's face pinch up. "She usually only looks like that when I get into her makeup drawer or jewelry box, sometimes when I leave my stuff all over the bathroom."

Derrick pushed the drone closer.

"You're going to hit them."

"I wouldn't have to get so close if you'd be quiet."

"We've got a problem," Maddie said as she popped the top of her next beer.

"Are the kids not working?" Dean

asked.

"Don't tell them this, but they're actually really great. Been working their tails off. It's nice to have help; I'm not quite as young and fit as I used to be." She rubbed her smooth, tight belly in a mock display.

"Then what's the problem? I just got off work; I'm tired and I'd like to eat something and relax," Sandra said.

"Wow, Mom really doesn't like her, does she?" Sam asked. "She still mad that her friend got bumped from the mission for Maddie?"

"What do you think?" Derrick shrugged.

"We're listening." Dean shot a heated glance at his wife.

"Oh, he's going to pay for that tonight," Sam hissed.

Derrick held his finger up to his mouth, hoping his sister would take the hint.

"Materials that shouldn't be rotting, not in this lack of atmosphere and not with this speed...well, they are." Maddie stopped to take a swig of beer.

"Perhaps if you maintained this place better, we wouldn't have a problem. Haven't heard from any of the other bases complaining about rust."

Maddie slowly turned her head to

Sandra. "I didn't say anything about rust, and there's nobody on this floating rock doing a better job than me, Sandra. Just because you're on the Ruling Council, don't go looking down that aristocratic nose at me."

"Oh shit." Sam put her hand to her mouth. "I don't think I've ever heard anyone talk to Mom like that."

"Is it, like, physically impossible for you to keep quiet?" Derrick asked. She stuck her tongue out at him.

"Please, can we act civilly here?" Dean said, attempting to be the peacekeeper.

"What do you think's causing the problem, Maddie?"

After a tense moment, Maddie turned from Sandra and spoke. "It's like some sort of dry rot. But in this controlled environment, without cold or high moisture, it shouldn't be happening. Equipment, components, they're crumbling."

"Which ones?" Dean asked with alarm. He understood how this could be a critical issue.

"That's the thing—it's random. There's no rhyme or reason. Couple of days ago a circuit board on the control panel for the door locks on one side of the base fell apart. And just today, I found a mop bucket, clear on the other side, part of it as thin as a sheet of paper. I almost only had to look at it hard to make it crumble."

"I do not see the problem," Sandra said, getting up and looking as if she were going to go down the hallway.

Derrick quickly maneuvered the mini flying machine so she wouldn't run into it.

"Oh, really? No problem at all, Sandra? What happens when whatever this is moves to our food storage cells? How about when it affects the shell of our quaint little biodome here? Then what?" Maddie said casually. Sandra froze in her tracks.

"That's not possible. The shell is designed with special polymers, innovative alloys, Kevlar; it's designed to withstand micrometeorites!" she fairly yelled.

"You talking about this innovative alloy?" Maddie reached into the front of her overalls and the large pocket woven there. She pulled out a block of metal some six inches square. She proceeded to make a fist, crumbling the material onto the kitchen table. "Metal, plastic, glass, nothing we have is immune."

Dean's eyes grew wide before he reached across the table; he appeared hesitant to touch it. "Have you sent this to the lab?"

"Did it with the circuit board, two days

ago."

"And?" He looked at her with an intense, questioning gaze.

"Inconclusive so far, but they're doing more tests. I'm here trying to get ahead of this. If we start having multiple failures…" she left it at that. "And your wife is right about one thing. What's going on here is not happening on the other sites, at least not that they've noticed. Although, I've put a message in to Clive over on Depot 5; haven't heard back, but that's not unusual. He's so remote and communication is sketchy, especially with the sunspot storm activity."

"I think I'll have a beer with you." Dean suddenly looked worried.

Maddie turned around and looked directly into the lens of the drone camera. She raised the empty beer can up as if she were going to toss it. Derrick turned the drone around and deftly flew it back under the door to his sister's room.

"Think she saw it?" he asked, his face flush.

"Yeah, but we've got bigger things to worry about," Sam said.

6

Don't You Want to be Something?

The low door swung in with a wooden creaking noise. Air thick with the smoke and scent of tobacco wafted out and up into a swirl that faded with the breeze.

"Money and time enough to buy more tobacco for his pipe," Thistle muttered. "Useless prick."

Arridon let his sister go in and then

followed, ducking through the doorway. He shut the door behind them and threw the bar, locking the outer world away. The first floor of their cramped home huddled around a large fireplace on one wall. Pots and pans hung on iron hooks and swings for cooking there, and the rest of the room was a mishmash of adopted furniture from neighborhood homes left empty when their owners left Mercy Point for a better life inland, or left for one of the Endless City's vast citadel-settlements. A few stained paintings their father had deemed "pretty" hung on the walls, and a worn spear with a metal tip rested on a pair of crooked wall mounts above one of the couches.

On the long couch below the spear—covered in a plaid blanket with multiple burn holes in it—rested their father. In one hand he held his smoldering pipe, and in the other, the handle on his tin cup. Both items were a moment away from falling.

Arridon went to the hand holding the pipe and took it out of his father's tired grasp. Thistle went to the hand with the cup and took that as well. She put it down on the slightly out of level table beside the couch, then sat at her dad's feet. An odor of grime pervaded the space around his body and he grumbled in protest as his relics were removed from his possession.

"Stop," he slurred. "Leave me with my things."

"Dad, you're gonna burn the house down," Thistle chided. "You fell asleep with a lit pipe and a cup of whiskey. It's like you're trying to kill yourself."

"No, that's mad talk," he said as he rolled onto his back, covering his eyes with a forearm. "I need to live as long as I can to protect you both. Take care of you until your mother comes home, or if the blood comes in on the tide."

"Getting drunk every night isn't taking care of your kids, Dad," Thistle said to him. "I'm sick of this. Sick of your uselessness and neglect."

He lifted his arm off his head and tilted his neck to look at his daughter. Despite being drunk, his face contorted into a mask of guilt. He dropped his head back onto the couch's armrest and sighed in defeat.

"It's okay, Dad. She's just having a rough day. More bullies."

"Are you alright?" he asked her, assembling control over his body enough to sit up. "Did they hurt you? Do I need to get out there and beat their asses?" He looked up to the spear.

"No, Dad. I don't need your protection. I can take care of myself," Thistle said to him before standing. "Arridon has been taking care of us for years now, in case you forgot."

"He's a good man," their dad said. "You're a good woman. Better sons and daughters don't exist."

"Have you eaten anything?" Arridon asked him.

"No. I drank a lot, though. Tummy feels full."

"You have to eat," the son chastised. "You can't live on mead and whiskey."

"So far, so good. Plus there's always ale to move on to. Gods called it liquid bread."

"Let's get you upstairs to bed," Arridon said to his dad. "You haven't slept in your sheets in a week. Your back must be stiff as an oar."

"Mm," he agreed.

Thistle and Arridon helped their father up off the couch, then held him upright up the steep staircase to the low-ceilinged second floor where their tiny bedrooms were. Their father started to snore before they got his head to his lumpy pillow.

Back downstairs, Arridon pulled up the cellar trapdoor and descended into the space to search for anything they could make for dinner. He moved empty glass jars around, then pushed aside wooden boxes nailed shut with decades-old memories their father couldn't let go of. He found a few dusty, heavy jars filled with some kind of food, and lifted them up to identify their contents. He grabbed a handful of questionable quality vegetables and examined those too.

"Find anything?" his sister asked.

"Two jars of pickled beets. A bunch of carrots that are starting to go soft. A few onions I can salvage some of."

"Perfect," she said. "Roast the carrots and onions, then let a broth form. I'll go down the street to old Miss Danno's home and see if she'll spare us some of her garlic."

"We can't keep getting handouts."

"I don't take anything for free, silly. I'm proud too. I help her with her laundry and pick up her floors for her. She has a hard time bending over, with her bad back and all."

Arridon appeared from the cellar, vegetables in hand. "Oh…that's nice of you. That makes me feel better. I don't think I could stomach owing people for something like food."

"Me neither. I do have to deal with her diatribes about how the gods left us to die, but she's mostly just out of touch. Plus, she grows some pretty delicious garlic."

"The price we pay."

"I'll be right back. You start cooking."

"Okay. If those assholes show up, just run back here and I'll take care of them, okay?"

"You don't have to protect me, you know. I can take care of myself."

"I believe that, but that's never going to stop me from trying to protect you. You're my sister. We half-gods have to take care of each other; no one else seems to want to. Besides, one day, all this anger I've been holding onto is gonna get out, and they're the best reason I can think of to set that monster free."

Thistle didn't reply to that. She just thought about her father, sleeping his poison off in his old, sweat-stained bed.

"She does grow a mean head of garlic," Arridon said after swallowing another mouthful of the meager hodgepodge vegetable soup. He brushed a lock of brown hair back behind his ear and listened as the growling in his stomach took a momentary break. The fresh silence in their house only had to contend with the crackling of the driftwood fire in the fireplace, and the sound of Thistle chewing her food.

"Will you take me to Ranmyr? Or the Citadel of the Temples?" she asked him.

"If that's what you want, yeah. I haven't been since last summer, but it's easy enough to find. The city walls go from one edge of the horizon to the other, and the channel between the two citadels can't be missed. Head north along the Trade Road. Watch out for bandits. Ranmyr is the one you want; the loonies at the Temples will all try and convert you to one of their religions."

"Thank you. When can we go?"

"Tomorrow morning?" Arridon said with a shrug. "All my things are in a single bag already. Just need the spear to protect us from any bandits on the road. Pack your things tonight and we'll grab some food on the way out of Mercy Point in the morning."

"Do we have enough money for this?"

"No."

"Then what will we do? How will we be able to eat? Where will we sleep?"

"Who cares? It can't be much worse than it is here now. Empty home, haunted by the ghost of a mother we barely knew and a father that's just waiting to die and join her," Arridon said. "We'll do what we always do. Find the work no one wants to do, and do it for money or food. I think we'll also find friendlier eyes there. Far more children of the gods in the city than here in the southern and central outlands."

"I'll get my bag packed after we eat. What will we tell Dad?"

"Nothing," Arridon said, dejected. "He won't notice we're gone for at least a day, and by then, we'll already be at the Endless City's walls. We could leave him a note, but that's assuming he'll be coherent enough to read it."

"You're right; I won't want to come back," Thistle said, dragging her spoon along the bottom of the wooden bowl, almost empty of the simple soup. "If I stay in Mercy Point much longer, I'll lose what little brains I have left, get pregnant with some idiot's baby, and that'll be it."

"I do not foresee you doing that," Arridon said. "You are not that woman."

"But every day I'm here, I feel like I'm slipping closer to that destiny, and that's worse than dying, you know? To live your life knowing that, no matter what you try and do where you are, you're always going to wind up being far less than you could've hoped to be, somewhere else. Don't you want to be something? Do something special? See the depths of the Endless City? Look for old golden relics? Own your own farm? Be the captain of your own ship? Learn magic? Something? Anything's better than dragging up empty nets day after day, or doing slave work for old vegetables, and moldy bread. Never mind being a parent to a father who can't be bothered to take care of his own children. I deserve more than what Mercy Point can offer, and you do too."

"Pack your bag. We'll go in the morning before Dad wakes up."

Thistle stood up from the small table and ran upstairs. Arridon heard her stuffing a bag with her most crucial of possessions, and before he could swallow the soup in his mouth, she was scampering down the stairs with her bag. Arridon watched his sister drop the bag on the floor near the barred door before she sat down to finish her soup.

"That was quick."

"The less I bring, the better off I'll be," she reasoned.

"Cool. Alright then. Eat up, and try to sleep. First light, we're out of Mercy Point and on the trade road heading north to Ranmyr and the Channel into the city ruins. We start our lives over. Leave this world behind."

Thistle bounced with excitement.

Arridon did too, but he hid it as best he could. Had to be the stoic older brother, after all.

Her older brother—by four years—made the effort, and slept upstairs in his bed one more time before leaving Mercy Point. Thistle couldn't. She went to the couch below the old spear and put her head on the same headrest her father had slept on earlier that evening. His scent clung to the rough material, and Thistle fought through the stench of tobacco and spilled whiskey just enough to give herself remnant memories of better times, as a very little girl, loved.

Comforting as those memories were, with their hugs and smiles, they didn't show her anything of her mother, and they failed to lull her to sleep. Her heart beat for the morning's journey, and as the minutes slipped into the void of the dark room, lit only by the embers in the fireplace and the flames on the larger logs she threw in, dawn crept closer, and eventually, the shutters on the windows flanking the tiny main door were surrounded by a blue border of dawn's light. Sleep had eluded her.

She sat up on the couch and looked at the light sliding underneath the front door. The slit of dawn went dark for a moment as someone walked past outside. The light grew bright again, then dark as someone else passed. After a minute of the alternating brightness, the light started blinking in and out faster as others came or went, running in the narrow street her home faced.

Voices began to seep through the crack. Short bursts of urgent communication, each charged with emotion whose origin she didn't understand. She jumped off the couch and trotted to the door. Bar undone, she pulled it open and took in the scene of the street.

"Stay inside," one of the lumbering fisherman said to her as he jogged past, heading towards the waterfront.

"What? Why?"

He stopped and faced her. In his hands he hefted a long, thin knife they used to cut fish. "The tide is in, and there's blood washing up on the beach and against the docks."

"Blood?"

"Blood. Thick and red they say. The war is upon us," he said. "The gods have failed, and demons are coming. I'm going to see for myself."

"I…" she tried, but couldn't find anything else to say. It couldn't be true. The war was a lie. No one ever went to it, no one ever returned from it. A great lie to keep kids in their itchy beds at night.

"Stay inside. Pack your things. We'll all be on the road going far from here before the midday. I wish you well," he said, then turned and ran towards the sea.

Thistle shut the door and slid the bar across the way. She spun in her simple cotton dress and went to the stairs. Once at the top she rapped on the door to her brother's room. She knocked three times, waited a second, then knocked again.

"Yes?" she heard Arridon croak. "Is it morning already?"

"Barely. Arridon, there's a bit of a commotion outside. I opened the door, and a man said there was blood at the beach."

She heard the bed's ropes groan in protest as he got to his feet. The door swung open. His face betrayed his worry. "Demon blood?"

"How would I know?"

"I have to see," he said. "And if it's real, then we need to get out of here as fast as we can. If it's blood from the gods' war, then the Bleed is winning, and it's close. And unlike gods…humans can be infected by their evil. One drop corrupts."

"Don't go to the shore. Let's just leave. Let's just go right now."

"I'm just gonna look. I won't touch the water, and if I see anyone turning into a monster like the legends say, I'll run," he said, pulling his boots on.

"We're gonna look. You're not going alone."

Arridon grabbed the spear off the wall before they bolted out the front door of their family shed.

7

London

They'd made it as far as Blackfriars and hadn't seen a soul between Trafalgar Square and the river. The streets were silent, as if everything living had been sucked up and swept away; no more soldiers or Special Forces or whatever else they were. No other people. Not even a single dog, rat or bird. Jenny was unsettled but kept it to herself. She heard nothing other than their own footsteps. The troops they'd seen a short while earlier, the thousands of people being evacuated from the city center, the helicopters they'd seen buzzing around the comet...they should have been able to hear *something*. This utter, impenetrable silence was terrifying. The temptation to turn tail and run was almost overwhelming, but the need to find out what was going on in the heart of her beloved London kept her moving.

It didn't matter that their phones were dead, because the way they needed to go was obvious. They paused when they reached Blackfriars Bridge and looked across to the other side of the river. The persistent green glow was coming from an area behind the Tate Modern, not far from the Shard. How that particular building, over three hundred meters, ninety-five stories tall and covered in glass, could have survived the arrival and landing of the comet so nearby defied explanation.

But even more distracting than the color of the sky and the desolation of the empty city was the stillness of the River Thames. It had stopped flowing. The water barely moved, hardly even a ripple. A pleasure boat sat motionless as if it had been sailing through jelly which had set mid-voyage.

"This is so fucked up," Jayesh said.

"I know. How can a river just stop?"

"What if it's worse than that? What about the oceans?"

"What are you saying? That the tides have stopped too? That's not possible."

"The tides have something to do with the moon, don't they?"

"They have *everything* to do with the moon. I thought everybody knew that. That's junior school science. They're caused by the gravitational pulls between the moon and the sun and us."

"So whatever that thing is out there, it's big enough to be fucking around with the very fabric of what holds the universe together."

"I'm going to find out."

"You'll get yourself killed."

"Very possibly."

Jenny walked on and over the bridge, pausing only when she heard noises again. She looked back and saw more of the black-clad soldiers chasing after them from the direction she and Jayesh had just come. Her pace quickened to a jog, then a run, then a sprint.

"He might be right," she said to herself, "you could be running towards your death." And yet she couldn't stop. Lungs and legs burning, she raced towards Christ alone knew what.

On the other side of the bridge she made

a sudden change of direction. "This way," she shouted back to Jayesh who'd lost sight of her momentarily. He caught up with her as she yanked open the door of a recently completed residential block. "We need to get up high," she said, breathless. "We'll have a better chance of seeing what's going on from up there."

"And you think the people who live here will have just left their doors open? Have you got any idea how much top floor apartments go for in a building like this?"

"Yeah, too much."

"We're talking a couple of million quid for a one bedroom flat in a postcode like this."

"And that matters because? I'm not planning on hanging around. It's just the height of this place I'm after."

She raced to the bottom of a staircase and started to climb. Jayesh, feeling the pace, followed. The close confines of the stairs made him uneasy. It felt like they'd been cut off from the rest of the world and were running blind.

"What exactly are you doing?" Jayesh shouted, desperately trying not to lose sight of Jenny.

"Trying to find out what's going on out there, because this is really frigging weird."

"Which bit, the comet or whatever it is

or the water flow stopping?"

"None of that. It's you and me. Okay, how's this…an hour ago we hadn't met, now we're up here together thick as thieves, maybe the only two civilians left in the whole of central London."

"What's your point?"

"My point is I don't know you, and you don't know me. One minute you're delivering breakfast to the rich kids in the City, the next you're running headfirst into oblivion alongside someone you don't know anything about. Anyone would think you're keeping tabs on me."

"It's just been one of those mornings, I guess. So what are you about, Jenny?"

She turned her back and started to climb again. "I'm nothing. Nobody. I sell overpriced fish and chips to tourists."

He caught up with her and they continued their climb in silence. She finally spoke again when they reached the top floor.

"Tell you the truth, I'm not the kind of girl who usually disappears off with blokes they've never met. Particularly when that bloke just tried to kill me."

"I didn't try and kill you."

"I know you didn't."

"I'm the one trying to get you to leave."

"It's just weird…I can't explain it, it just

feels like...like I was always supposed to be here."

They stepped out into a sun-soaked vestibule at the top of the building with floor-to-ceiling length windows at either end. They were rewarded with glorious views over the empty city. The clouds of dust had settled, leaving everything coated with a layer. Apart from the lack of movement, the streets filled with unmoving traffic and the unnaturally gelatinous river water, it looked like the iconic view they'd both seen a thousand times before. All the expected landmarks, all present and correct. Together they crossed to the other side of the building, where everything had changed.

"Fuck..." Jayesh said, open-mouthed.

Their position from up on floor thirty-something of the luxury apartment block was terrifying and exhilarating in equal measure. Down below them, a vast expanse of land had been reduced to rubble. And at the center of it all was the comet-thing. Girders had cupped it like the massive frozen fingers of a twisted steelwork hand.

"It's half the size it was," Jayesh said.

"Less than that. When that thing first appeared, it was fucking huge. I reckon it's only a few meters across now. Christ, it must be so heavy, so dense. It's a wonder it doesn't fall through to the center of the earth."

"I don't think it's interested in obeying the laws of physics, do you?"

"I don't think it cares," she said. "See how it's only destroyed one building? The level of control is incredible."

"'Control' as in someone piloting it? Little green men and all that?"

"Or little green women," she corrected him quickly.

It was as if they'd been vacuum-sealed up here. Their viewing platform felt deceptively safe. For the first time, they felt able to stop and stand still and take stock of everything. Below them, the mysterious object had lost much of its green hue and now looked gray, like stone. It was smooth. Featureless.

"It definitely was controlled," Jenny said. "If it had come down with any force at all it would have been buried. That thing carried out a perfect touchdown."

The spherical mass looked like it had been there forever, as if the rubble around it was the remains of the buildings which had tried to compete with it and had failed.

Jenny became aware of a sudden change in the light, the atrium filling with shadow. She looked around and saw a helicopter level with the top of the apartment block. It was black. Almost featureless. Definitely military. It was like something out of an action movie, the way it hovered, holding position and facing them like an enormous insect, ready to take a bite or plant a sting. It hung there ominously, swaying slightly but going nowhere.

"Do you think—?" she started to say, before it opened fire. Jayesh lurched to the right and dove on top of Jenny, both of them skidding across the marble then coming to an undignified halt when they hit the nearest wall. Jayesh pulled her to safety. The air—so still and deceptively calm just seconds earlier—was now filled with the combined cacophony of gunfire, shattering glass, and the ear-splitting *thump-thump-thump* of the helicopter's rotor blades.

"I'm starting to think someone's got it in for us," Jenny said, covering her head and protecting her face from shards of glass and sharp daggers of concrete. She got up, grabbed his hand and dragged him down the staircase they'd spent so long climbing up. She was momentarily aware of a flash of light and a high-pitched shriek as a missile hit the top floor of the building.

"Do you have a price on your head or something?" Jayesh asked as they thundered back downstairs. He was so scared he could barely coordinate his legs. His escape was more as a result of gravity than control.

"I already told you, I'm nobody. Anyway, who says it's me they're shooting at? Who the hell are you?"

The noise in the stairwell was unbearable. The entire building shook precariously as missile after missile was fired, the helicopter crew working their way down the length of the apartment block. Both Jenny and Jayesh knew that it was only a matter of time before the whole structure came crashing down, but neither allowed their fear to delay them. If anything, the terror was an accelerant. Over and over, turn after turn, step after step and flight after flight — their rapid descent became a breathless blur of walls and floors. Jenny lost sight of Jayesh, and losing him spurred her to run faster. Another missile hit, and this time it felt like the whole building was swaying, about to be felled.

Jenny couldn't see Jayesh when she reached the ground floor. She didn't have time to care: *get out of the building, then worry about everything else.* She caught a glimpse through a dust-covered window of black-suited figures swarming outside and turned back on herself to find another exit.

The doors will all be covered, she guessed. She needed a less obvious way out. A huge chunk of masonry dropped from the ceiling and hit the ground just a couple of meters ahead of her, blocking her way through, but giving her a little unexpected cover. The force of it nearly knocked her off her feet. Moments later and she'd have been right under it. *At least I wouldn't have known anything,* she thought. She'd have been wiped out like someone had switched off a light.

The door to a ground floor flat had been left propped open, no doubt in the haste of the occupant's frantic escape. Jenny didn't think—she just burst into the flat and ran towards the light. Most of the windows in the apartment were locked, but she was able to force one open in the bathroom. It was narrow, and she could only reach it by climbing on top of the toilet cistern and hauling herself up, but it was enough. She was on autopilot now, kicking and thrashing to get out before what was left of the building came down on top of her. She stretched her arms out, reaching down the other side of the glass, trying to guide herself out but failing miserably. She overbalanced and flipped, landing on her back on the ground. The force of impact knocked the breath from her lungs and for a few precious seconds, she just lay there, looking up at the building coming down.

No time to think.

Jenny scrambled back to her feet and started to run. She zigzagged wildly, boulder-like chunks of concrete falling around her, forcing her to change direction at every turn. And then the most awful noise...a sound so deep and low and ominous and all-powerful that she could feel it as much as hear it. A prolonged, sonorous din: the dying groans of the apartment block.

She kept going for as long as she could, then threw herself down and covered her head as the building collapsed. She glanced back momentarily, certain she was about to be crushed, then did a double take. Bizarre. The building wasn't falling towards her, thank God. Instead, it was tipping sideways. She climbed back to her feet and watched as what was left of the apartment block collapsed into its nearest neighbor.

And then, on a day where every minute seemed more surreal than the last, the first building fell onto the second as if had been pushed, and the force of that impact made the second building come down on a third. Then a fourth. And another and another and another and...and it was only when Jenny had turned through a full three-sixty and she was looking back at the ruined stump of the building she'd originally escaped from, that she realized a complete circle of buildings had come down all around her. In the madness, she almost forgot about Jayesh. She'd had such a breathless and remarkable escape that she couldn't imagine he'd been as lucky. Poor sod. What if he'd still been in that building, looking for her? She felt a sudden pang of guilt, as if all of this was somehow her fault.

Jenny's sadness and regret didn't last. Her overriding emotion now was fear. She was trapped; imprisoned by a towering wall of debris on all sides. Isolated. Completely alone and totally exposed.

And that wasn't the worst of it.

As the dust settled and more of the devastation around her came back into focus, Jenny realized she'd fucked up badly. She'd intended on retracing her steps and running towards the river, but in the chaos of her frantic escape, she'd taken a wrong turn and gone the other way.

Next to her now, right at the very center of the ruination, just a couple of meters from where she was standing, was the comet-thing.

Her brain screamed at her not to get too near, but her heart said something different.

She couldn't be this close to the thing which had triggered all this madness and not touch it, could she? She knew it might burn her or poison her, but that didn't seem to matter. She might already be breathing in toxic fumes or absorbing deadly levels of radiation, but the risk felt inconsequential.

I've got this far and I'm still alive, she thought. *I've survived being shot at and crushed. What's the worst that could happen?*

It was beautiful.

Until now, she'd only seen images on TV and glimpses of the object when it had first appeared in the sky over London. It looked so different that she questioned whether it was the same thing at all. Its diameter now, she estimated, was between four and five meters, a fraction of its original size, but still enough to dwarf her. It was resting in the hollow it had made on impact, the dip cupping it from rolling away. Jenny had visions of *Raiders of the Lost Ark*, of her getting too close and disturbing it, then being chased by it for miles through the ruins until it rolled her over.

Again she thought of Jayesh. *Poor guy.*

She was up close now and could feel a residual heat coming from the surface of the thing. What was it made of? It was perfectly spherical, machined to the smoothest of finishes like a huge ball bearing. And that thought caught her off-guard; the fact it had been purposefully designed and built. She knew it wasn't here by chance, that all of this had been planned by something or someone. It was supposed to have arrived in London this morning, and she was supposed to be here with it.

Stone or metal? Some kind of plastic? A previously undiscovered material? The quality of its surface made it impossible to tell without touching. Standing in the immense object's shadow, Jenny lifted a hand but paused just before making contact with her fingertips. For such a small movement, it felt like she was about to take an improbably large leap of faith. The next few millimeters felt like they would define the rest of her life or end it. The danger was unparalleled, and yet she felt no fear. She couldn't imagine getting this close and *not* touching it now.

So she did.

The surface of the orb was so smooth, so completely frictionless, that it was almost as if she hadn't touched it at all. When she felt no immediate heat or pain, when she wasn't shocked or repelled or electrocuted or vaporized, she pressed her whole hand flat against it. It felt as if her skin had become welded to the thing, and she quickly withdrew to make sure that it hadn't. She inspected her palm for signs of injury, but there was nothing, and she risked touching it again. This time she left her hand where it was, but pushed down harder and for longer. When she stepped away she saw a faint, luminous green glow where her palm had been.

Jenny's phone began to ring again. *Of all the times...* She felt it vibrating in the back pocket of her trousers and immediately reached for it. *Funny,* she thought, *how conditioned we all are to react.* There she was, standing on the threshold of something either dreadful or transcendent, and yet her phone was still a distraction impossible to ignore. It must have re-started itself. Last time she checked, it had been dead.

It was Dad. Again.

"I told you to come home," he yelled. His voice sounded remarkably clear, like he was standing next to her. She wished he was.

"I'm on my way," she said. "It's mad out here, Dad."

"Don't lie to me, Jennifer."

"I'm not...."

"You *are*. I can see you on the bloody television."

"How?"

"Look up," he told her. She could see drones drifting high overhead. "You don't know what you're messing with."

"And you do?"

"Yes," he said, and the firm authority in his voice took the wind from her sails. "They're careful how much they show on TV, but I know that helicopter was firing at you. They made it out to look like they brought down the buildings to keep the transport contained, but all they're trying to do is stop *you* getting to it."

"The transport?" she interrupted. "What is this thing?"

"Get home and we'll explain everything."

"We?"

"Now's not the time to argue. Please just do what I say. I'm scared for you, Jen."

It was at that precise moment that all the nerves she'd managed to either suppress or ignore came crashing over her, a tsunami of guilt, regret and stupidity. It hit her like a wall, and yet, at the same time, she felt vindicated. She knew she had to be here. The fact that if Dad could see her then it was likely the rest of the world could too barely even registered. The moment felt enormous on so many levels.

"I'm sorry, Dad. It's hard to explain. It's just I—"

A screeching blast of static ended the call. She held the phone at arm's length, recoiling from the godawful, ear-piercing feedback.

The ground began to shake.

Jenny looked up and saw that her handprint on the side of the sphere was still visible, and that the glow from her fingers and palms had increased in intensity and had started to spread across the globe, illuminating previously unseen channels, lines and grooves. It looked the way she thought daybreak would look if viewed from space; the way daylight eats away the dark, steadily waking the sleeping world.

But Christ, she was really starting to think she might be in trouble now.

Unless she was going completely mad — and that was looking like an increasingly likely explanation for the events of the day so far — the huge ball had climbed to be perhaps a meter up into the air, high enough that its full shape was again above ground, and it was starting to spin. Faster and faster it went, the green light becoming brighter and brighter and turning to white. Grit, rubble and dust was being whipped up furiously around the shape, held in orbit as if trapped by some invisible magnetic force. It whirled around the orb in the opposite direction to that in which the ball itself spun. The speed of everything continued to increase and a ferocious wind blew, but Jenny stood her ground, defiant. Faster and faster and faster until her eyes could barely focus on any detail and all movement had become a single relentless blur.

And then it stopped.

The light disappeared and the clouds of impossibly contained debris dropped as if whatever had been holding them had become bored and walked away.

The orb was gone. There was nothing left now but a hole in the ground. Jenny edged forward and peered down. She started laughing — partly through nerves, but mostly because all she could think about was a scene from *The Terminator*. The original had always been one of Dad's favorite films, and she'd watched it with him hundreds of times. Now, right in front of her, on what felt like the very edge of Armageddon, some random guy was mimicking Arnold Schwarzenegger: down on one knee in an area of ground burnt away through the side-effects of some ridiculously futuristic mode of travel, butt naked. The person definitely wasn't Arnold, but otherwise the resemblance was uncanny. He was clearly powerful, athletic looking. His head was bowed as if he was composing his thoughts or otherwise recovering from his chaotic, otherworldly arrival in the center of London.

"Not one scrap of this makes any sense," Jenny said to no one in particular. "I've lost my mind. Maybe I died when I got knocked down? Maybe we all died...?"

The man in front of her lifted his head and fixed her with an intense, yet oddly reassuring look. Her feet remained rooted to the ground while a thousand screaming thoughts ran around inside her head: *Run! Get away while you can! Disappear like everyone else did.... He's going to kill you....*

But somehow she knew that he would never hurt her.

He climbed out of the hole and stood upright, towering over her.

"Hello, Jenny," he said, and in the madness of the morning so far, she didn't even stop to wonder how he knew her name. His face was beautiful and strong; unique, and yet, that of an everyman at the same time. She should have been terrified. She should have run for her life. Thing was, she was exactly where she wanted to be.

"Who the hell are you?" she demanded, sounding more confident than she felt.

His answer was simple, yet impossible. Crazy, but unquestionably honest.

"I'm God," he said.

8

The Moon — Clive Barrow

Clive Barrow had been a nuclear physicist on Earth; he'd helped create some of the most inventive forms of new energy the planet had seen in over seventy-five years. So it came as no surprise when two government officials came to his modest home in the mountains of Idaho with a request to fly immediately to Washington,

DC, to sit in on an ultra-secret meeting.

Curiosity had won out over his desire to be left alone in his remote location. He'd been intrigued by the notion of life on the moon, but that had stopped at the foot of reality. He knew the days of Earth remaining sustainable were numbered, but according to his calculations, even if he lived to the furthest extent of his days, he could pass some twenty years before the earth became the wasteland it was rapidly heading toward.

His motto had always been "What I can't see can't hurt me," a strange adage for one that worked with things at the molecular level, though he never did see the hypocrisy. He'd refused their offer over a dozen times during the week, no matter how sweetened the pot had become. It wasn't until they'd flown him home that he changed his mind. His home of thirty years had been broken into and everything of value either stolen or destroyed. The monsters (for that's what he thought of the people that had done this) had urinated on his couch and defecated on his kitchen table and bed. No matter how well he cleaned the surface, he would never be able to get the imagery of that curling shit out of his mind. He'd never have another pleasant meal or a good night's sleep again. Not there.

He'd been on the moon some six months before it ever dawned on him that, in all likelihood, it had been the government that deliberately vandalized his home. They'd read his dossier and were very familiar with his peculiarities; his fear of germs and obsessive-compulsive disorder would make dealing with a filthy desecration almost unbearable. As soon as he'd come to that dark realization, he retreated to the colony's Energy Housing Compound. It had never been designed for permanent lodgings, and the nuclear cell was so well designed and needed such minimal maintenance that it only needed to be checked on a couple times a year. There wouldn't be a problem. He'd become bitter with the people he'd worked with, convinced that they'd had something to do with the government's nefarious plans, so he opted to move as far away from them all as he could. Daily he fantasized about the notion of crippling the cell and destroying the entire colony in one fell swoop.

"Would serve them right," he said aloud as he looked upon the various gauges, inputting the data into a spreadsheet he had created to search for any irregularities in the output.

"What's this?" he asked, looking at the

ground. He bent to run his fingers over the metallic shavings. Clive looked to the wall that formed the protective housing for the energy and noticed a rough-looking area. He ran his hand along the surface; more material fell to the floor. "That can't be good. Better call Maddie and have her check it out." As he stood he felt lightheaded, he canted to the side, his head rapping lightly against the wall. As he began to sink down, he looked over to his workbench and the foil-packaged energy bar he was supposed to eat that morning to keep his blood sugar level from dropping.

"Fucking diabetes," were Clive's last words.

9

The Red Tide

Spear in hand, Arridon led the charge back down the narrow streets of Mercy Point in the direction of the calamity happening at the water's edge. He took the same route in reverse he'd taken the day prior, but instead of continuing forward toward the docks and the rising sun, he took a left and headed north towards the rocky jetty and the small beach beyond. On his heels ran Thistle, carrying their family kitchen knife, still covered with bits of raw onion and carrot.

What little crowd the village could muster had gathered there, looking down on the lower, sandy shore from the higher, drier position above the water. Gossip-loving old biddies stood beside curious teenage boys, who stood beside brave men and women holding bandages and weapons, ready for a war that may or may not be about to erupt.

Arridon reached the crest of the low bluff and pushed his way through the crowd with grace. He slid past one, then two of the villagers, then more, until he started going downhill with Thistle. Her feet padded behind his in the grassy sand as they walked to the water's edge, but their movement ceased when their eyes rose to the shore.

"Bloody sand," Arridon said. "Oh *fuck* no."

Bloody sand it was. Stained pink by the red froth of the alarmingly crimson water coming in wave after wave, the coagulated runners in the wash tracked and wiggled like tentacles where they caught grip of something to hold on to. The smell of it all, salty like the sea, but coppery like a bitten lip and a bloody nose, combined to make the scene unbearable. Too real. Too true.

A single spear floated in on the water until it reached the sand, and its metal tip lodged in the beach.

"Halfsies," a man's voice called out to them. "Golden eyes."

Arridon and Thistle turned to look at the speaker. Neither brother nor sister knew the barrel-shaped man's name, but they knew he frequented the inn taverns near the docks, and often took jobs on ships that left quitting sailors on shore. His eyes were fixed open with fear.

"Ya know more of the gods' war than anyone else here, I reckon," he continued, "half-blooded as you are. Is that what we're seeing? Is this the spilled blood of gods and demons? Ya?"

"I can't say for sure…but this is what my father said would happen if the demons ever started to win. They're coming up and over the edge of the world, at the ocean's edge to the east where the water turns cold, and the void meets the land. That's where the battle has raged for our whole lives. This same ocean," Arridon explained. "And that spear…it wasn't on a fishing boat. If the legends are true, we mustn't touch the water. Mortals can be infected by the madness in the blood of the demons. You'll turn into one of them; a monster."

"Just mortals are in danger?"

"Gods were immune, as I understand it."

"What about halfsies?" he asked. "Are ya immune to this monster curse like yer god-kin?"

"I...I don't know. I have no plans to find out. We should leave. All of us, the whole village. Head inland. Head to the city, head anywhere. If the blood is here, then the madness and the war cannot be far behind. If we want to live another day, we shouldn't plan on that day being here at Mercy Point," the young man counseled.

"Alright then," the sailor agreed. He turned back towards the silent, watching crowd and waved them away. "Half-bloods say the water's tainted and we need to go. Abandon Mercy Point for safer refuge, ya. No harm in leaving for a few days to see if they're right."

"Bah, bullshit," one of the other sailors hollered. A drunk, judging by the loose quality of his words. "Just a red tide at night. We had them a decade ago one warm summer. Turned out to be a dead whale a dozen yards offshore. They just want to ransack our houses when we leave. Take our food and heirlooms."

"We don't want your trash," Thistle yelled back at the man. "And look into the surf; there's no whale a dozen yards offshore. Our bags are packed, and we are leaving on the trade road right now. Come on, Arridon. I've had enough of this town and its thanklessness."

"Lies," the man returned in a shout. He shoved his way through the people around him and strode down to the red sand and the crimson ocean waves lapping up atop it in the dawn light. "They're thieves, like all the half-breeds we've ever seen. Look here; I'll touch this demon water. Show everyone their falseness. Watch."

"Don't do it," Arridon warned him. "You'll be dead in a minute. Or worse than dead."

"You right fuck off, thieving halfsie," he called back, and awkwardly bent over to stick both hands in the surf.

"Uncle, no!" a teenager called out, and the man paused. Arridon and Thistle looked to the new speaker. The nephew was Sebastian, the boy from the street the day prior, and he pleaded again. "Please. Don't."

"Watch, boy, and learn," the uncle said, and plunged his hands into the bloody surge of water just at his feet.

Not one of Mercy Point's citizens drew breath as the rebellious man rubbed the viscous surf water over the front and back of his hands, then up and down his forearms. Where he smeared the substance, it stuck like real blood, and when he got to his feet, his arms remained filthy with it. He shook them off, to no effect, and stared down Thistle and Arridon.

"See? Nothing to fret over. Just two pieces of halfsie scum trying to use a perfectly natural bit of weather to rob us blind."

The gathered crowd found their voices, and used them to laugh nervously. The laughter turned into mocking of the brother and sister, and before long, many of the half asleep, deluded villagers were yelling slurs at them, and threatening the brother and sister if they didn't leave.

"Come on," Arridon begged his sister. "It's long since time for us to leave."

They made their way in a wide circle around the thirty or forty angry villagers to head back to their home and their belongings. Arridon kept his eyes fused on the man who'd stuck his arms in the water. He went to his nephew Sebastian and embraced him, laughing with a touch of mania, like a man who'd bet his life on a card game, and stole the win with an improbable hand.

"He's the thief," Arridon whispered, "taking the trust from everyone." Just as his words were spoken, the man's head twitched to the side in a spasm.

"What?" Thistle asked her brother.

"Nothing…or, well, does he look okay to you?"

They slowed the pace of their escape and watched the man as he allowed his embrace with his nephew to slip to an arm's length. He grinned at Sebastian—not a smile, but a drawn grimace, like a greed-driven hyena feasting on a hare—then a trickle of dark heart's blood issued from one of his nostrils.

"Bleeder! He's changing!" Arridon screamed, jabbing the spear's tip in the direction of the man.

The sound of bones cracking drowned out the splashing of the waves coming into shore.

The gathered, jeering villagers turned in time to watch the first of many murders happen that morning. He dove forward with his head, burying his grinning, now fanged teeth into Sebastian's chest where it met the neck. The boy yelped out in pain, then bellowed in choked misery as his uncle used new teeth to create new wounds in his flesh. His cries of pain split the morning sky in two and silenced the sound of the sea with its raw agony. More of the idiot uncle's skeleton broke and fused to make his body twisted beyond recognition, completely new.

Arridon was overcome by an urge he'd never felt before. He strode forward, away from his sister towards the man attacking the boy he himself had wanted to hurt just the day prior. In his strong hand he spun the spear around for throwing, and when he felt he could make the throw, he stepped into it and hurled the sharpened, steel-tipped shaft of wood with all his might.

The spear whistled through the damp, summer morning sea-air, and knifed its way into the side of the man with the bloody hands, lodging in his ribs, a foot of spear coming out his back on the opposite side. The mutating sailor let his nephew go without shout or cry of pain. Sebastian fell to the grassy sands, clutching at his raw, pulped neck as the monstrous, murderous uncle turned to face Arridon.

His face had abandoned all sense of normalcy in short seconds. His jaws had thickened, and grown, jutting forward so they could bare the massive fangs the mouth had grown. Thick, protrusive ridges of bone and horn erupted from his brow, and worst of all, his eyes had shifted into something evil, something beyond human. Yellow centers, bright as the sun and glowing were surrounded by swollen, ruby-crimson flesh where the whites once were. Black pricks at the center of the light stared at Arridon, oozing hatred as deep as the pit on loneliness in their father's heart.

He locked eyes with the speared monster, and the world froze. A voice manifested in his ear, as if whispered by someone standing at his side.

Half breeds die first.

The voice changed, and shouted to all those gathered: *Kill the half breeds, and you shall be allowed to worship me as slaves instead of serving as my sustenance.*

Then the world returned at full speed. None of the crowd rushed to do the monster's bidding, but they looked to Thistle and Arridon, and their thoughts shown in their eyes.

Then chaos was upon them. The man-turned-demon, infected by the Bleed, turned and ran straight past the now-screaming and running crowd towards the unarmed Arridon. Yellow-red eyes fixated on the young man's thin neck, it loped, leaping as its posture broke down, turning it into an even more monstrous, contorted, wrong-bodied horror from the void.

"Run! Home!" Arridon screamed at his sister, and she listened.

Over the grassy sands then over the rocks they scrambled. They ran as fast as their bodies allowed, and then pushed harder. All the while, with each desperate, pained and frightened stride, the monster remained on their heels, just steps behind, snarling, raging, frothing, speaking in a wild, nightmarish tongue that somehow charred their frayed nerves and made the fear inside them threaten to choke them into apathy. Through the streets of Mercy Point they ran, past closed doors and shuttered windows. Past the frightened cries of hiding citizens, and even past an old man watching it all with uncaring, ready-to-die eyes.

The old man and his eyes got their wish as the demon's unending hunger and hatred for humanity spied an easy target. Behind Thistle and Arridon, it tilted its murderous path and crashed into the gray-haired man, smashing the life from him and beginning another blood-spilling feast. The urge to stop and help nearly overwhelmed Arridon, but he saw his sister's face contort when the sound of the beastly mauling hit her ears.

She was the one he had to save, not the old man.

They rounded one last corner as meat was torn apart, and several small houses later, they crashed into and through their own front door, slamming it shut behind them. Arridon jammed the wooden bar into the brace across the frame, and dragged the closest couch over to block the door further. With his long arms and legs, he dragged a hutch to block the window beside the door. He collapsed into the plaid couch, panting as Thistle leaned on their small table, hands placed between the two wooden bowls they had eaten soup from only the night before.

"What the fuck?" she cried out in a voice mixed with sobs and laughter.

"What's happening outside?" their father asked from the base of the stairs. His voice rang with urgency, and clarity. No sound of any alcoholic influence could be heard.

"You're awake?" Arridon exclaimed.

"I am. I heard screams. Answer me. What's happening outside?"

"The shores are bloody. A man touched the water, and he started to…started to change," Thistle said, her voice breaking. "This isn't right. It's not real."

"The eyes?" her father asked, monotone, his expression locked and serious. "What did his eyes look like?

"Red and yellow and…lit by a light from within. Like…staring into a sun from another world. Here, but not here," Arridon explained. Outside, the far-off cries of the elderly man finally halted. Their disappearance caused no relief.

"You're right about that," their father answered. "Your mother's greatest fears. Damn it. Time for us to leave." He walked over to the cellar door and lifted the handle so he could descend.

"Dad, this is not the time for you to look through our empty root cellar," Thistle chastised.

"Daughter, you've no idea what I'm doing. Get rid of that knife. Cutting him will only spill his blood and put yourself and others in danger of infection. Grab a bag and pack it to travel fast and light. Our best weapon is speed."

"I'm already packed," she shot back at him.

Her dad stopped, and looked at her. His dark hair seemed a touch grayer for her comment. "Oh. That's good, I guess."

"What's in there you need? We don't have any food to bring. We're gonna starve fast, if those things don't kill us," Arridon said.

"Oh, they're going to try and kill us; that's for certain. Eating is a secondary concern. All we can do now is run to the city and try and find a way out. Your mother left me with some instructions."

"A way out? What do you mean?"

"The Bleed is not of this world. Not of this universe. It and the creatures that serve it are from the realm the race of gods came from. The gods came here to escape it, but the Bleed found a way to follow them. The gods built several ways out of this world. Places to escape to if this ever happened. Another chance to start over."

"This is the Gods' War?" Thistle asked him.

"Not anymore," he replied, and then looked into her golden eyes. "Now it's our war." He ducked under the floor, into the cellar, and started to move wooden crates and boxes around in a search for something important.

The front door began to shake as the demon smashed into it over and over.

"Hold the door closed. Keep that thing at bay," their father called out from his search in the cellar.

"I'm doing the best I can!" Arridon shouted as the demon in the street crashed repeatedly into the wooden door. The wood bent and cracked with each impact, the grains protesting louder and louder. "Time is something this door can't give us."

"Found it," their dad said, and ran up the few stairs to the living room proper.

He rushed to the small dining table and wiped the two bowls off to set down a small wooden box. Arridon had moved the box aside in his search for vegetables just the night prior and thought nothing of it. Their dad picked up the knife Thistle had sat down and used it with remarkable precision to pry up the edge of the nailed-shut box. The nails creaked in concert with the groan of the besieged door, and the cracking of the bar holding it shut for the moment. He got the lid up high enough to get his fingers under it and ripped it free.

He pulled from the box a strange metallic device foreign to both Thistle and Arridon.

"God-tech…" Thistle said, trailing off and staring at the thing.

Shaped like an uppercase L, with the short end covered in a dark, matte material resembling fabric, he hefted the weight of it in one hand. With the other, he pulled on the longer branch of the metal; it slid backward then snapped forward with mechanical perfection. He clicked a tiny lever downward with his thumb and pointed the long end at the door.

Arridon spotted a hole in the end of the metal and instinctually moved away from the couch where the opening pointed. The menace of the device radiated into the brother and sister without evidence or cause.

"What's that thing?" he asked his dad.

"Your mother left it with me. It's a

weapon," he answered.

"What's it called?"

"A gun. She called it her 'Colt,' named after a creature called a 'horse.' Your mother said they were beasts of burden on some of the worlds she visited before we met."

"Mother traveled the worlds?" Thistle asked as the door crashed inward once more. It burst off its hinge-moorings, saved upright by the pressure offered by the couch pushing against it.

"She did. Cover your ears. When this weapon fires, it's deafening."

"You're gonna—?" Thistle began, but when the door smashed again, and the wood at its center cracked apart, her father fired the God-weapon.

A flare of light erupted out of the tip of the weapon, its brightness only exceeded by the volume of the explosion that tore through the small home. Thistle—who was closest—shot her hands up to cover her ears as she screamed in both pain and shock. Arridon dove to the floor, yelling at the world in confusion and fear as he, too, was shaken by the gun's discharge.

Simultaneous with the firing, the monster invading their home screeched out an alien, guttural roar of pain. A massive burst of dark blood erupted into their space, covering the couch Arridon had only just vacated. The fabric hissed as the monster's life blood sank in.

The screams from the broken demon's face continued on, and their father shot once more, piercing another hole through the torn shirt the old, rebellious sailor had worn when he was still human, and not a nightmare. But all nightmares cease at dawn, and this monster was no different.

It fell forward into the hole it had smashed in the door, and hung there, one bony, claw-ended arm draped over the couch, twitching. Its blood ran down in tiny rivers.

"Well shit," Arridon said, breathless. "That thing…that *weapon* was in the cellar the whole time?"

"Sure was. Not that you'd have been able to operate the gun if you'd found it. I'll have to teach you both how to use it. It's one of the few weapons that can kill a demon fast, without too much risk of getting their blood on you."

"Gods' power," Arridon muttered. "I'm in awe. Mom…it's from mom?"

"It is. If you think this thing is impressive, you should've seen the one she brought to the world's edge. She left this one with me to protect you two, in case the war ever reached the mainland again."

"Again? What?" Thistle asked.

"Our world's history is a lot more complicated than you know. Suffice to say, the demons of the Bleed and the Bleed itself have been around a long time, and the war against them encompasses far more than the edge of our tiny world."

"Who the *fuck* are you, and what have you done with my drunk, piece of shit dad?" Arridon demanded as he got to his feet. "You're far too smart and capable to be him."

"I'm…" he started, but his eyes dropped to the floor, upon the corpse of the monster he'd just ended, and he had to pause. He looked up after catching his emotions. "I've been a terrible father. I've kept terrible secrets. Secrets it's time I shared with you. Gather your things as fast as you can. Carry only what you can run with. Bring the spear," he said, looking at the blank space on the wall. "Never mind. Grab the axe from the woodpile at the shed when we get outside. Thistle, no knives. They'll bleed on you, and we don't know if your mother's immunity was passed on or not. Get a…get a pitchfork. Or a shovel or pickaxe. Nothing too heavy. I'll gather my things, and we'll get those tools on the way out of town."

"You have a plan for this?" Thistle asked him.

He looked her in the eyes. Hers gold, his gray, like his family name.

"I've been dreading this every year you've been alive, the both of you, and I've made a hundred plans for each of those years, yet all those plans together seem like they're just not enough. But we will not fail. Now, let me gather my things, and we'll head out of town as fast as we can go along the Trade Road." He took off for the stairs.

"What then?" Arridon asked him. "Where do we go?"

"We head north until we hit the channel between the two citadel-cities. Then, so long as the war hasn't spilled into the city there, we try and make our way into the depths of the ruins to find one of your mother's portals."

"What's a portal?" Thistle asked.

"A gateway into another world. Somewhere we can escape where the Bleed can't follow. Can't follow fast, at least. The Bleed gets everywhere, eventually. The best we can hope for is the rest of our natural lives." He went up the stairs to get his things.

Arridon and Thistle looked at one another then at the corpse of the monster that had tried to tear them limb from limb just minutes before.

Its blood still hissed where it ate away at

the fabric of their sofa.

First they removed the couch, taking great care not to touch the spilled blood. Second, they pulled the door inward, heavy with the no longer human body stuck between its splintered middle. Trapped by the jagged shards of wood it had fallen on, coupled with Arridon's broken spear still halfway through its midsection, it remained still, dead, and hung like a scarecrow in the fields.

"It smells of blood, and low tide, and rot," Arridon whispered as they slipped out into the abandoned streets. From over the roofs they could hear distant screams of pain and fear. Violent sounds followed, like echoes born from the depths of the void.

"Get around the corner to the wood axe," his dad counseled.

Arridon and Thistle moved to the corner of their house and dipped into the narrow space between their home and the next. Home to a tiny garden, blocked in by an equally tiny shed, they tiptoed through the meager, unripe tomatoes until they reached the thin wooden door to the storage outbuilding connected to their house. Arridon grabbed the handle to the door and pulled it open slowly. It squeaked a tinny noise as the metal hinges ground a layer of rust away, and the brother and sister winced at the offense.

Thistle reached past her brother and grabbed a pitchfork from the shed. She stepped back to her father at the corner of the house, who still held the Colt gods' weapon at the ready. Arridon grabbed up their largest hatchet with the long handle and returned to his father and sister. In his hands, the cold wood of the tool's shaft felt reassuring, and the steel head heavy, and deadly. He did something strange then. Something he hadn't done in…memory. He smiled at his father. Awkward as it might be, it was still a welcome sight.

"What now?" he asked his dad, whispering underneath the distant sounds of growling half-men, and the meals they made of Mercy Point villagers. From the sounds of the screaming, it seemed not all of the villagers were killed.

"We run. As fast as we can until we get to the crossroads, then we take the north branch to the Endless City."

"That's it?" Thistle asked. "We just run away?"

"For now, yes. There's no fighting to be made here. Getting their blood on you can kill you, or turn you. We run, get to where your mother said a portal was, and try to activate it to leave."

"This feels a whole lot theoretical," Arridon said. "I would've thought the gods would have had a better plan than this."

"The 'gods' were hardly gods. Just a race of magically gifted, technologically advanced humans from another realm. We put them on pedestals and worshipped them because they taught us sciences and elevated us by several hundred years. When the Bleed came to their first home, they reacted just like we are right now. Running scared, and trying to save their loved ones. Now, let's save the chatter for when we leave the village. The further we are from here the better, and the faster we get away, the less likely we are to get eaten alive—or worse."

"Let's go this way," Arridon said, pointing at an alley across the street that he knew led to a path heading out of town towards the Trade Road.

"Streets are faster," his dad said, ignoring him and heading out and up the main thoroughfare their house sat on. He stopped when he realized his children weren't following. "Come on. I know what I'm talking about. Follow me."

"The fuck you do," Arridon said. "You haven't been out of the house, sober, for a year at least."

"Arridon's right. The path that way is much faster, and won't reveal us to anyone else walking the streets," Thistle added.

"Okay, fine; you're probably right. Lead on."

A hesitant Arridon led them, axe in hand. One by one they ran across the street, diving into the space between the houses. The grassy yard gave way to a hard packed alley framed by tall wooden fences, keeping neighbors at a distance. The equally tall young man led his family down the weathered wooden passage. On each side of the fence, in the hidden world of the village below its height, they could hear more and more of their friends and neighbors succumb to the feast of demons. They passed one house, then two, then ten. They neared the fence bordering one of the last houses in Mercy Point.

"Please, no," they heard a woman call out from just on the other side of the wooden wall, not ten feet away. "You know me, Brendan. You know my daughter. You can fight it. Whatever's happening to you. Fight it!"

"You don't understand, meat," a man—presumably Brendan, or whatever was left of him—said back to the woman. "I have joined with the Bleed, and now, so will you."

Arridon stopped and looked back at his family. His eyes told them what he had to do.

"No," his dad said, his voice barely audible. "We. Must. Escape."

"Let us run," the woman pleaded as her daughter started to cry, a sad, low cry of a child who dreads something they come to realize they cannot escape. "I'm begging."

"Beg all you want," the Brendan-thing said. "Your desperation will only make your flesh sweeter, or your servitude that much more valuable to the Bleed. Choose: worship, or feed."

Arridon didn't think about or plan what came next. His response was entirely subconscious, autonomic, like the beat of his heart or the blink of an eye. He raised one thin leather boot up and kicked the tall wooden fence with all his power, shattering two of the boards with ease. He leaned into the space between and found the monster lunging forward, about to eat the woman.

It no longer walked on two legs, having made the choice to grow several new limbs out of its hips and lower abdomen. Hands grew out of its arms in strange places, at strange angles, and Brendan's face no longer looked human either; he'd exchanged two human eyes for four red and yellow ones, and a head covered in dark hair for a cracked wig of dry, rotten flesh from which his skull shone through. Mandibles jutted from his cheeks, and they twitched in hunger.

"Eat this, freak!" he screamed through the hole he'd made in the fence. Arridon kept his eyes wide so their golden hue couldn't be missed.

The creature reacted to the sight of the man appearing like a fire that had oil put to it. It roared in a skittering, hitched rage, and leapt at the fence with its numerous legs, limbs, and clawed hands in a wide, aggressive stance.

Arridon ducked back, yelling in fear as the massive monster slammed into the feeble fence, smashing into it and shattering a ten-foot length of boards, tipping a wide section of the fence straight over and into the narrow alley, and cutting Arridon off from his sister and father.

The monster got to its many feet, and swung its head side to side, hissing and spitting a vile, green and yellow bile at the family.

Half breeds die first, the creature said in their minds. *Right in my belly, where they rot to delicious oblivion forever.* It tilted its strange head back and screeched a battle cry into the sky, alerting all of the transforming denizens of Mercy Point to its location, and the special, rare meal it was about to consume.

"Oh fuck right off," Gray said, and blasted the monster in the side of the head with his wife's pistol.

10

The Moon

DAY THREE / 5:15 AM

"Come on, you two turds," Maddie said. "We can only keep this mower for another three days."

"It's so early." Sam yawned.

Derrick grabbed the toolboxes and placed them in the back.

"Well, you'd both still be sleeping if you hadn't stolen the vehicle then wrecked it."

"Tyler wrecked it. How come he isn't he going out to get the axle?" Sam whined.

"You can trade places with him if you want," Maddie responded.

"Um, no, it's cool." Sam knew Tyler was working in the wastewater facility, cleaning the machinery.

"Didn't think so."

Derrick began to nervous sweat, just thinking of going back out the dome.

"Don't worry, you're with me, drone-boy, and I'm not going to flip."

"How…how did you know?" Derrick asked.

"Low pitched hum, hard to miss. How much did you hear?"

"Enough to be worried," he said honestly. "Should I be worried?"

Maddie did not reply.

"What happens if it keeps, you know, spreading?" Sam asked.

There was a pause. "It can't," she finally said.

"Well, that's good to know." Sam was relieved.

"Because if it does, we're all in a lot of trouble," she added.

"And you have no idea what it is?" Derrick asked.

"Don't know…faulty materials? Some bacteria on the surface we didn't know about? Sabotage from Earth? It could be any one of those or something we haven't thought of yet. The why doesn't matter; how we stop it does."

"And getting this axle, what's that going to do?" Sam asked.

"It gives us the ways and means to move somewhere else if we need to."

They moved along the surface at a somewhat safe speed. Maddie was going faster than she wished, but she felt like there was a large clock over her head, and it was ticking loudly to a countdown she didn't know the final results of.

"Can't we just wait for the replacement?" Sam asked, referring to the supply ship due out next month.

"Quit your bellyaching. We're here now, and, no, I don't think waiting is a good idea. I don't like being this isolated from the other bases. Something happens and we won't be able to get out."

They were heading to the moon's garbage graveyard. Out of necessity, they did their best to repurpose everything, but there were some things that just weren't salvageable. The cargo hauler was one of them. It had caught fire and melted anything of value. The rear axle wasn't quite the same as the mower's, but it was close enough that Maddie thought she could retrofit it.

"Been here a little over twenty years, and we're already mucking the place up," Maddie said as she stepped out of the vehicle and looked upon the expanding trash heap. "I don't think, as a species, we're ever going to learn. No matter what anyone says, when it all comes down to it, individuals always put themselves first over the betterment of the populace."

"That Marx?" Derrick asked.

"Maddie," the woman laughed. "Let's get this done. I've got a batch of brandy stashed and I want to drink some before the end of the day."

"How can you like that stuff? Smells like diesel fuel."

"Funny you should say that. Ratchet." Maddie had her hand out as she waited for Derrick to give her one. "Eighteen millimeters. Help me," she grunted as she tried to break the nut's hold. Derrick went stumbling off as it finally gave way. Within the hour, they had removed the axle and loaded it on the cargo trailer they'd brought with them. "That went quicker than I expected." Maddie stood and stretched her back.

"Great...we can go back and I can get some lunch and then a nap," Sam said.

"She always sleep this much?" Maddie

asked.

"You have no idea. I think the only reason she wanted out first when we were born was so she could get into the crib."

Sam stuck her tongue out at him.

"Plus, I think she wants to see Tyler."

"Trust me, you're not going to want to be anywhere near that boy for the next few days. The wastewater facility has a way of sticking with you after you leave, if you know what I mean," Maddie said.

"Oh, yuck." Sam wrinkled her nose.

"I think we've got enough time." Maddie looked off to the west.

"Enough time for what?" Derrick asked.

"We're going to the Energy Compound."

"Seriously?" Sam asked.

"I haven't heard from Clive in three days; that's not overly unusual, but right now, I don't like it, not one bit. You can sleep while I drive. Let's go."

"You think something might be wrong with him?" Derrick asked.

"That's why we're going."

In minutes, they were all back in and traveling the fifty miles to the energy compound.

"I've never been this far out," Sam said, taking in the surroundings. She leaned over Maddie's seat and looked out over the terrain.

"It's the moon. It all looks the same. Now sit down," Maddie said. "This is weird…." she said as they approached Clive's impromptu home.

"What?" Derrick asked.

"All of the mowers have transponders on them. Clive should have known we've been coming for the last half hour. That he's not out here wondering who it is and why we're bothering him…that's strange."

"Maybe he's sleeping," Sam offered.

"Not everyone is you, sweetheart." Sam poofed out her lower lip to Maddie at the jibe.

"Could be because he's strange; that might explain it," Derrick said.

Maddie looked at him sharply. "You don't know what the man has been through. Don't be so quick to judge."

"I don't know him at all, other than he's decided to be out here on his own when he doesn't have to be," Derrick attempted to defend himself.

"It got him away from the likes of you and your sister; I'd say he knew exactly what he was doing."

Sam was the first to put her suit back on and head out the airlock. She waited by the door for the others to join her.

Maddie input the code to the building

and the door opened soundlessly. She waited until they were out of the airlock before removing her helmet and calling out.

"Clive!" She ushered the two teens with a sweeping motion of her arm. "Stay behind me."

"What? Is she afraid there's a moon monster or something?" Sam was smiling, but the more she thought about it, the more concerned she got. "You don't think there is, do you?" She was so close to Derrick she barely had to whisper the words.

"Shut it, girlie," Maddie said. She stopped and reached her hand down to a holster she no longer wore.

Sam gasped as she looked past Maddie.

"Shit," Maddie said before moving towards it.

Clive's purple and bloated body was on the floor.

"Aren't you going to help him?" Sam asked, though she had not moved.

"He's way beyond anything I can do." Maddie grabbed a shirt strewn on the floor and covered Clive's face.

Sam could not stop looking at the mottled and discolored hand, the index finger curled in a gesture that was beckoning her to come forward.

"What happened?" Derrick asked, doing his best to not look at the body.

"By the looks of it, diabetic shock." Maddie looked over to Clive's workbench and the large candy bar that sat untouched.

"So, not a moon monster?" Sam asked.

"Are you sure you're my sister?" Derrick asked her, doing his best to ignore the body.

Death was rare on the moon, but it had happened. Most candidates had been pre-screened to make sure that they were in peak shape, but sometimes it was necessary to take people who had some ailments, as experience in critical positions was of more importance. Sometimes none of those things mattered. Major Carlsen had been the leader of the entire expedition and arguably one of the fittest men the Army ever had within its ranks. Before the war, he had continuously run in Iron Man competitions for the fun of it. The first month on the moon, he had been upset with the lack of progress the rest of the team had with setting up, and he decided to lead by example. He was moving a stack of boxes when a fifteen-pound spanner wrench fell off the top and directly onto the dome of his skull. The head of the wrench drilled neatly into his brain, damaging his motor skills. He died ten agonizing days later. Of the eight deaths on the moon, including poor, diabetic Clive, seven had been accidents.

"This is bad," Maddie said.

"You think?" Sam answered. "He's dead; doesn't get much worse than that."

"You'd be surprised," Maddie told her. "And I'm not talking about Clive. His problems are over, but ours are just beginning."

"Why? Diabetes isn't catchy," Derrick said. "Right?" He looked at his sister.

Maddie was looking to the nuclear cell containment housing; she saw a faint glow on the side.

"That supposed to look like that?" Derrick asked.

"Everyone out, now." Maddie pushed them when they didn't move quickly enough. "Get your dad on the radio." She was powering the mower up.

"Everything all right?" Dean asked.

"Far from it. Clive is dead." Maddie heard Dean wince on the other end. "That's not the worst of it. The rot I was telling you about…" she looked over to the kids before continuing. At this point, the truth couldn't be hidden; shielding them from it was not going to do anyone any good. "It's on the containment unit."

"Is it inside as well?" Dean's alarmed voice rang through clear enough Sam and Derrick heard it.

"I'm a mechanic, not a nuclear engineer, and even if I was, I didn't stay around long enough to check. I could see it glowing."

"Glowing?" Dean asked. "Are you sure?"

"Haven't started drinking yet, so, yes, I'm sure."

"I wasn't implying that…it's just…a disaster of this magnitude? I'll have to assemble the committee."

"Out," Maddie told Dean as she hit the accelerator.

"Where are we going?" Sam asked.

"Back to the base. We're going to need a lot of supplies if we're going to get through this."

"*Get through this?* We lose power and there's no getting through this," Derrick told her.

"Lose power? There are solar and battery backups; won't we be fine?" Sam asked.

"For a while." Maddie thought furiously. "We'll have the power for life support and some extras, but beyond that, we'll be living on top of a graveyard."

"What's that mean, Derrick?" Sam asked.

"There won't be enough juice for the T3s."

"That's one problem. The other is if the

power station blows, it could wipe out half the bases in the area and, more than likely, most of the solar array. I *told* them, I fucking told them to put the panels farther away, but the lazy idiots didn't want to haul up anymore cable than they already had. Granted, I wanted the panels where they would get more sun, not because I thought they'd get destroyed in a nuclear explosion, but still."

"This can't be happening. My parents will fix this."

Nobody answered Sam. Not Maddie, because she didn't think that could happen, and not Derrick because he hadn't completely processed what was happening.

Maddie didn't slow down. "We have some tough decisions coming up as soon as we reach the base."

"What do you mean?" Sam asked.

"This vehicle, with all the supplies I plan on stuffing in it, will only hold five people at the most."

"There's sixty-four in our base alone," Derrick said.

"As soon as your father alerts the council about what is going on, they are all going to want out, and this is the only means available."

"Can't we get everyone out of there?" Derrick asked.

"To shuttle that many people to Base Delta, even if we crammed in five people per trip…" Maddie was doing the math in her head, "…it'd be close to four or five days if you factor in the charge time for the mower. And just looking at the nuclear cell, I don't think we have anywhere near that much time."

"Our parents," Derrick said.

"Tyler," Sam said at the same time.

"If they go by seniority or importance, none of us are going to make the cut. Maybe your parents make it out on the second or third trip, but there will be a whole lot of boom before we get our chance."

"But…but, wait." Sam had her tongue firmly entrenched between her teeth. "Without an atmosphere, I mean, even if the nuclear cell explodes, it won't do anything, right?"

"You're forgetting the T3s," Maddie responded. "There's just enough atmosphere to bring shock waves and radiation across a fair portion of the surface."

"We can't just take the mower and leave everyone else behind," Derrick intoned.

"What's your answer, kiddo? We hand over this mower, we die."

"I don't want to die," Sam replied.

"None of us want to, sis, but we can't just take this and leave everyone to what happens next."

"I like your empathy, kid, I do; if you want to give up your seat for another, I'll understand completely. I, for one, am holding on to this with both hands."

The base rapidly came into view as Maddie pushed the machine to its limit. The over-sized garage door trundled open, then Maddie waited impatiently as the door behind closed and the pressurization stabilized before opening the door that led into her garage. She quickly opened the hood and attached the power pack. Sam and Derrick were outside the vehicle looking at her.

"If there is anything of importance that you must have with you, I suggest getting it now. If you're not back in an hour, I will take that to mean you want to give up your seats to someone else."

They both left quickly.

11

Coronation

The boy—or rather, what his uncle had left of him—twitched and cried in the grass just near the beach and its bloody shores. His sobs wracked his frail body, and pulsed his heart, which set free surge after surge of his life's blood. The precious fluid ran down his neck and chest. His milky blue eyes pointed up at a dawn sky that mirrored the color, though they saw nothing as his life slipped further into oblivion.

I can save you, a voice whispered in his ear. His addled thoughts struggled to mine the tantalizing worlds for their meaning, but poor Sebastian had too little left to assemble anything.

Then, a tingling sensation rippled over his body, starting where his uncle had ripped the skin off his collarbone and neck. The feeling of pins and needles overcame the mind-wrenching agony that had consumed him, and that gave him clarity for a moment.

See? I can take away your pain and give you strength. All you have to do is serve me on this world until it is in my belly for eternity. What say you?

"I...who are you?" he whispered, freeing up a spatter of blood from his mouth. His eyes remained fixated on the clouds filling the sky.

I am the Bleed. Eater of flesh, eroder of mountains, drinker of seas, suffocator of hope, and penetrator of all realities. The endless hunger. I am the end. I am the end of endings.

"You're not real."

I am the only thing that is real, and only I can save you. Only I can give you power. Only I can give your life purpose for the remainder of time, so long as time serves me.

"No," Sebastian protested weakly.

You are already mine. Your meat belongs to me. All you've left to do is to give me your will, so that I might have greater purchase in the waning hours of this world's war. A willful general. A hunter of souls who choose to fight back. A face to be seen. A mouth to speak. A presence to be feared. A prophet to set the worship of me afire.

Sebastian's thoughts raced as the tingling faded, and the pain returned tenfold. He cried out, then whimpered. Then, the agony faded away just as fast as it had appeared.

See? Your flesh is mine to do as I wish. Now gift me your will, and you shall have such power as my servant. Or, if you prefer, I can return the worst moments of the pain and prolong your death until the crabs walk up from the bottom of the sea and eat you bit by bit.

"Can't you just make me do what you want? Why…why this silly game?"

Fear is delicious to me, like salt on a steak, or caramel on ice cream on your tongue. The same I will say about willful servants. I have eaten worlds a billion times over, and all are a challenge I relish. Your world is no different, and I shall have my treat as I consume everything on this table of a planet, and the universe surrounding it.

"Will…will I hurt my mother?"

No. You will not harm your mother.

"You promise?"

I speak in absolutes. You can do your mother no harm, for she serves me at my side already.

"Okay. Fine. I'll serve you. What do I have to—" Sebastian's weak voice died away as his body was seized by the entity speaking to him. Power erupted through time and space, crushing into him, filling every nerve, muscle, and bone, draining away the pieces of him that didn't need to be there anymore, purging the parts that could fight back, voiding the compassion and fear that didn't serve the monster's purpose.

In the absence of his humanity, the Bleed left him with power, malice, and one bit of knowledge from his recent past needed to see the world ushered into oblivion.

When the coursing power of the creature from beyond finished its agonizing, annihilating work, Sebastian's body had healed back to whole. Under the skin, his shoulders had hardened into the first signs of his knight's pauldrons, and under his hair, his helm of scale and bone began to form as well. When grown, it would be fitting garb for a warrior king of the Bleed. He stood up from his near-grave on the shore and brushed the sand off of his bloodied clothes. Most of it came off, and what remained he ignored.

Sebastian surveyed the area around him, and nodded in satisfaction at the piles of bodies that once had names he knew. He counted the corpses — 41 — and knew the village had ten times that number of slaves or meals remaining, not accounting for however many were infected by the blood tainted with his master's unending power.

Those who were infected became one with the Bleed, serving it as mindless minions hell bent on ruination and murder. They were the foot soldiers of the apocalypse, the same as a billion-billion others in a billion dimensions before, fueled by instincts given them by the taint of blood. Soon, all the living souls of the mainland would be dead or absorbed into the Bleed's ever-growing horde.

And of all those souls, the most delicious, most coveted, were the cowards than had run from a lost world long before, and their unwitting spawn, birthed in the wake of their parent's shame.

And Sebastian knew where two half-gods were headed.

Over the crest of sand and grass, two of the villagers who had been infected and twisted into monstrous caricatures of their former selves loped and crawled on limbs that failed to match. Two more followed suit as they reached the top of the rocky outcrop that split the beach in half. They seemed more crustacean than human, save for the original, pained, confused, pink faces of the children they once were erupting through the fronts of their reddened carapaces. Another pair of the mutants—these two simian and horned, but covered in patches of reptilian scales that oozed streams of infected pus from their edges—approached from the direction of the village.

All were covered in human blood, and all were drawn to his presence, like wolves forming a pack around the scent of their undisputed alpha. They came nearly within touching distance, and supplicated themselves, dropping down on whatever bended joint served best to show fealty to something even closer to their god than they were.

"Our lord and devourer has smiled down upon us this morn," Sebastian said, using words and sentences that came from a place in his mind that didn't feel entirely his own. "Our victories here are almost complete, and this world almost another meal."

They howled as they cheered, like animals struck by whips.

"And yet for us to carve out the choicest

of meats from this meal, we must find those who will bleed the best for us. We must find those of the wild eyes, and cut those eyes from their skulls, and suck the juices from those precious little jewels. We must scalp their manes and eat their flesh, for they are the children of the children of another realm, they are prey on the run as they flee, and the Bleed leaves no drops unspilled."

The whips freed more raucous screams of angered joy, and they leapt and cavorted like the nightmares they were.

A sharp tug at the back of Sebastian's mind brought him to the prior day's events. The warmth of the summer sun on his face as he spoke to the one named Thistle, the girl with the golden eyes. Lust—primal and hot, making his loins throb with unnatural breeding urges—struck him, and he pushed his hips forward in a sexual thrust without thought. He let his memories linger at the surface, letting the scene play out once more, right up to the moment the whore's brother grabbed him by the throat and made him stop. He memorized the faces of the two family members with equally odd metallic eyes from his dream-moment, and let the desire to fuck Thistle blend into the desire to maul and murder Arridon. His hips still swayed back and forth in the rhythm of procreation. His cock rose up and pressed against the tattered crotch of his trousers. A banner for a different kind of war.

No longer was their death an abstract thought, or the driving ambition put into him by a master from a million dimensions away. Now…it was personal. He had hatred and lust to fill his belly.

He turned to the shore and watched the thick sludge of life's blood roll in, wave after wave. The curdled, coagulated bodily fluids came and went, carrying dropped spears, arrows, bows, and other weapons light enough to float from the final battle in the deep sea to the shores at Mercy Point. He laughed deep and long as he took stock of all the weapons the so-called gods had left as garbage in the wake of their pathetic deaths.

"All will be in the belly of the Bleed," he said, and the monsters cheered again. "Now, ocean of blood, give me a suitable weapon to strike down the fools who think they can make a difference."

As sure as the winds blew in the skies above, a wide wave carried into shore, and deposited a weapon in the sand that could never have floated.

A greatsword — too long of blade to be wielded by a single human hand — washed in, gleaming like metallic-ruby death. The wave's crushing weight stuck the blade into the flat sand, and pushed the hilt upwards towards him like a flag raised over taken territory. The sword was an offering.

"The Bleed provides for those who serve," he prophesied as he reached down to pluck his new blade from the ground. The words were spoken partially for his own ears, or at least the tiny part of Sebastian that remained.

The invisible whip cracked again, and his misshapen foot soldiers cheered and chortled as he drew the blade out from the sandy flesh of the shoreline. With one powerful hand he held it aloft and towards the late eastern sunrise. Blood and pink sea foam dripped off the thick blade and gem-encrusted hilt, hitting the ground with a steady pitter-patter that made him smile yet again.

"Find the halfsie trash. Find the children of the scum that let slip, and devour them. Turn all those who stand in your way, but find those who claim the gods' blood and see to it they are torn limb from limb and eaten as the precious morsels they are. Then, we shall dance on their broken bones."

The monsters cheered, and screamed, and threw their hands into the sky, praying and celebrating and tearing into their own flesh with claws borne of evil from the madness of it all. Their blood mingled with the land, and left a pox where it sank deep.

"Seek them out. They flee to find safety behind the walls of the dead city, atop the bones of their dead ancestors."

Sebastian lowered the sword, and thought again of Thistle. Her brown hair tied back into a ponytail and the fierceness built into the line of her jaw. He thought of her as she tended the garden outside her family's little home on the fringe of the coastal village, and he remembered sitting in the single room schoolhouse next to her where they were taught basic reading and writing and mathematics. Her face would tighten up as she counted on her fingers, and he always looked away so as not to embarrass her.

The Bleed within him indulged those fond thoughts, and sucked on the marrow of them when they faded into sadness.

Soon, Sebastian would suck on the actual marrow within her and her brother's bones, and that would be such a sweet dessert on the tongue.

"GO!" he screamed, and monsters did the bidding of their armored prophet.

12

London

How the hell am I supposed to reply to that?
"Yeah, right."

"I don't expect you to believe me," he said. He looked up, and she followed the line of his gaze. There were more drones buzzing overhead. Another three Chinooks too. More black-suited soldiers had appeared on the peaks of the rubble mountains that surrounded them.

"Never mind believe you; I don't

believe *in* you."

"I know I've not been around much. I should have taken more of an interest."

She laughed at him. "This is absolutely crazy."

God looked around, calm and serene. "I'll explain everything."

"You need to be quick. Have you seen how many soldiers there are around here? Oh, wait, I forgot. You're all-powerful."

"I understand your skepticism."

"Well that's a heck of a lot more than I understand right now. Don't you think we should do something?"

"We should always do something," he said. "Doing nothing is never an option."

Jenny rolled her eyes. "Oh, great. I'm about to die and I'm going to spend my last seconds with a guy who thinks he's God and speaks in clichés straight out of fortune cookies."

"You're not going to die. Not yet, anyway. And I'm sorry you don't believe in me, but you're going to have to make some adjustments to your belief systems."

"It's not you as such...or maybe it is...it's religion in general I have a problem with. I've never understood it."

"Tell you the truth, neither have I. I don't get it everywhere I go, just in places like this."

"What, London?'

"No, this planet. That's the problem when you get a species with some degree of intelligence. They have this irritating need to explain things, and when they start out they almost always pin the blame for everything on the gods. And then as time goes on and they start to understand a few things, most of them are too scared to let go of the ideas they've been clinging on to for hundreds of years."

Jenny looked around anxiously. More soldiers were rappelling down the rubble towards them. "You sure we're not going to die?"

"Not today, Jenny."

Weapons were being raised and pointed in their direction.

"How exactly do you know my name?"

"How exactly do you come to be here? Of all the places and all the people, why you, why here, and why now?'

"I think they're going to kill us."

"Oh ye of little faith."

"Is that supposed to be funny?"

"Yes, actually."

"Well it wasn't."

God reached out and grabbed Jenny's hand and pulled her closer. His grip was strong, but gentle. "Follow my lead."

"What are you doing?"

"Convincing around seven billion people of my existence, getting us away from here, then saving the world."

"In that order?"

"Yes."

"And the world needs saving, does it?"

"It does, as it happens."

"From you?"

"No...from something far nastier than me."

Jenny was about to speak again when a lone voice cut through the uneasy silence. "Stay where you are and put your hands in the air."

"They'd be so embarrassed if they knew," God whispered.

Jenny couldn't help herself. "You can't be *the* God. You're a bit of a dick."

"Sorry to disappoint."

A female soldier approached, flanked by countless others. God gestured for Jenny to get behind him then held out his hands to the sides, unashamed of his nakedness. "Don't move," the soldier barked at him. "Stand still or I'll open fire."

"Do not fear me," he said, pretentiousness dialed up to the max. "I'm not here to harm you. I am your god, and I've returned here today to—"

God didn't reach the end of his sentence.

"OPEN FIRE!"

Behind him, Jenny screwed her eyes shut, braced for the inevitable. The soldiers opened fire, and every weapon they had unloaded on God. Jenny heard every single blast and even felt the air burning as munitions and missiles crisscrossed all around them. The non-stop blitzkrieg continued for what felt like forever, but not a single bullet got through.

"Okay!" she said, screaming to make herself heard over the din of war, "I take it back! I believe in you. You're all powerful etcetera etcetera…but why are you here? And what's any of this got to do with me?"

"The human race and this entire planet is in grave danger," he explained, his voice rising above everything else. "And you, my dear Jenny, are pivotal to its survival. We need to talk."

"We need to get out of here first. You might need to crank up your comet — or whatever it is — again, pal."

This time God didn't say anything. He just grabbed her hand again and then they were somewhere else.

Phillip Allsopp had been dreading this day. Everything changed today, as he'd always known it eventually would. Nothing would ever be the same again. *Maybe I should have told her*, he thought. He wished things could have been different. The inevitability of it all was hard to handle.

Half of the kitchen and part of the living room of the flat disappeared in an impossibly powerful, yet perfectly contained, burst of energy. When the light faded, all that remained of that part of the flat was a hole. And Jenny and God. Phil looked up and saw that the incandescent sphere had eaten away swathes of the ceiling and floor.

"You fucked that up," he said to God.

"Sorry about that," God said. "Good to see you, Phil."

"Wish I could say the same. You okay, Jen?"

"I will be when someone either wakes me up or tells me what's going on."

She left God's side and went to hug her dad.

"I'm sorry, love," he said to her.

"Sorry? What have you got to be sorry about?"

"It's my fault you're mixed up in all this."

"*Your fault?* And what even is this all about? By the way, Dad, this is—"

"Yes...we've met. A typically understated entrance, Thirnas."

"Thirnas?" Jenny interrupted. "He told me he was God."

"*A* god, not *the* God," Dad explained.

"You knew this day would come eventually, Phillip."

"Yes, but I hoped with all my heart it wouldn't."

Jenny stood open-mouthed between the two of them. "Would one of you please tell me what the fuck is going on here?"

"Don't swear, Jennifer," Dad said, sounding disappointed.

"Don't swear? *Don't swear?* For fuck's sake! Do you know what kind of a day I've had? I've been knocked down, almost died a few times, almost been crushed by a building, been shot at...then I meet God, and it turns out he's best friends with my dad. You work in a call center, Dad, for crying out loud. I think that today of all days I can be forgiven for using the word fuck as many times as I want. If I wanted to I could even say cun—"

"Jennifer, enough," Dad interrupted, just at the right moment. "Things are going to get a lot more complicated yet."

"She does have a point," Thirnas said.

"You stay out of this."

Jenny had had enough. "I don't care

which of you does it, just stop bickering and tell me what this is all about."

Thirnas looked at Dad. "I'll tell her."

"No," Dad said, "you won't. You've done enough damage."

The god was relegated to the corner of the room like a petulant child. He leant against the wall and gestured for her dad to continue. Phillip cleared his throat, sounding suddenly unsure. He appeared more nervous than Jenny, even. The two of them sat together on the sofa. There had only ever been her and Dad. They'd sat here together to watch TV and eat dinner and open Christmas presents and...and she couldn't help thinking that all that and more might have been lost forever this morning.

"You and me, Jen, we're not from 'round here," Dad started to explain.

"We moved up from Brighton when I was a kid, I know."

"No, we're originally from a little further afield than the South Coast."

"What's that supposed to mean?"

"This is going to take a bit of explaining. You might not believe everything I'm going to tell you."

"Well, I just met God and he turned out to be a trainwreck. After this morning I think I can handle just about anything you can throw at me."

"Okay. Here goes. First thing you need to understand is that the shape and structure of your reality is far more complex than you might have imagined."

"Can't say that's something I've spent a lot of time imagining, Dad, but go on."

"There isn't just one universe."

"Okay..."

"We live in a multiverse, but inter-dimensional travel between different universes is generally impossible.'

"Unless you're God," Jenny said.

"She's smart, this one," Thirnas interjected.

"Not quite," Dad said to Jenny, ignoring him. "Unless you're *a god*."

"There are more of them? You know I'm an atheist, right? I don't buy all that crap."

"I know. You must have told me a million times. Ever wonder why I was so non-committal?"

"I thought you were just doing the good parent thing."

"Partly. I had to be careful not to influence you, so I sat on the fence."

"You mean you neglected to mention you were best mates with God."

"Don't get hung up on the definition of 'god' you've grown up with. Gods are a different species, that's all. A different creature at a different stage of evolution."

"If you think I'm some omnipresent busybody who sits around pulling the strings of several billion people's lives, you're very wrong," Thirnas explained. "I'm not an interventionist; never have been. I'm only here today because I don't have any choice. In a civilization as complex as this one, we gods tend to get promoted by default. It's easier for many of the people on this planet to convince themselves they're being looked after by some unseen all-powerful being than to face up to the reality that they're wandering alone through space, no one in charge. I'm here to help and guide and protect, sure, but if I had to respond to every prayer, take out every evildoer and reward every good deed, I'd never get anything done."

"So why are you here today? If you don't care about anyone else, why bother?"

"Who said anything about not caring? Pay attention, Jenny. I just told you, I'm here to protect your planet."

"From what?"

It was Dad's turn to take over again. "From demons. It's not just the gods that can move between dimensions."

Jenny laughed out loud. She couldn't help herself. "Demons?! Come on, Dad, cut it out. Have you got any idea how stupid you're sounding?"

She could tell from the look on his face that he was deadly serious. Thirnas, too, was now equally intense.

"This is serious, love. Gods are real, and demons are too. They're the most dangerous creatures in the entire multiverse. They're gods without a conscience, and they exist in massive numbers."

"They wreak havoc wherever they go," Thirnas said. "There is a vast army of them out there. Vile, parasitic monsters that are able to slip between existences, destroying age-old worlds and civilizations in seconds."

"And they're coming here, I take it?" Jenny said.

"Yes, Jenny," Thirnas said.

"The soldiers that chased us across town this morning? The blacksuits?" she asked.

"Merely foot-soldiers, not demons. An advance force. They've been here forever in some way, shape or form. Your world has always managed to sustain a kind of equilibrium, but you're on a knife edge. Childhood cancers, political rifts, natural disasters, wars...they're all precursors to the Bleed, but you've so far been able to counteract the evil with good and maintain the balance. Until now."

"Wait. What's the Bleed?"

Dad again now. "A name for the evil. It's the way they seep between dimensions like an infection. Their scourge taints everything it comes into contact with. If the demons are allowed to get a strong enough foothold here, the whole human race will fall. The planet, then the solar system, the galaxy, then finally this universe. Everything."

"Are you sure about this? I know they came after me all guns blazing, but I watched the blacksuits helping to evacuate the center of the city this morning. And if I remember rightly, Thirnas, it was you causing most of the panic in your bloody comet or whatever it was."

"I had to make an entrance. I had to get your attention."

"You did that all right."

"Those people the soldiers were evacuating," Dad said ominously, "I worry what might have happened to them."

"What do you mean? They were just getting them out of the city, weren't they?" Jenny said, shocked and concerned.

"Yeah, I'm sure you're right. Just my mind running away with itself as usual. I'm stressed, that's all."

"And you're right to be concerned," Thirnas said. "We have to be ready for an incursion. I'll do everything I can to hold them back, to prevent the Bleed from spilling through."

"And how will you do that?" Jenny asked.

"For this reality, water is the key," Thirnas answered.

"You've seen the Thames this morning, I take it?" Dad said.

"Was that your doing too?" Jenny asked the god.

"Yes. A precautionary step. I've held the tides steady for now, but it's only a temporary measure. It'll do irreparable damage if I don't release them again soon."

"Not as much damage as the Bleed will if it reaches here," Dad said.

"So how do we stop it? And for the last time, what do I have to do with any of this?" Jenny asked.

Thirnas went to leave. Dad just looked at him. "Oh, that's right. Always disappearing when the conversation gets really difficult."

"You know I can't stay."

Dad shook his head, regretting his words. "Yeah, I know."

"I'll leave you to tell her," he said, and he ducked under what was left of the door frame and disappeared into the kitchen.

It was strange—of all the things Jenny

had been bombarded with this morning, nothing worried her as much as Thirnas's sudden change in demeanor just then. It didn't take a genius to work out that he was leaving her alone with Dad so the two of them could talk in private. She put two and two together and came up with an answer she didn't like. Dad had been keeping huge secrets from her for all of her life so far, so what else hadn't she been told? She braced herself as he began to explain.

"First things first, love, I need you to understand that I've kept this stuff from you to protect you, not deceive you. Your mum and I always wanted you to live the best life you could, free from any unnecessary pressures or responsibilities."

"So why do I get the feeling you are about to unload a whole load of pressures and responsibilities onto me?"

"You're so smart, Jen. Nothing gets past you, does it?"

"What, apart from the fact you're best mates with God?"

"Yeah, apart from that. Fact is, he couldn't have come back here if it wasn't for you. You're a key. You're the link that allows a connection to be made between the gods and the mortals here on Earth."

"Why me?"

"I'm coming to that."

"Has it got something to do with Mum?"

He paused, then answered. "Yes."

"And did she have something to do with that god in the kitchen?"

"With another god, not him. Not directly."

"That's a relief, I guess. So, is this the part when you tell me about my mysterious parentage and finally explain what really happened to her? You know, like they've done in about a thousand crappy science-fiction and fantasy films."

She was waiting for him to tell her to stop being stupid.

"Yes. That's right," he said instead.

"Jesus."

"Your mum was in love with a god. She fell pregnant, and you were the result."

"And where were you at this stage?"

"That's not important right now."

"So you're not my dad?"

"How do I answer that?"

She was starting to sound angry now. "You could try with the truth. You've had twenty-two years to get your story straight."

"I know. And I've rehearsed in my head what I'd tell you pretty much every day of those twenty-two years."

"So, answer."

"Let me start by telling you that I love you more than anything else in the world. In any world, come to that."

"But not enough to trust me with the truth?"

"It's because I love you so much that I didn't tell you. Did you not hear me earlier? I'd hoped this day would never come. You could have suffered years of confusion, doubt, anxiety. By not telling you, I gave you a normal life."

"You deceived me."

"I *protected* you. Your father died and I was there for your mother. You were just hours old at the time. All I wanted was for you to lead a normal life."

"Normal?"

"Please understand, love, this kind of thing happens all the time. Your mum lost her husband, then I came along and things just clicked between us. We were just two people who fell in love under unusual circumstances."

"You can say that again."

"I wish with all my heart that you were my natural daughter, and as far as I'm concerned, you are."

"So who was my father?"

"Thirnas's brother. He was killed by the Bleed. He died stopping it from breaching into our dimension. This isn't the first time we've been in this situation."

She got up and paced the room, then stopped, turned back, and glared at him. "Wait...are you saying I'm half-god? Is there such a thing?"

"Yep. That is exactly what I'm saying."

"Fuck me."

"The only one on the planet, as far as I know."

"Seriously?"

"Seriously."

"How can a god die, anyway?"

"Like I said, they're another species. Immortality and divine protection is the stuff of legend. It's mostly rubbish thought up by people who only know half the truth, people who are trying to keep other people in line with threats of damnation and promises of rewards for devotion."

"And you didn't run a mile when Mum started talking about gods and stuff like that?"

"I already knew about the gods and demons, and about the Bleed. If we're going for complete transparency, I should tell you I'm not from this reality either."

"Oh, this just gets better and better…"

"You never wondered why you've never met any of my relatives?"

"You told me they were all dead—"

"They are."

"—but you didn't tell me they were aliens."

"There are gods on other planets, and there are people like us on other planets too. The multiverse is an impossibly huge place. Like I said, I wanted you to lead as carefree a life as possible. Your mum and I came here so we'd have the best chance of blending in and giving you that life."

"Until today?"

"Yes, until today."

A pause. A chance to breathe. A chance to try and make sense of the tirade of madness that the day had become. Jenny got up from her seat and paced the room.

"Okay. Assuming you and the big guy are telling the truth...."

"We are."

"...then for the last time, Dad, what's my part in all of this?"

"Like I said, you're the link between this world and the others. You're a half-breed with a foot in both camps. You're the key to everything."

"How?"

"The vessel he arrived in—he was reliant on you unlocking it."

"Seriously? He's all powerful and still I have to let him out of his own ship? That makes no sense."

"There's a lot about interdimensional

travel that doesn't make much sense. Every plane of reality has different rules and laws. Physics, chemistry…it can be different everywhere."

She laughed at that. "Honestly, that's just stupid."

"I think you've seen enough so far today to know I'm telling the truth."

"Fair point. And now there's a god here my job's done?"

"I wish that were the case. You facilitated Thirnas's arrival back on Earth, but you have to understand the power that gives you. You're just about the only one who can give the gods and demons access to this planet. You can let them in, or you can keep them out."

"So it's all on me. Is that what you're saying?"

"You're the conduit, Jen. You're the one who creates the link between one reality and the next. And that means…."

"That means what? Say it, Dad. Tell me."

"That means it'll be you who stands in the way of the Bleed when the time comes. I'm sorry, love."

Not for the first time since the comet had appeared over the London skyline, Jenny found herself struggling to make sense of the insensible. "What do I have to do?" she eventually asked.

"Just stop them getting through. I wish I could be more specific. For now, though, the key thing is keeping you safe. I'll do everything I can to look after you, love. I always have and I always will."

"I know."

"We need to speak to Thirnas and find out what he's planning. He'll have his next steps already mapped out."

Jenny went into the kitchen to see him but returned just seconds later. Dad could tell from the expression on her face that something was wrong.

"What is it, love?"

"God's run off."

13

The Moon

DAY THREE / 4:45 PM

Maddie was placing food stores and other supplies into a small sled when she felt the presence of another in the garage. She turned to see a small-caliber handgun pointed at her.

"Didn't think you had it in you," she said as she stared at Sandra.

"Get away from there," Sandra said

frostily.

"And if I don't?"

"I'll shoot you."

"In cold blood? What will the rest of the council think?"

"According to you, that won't be much of a problem soon enough." Sandra motioned with the gun.

"Sandra?" Dean asked. "What are you doing?"

"Getting us out of here.

"We have an emergency meeting in ten minutes."

"I love you, honey, I do, but screw the meeting. We don't have time to discuss how we're going to die."

"We don't know that," Dean answered, but there was not much sincerity in his voice.

"We just looked at the computer models; there's less than a two percent chance of this post surviving. That's not nearly good enough. And look, Maddie has been kind enough to pack the mower with the supplies we're going to need."

"And the rest of the people here?"

"Besides the kids and you, fuck 'em."

"Real altruistic nature you got going on there," Maddie replied.

"Me? And pray tell us what you were about to do, Maddie? Got that all packed up like you're heading to the hills for an extended stay. I may have said it aloud, but it looks to me like your actions say it all."

"Got me there."

"We...we can't just desert everyone," Dean pleaded.

"That's your problem, my dear, sweet husband. You're always putting others before yourself. That's why I'm here to make sure our family survives."

"What makes us more important than anyone else?"

"Someone has to live. Why shouldn't it be us?"

"I...I don't know how I feel about this. This...this can't be right, Sandra. We vote, we do shuttles, save as many people as possible."

"So you're saying we leave it up to fate? You realize that the kids will be considered last to leave, right? The 'success of the mission' and all that. Technical personnel first."

"Mom? Dad? I've been looking for you." It was Derrick. "What's going on?"

"We're just getting ready to leave and quick thinking Maddie here had got our transportation all ready," Sandra replied.

"And the gun?" he asked.

"Insurance. Now, where's your sister?"

"I would imagine looking for Tyler," he

told her.

"Shit, she's going to ruin everything. Everyone is going to know what's happening before she gets back. We're going to have to leave without her."

"Holy crap," Maddie said. "I had you pegged as cold-blooded, Sandra, then you almost had me convinced maybe you had a soul in there somewhere. I mean, understandable, pretty admirable, in fact, trying to save your kids and all, but then come to find out it was all an act… a pretense to get your own scrawny ass to safety. Sacrificing your own daughter… that's some serious biblical stuff right there."

"Doesn't matter to me if you're dead before the explosion, smartass. I said move away from the mower."

Maddie had her hands up in the air and did as she was told.

"Get in," she said to her husband and son.

"Without Sam? Not a chance," Dean told her.

"Fine. Derrick, move!"

"Mom?"

"Don't be stupid, Derrick. We leave or we die."

The boy didn't move.

"Good to see not too much of you

rubbed off on them," Maddie smiled.

"Dying funny to you, grease monkey?" Sandra moved for the driver's seat.

"Not really. The thing is, Sandra, that after your little darlings stole a mower, I retrofitted all of them with a security device. You need to key in a code to start them."

"No shit Maddie. I was at the meeting when we discussed it." Sandra sat in the seat and pulled up the control panel.

"See, the thing is, I have the master code, which means I have the ability to change them."

Sandra set her jaw and entered in her invalid code. A red warning message flashed on the display screen.

"Two more bad entries and the machine shuts off for half an hour," Maddie said after Sandra once again input what she thought was the correct code and was greeted with a loud chirp.

"Give me the damn code, Maddie," Sandra hissed.

"Not a chance. If I'm going to die, you're coming with me."

"I will blow your fucking head off!" Sandra extracted herself from the vehicle.

"What are you going to do then? Sift through my leaking brain for the answer? Doesn't work like that, sweetheart."

Sandra advanced on Maddie, gun extended. "You're going to give me that code and then myself and whoever is smart enough to go is getting in with me."

"Since the day we arrived, Sandra, I've watched you. You're smart and manipulative and if you don't get what you want by conventional ways, you are more than adept at using back channels."

"What can a wrench wielder like yourself, possibly know about it?"

"Oh, you'd be amazed. Like that council seat you 'won.' I saw how badly you wanted to be on the governing body, but you just couldn't get the votes. Seems that hard as you tried, people were still able to see through the veneer you wear and to the root of the person underneath. You want me to continue?" She gave a sidelong glance to Dean.

"What's she talking about, Sandra?" Dean asked.

"Hopkins was a shoo-in for the council. He was a doctor, Mayor of his hometown, well-respected and genuinely cared for his patients and constituents."

"Hopkins died in a carbon monoxide accident," Dean responded.

"Wasn't an accident," Maddie said.

"Are you saying I murdered him? Because that's preposterous," Sandra said.

"No, not directly. Not that I don't think you're capable of it, you just went about it in a different manner."

"You shut your mouth." Sandra came menacingly close to Maddie, the gun mere inches from her face.

"You can't be this clueless, Dean, can you?" Maddie asked, turning away from the gun. "Your wife isn't well-liked. She's a brilliant molecular scientist, but she's as cold as the dark side of this rock."

"I say what needs to be said. I don't have to be liked to lead." Sandra angled to get between Maddie and her husband.

"Hopkins was in. Hell, I was going to vote for him. Thought it was particularly strange when he dropped out," Maddie said.

"He said he was going to be too busy." Dean looked perplexed.

"Too busy doing what? At that point, I don't think anyone had suffered so much as the sniffles. I was slightly curious at that point, but it was his decision to make. If he didn't want to be on the council, so be it. I could see his point; the less interaction with people, the better as far as I'm concerned. But as soon as I started hearing about how Sandra was picking up support, that got me thinking, because, well, honestly, she's a frosty bitch and about as likely a choice as me. Started digging. I wasn't much of a Nancy Drew fan, but I'd read enough of those books to know something wasn't quite right. Whoa…and was I ever right. I know you thought you covered your tracks fairly well, but not many devices these days aren't connected to the mainframe hub. Even little hidden cameras. And if you know where to look, you see things you, unfortunately, can never forget. One of them being that concave thing you call an ass riding up and down on quite the prodigious member, if I do say so myself."

"Wha…?" Dean had a confused expression on his face.

"Are you still not following, or is it stemming from a desire to remain ignorant?" Maddie asked.

"That's enough!" Sandra pressed the pistol up against Maddie's head.

"Was wondering…" Maddie said as she twisted quickly, bringing her hand up and knocking Sandra's arm away. The handgun erupted as the woman sent a round into the ceiling. With her left, Maddie threw a punch into Sandra's nose. Blood sprayed from the blunt force and the pistol fell to the floor. Maddie was quick to pick it up as Sandra's hands flew to cover the injured area.

"You broke my nose, you bitch!"

Sandra's words were muffled.

"She slept with the good doctor, then threatened to give his wife the proof. Now, this part is conjecture, but I don't think you need to be the Hardy Boys—now them I liked—to figure out what was going on. She blackmailed Hopkins for his support. I figure guilt or disgust got the better of him so he offed himself. Not sure why being on a council of what's basically a well-oiled machine was so important to go to such great lengths for, but there it is. So it shouldn't come as any great shock what she's willing to do to preserve her own life. And that, my good folks, is why I changed the code." She made a half bow.

"Is that true, what she said?" Dean was shocked, and hurt.

"I'll kill you for that." Sandra rubbed the wrist Maddie had hit and dragged a sleeve across her still bleeding nose.

"Which part? Ratting you out or breaking your ugly nose?"

Sandra sneered.

"Go, go to your husband. He's hurt, wounded, really. See if you can muster up some of that steaminess you did for Hopkins. Honestly, I don't know what he was thinking. His wife is a knockout, and, well, you're you. But that's men for you, isn't it?"

"Any man would be happy to be with me!" Sandra said proudly.

"Pah, Don't go thinking you're all that. I once saw a video where a guy fucked a cabbage. Just goes to show they'll stick it in just about anything."

"A what?" Derrick asked.

"Sorry, that wasn't meant for your ears." Maddie looked slightly embarrassed.

Sandra realized her secret had been shared and that she'd lost the upper hand. She went to her husband.

"Don't," he told her before staggering out the door. She followed.

"Where's your sister?" Maddie put the gun's safety on before placing it in her pocket. She went back to what she was doing as if nothing had happened.

"My mom cheated?"

"If there's a sliding scale of the crap your mother has done, I'm sure that's on the lower end of the spectrum. That was kind of harsh, but she was pointing a weapon at me. I don't see any bags with you kiddo; you planning on coming or not?"

"I can't just leave."

"This is weird for me to say, but, you and your sister are the only two people on this whole base I trust now that Clive is gone. I can survive on my own, been doing it in hostile environments for most of my adult life, but it's easier with help. You should reconsider."

"You'd just leave?"

"Should I sit around and wait to die? What are you expecting me to do?"

"Not what my mother would have—just leave us all here!"

"I am not your mother," she replied evenly.

"Then prove it. Wait to see what the council has planned."

"The same council that your mother—who was about to leave you and your sister behind, by the way—sits on? That council? Do you think any decision they come to is going to benefit the likes of us?"

"I have to trust that what they decide will be the best thing for everyone. You aren't even going to give them the chance to do what's right."

"What's right, Derrick, is us getting out of here."

"No, the right thing is all of us getting out of here."

"You're just a kid, what do you know? Now get in."

"Not a chance."

"Your funeral. I'll lay some plastic flowers over this general area once the radiation dies down in a few hundred years and I can get close enough to do it."

Derrick watched as Maddie strapped herself in, remote opened the inner door to the airlock and drove through. The inner door shut and the yellow warning light began to strobe, indicating the outer door was being opened. He didn't bother to watch her drive off before turning to look for his sister.

14

The Trade Road

"It's pointless to run," the distraught mother sobbed as she shuffled along at the back of the small pack of Mercy Point survivors heading north. "They run so fast. And they kill so fast. How can they?" she asked, pointing her anger at the sky with hands made into claws. "They were our family, our friends. Can they not see who we are? Have they abandoned who they were?"

"Stop," Arridon called out to her. "Your despair ruins our calm. It hinders our pace. Save your breath if you want us all to reach the city in safety."

"How dare you?" she called out to him. "Did *you* lose a child today? A husband? Do not dare to tell me I cannot grieve when the end is here."

The dozen survivors walked at a brisk pace, heads looking over shoulders in small groups of familiar faces, shied away from the tall man and the crying, manic woman. They were ten miles inland on the Trade Road away from Mercy Point, amongst the fields of wild grass and sparse bushes that were in bloom with pink and white flowers. The scent of the blossoms allayed the dense, clinging smell of death in their noses.

"You must grieve, ma'am," Arridon said, trying to soften his tone and succeeding somewhat. "But now is not the time. You are ranting and raving, making noise we can ill afford to make, and lamenting events we can do fuck all about. We *can* run. We *can* reach the city, and find assistance there, but only if we maintain our pace, keep watch, save energy as best we can, and trust one another."

"Kindly, child, go to the closest edge and take a long walk off into the stars," she hissed at him. "You'd be served by such an act. Save yourself the time it'll take for the monsters to bleed you dry."

"Enough," Gray barked. "I have woe for your losses, madam, but I will not have you speak to my son in such a way."

"Oh, such firm words from the village drunk," she said with a laugh. "How long will you be so brave and forthright, Gray? Until a half empty bottle calls you to a ditch along our pointless journey to the Endless City, with its giant walls and crowded streets? How long will you remain so strong and brave, knowing that there's a mouthful of whiskey to be had?"

Gray stopped walking and stared at the woman. "Your losses came today. Your wounds are fresh," he started. "And that pain is terrible, and I know so. My wounds are fifteen years old, and they are toughened scars that I suffer with every thought and step. To alleviate that pain I turned to wine, and mead, and worse, and I will forever be ashamed of that choice. Know this; my mind is clear, my soul unburdened by drink, and we are heading north to the city to find refuge from the Bleed. I will earn my forgiveness, if those whom I have wronged most deign to give it."

"For how long will that refuge last?" she asked in earnest. "Those monsters will climb the walls and tear the gates open eventually."

"Truth. I fear this world's story is all but written, but there are other worlds we can flee to. Worlds where we might start anew."

"Speak of this more," an elderly man asked the father. "What worlds? Islands at the opposite cold edge we can set sail to? Some place deep in the Endless City?"

"Both of those ideas have merit, and surely will buy you time before the servants of the Bleed reach you, but no, that is not of what I speak. My wife…she was…."

"A god. One of the gifted from the Endless City. Your children bear her eyes," the balding man at the back of their pack said, lifting his cane high enough to gesture its handle at Thistle's face.

"Yes, and they are such amazing eyes," Gray said, looking to his children with pride as they walked near his shoulders. "The gods are not from our world. When the oldest trees were but saplings, their ancestors came here from a different realm entirely."

"Like, from the heavens?" the grieving woman asked.

"Something to that effect, yes," Gray answered her. "Using their magic, and science, they pierced through the fabric between worlds, escaping their inevitable destruction when the Bleed invaded their world, as it has invaded ours now."

"So this...invader, the Bleed, it made the gods turn tail and run?" Arridon asked his father. "They left a whole world to die?"

Gray nodded in shared shame. "The Bleed wages more than just war on the living, son. You've seen some of what it can do, and based on the gods' legends, the Bleed can do much more. There is only running when it arrives. Taking a stand against it might push it away for a time, but it will always return. It is a...sentient, wily infection of pure evil that ruins everything, and for which there is no cure."

"What is the Bleed?" the grieving woman asked.

"It is the entity that creates demons. It seeks to destroy everything. My wife tried to explain it to me when our first—Arridon—was born. I lacked the wisdom to understand what she said then, but I gathered that it is a great being of terrible hunger and avarice who has learned to pierce through to other worlds. Perhaps it is the one true God."

"To wage war?" the elderly man asked.

"To feed," Arridon answered. "That's why, isn't it? Because its hunger knows no end."

"I believe that's what your mother

said," Gray replied to his son.

"So knowing this, if it's the truth you speak, what hope have we?" the elderly man asked after stopping and leaning on his cane.

"My wife told me of a place where a portal could be opened once again. A portal she created with the gods' magic and science. A door that will open only for Arridon and Thistle, and only again if they are alive."

"Where is this door to safety?" Thistle asked her father.

"The Endless City is massive, sprawling beyond anything you can imagine. We could walk its winding streets, search the miles-wide citadels in the shade of the miles-tall tower kingdoms which lie within its god-made walls for a year and then ten more before finding it."

"How then have we any hope?" Arridon asked. "We're fucked, then."

"No…because I know which specific building we seek, and remember much of the way to return to the area it resides within."

"You do?" Thistle said, then skipped ten paces ahead in pure joy. She stopped and waited for the rest of the beleaguered, tired, and dirty party to catch up.

"It's in a keep?" Arridon posed. "A

castle or tower?"

"It belonged to your mother's family. Makers of devices and spells that counted time and space, they were. Influential, and wealthy."

"Mom was a rich god?" Arridon asked.

"That she was. Her family owned one of the great citadels in the center of the Endless City, and we seek that citadel. Within there is a central spire, and atop that spire—a mile above the ground, if an inch—is a great clock made of glass. And behind that clock is the portal we seek."

"How long a journey?" Thistle asked.

He thought. "If we maintain this pace, and if the infected denizens of Mercy Point do not catch up to us, we shall arrive at the walls of the Endless City by dusk. We shall tell the guard there of Mercy Point's fate, and perhaps rest and supply ourselves for the rest of our journey in the morn. From there, barring setbacks within the city ruins…we could arrive at your mother's tower in perhaps two days. Ascending to the top…that is a task I cannot surmise the difficulty of. It will be exhausting."

"Ruins…" Arridon muttered. "Why is the Endless City in ruins? I know the gods left their city to fight the war on the edge of the world, but how did the city become ruins? It couldn't have fallen apart in just my lifetime. What happened?"

"The Bleed."

"What?" Thistle asked. "They attacked the city?"

"In the far west of the Endless City, on the other edge of our world, the Bleed found a way in, and made war against us."

"Us?" Thistle asked. "You and mother were in the Endless City together?"

"Your brother was born in that tower I speak of. We fled not long after, when word of the Bleed's arrival reached us. Her family —your family—remained behind to fight while we fled to Mercy Point to wait it out."

"Then I was born," she said.

"Years later, yes. And we settled in. Made the village our home. But, as you know, the war didn't end, and in the face of a threat to her children, your mother left to do her godly duty. She went back to the city, laid the necessary preparations to open the portal, then headed to the new front on the eastern end of the world, where the Bleed had crawled up and over the edge and began to eat away at the very seas."

"And here we are, having lost the Endless City, and now the Eastern Sea," Arridon said, looking over to the grieving woman who now sobbed into her hands. "And for us to have any chance at all, we must venture into the depths of a city we know to have once been overrun by demons and find a citadel with walls a mile high, then hike to the center of that fortress, and ascend to the top of a tower that may or may not still have a portal that will allow us to run away like cowards?"

Gray stopped and took his son by the shoulders. "If your mother and I had been of sound mind the day we fled the city with you—a tiny babe—in our arms, we would've used the closest portal that went to anywhere and left on the spot. Instead, we had faith that the gods could turn the Bleed away. Gods are immune to the infection, and had many weapons they could fight well with. We were not brave to stay, and we would not have been cowards to have fled that day. When you are a parent, the only thing that matters is taking care of your children, whatever the cost. I wish one day for you to understand that."

"But when you have no children, maybe the only thing that matters is taking care of your world," Arridon said. "Whatever the cost."

"Some truth there," the mother without her children said as they reached a low, dry stone wall that ran alongside the well-traveled road. She moved to it and rested herself atop a smooth stone, wiping sweat from her brow. The old man she'd kept pace with stopped to regard her place of rest.

"Come on," Gray said to her, extending a hand. "We mustn't slow in the least until we pass between the citadels and enter the city. The infection spreads like wildfire amongst our blood and it will surely catch us if we slow."

"I think I'll rest right here. You all go ahead now," she said, tired, but proud.

"Why?" Thistle asked her. "You're killing yourself if you stay behind."

"I've nothing left to run for," she said with a shrug. "I fear running for a refuge where all that will be left me is to mourn and then die." She shook her head. "I have no interest in new worlds. All I ever wanted is gone or is on this road trying to find me. Perhaps it is best that I find them, too. You see, I have this knife," she whispered, then produced a small blade that likely had only ever cut bread on a cutting board. She looked at it and fiddled with the feel of it before letting her hands drop to her lap.

"You'll turn into one of them if their blood touches you," Gray explained.

"The knife won't just be for them, if you understand my purpose," she said, then smiled. "You go on ahead, ya? You take care of your boy and girl first and foremost. You find no more grief for you. You take them all to a place where the sun shines, and the only blood is from skinned knees, ya?"

Gray wiped a tear that escaped from his eyes, and nodded at her. "Ya. Be well, ma'am. I will remember you."

The conversation died on the altar of Gray's statement, and without the lady and her knife, they ushered themselves forward towards the hope of salvation within the Endless City. Tears flowed, feet ached, and sweat ran on hot skin.

At their heels, miles behind them on the same road they walked, monsters followed their scent.

Following them was Sebastian, voice of the Bleed, sword in hand, hate in heart.

15

London

The broadcast (if it could be called that) was shown on every screen in the world, the source of the signal unknown. Best-guess approximations suggested it was coming from somewhere in the middle of the Sahara; somewhere there wasn't anything other than sand. It interrupted and overtook every other signal. Not just on TVs; the message was also relayed to phones, watches, computer monitors, cinemas, outdoor advertising, tablets, trains and airport departure displays…Thirnas's face was literally everywhere. And he spoke to everyone at the same time, though not in the same language and not with the same voice.

The message was continuous, though.

As was the warning.

"I am your God. For many thousands of years I've left you alone to grow, safe in the knowledge that I've always been there and I've always been watching. I've watched you learn and develop. I've watched you flourish and create. I've watched you become more sophisticated, more understanding, to the point where you're pushing the boundaries of your own mortal restraints. I've watched you live fully and love passionately, and it has been a wonder to do so. It was important to leave you to do this by yourselves, though. The lessons we learn mean more when we find the answers for ourselves. Had I held your hands too closely, I would have denied you countless experiences and discoveries.

"I understand you may be dubious. A message from me was the absolute last thing you will have been expecting to see today. For many, I know that this will cause a profound emotional stirring. I'm probably not what you expected, or what you'd hoped for. I may be more than you'd imagined; I may be far less. I know that many of you will question your beliefs now that you have seen my face and heard my voice. Many of your principles will have been shaken, but I need every last one of you to know that I am here to reassure and to help you. Your relationships with me—collectively and individually—will be enhanced by this interaction. In answering many questions about me, you'll also discover many more questions you've yet to ask about yourselves. This will be a wonderful time we share together. This is the dawn of a new age for the people of Earth.

"But, I'm afraid there's a reason for my visit to you today."

The momentary pause before Thirnas's next words felt like the largest collective intake of breath in Earth's entire history.

"All of creation is held in a delicate balance. Light and dark, right and wrong, good and evil. There are times when events conspire and the balance is tipped. For a long, long time, the equilibrium has been maintained, but now, unexpectedly, the corrupting force of evil has managed to get a foothold and threatens to consume the earth. I cannot allow this to happen. I will not allow this to happen. I am here to protect you, my children. War is coming."

"He's so far up his own ass at times," Dad grumbled as the two of them sat watching the TV. "Switch it off, will you."

Jenny didn't need to be asked twice. She pressed the red button on the remote. The TV power turned off, but Thirnas's image and voice continued uninterrupted. "That's really annoying," she said. She went to check her phone, but he was there too.

"Shall I put the dinner on?" Dad asked. It was getting late. Darkness had set in outside. The day had slipped by without either of them noticing.

"How can you think about food at a time like this?"

"I can think about food at any time. If I'm honest, I'm nervous. Food is a distraction."

"I don't think I'll be able to eat a thing."

Dad got up and went to the kitchen. Thirnas was on his iPad too. He turned it face down and looked through the cupboards for something to cook. "I'm worried how his pontificating is going to go down," he said. "He has always been an arrogant bastard. Rather abrasive. I expect there will be plenty of people who won't react well to seeing him."

"Yeah, you, for a start."

"I'm serious, love. He needs to bring people together and get them on side, not push them away. Everything's changed since the gods were last here. People are far less accepting, less superstitious. We've grown past the need for God. He's likely to encounter far more resistance than before."

Jenny stood in what was left of the energy-damaged doorway and watched her dad chopping vegetables. He was concentrating a little too hard for Jenny's liking. She knew him better than anyone. When he was quiet like this he usually had something to say, but he either didn't want to say it or didn't know how. It made her feel nervous.

"There's one part of this I still don't get."

"Just one part?" he said, not even looking up.

"Why now?"

Still nothing. The silence was worse than anything.

"Dad, answer me."

"I'm scared, love," he eventually admitted. That took her by surprise. She'd expected him to say plenty of things, but admitting he was frightened hadn't been one of them. "I'm scared because this day was never supposed to happen, and I'm scared because you're right at the center of it and there's little I can do to help you. The gods have been keeping the Bleed under control all this time, but him turning up here like this today means the gods are on the back-foot. They're getting ready for an attack."

"So what am I supposed I do, Dad?"

He put down his knife, walked across the kitchen and hugged her tight. He looked deep into her eyes, and everything he'd told her earlier about her parentage was forgotten. Jenny knew this man would do anything to keep her safe. He'd been looking after her for her entire life and she had no reason to think he'd stop now. But what worried her most was that this war between the demons and the gods, no matter how far-fetched it sounded, was unquestionably bigger than Dad. And for all the love in the world, he was never going to be able to protect her forever.

"Do you know why you did what you did this morning, Jenny? Why you went the opposite way to everyone else?"

"I didn't think about it. It was natural. Instinctive."

"That's right. It was a response that's hard coded into your very being. It's running through your DNA. You can't help it, and you can't fight it, and that's what scares me more than anything. When the shit hits the fan, you'll inevitably be right in the middle of it all."

She sobbed involuntarily. This was too much to take in.

"You have to promise me something," Dad said.

"Of course. Anything."

"Don't sacrifice yourself. If things look lost, don't throw it all away and give up. Promise me?"

"I promise," she said, though she didn't know if she could.

"You trust no one. Remember that the demons will be looking for you to allow them through a rift, but also remember that doors are two-way. The same interdimensional links and leaks that will let the demons in will let you out."

"*Us* out."

"Hopefully."

"So, where do I find them?"

"Up high. Very high."

"What, like mountain high?"

"Are there mountains in the middle of London?"

"No."

"So think logically. Skyscrapers, landmarks...there are enough tall buildings around here. You'll know when you see it.

You'll feel the same pull as the one that led you to Thirnas."

Dad put the vegetables into a casserole dish along with chicken portions and stock. He then started peeling potatoes.

"What aren't you telling me?" Jenny asked.

He shrugged. "Nothing."

"Don't, Dad, please. You're cooking comfort food. You do that when you're worried."

"You're imagining things."

"I'm not. Whenever I look back and something shitty has happened, you always cooked chicken casserole. You did it when you had all that grief at work earlier in the year, and when I broke up with that Colin guy."

"Never liked him," Dad grumbled.

"That's not the point. Point is, you cook food like this when you're worried about something."

"And you don't think I'm entitled to be worried today?"

"There's something else. I know there is...."

"You're just imagining it."

"I don't think so. I think you're expecting—"

Her words were interrupted by a knock at the door of the flat. Dad picked up his knife again. Jenny went to answer it, but he overtook and gestured for her to stay back.

He peered through the security spyhole, then relaxed. It was Veronica Allen, the woman who lived in the flat below. He opened the door for her and let her inside, hiding the knife behind his back.

"Veronica, this is an unexpected surprise."

"Not as unexpected as the surprise I got earlier today. What's going on in there?"

She stood on tiptoes and tried to look over Dad's shoulder, deeper into the flat.

"What do you mean?"

"There was a heck of a lot of noise this morning, and I've got a problem, too."

"What kind of problem?"

"Some damage to my ceiling."

"Ah, yeah. Shit. Sorry about that."

"I was just sitting there minding my own business when the TV went haywire. The lights started flickering and they're still not right. Then this bloody big stain appears on my ceiling and I smelled burning."

"I can explain."

"I hope you can, because when my landlord sees the state of my place, he'll go crazy."

"I know. I am sorry, truly. I had a bit of an accident up here, and I'm still trying to get myself straight. I've just put dinner on. What do you say I come down now and see what I can do, then you come back up later and have dinner with Jenny and I? It's the least I can do."

"That's very kind of you."

"Like I said, it's the least I can do."

"You're sure?"

"Completely."

"What about dinner?"

"What about it?"

"You said you've just started cooking."

"That's okay. Jenny will keep an eye on it."

"She's here, is she?"

Dad realized too late that he'd been tricked. He pushed Veronica back and slammed the door in her face. The force with which the door shut was nothing in comparison to the force that came back the other way as Veronica headbutted the door again and again and again.

Jenny was at the far end of the hallway. "Dad, what's going on? Was that the lady from downstairs?"

"Get your stuff together," he told her as he locked and bolted the door then dragged a heavy oak table unit across, blocking the way in and out. The door rocked and shook every time the woman on the other side smacked her head into it.

"Why? What's wrong with her?"

Dad went back into the living room and opened a window and looked down. He pulled his head back fast. "She's the least of our concerns. We've got a problem."

"Worse than our neighbor using her head as a battering ram?" she asked as she squeezed past him to see.

The streets around their block of flats were filled with people. And this wasn't just a busy night out in London, this was something entirely different. The people weren't milling aimlessly or on their way somewhere, they'd specifically come *here*. Hundreds of them, all converging on this place.

Jenny went through to her bedroom, the next-door room with a window on the adjacent wall, high above the main entrance to the block. She knelt on her bed and looked down. There were more of them out there. She craned her neck, and although she couldn't see all the way around their building, she already knew they were surrounded. The hordes outside were hardly making any noise. Out on the landing, on the other hand, Veronica was still smashing her head against the door.

"Tell me this is just a coincidence," Jenny said, frantic, but she already knew that it wasn't. "What do they want?"

"You, love. Have you not been listening to me? Bloody hell, Jenny! You need to start paying attention. This isn't a game, you know."

A dull roar came from outside, audible even from this distance high above the crowds. Jenny looked down again and saw that the main entrance to the building had been forced. Although it was dark out there, the streetlamps and other random lights provided just enough illumination for her to be able to make out what was happening. A surge of movement appeared as people began to flood inside.

"Who are they?" Jenny asked.

"My guess is these could be the people you saw being evacuated this morning. Conscripted by the blacksuits you were talking about, I expect. A new army, controlled by the demons. They need you to open the portal and let in the Bleed."

Jenny had to stop herself. It all still sounded so ridiculous, but she could tell from the desperate expression on Dad's face that every word of it was true.

The sound of wood splintering from the hallway. Jenny couldn't help but look. Veronica had managed to smash her head completely through the door, doing as much damage to her face in the process. Blood was streaming down from a jagged gash across her forehead. When she saw Jenny, she smiled with a mouth full of broken teeth.

"I see you!" she cackled, then she pulled her head back out of the gap to shout to the crowds gathered below. "She's here!"

"You have to go," Dad said. "Get away from here and find somewhere safe. Keep away from everyone else, especially me. And if things get any worse, find one of the gateways. Doesn't matter where you end up, anywhere will be safer than here. The boss will try and find you and help you. Just stop the Bleed from getting through."

"I can't just leave you."

"Yes, you can. Now move!"

She grabbed the sports rucksack she kept under the bed then half-filled it with clothes. From the kitchen she took food and water, enough to keep her going for a few days in hiding.

Veronica was still yelling out on the landing. And then she stopped. There was a momentary silence, followed by more hammering and banging, this time far louder than before. Where there had been one person trying to get into the flat, now there were many.

"They're here," Dad said. "Go."

"But how?"

He took her to the part of the flat which

had been damaged when she and Thirnas had arrived earlier. The circular energy burst caused by their arrival had burnt away part of the ceiling, walls and floor, leaving a perfectly spherical space. Dad stamped his boot repeatedly onto the deepest part of the burn where the remaining floor was thinnest. It only took a few frantic strikes for him to have kicked his way through.

"Remember, they might not know what you look like, they just know where you are."

"I was on TV though, wasn't I?"

"Yeah, but the focus was on the other guy. Right now you've still got a degree of anonymity. Get out there and make the most of it before it's too late."

He pushed her down towards the hole in the floor.

"I can't leave you," she said.

"You can and you will. I'll be okay. Now go."

"But, Dad..."

"Go," he said again. "Run and keep running until you're far from here. This is bigger than you and me, Jen. If you don't do this, we're all dead anyway."

He kissed her forehead then helped lower her down. She dropped into Veronica's flat, cushioning her landing on a sofa then falling forward onto the floor. She heard a horrific thump and crash from upstairs and looked through the hole she'd just climbed through. She caught a glimpse of Dad running for cover as their apartment filled with people.

Got to move.

The landing outside Veronica's flat was so full of people that it was almost impossible to move. Unable to fight against the irresistible, slow flow, Jenny dropped to the ground and crawled through the forest of legs, expecting at any moment to be recognized, dragged back up, and lynched. She kept crawling, going as far as she could until she reached the wall, then managed to find a small alcove in front of a maintenance hatch. She picked herself up and tried to disappear into the shadows.

What the hell was wrong with all these people?

They looked like regular folks, but their faces were drained of all emotion. Their expressions were frozen, eyes unblinking. They appeared puppet-like, manipulated and controlled from elsewhere. They continued to converge on her flat, and for a moment the temptation to go back up there and try to help Dad was hard to resist. But what could she do? The number of people flooding through the building appeared incalculable from her limited viewpoint and she realized they'd soon reach a point where the entire block was clogged with human flesh.

So how was she going to get out?

The fire escape.

It was the only other option, but it was on the opposite side of the building to where she was currently hiding. Before she could talk herself out of it, she turned up the collar of her jacket, pushed herself away from the wall, and merged into the crowd, letting their movements carry her forward. Almost as one they were shuffling up the central staircase, but their massive numbers forced them to spill out onto the landings and fill other communal areas. She could see the fire escape and wanted to bolt for it but knew she had to match the pace and intent of everyone else. The temptation to run was almost impossible to fight, if she only had an opening. Harder, almost, than stopping herself going back up to Dad.

She was almost there, level with the front of the lifts. In a moment of madness she looked for an alternative method of escape. Nonchalantly, she stretched out a hand and called the lifts, hoping that one of them might have stopped on this floor and that the sliding doors might open immediately and let her get away. Over the unnaturally quiet hum of the crowds and the shuffle of their feet, she thought she heard the reassuringly familiar sound of the elevator climbing towards floor fourteen, and she slowed her pace even more to try and stall her progress. One of the lifts was definitely close, she was sure of it, but the single-minded will of the crowd kept her moving.

As she drew level with the final lift, she heard the bell ring and the doors of the first one opened behind her. Jenny turned around to dive into the lift, and immediately wished that she hadn't because that single movement, that sudden change of direction, was enough to mark her out to the massed bodies as something different. As *someone* different. As *the one* they'd been looking for.

They came at her *en masse*, all directions converging. They had a new found collective purpose and speed. A confusion of grabbing hands came at her from all angles, and she fought to get through them. Several of them caught hold of her backpack and she wriggled free from the straps then dropped to the ground again and dragged herself along the grubby floor of the atrium on her belly. It was as if these people had lost the ability to think with any complexity or depth, because they struggled to see where she'd gone, as if their reactions had been dulled by drugs or booze. And then, when they did see her, they got in each other's way and blocked themselves. It might have been comical, Jenny thought, if it hadn't been so absolutely fucking terrifying.

She made it to the fire escape and used the exit bar to drag herself back up onto her feet. Then she pushed through and out onto the stairs, setting off deafening alarms in the process. Frightened, otherwise blissfully unaware, residents emerged from their apartments to evacuate, their numbers adding to the masses already filling the building. Though every scrap of space in the public area was now heavily congested, the fire escape was not. Jenny threw herself down the steps, aware of countless others racing down after her. She didn't dare look back to see how many were following, but then again, she didn't have to. Their numbers were such that the pressure forced several of them over the balcony. Bodies dropped around her, some hitting the steps, others falling through the gaps between, dropping all the way down to ground level. The noise as they hit the deck was nauseating. Wet slaps. Bloody pops as heads burst. Vicious cracks as bones snapped.

But no cries of pain.

Everything that had made these people human had been stripped away. They were shells now. Emotionless and cold. She knew they'd kill her if they caught her.

Jenny forced herself to keep running. Could this day become any more terrifying or bizarre? She'd already lost Dad and her home...did she have anything else left to lose? She knew that she did. Dad would have wanted her to keep running and fighting, to never give up. She wasn't sure if she could.

By the time she got to the bottom of the staircase there was a pile of fallen bodies as high as her waist. Most were dead or buried under others, but some continued to reach out, fighting to get at her through the chaos of twisted and broken limbs. There was just enough room to skirt around the edge and avoid them, and as she slid along the wall, expressionless eyes locked on to her. Outstretched fingertips brushed at her clothes, not quite far enough to grab hold.

She burst out onto the street, and the coolness of the air and the feel of misty rain on her face came as a blessed relief. She saw from the movement of the remaining crowds at the front of the building that they were still trying to get inside to get at her, but they were so preoccupied getting in that none of them noticed her getting out. She shut the fire escape door behind her and jogged away into the night.

16

The Moon

DAY THREE / 5: 15 PM

"Is it true?" Dean asked as Sandra caught up to him.

"Does it matter?"

"You're not even going to deny it?"

"I will if that makes you feel better."

"He killed himself, Sandra. A highly qualified doctor and surgeon killed himself because of you. Not to mention breaking the trust of our marriage!"

"The trust of our marriage? Oh, I think that's been gone for a good long time, don't you?"

"That was fifteen years ago, Sandra. I thought we'd moved past it."

"Maybe I had, right up until I realized that you were trying to get her onto this mission. You can thank me for making sure she dies in squalor on Earth."

"She's arguably the brightest and most forward-thinking person in astrophysics. She was necessary to make all of this successful!"

"You say potato, I say slut."

"I've got to go." He looked down at the hand holding on to his arm.

"We're going to the same place, and for all of our sakes, maybe we should present a unified front."

"There was a time I would have done anything for you."

"I don't recall my ever asking for you to do Catherine Anders."

"If we make it through this, I want a divorce," he told her right before they were to enter into the conference room where the other members awaited.

"Oh, I don't think so, Dean. I have more dirt on you than your reputation could possibly survive. And I won't even bring up where you like my thumb during sex."

He opened the door to four people who were doing their best to pretend they hadn't just heard the last words of the heated conversation.

"Hello, all," Dean said through pursed lips.

"What's this all about?" Janice Younger, the senior scientist and molecular biologist who took Catherine's place when Sandra sabotaged her application, asked.

"Our power supply is very much in danger of a catastrophic failure," Dean relayed to them, then gave a quick recap of everything that Maddie had told him.

"Can't we just shut it down and make repairs?" Janice asked.

"Quite possibly we could have, if Maddie hadn't stolen our only mower to make her escape," Sandra shot out.

Dean wanted to tell them if it hadn't been Maddie, it would have most assuredly been his wife, but he kept silent, fearful of what she could say to the committee.

"Where is she planning on going?" Shen Bonsoon, a field researcher and doctor in training, asked.

"We can track her, but right now, we have more important things to be concerned about. Once this crisis is averted, she'll be dealt with," Dean told the group.

"I'm going to vote for the death penalty." She looked at Dean. "What? She's risking all of our lives; it only makes sense."

Janice tried to steer the conversation back. "There are fail-safes within each satellite base, can't we shut it down from here?" she asked.

"Remote shut off was the first thing we tried as soon as Maddie called in with the report. Whatever is happening is not allowing us that alternative," Dean replied.

"And if we radio another base? Can't someone else shut it off at the source or possibly remotely? Maybe the problem is here." Bob Granger wanted to know. He was at the top of his field in horticulture.

"The person best able to do that has died, most likely from diabetic shock. There's a chance one of us could be walked through the procedure. As for the remote shutoff, this hub is the only place that was set up for that; the redundancy would have been appreciated, but we all know that many things were sacrificed in the name of weight," Dean told the group.

"Then, being walked through it is what we're going to have to do," Janice replied.

"Great. Looks like we have our volunteer," Sandra said.

"I wasn't implying…"

"What's a little radiation among

friends?" Sandra replied.

"How do you suggest I get there, Sandra? Fly over on your broom?" Janice asked. Bob coughed loudly as he choked on a swallow of water.

"You're…" Sandra started just as an alarm began to ring and the lighting in the conference room flashed.

The door burst open. A shock of red hair was the first any of them saw as Geoff, one of their computer engineers, rushed in. "You should come quick!" The entire group trailed the young man as he ran down the corridor to the control room. The alarm had not ceased, though the lighting had remained steady. "We've got spikes in power. Our nuke is looking like it's going to go super nova." Geoff was pointing to a line on a screen that was incrementally getting higher.

"Will shutting down our draw of power do anything?" Shen wanted to know.

"No, at this point, that's like pulling the plug out of the wall after the toaster is on fire," Geoff replied.

"So, what can we do?" Dean asked.

"I'm agnostic and I've started praying; that would be my suggestion for the rest of you," he replied.

"How much time do we have? Is it worth suiting up and running?" Janice was intently watching the screen.

"I don't think you'd get far enough, and none of the other satellite bases in the area are going to come to our aid, as they're busy evacuating those that they can." Geoff finally turned from the console. "I'm, um, going to go to my room, maybe play some video games, keep my mind off the inevitable." He stood and was heading for the door.

"That's your answer? Virtual reality isn't going to work in this instance," Sandra was nearly shaking.

"I code machines. Software is all I have ever known. If this was some disaster revolving around a crashing program, I could guarantee I could reduce it down to its smallest pieces of code, fix the problem, and have everything running smoothly in under an hour, and trust me, I tried that here. This isn't software; this is a hardware problem. The containment area has been compromised, and the cell itself is acting erratically, possibly due to the same set of circumstances. There is no way to shut it down, so I'm not seeing the point of staying here. Even if my life is now being measured, I would rather the end came as a surprise." With that, he left the room.

"Dean, stop him." Sandra was pointing to the door.

"For what?" He suddenly felt and looked weary.

"I'm going to be with my family," Shen spoke, her head down as she left.

The rest followed as Sandra continued to stare hard at the board, believing her will alone would be enough to force the energy source into compliance.

"Enough," Dean said. He placed his hands upon his wife's shoulders; she immediately shrugged them off. She gave him a look that froze his heart. He raised his hands in surrender, defeat in his eyes.

"I'm…" he got choked up. "I'm going to say goodbye to the kids."

Sandra did not reply. Instead, she moved over to a different area on the console. She typed in a few commands and waited. "Well, what do we have here?" she asked as she looked at a blinking icon. She ran quickly out and headed for the surface suit-up area.

17

The Channel

Stone ripped from the earth and arranged into walls, reached up to the skies, and headed off to the horizon in both directions until the length exceeded anyone's ability to see its end. A wall too large to climb, too massive to breach, too immense to truly understand.

"How did they build the walls that tall?" Thistle muttered as the crew of survivors shuffled up the carved, sloping road that led between the twin circular citadels, each wide enough to encompass the entirety of their home village of Mercy Point, docks and ocean included. "Do the tops touch the clouds?"

"They do," her father answered. "We can't see them yet, but deeper into the city beyond these citadels, the gods' towers grow even taller. Twice the height of the enchanted walls we see here. Streets large enough for a dozen wagons and sixty oxen to walk shoulder to shoulder." He paused to help the old man with the cane up a steeper portion of the gentle slope that led into the channel where the rounded walls of the two citadels dived close to one another. "At dawn, the clouds cling to the spire peaks like cotton balls."

The gap between the two massive god-made structures seemed small at the mile they were distant from it, but in truth, the space between the mile-tall fortifications was still hundreds of yards wide. Wide enough for several of the streets Gray mentioned.

"How?" Arridon asked, his eyes taking in the scene of unfathomable scope. "How did they build it?"

"Magic, for the greater part, so I understand," the dad explained. "But some of the gods' machines, too, I think. I saw one as big as castle. Those are gone now. Rusted away and never remade to build again. The city walls are impregnable, as the legends say. You cannot invade where you cannot pass."

"They're so smooth," Thistle said. "And no windows. I always imagined the citadels would have windows. People live in them, right?"

"In a fashion, yes," Gray answered as he shepherded his following up towards the commotion that resided in the channel between the two titanic towers. "Citadels are...like towns. Neighborhoods within the Endless City. Each is different on the inside, but these round walls simply serve to section off a portion of the city's footprint for one purpose or another."

"Noble kingdoms," the old bald man said, hoarse from the dry summer day. "Mercantile empires. Schools. Some citadels were built around mountains or lakes. They are closer to gardens, not castles."

"You've been to the city before?" Arridon asked the old man as he took his hand to help him up the slope to the level the city began on.

"Ranmyr, there," he said, pointing to the massive edifice to the left of the channel. "I was a squire in their alchemical laboratories before the war broke out."

"You were an alchemist? You knew the war was real?" Thistle asked him, shocked. "Why haven't I talked to you before, back in Mercy Point? You could've convinced me everything was true."

"Doubtful," Arridon shot back at her. "You'd have called him an old, clueless twat two days ago. You've changed since the blood washed in."

"What do you know?" she said to him.

"I know my sister," he replied, helping the old man.

She shot his back a middle finger then looked to the old man. "What's inside Ranmyr?"

"It used to be oh...perhaps ten buildings, maybe twelve. Most tall, like your father says. Twenty, maybe thirty stories. Five minutes to walk one side. A few shorter and wider. Those were the labs where the gods and the humans in their employ worked as they brewed potions and mixed substances for many purposes. Gardens grew crops of immense rarity in all directions and the inner walls of the citadel were covered with fruit-bearing ivy. Myriad were their minds, the gods. Always wondering what to improve on, what to grow or what illness to try to cure next. Curious people, the gods. Always curious."

"Ranmyr sounds like paradise," Thistle

said.

"It once was," the old man mused. "Now…with the gods gone, and the citadel left to the uneducated hands of us poor, simple folk…who can say what lies within Ranmyr's walls?"

"There are many, many people heading into the channel," Gray said. "Look," he gestured to the east, in the direction of the Eastern Sea, then to the west, along the plateau's edge where the city wall faded into the sunset. He pointed over his shoulder as well. In each direction there were strings of travelers, all walking, or riding oxen towards the city's entrance. Hundreds, if not thousands of moving people dotted the landscape.

"City's a busy place," Arridon offered.

"No. Not like this. Look at them," the father said, and they did. They walked for several minutes in silence, staring at the approaching groups as they all converged in the gap between city-towers. Uneasy became their way as their gait slowed, fearful to get closer, fearful to stay away.

"I don't see anything," the son said.

"Their wagons are empty," Thistle said. "Is that what you mean, Dad?"

Dad. The simple word and title sounded strange to both brother and sister when said without the normal frustration that usually accompanied it. Arridon was right. Change *had* come with the bloody tide.

"Not just that. They carry weapons or tools as such, and too few carry bags on their backs. These are not common travelers, and certainly not traders."

"For a guy who spent the last ten years or so on the couch, drunk as a pickle is pickled, you sure are sharp," Arridon said.

"Your mother didn't marry me on account of my looks, kid," Gray answered his son after rubbing his temples. "You both look like her, thank the sea. But oh, we were a pair."

"I bet," Arridon said, and meant it.

"Watch yourselves," Gray cautioned. "They're running from something, and on a day such as the one we've had, I'd wager they're running from the same thing we are."

"What should we do?" Thistle asked him, hefting her pitchfork in nervous hands.

"Watch out for blood. If you see blood on anyone—fresh blood, for any reason—you holler out, and you run like riptides are pulling you out to sea, you savvy?"

"Savvy," brother and sister answered.

"Old man," Gray said, addressing the fellow with the cane. "Were you around in Ranmyr when the demons hit the city's western edge?"

"I was not. I had retired from the city life, but I had friends who remained behind. We exchanged letters about it for a few years. They spoke of the horror of it all. Thankfully, the minions of the Bleed never reached this far east. Perhaps they were of weaker stock."

"No, we are weaker than the gods were. So you know, no blood can touch your flesh, or you'll suffer the change. Do you hear that everyone? No blood can touch you."

"Hardly matters to a man my age, but yes. If they blood hits me, I will see to it I am put down with haste."

No one answered him. They kept walking up the hill towards the city that ate the horizon and swallowed the clouds above. As they walked, Gray rubbed his temples again and kept his eyes shut against the darkening light of the day.

"You wanted markets full of vegetables and fruit, right?" Arridon said to Thistle. "Here's your market," he said as he poked the handle of his axe into an empty wooden basket on a long wooden table beneath a cheap fabric canopy that should've been filled with brimming baskets. "I don't hear any musicians or see any artists. I'm sorry."

"No fruit or vegetables either," Thistle replied as she stepped out of the way of a trio of running girls. Their wild black hair suggested they were sisters.

On all sides, the throngs jockeyed to move deeper into the city or closer to the few tents in the channel still selling something of value. Each face wore a grimace of worry, and each person moved with the frail control that held violence only a bit at bay. Hands snapped at goods while other hands snapped at wallets or coin purses. Voices called out in every direction—spoken in accents the brother and sister had never heard—and those voices sounded the alternating pitches of the clarion bells of fear.

Goods purchased at a gouged price, or stolen, the shoppers disappeared into the crowds and headed deeper into the channel, and deeper into the Endless City. They sought refuge from the burgeoning chaos.

"None were stained by the blood of others," Gray said, his eyes searching for the mark of doom. As he searched those around him, he held his hand down at the waist of his trousers where the Colt pistol was tucked out of view. He could draw it and fire the monstrous weapon at a moment's notice.

"Not yet at least," Arridon said as his company slowed in the crowd. Ahead, a fight had broken out between two small groups. The taller Arridon watched as they struggled over a handful of belts and a leather bag. The argument turned into shoving, and fast punches were thrown. They were stalled out until the fight found an ending.

As they watched, Arridon couldn't but notice his father's clothing. Hot sweat stained the simple sand-colored tunic Gray wore in dark rings around his neck and armpits. He'd put out two or three times the water over their journey anyone else had, and now that they were at the channel, with its walls soaring straight up above and dropping them at the bottom of a chasm, Gray had fallen into the habit of rubbing at his head near constantly.

"Are you okay?" Arridon asked his father as they waited for blood to be spilled in the scuffle.

"Fierce ache in my skull. Tongue's dry as autumn wheat…and I feel ill. Look at my hand," he said, holding up his fingers. The whole of it trembled as they stood in the center of the crowd.

"Something you ate?" Thistle asked

him.

"Something I didn't drink," he answered, then sighed. "I'd kill for a drink right now. This has happened a hundred times. Each time I've tried to walk away from the drink. I fight the tremors. I fight the vomiting. I do my best, but in the dark of the night with the despair strongest in the silence...I pull the cork, and pour salve on the wound. My weakness. My sickness."

"This is what happens when you drink too much and quit?" Arridon asked.

"Aye," he said and closed his eyes against the pain behind them. "At least, it's what happens to me. This time, I must forge forward, without the salve. None to be had, and if there ever was a day to suffer for good reason, it's today."

"Well if it gets worse, you say something," Thistle said to him. "We'll find you a medicine of some sort. Somewhere."

"You've taken far too good a care of me," Gray said, eyes getting acquainted with his feet for a moment. "I'll be fine. Just need water. Should be some freshwater fountains ahead once we get past the channel here and inside the city proper. I'll drink my fill, and be better for it."

Arridon looked from his struggling father to the crowd pressing in on all sides. His skin crawled with itch as a mother and father—not much older than he—pressed into one shoulder. At their feet stood a little boy and girl, dirty and blonde like their mother. Their awkward agitation as they tried to console their confused children made Arridon uncomfortable in a different way.

"When do we start shoving through?" he asked.

"The brawl is over," Gray said. "I see no bloodied noses. The gawkers are moving. We'll be on the march in a moment."

Arridon looked over to the young family as the father peered out over the crowd, just as he had. The mother pulled her children into her dress, pressing their heads against her thighs to shield them from the commotion and anarchy threatening to roar up and out of control.

"Too many people, too few supplies," he muttered. "Why are you here?" he asked the mother.

"We're fleeing. Our village on the wall to the east was…destroyed," she said, loud enough for just those nearby to hear. "Monsters," she hissed. "These walls are the only thing that can keep us safe."

"Stop," the father said to her. "It's not wise to tell others what we're thinking. What if they're bandits? You don't know him. He could be a murderer."

She glared back at him, but said no more to Arridon.

"I'm sorry. We're trying to get into the city for the same reason. I was...curious, sympathetic. Forgive me," Arridon said to the man and woman.

"Mind your business, kindly," the man replied. "Until this passes, trust isn't something I'll give freely to strangers. I'm certain you'll find others acting the same."

"This won't be passing," Arridon said. "This is no storm. The Bleed is here. You should run as fast as you can. Run as far as you can, and hide until the gods can figure it out. They can save us."

"With eyes like yours, you'd say something like that," the man shot back. "If this is the Bleed, as you say, then the gods have failed us, and I've no faith in their children, either. Come, let's go," he said, and took his wife's hand. They pushed off through the throngs starting to move forward.

Something on the mother's face caught Arridon's eye. He dipped his head and swung it a bit to the side to get a better angle as she walked away, but when she looked over her shoulder at him, he saw a red rivulet of blood just below a nostril.

"She's bleeding," he called out.

"Who?" his father barked, grabbing his

arm and brandishing the pistol.

Arridon pointed at the woman and lifted the axe as a ward against danger. The crowd directly near them pulled away as if they'd all gotten vomit at their feet.

"God-weapon!" someone called out, pointing at Gray's pistol.

Gray muscled Arridon aside to see the now petrified woman. She shot a hand up to her face to feel for what Arridon spoke of. She looked at the blood on her finger and tried to cover the bloody nose, but it had been seen.

She twitched.

"RUN!" Gray screamed.

18

The Moon

DAY THREE / 6:16 PM

"Shit." Maddie lightly punched the steering wheel. She'd driven a mile away from the station and stopped. She'd been honest with Derrick when she told him it would be easier to survive with extra hands, but she'd also come to like the two little brats and leaving them to fry like microwave popcorn was not sitting well with her. She was stuck. She couldn't force them to come with her, and if she went back now, there was a good chance the mower would be overrun like a lifeboat from the ill-fated Titanic.

"Wasting time, woman! You need to make a choice and make it now." Still, she sat for another five minutes. "Now. Now is the fucking time I develop a conscience," she said as she spun the mower around. "What are the odds I don't regret this? Zilch, but at least it won't be something that keeps me up tonight." She laughed at her grim joke. "Can't imagine we have more than a half-hour." She had heard the alarm being broadcast and the warning that went with it. Her mower had the ability to tap into the network and look at the same dire readouts, but she didn't see a reason to bother. She'd made up her mind; she needed all the time she could to grab the little ingrates and get reasonably far enough away from the oncoming blast, otherwise none of it mattered.

"Last chance," she bemoaned as the outer doors rolled up. The exterior door had just closed and the inner was beginning to go when she saw the barrel of a large caliber weapon pointed directly at her head.

"Good to see you again!" Sandra

shouted through the helmet. "Now get the fuck out." She pulled the door open and stepped back quickly. "I know you're thinking about it," Sandra said as she watched Maddie's eyes look down at the door controls. "How many bullets do you think I can put in you while you wait for the door to open? This gun holds eight and I'm what, five feet away? Even if I was untrained and shot wildly there's no reason to think I couldn't get four in you. But seeing as I learned how to shoot when I was seven and have been continually training for most of my life, I think it's safe to say I'd only need one well-placed. Now I'd rather not have to clean your blood and guts out from inside there but I will. Just come out here and fry like the rest. Leave it running; don't want to have that little problem again, do we? That's a good girl," she said, backing up further as Maddie emerged. "Don't do anything that's in line with your character flaws. I can and will gladly shoot you. Won't be anybody to lock me up for the crime."

Maddie walked over to her workbench. Suddenly she felt incredibly tired as she sat down.

"Just out of curiosity," Sandra asked as she stepped in. "Why'd you come back?"

"Your kids, remember them?"

"Survivor's guilt eating you up? Don't look surprised, I gained access to everyone's files. A lot of tragedy in your past; at least your suffering will be over now."

"Ah, look at you doing me a solid." Maddie flipped Sandra off.

"That's the spirit, last act of defiance and all."

"You're not even going to try and get your kids?"

"I'd like to, but you can hear the alarm as well as I can. There's no time, and if left to go looking, you would obviously have to die."

"Obviously."

"But who's to say someone else doesn't get a notion to take the mower, and where's that leave me? This has been a great little talk, very helpful. Ta-ta, Maddie. We'll do lunch some time, or not." Sandra prepared to close the door to the vehicle.

"Mom?" rang out from the far side of the garage.

"Shit, how much did she hear?" Sandra asked, not expecting a response. She slid her faceplate up.

"Enough that Mother's Day is going to be awkward," Maddie responded.

Sam had Tyler and Juan with her.

"Where's your brother?" Maddie asked.

"He's looking for Dad," Sam told her. "Mom, what are you doing?"

"I was getting ready to get my babies and get out of here." Sandra fluidly slid smilingly into the persona of a loving mother.

"As if," Maddie snorted.

"Don't you dare." Sandra exited and was holding the pistol on the other woman. "Come on, we have to go." Sandra was waving her daughter on. Tyler and Juan were in tow. "Not you two, just my daughter." She turned the pistol, all three stopped their advance.

"They're coming with us, Mom."

"The mower holds four. After your brother and father; there's no more room. Five is too crowded and no way with six."

"What about Maddie?" Sam asked.

"What about her? You realize she left without you, right?"

"Huh?" Sam asked.

"Going to be tough to convince her of that, considering I'm sitting right here." Maddie somehow found the ability to laugh through it all.

"I chased her down, baby. I got her back here for you, for us. For the family."

"You've got the looks. I'll give you that, but you don't have the chops for it," Maddie said.

"What are you talking about!?" Sandra shrieked.

"The acting. It's not believable. It rings hollow to the ear."

Sam cried out when Sandra fired a shot, blowing a hole in a canister of penetrating oil, sending it spinning wildly away.

"Let's go, Sam!"

"Not without my friends or family or Maddie."

"You stupid girl. I thought I taught you better than that. Now get in this mower or I'll shoot you in the leg and drag you in."

"I think your mom has lost her mind," Juan said. "We should get out of here."

"And go where? This place is about to blow up," Sam told him. "Look, Mom, we'll all just cram in there, just until we get to another satellite station. It'll only be a couple of hours at the most."

Derrick came barreling in, slamming into the side of Tyler as he came to a stop. "Dad says he isn't coming. He's going to do everything he can to save this place."

"Fool," Sandra said. "Let's go."

"You're not going to try and get him?" Sam asked.

"He made his choice, and besides, there's no time. What is with you? Let's go!"

Sam moved closer again; Tyler and Juan

did as well.

"How are any of you failing to realize I have a gun? Sam, ditch the baggage or I'll get rid of it for you."

"They're our friends." Derrick stepped in between the group and his mother using himself as a shield. "You're right, Dad made his choice, but him not coming opens up space. Dad said we have maybe fifteen minutes to get as far from this place as possible. We have to go. All of us. Or none of us."

"What does that mean?" Sandra asked suspiciously.

"It means, Sandra, my dear, that as soon as you shut the inner door, he's going to manually override your ability to open the outer door. Am I right, kid?" Maddie asked.

"I'll…" Sandra was at a loss for words.

"What are you going to do? Shoot us all?" Maddie immediately regretted saying that. She didn't think the other woman would resort to that extreme, but why put an idea, no matter how abhorrent, into the mind of someone that clearly did not think along the lines of social norms?

"Clock's ticking, Mom. Hurry up and choose, because if we're not leaving, I'd rather spend the end with Dad," Derrick told her. That seemed to be the only thing that cut through the jumble of emotions.

"In, let's go, everyone in!" She was waving her gun around. Nobody moved; it's difficult to trust someone that has been pointing a firearm at you.

"I'll drive." Maddie got up and walked over.

"Sandra — put the damned gun down," Dean spoke through the intercom system, he'd been watching the whole thing transpire over the network. "The readouts have pushed into the yellow; I don't think I need to tell you what's going to happen when they get to red. Pretend you're a mother for five minutes and get your kids to safety!"

"Bye, daddy!" Sam was crying as she got in.

"Maddie, I can't get Satellite Station Etna to pick up, but that's your best bet. They're far enough away that the initial blast won't be a problem, and the radiation should be low by the time it travels there."

"Not Terrapin?" she asked as she strapped in.

"The computer models show that the way they are connected to the energy source could be problematic."

Maddie knew enough that "problematic" could potentially mean catastrophic. Everything in space was magnified.

"Oh, I don't think so," Sandra said as Sam climbed atop Tyler's lap. "Get up front," she told her daughter. Sandra ended up on Derrick, Juan on Tyler.

"Yeah, this is perfect," Tyler said sarcastically.

"Because it's so much better for me," Derrick told him.

"Everyone in? Godspeed, Dean," Maddie said, and in less than a minute, they were racing along the lunar surface. She knew the terrain better than anyone, but even she was not happy with how fast she was pushing the vehicle.

"How are you going so fast?" Sam asked.

"I removed the governor…had a hunch that speed was going to be needed."

Sandra looked over Maddie's shoulder. "A hundred and ten? Is that safe?"

"Safer than being vaporized."

The mower used gyroscopic devices in the wheels and powerful electro-magnets to deal with the lack of gravity, making every bump they hit feel like they were inside a paint shaker.

"How can you even see?" Sam asked, her vision bouncing wildly.

"Can't." Maddie had both hands on the wheel. She was more holding on for dear life than steering; if a moon moose stepped into her path, there would be little she could do to avoid it. This was the first and only time she was thankful there was no wildlife on the moon.

"You're not far enough away," Dean said over the radio.

"I can't go any faster," Maddie told him.

"The cell is going critical quicker than we expected." He left the rest unsaid; wasn't like it needed to be spelled out.

"You can't seriously be thinking about going faster, can you?" Sandra asked.

"Sure am. If we have an accident, maybe you'll break your neck." Maddie couldn't focus well enough to see the readout, but she felt like she was pushing close to a hundred and twenty.

"Maddie, we're in the red. Kids, I love you both with all my heart." Dean hitched, the strain in his voice clearly audible even over the jumbling of supplies inside the mower.

"We love you too, Dad." Sam was crying. "Daddy?" The other end had become laced with static.

"Maddie, faster!" Derrick had turned around. The horizon behind them was now illuminated in angry reds and violets.

"I don't think I can." Her arms shook as she death-gripped the steering wheel. "I wouldn't go this fast on the highway, and this is far from a highway."

"Look in your mirror." He turned back to the nightmare rapidly approaching.

Maddie spared the briefest of glances; she wasn't even entirely sure of what she was looking at, only that her mirror appeared to be illuminated. Her heart leapt in her chest as she pushed the pedal to the floor. "Not going to be enough." She was now dividing her time between the ground ahead and the impending explosion behind.

"You're going to kill us!" Sandra yelled.

"That's helping," Maddie hissed.

"I think Juan's dead!" Tyler cried out. "Oh, fuck, oh fuck…."

Maddie couldn't spare even the slightest glance over, and anyway, there wasn't a thing she could do about it. Not now, maybe not ever.

"He hit his head on the roof! Someone has to help!" Tyler was desperate. He started sobbing as he held his friend.

The bright line on the horizon had become a full-fledged firestorm, taking up nearly the entirety of the mirror.

"We can't outrun it," Maddie said. "I can guarantee none of you are going to like this." She began to slow down.

"You can't give up," Sam begged.

"Not giving up, trying a new tactic," she

replied. When she got the mower down to an acceptable speed, she started quickly pressing buttons on the onboard computer, migrating deep into the operating system. She hoped she'd be able to do what needed to be done before the onslaught caught up.

"Don't like this, Maddie...." Derrick could not keep his eyes off of the impending disaster.

Once she was satisfied she'd done all she could, Maddie began to speed up.

"Something doesn't feel right," Sam said as they sailed over some rough terrain.

"Oh god—you shut off the magnets," Sandra said. "You can't do that, you idiot! We'll go flying off into space!"

"That's the idea. Have the blast launch us instead of taking us over and burning up in a radioactive firestorm."

"You're insane!"

"What about Juan?" Tyler was attempting to shake his friend awake.

Maddie had the machine back up to a hundred. She didn't need the mirror any more to tell how close the blast was, as her entire field of vision was so bright she had to squint.

"You can't do this!" Sandra was reaching up to pull Maddie away from the controls. Derrick wrapped his arms around his mother and held her tight. In this moment, and possibly every future moment, he trusted Maddie more than his mother. "Derrick, you can't be this stupid!"

"Might be the smartest thing I've ever done." He wrestled her tighter to him as she tried to squirm free.

"Do you know who I am?"

Maddie couldn't help herself; she had to look at the bug-eyed woman behind her who was clearly on the verge of mentally collapsing.

The mower—which had already been shaking uncontrollably—began to be buffeted by three hundred-plus miles per hour winds. The vehicle had lifted off from the ground. Maddie was fearful her idea was going to get them killed quicker; instead of shooting straight ahead, they were being tossed intensely back and forth like a tennis ball during a rigorous game. Her head smacked against the side window hard enough she saw stars. The mower shuffled back and forth, sometimes twenty feet in one direction before being pushed the other way. She knew it was only a matter of time until pieces of the vehicle were stripped free, exposing them to the deadly outer elements. And the only one who had any protection was Sandra, though where her helmet was, was anyone's guess.

Looked good on paper, she thought sourly. Her neck ached from the whiplash, her teeth hurt from them being clenched so tightly, and she was certain that, when her body was found years later by archaeologists, her hands would be melded with the steering wheel. They were now encased entirely within the blast. Burning rocks and tumbling boulders flew everywhere, some striking the rear of the mower; the heavy-duty safety glass had starred in more than one place. Soon, metal-melting heat would rush through the opening, ending all their troubles instantly as they became liquefied. The noise had become so all-encompassing it had become silence; it was a strange phenomenon. The human mind, its inability to process one further ounce of stimuli, reduces all sound to one solid wall of white noise. Maddie felt her heart and stomach lurch as the mower did what she thought it might. They were ten feet off the surface and gaining altitude at an alarming rate.

Alarms began to ring as the collisions of rocks lessened. She thought they might be out of the worst of it until a boulder, nearly the size of the mower itself, bashed into the rear end with enough upward force that the car spun in space, ass over top.

"Maddie, make it stop!" Sam begged.

She'd been about to do just that by turning the gyroscopes back on, but the last hit had killed the power. With the life support systems off-line as well, it was quickly getting cold inside. Maddie could see her breath as she did what she could to restart the machine. Tyler vomited, adding his stomach bile to the churning mass of material within the vehicle.

"We'll be breaking through the moon's gravitational field soon," Sandra said.

"I don't need a play-by-play, Sandra; I need a way to turn this bucket back on so I can get us stabilized and back down."

"Then do something!" Sandra ordered.

Maddie began working on the two thumbscrews located beneath the steering wheel. She pulled a small panel away and tried to put her hand in but couldn't get much more than three fingers in.

"Sam, I need you over here."

The girl unbuckled and picked her way over, doing her best to avoid her boyfriend's stomach butter. "Ew, so gross!" she said as a thick, viscous chunk smeared across the side of her face and up over her head.

"Come on, girl, you can worry about getting cleaned up later," Maddie told her. She grabbed her helper by the arm and forcibly pulled her close. "I need you to put your hand in there." Maddie held Sandra in tight to keep her from spinning away.

"I can fit four fingers; what am I trying to do?"

Maddie couldn't see past the girl to tell what she was doing.

"I'm thinking…okay, there are three small circuit boards. You need to pull one of them out."

"I…I can…yup. There's one." She shifted. "Okay, I feel another…I can sort of touch a third, but I can't go any further."

"You need to pull one of the two."

"What? Do you even know what you're doing?"

"No, Sandra, I don't. At no point have I ever had to remove the electronic safety lock-out board because of a nuclear disaster. Either an EMP took out the circuitry or the rock shorted the board. The only way I have the remotest chance of getting us power is to bypass the safety. My best guess is we have less than five minutes before we've left the moon's atmosphere for good, so I'd appreciate it if you'd shut the fuck up."

"Which one do I pull?"

"Fifty-fifty chance."

"What about the one she can't reach?" Derrick asked.

"Can't factor in what we don't have control of," Maddie replied. "Pull one, Sam."

"What if I pull the wrong one?"

"Can't get worse than it already is."

"I hate this."

"Do it," Derrick told her. "I trust you to make the right choice."

"Were you on the right or left inside, Mom?"

"Huh? Do you mean looking straight on, or from her perspective?"

"Left it is," she said without waiting for a response. "Got it." Sam was in an awkward position, looking up at the roof, her tongue firmly gripped between her teeth as she pushed in as far as she could. Somehow through the din, they heard the crack of plastic as it was not only pulled from the board, but broken. She triumphantly pulled the piece out of the opening.

"You can celebrate later." Maddie pushed her back into her seat.

"Rude." Sam grabbed hold of her belt to keep from becoming just another drop of floating debris in the sea of it.

"Was she right?" Derrick questioned.

"Don't know, might never know. Not even sure this is going to work."

"Then why'd you bother?" Sandra cried

out.

"Well, I guess I could have flailed my arms about wildly and hoped that worked." Maddie grabbed the compact multi-tool she carried with her everywhere from its holster on her belt and pried part of the dashboard off. "Shit," was her only response as she looked upon a jumble of circuits.

"Do something! You're a mechanic!"

Maddie wanted to tell her to shove off. Yeah, she was a mechanic, but this was a workaround she'd never done before. Also, it didn't help that they were spinning wildly out of control, mere moments away from being lost to the vacuum of space while simultaneously riding a wave of nuclear radioactivity and debris. She saw the two chips she needed to bridge from, neither bigger than a dime, and each had over twenty pins. She had a vague idea about which pins she needed to short together, but also knew if she hit the wrong ones she would fry the electronics entirely, and she'd never get the machine powered up.

"What are you waiting for?"

"You in a rush to get back down there?" Maddie hadn't looked, but it was impossible to miss the glow each time they flipped toward the surface. The moon was on fire. She wondered if the people on earth could see it, then she figured that those still alive didn't have enough frivolous time to look to the sky.

"I don't think I'd mind." Derrick couldn't help but notice that with every revolution, they were getting further and further away from their home.

Tyler had got his stomach under control and was holding the limp, unresponsive body of his friend as he cried into the other's back. There was a flash of light in the cabin; Maddie swore as a shock zapped her fingers and traveled up her forearm. Her fingers had constricted to the point where she thought they might snap, and once she was able to pull free, they popped open and she lost her grip. The multi-tool immediately got lost in the rest of the debris.

"According to what you said, we only have a minute left." Derrick spoke through gritted teeth; he was trying not to let the panic welling up in him spillover.

Maddie had used the number as an approximation; she had no way of knowing for sure. They could already be well past that threshold, and what she was doing now was nothing more than applying some window dressing while the world around her fell. Sam deftly snagged the pliers out of the air and thrust them back to Maddie, who was reluctant to jolt herself again. A crack in the window next to Derrick's head elongated, traveling nearly the length of the window. He was certain anything more than a feather tapping the glass would cause it to shatter.

Maddie lined up her pliers as best she could. She wanted to pray but wasn't sure who was the patron saint of wayward space travelers. She chipped a tooth as her mouth clenched tightly shut from the current that ran through her body. The lights flickered, went out, flickered again; acrid smoke began to pour forth from the opening. Something was frying; there just wasn't anything she could do about it.

"It's not coming on!" Sandra yelled.

"That's not helping, Mom," Derrick told her.

Maddie was finally able to let go of the pliers. They stayed in place, as they had now been fused to the board.

"Now what?" Sam asked; they were both looking at the grip to the pliers.

"I'm out of ideas," Maddie said.

"Some mechanic you are! How could you be the best Earth had to offer? Can't tell you how glad I am that they brought you up here." Sandra pulled free from Derrick's arms. She moved over the back of Maddie's seat; the other woman put her arms up to deflect the blows she figured the other was about to rain down on her. Instead, Sandra lunged for the dashboard, which she beat repeatedly. The lights flickered as her anger and frustration began to peter out.

"Keep doing that!" Maddie urged, moving out of the way as best she could.

Sandra slammed her hand again, this time catching the edge of the panel, and slicing neatly through her glove and the side of her hand. She winced in pain but continued. Fat globules of blood formed into perfect spheres and hung suspended in mid-air.

"Fucking..." *smack* "start..." *smack*. "You." *Smack*. "Piece." *Smack* "Of shit!" She hit it hard two more times. One more flicker, then nothing.

"Back up, Mom. I saw something," Sam said. "This is going to suck, I think, I sure wish you were up here," Sam said as she reached for the pliers. "OWWWW!" she yelled as the lights came on.

"I'll be a..."

"Just get us going! This hurts and my arm is going numb."

Maddie went through the controls and the thirty-second warm-up process before engaging the engine. "Holy shit...it worked."

"I don't think I like that you're this surprised," Derrick told her.

"How would you feel if you correctly solved a calculus problem, blindfolded? That's this," Maddie told him.

The vehicle began to shudder as Maddie fired up the gyroscopes and the mower sought equilibrium. The spin slowed and finally righted itself. Juan's head fell against the window and he let out a low groan.

"What's...going on?" He hadn't opened his eyes.

"Oh man, oh man...I thought you were dead!" Tyler was ecstatic.

Maddie didn't have the heart to tell him that they were far from out of the woods. They were still very much in the forest being chased by a pack of starving, rabid wolves that would not be content until they had devoured them completely.

The explosion behind them had begun to fade, but they were still being hurdled through space.

"Umm...Maddie? Aren't we too high for the magnets to be effective?" Derrick glanced out his window at the rapidly retreating surface.

"There will still be *some* pull...I think." She engaged the magnet drive. While it was true that there would be some pull, she feared it would be too little to stop their escape velocity.

"How long?" Sam asked. Maddie didn't respond. The time for a B.S. answer was past, and she hadn't a clue.

"Oh, come on." Maddie was looking at the battery readout, which was heading into the red.

"How long is the cable on the winch?" Derrick asked.

"A thousand feet, give or take," Maddie answered from rote, though she had no idea where the question was leading.

"And the towers, how tall are they?" he asked.

"A couple hundred feet," Sam replied.

"Are you insane? What do you think the odds are of a trailing hook catching a tower?" Sandra asked.

"Better than the current odds we have," Maddie told her as she let out the cable.

"This is insane! It won't work!" Sandra was getting hysterical.

"Neither is your shouting, Mom," Derrick told her calmly. "I would rather die trying."

"Not to be a sourpuss," Sam stated. "But if…"

"When," Maddie corrected.

"When we hook on, what happens then? Won't we be pulled into the ground?"

"That's if the front end stays on,"

Maddie told her.

"Thanks for that. I didn't even think that might be a problem. Shit," Derrick muttered.

"We've got to be traveling over a hundred miles per hour. The force alone when we stop will break our necks!"

"Sandra, you really need to shut up now," Maddie told her. She was watching as she let out the cable. There was a solid *thunk* as it came to the end of the spool. It didn't look to her like it was low enough; she could only hope the magnets and the gyroscopes brought them close enough to the surface for their last-ditch effort to work. The interior was preternaturally quiet as each passenger was lost in his or her own thoughts; it was a waiting game, and nothing they could say or do now was going to make even the slightest difference. The powerful magnets were doing their job admirably, but Maddie could not shake the feeling it wouldn't be enough.

"There are some towers coming up." Sam pointed to a line some miles ahead.

"We're too far over." Derrick was straining to look past his mother. "Spin the left wheels."

"We're in the air; what is spinning the wheels going to do?" Tyler was panicked.

"I'm hoping inertia pulls us in that

direction."

Maddie sent power to the appropriate wheels; there was an electric whir, but if they were moving in the correct direction, it was not anything that was happening with speed. It was frustrating as everyone subconsciously leaned to the left, but it was as if the mower didn't understand the sense of urgency.

"Everyone get a helmet on," Maddie told them. "Now!"

"Oh, gross—mine has puke all over it," Tyler whined.

"At least it's yours." Derrick wiped the side of his on the seat.

"Don't worry about that, get them on!" Maddie urged.

"There are only four helmets." Sam looked around, the only one without was her mother.

"Tyler, Juan, how long can you hold your breath?" Maddie asked.

"I don't know...thirty seconds? Never really timed it," Tyler responded.

"My head hurts...seeing double," was Juan's response.

"Tyler, give your helmet to Sandra. You don't have a suit on, won't matter."

Sandra had no sooner clicked her helmet into place when Maddie overrode the door locks on the left side before opening them remotely. Brutally frigid, freezing cold filled in the vacuum created by the escaping oxygen. Tyler began to hyperventilate as fear coursed through him.

19

Walking Through Walls

Thistle turned away from the direction the bleeding woman stood and took off as fast as she could. She got three steps into her escape before slamming into the back of a large man. He spilled forward into a pair of men and all three turned and hollered at her in anger. Blades slid free from sheaths at belts and within the blink of an eye,

Thistle was staring down three men threatening her with violence.

"Fuck off! Out of our way or run," her father screamed at them. In her peripheral vision she saw the shiny metal barrel of her mother's pistol appear near her shoulder. He pointed it at them.

"Run, be gone! She's bleeding," Thistle said to them. "She could turn into a demon and we'd be done for. Come on, move!"

"I'll not suffer a girl ordering me about," the largest of the knife-wielding men said. His voice stank of cheap alcohol. Reminded her of her father…or her father as he used to be. "Shut yer mouth and head that way, or I'll cut ya open, and we'll find the demon inside you."

The sound of her mother's pistol clicking into the dangerous state scared only her, and perhaps her brother. Maybe it was the deafening din of the crowd moving forward, or moving away from yet another confrontation, but the weapon wasn't being respected the way it should've been.

"How many times can the weapon be used?" she asked her father, fast and hushed.

"Twenty more times."

"Don't waste any of those times on these thugs. Push in the opposite direction," she said.

"The woman is starting to twitch faster," her brother said. "She'll shift and then we're bent. One spray of blood and a hundred demons will surround us. We have to *move*."

"Follow me," a firm voice suggested.

When the family turned they laid eyes on a man of unclear age and medium height with a shaved head and clean chin, wearing a long white duster that near-sparkled in the dimming light of the day. He had wide, bright eyes that looked as if they were made of polished steel, and he seemed happy to be in their presence.

"Who are you?"

"A man whose father was a god, and one who can get you to the other side of that wall," he said, looking at the towering, smooth stone side of the Citadel of Temples, "where the demon that woman is about to become cannot follow. Now, what is your answer? Speak now, or I'll leave you where you stand to fare as you will. No sense in sharing a fool's fate."

"Take us," Thistle answered without hesitation.

The man grinned and snatched the hand Thistle wasn't holding a pitchfork in. He made a direct line at the men with the knives, and, unlike how they'd reacted to Thistle alone, they scrambled to get out of his way. Their knives disappeared into sheathes, and they held their hands up in supplication as someone cried out in pain behind them.

The crowd erupted in fear, and as the screams spread in every direction, so too did the scattered people, all trying to get away from whomever was meeting misery.

"Run," the stranger said, and he took off, dragging Thistle through the now parting crowd as they pushed away from the area they stood in.

He dodged them left and right, sprinting as they passed through clusters of fleeing people, and around market stalls with the gall to have been built in their way, long before their time of need. He had a path in mind and moved with purpose towards the wall that reached so high up they couldn't see the top of it. He darted left then right, all the while holding her hand with a grip nearly too tight. Then, just as the screams of pain and suffering, behind the stalls he ran them past, grew to a crescendo of nightmare-inducing proportions, there they were, standing mere feet from the blocks that formed the cells of the wall.

She hadn't seen them from a distance, but inscriptions and markings covered each perfectly matched stone. Bordering them like a frame, and filling the center space with an unreadable message, the symbols were entrancing, seeming to speak magic aloud without having a voice to do so.

"Follow me," the man said to her with a smile.

He let go of her hand and bent his fingers on both hands into a specific organization of position. Some fingers were up, some bent, some down, but the left hand matched the right. He swung his arms in circles, up and around, smaller then larger, all the while using his voice to speak in a language that no one in the gathered family could understand. His words resonated and vibrated, and as he etched time and space with his movements and presence, in front of him, a portion of the wall the size of a ox's stall grew translucent, then clear and pristine like fine glass, and then finally it disappeared, leaving a dark tunnel thirty feet deep which opened up into a lush, green garden that spilled out of view, miles away.

"Please, we must hurry and take shelter inside the Citadel of Temples. We can gather at my place of worship."

"Go," Gray ordered then looked over his shoulder at the mob of screaming people at the center of the channel. Cries of pain were hundredfold.

"We don't know who he is. What if he's a crook? He might take a life over nothing," Arridon said.

"If he's a murderer, he's one of a thousand in this valley between the towers, and I'll take my chances with this one on the other side of the wall versus the thousand on this side. Now go."

"Magical door away from danger? Yes please," Thistle said, and stepped into the passage through the stone.

The moment the barrier of the wall was passed, she felt a burst of energy course through her body, head to toe. The sensation left a coarse, tingling shudder inside her skull and opened a door into memories she'd long since suppressed. The scent of her mother's hair, the feeling of a skinned knee after a spill during yet another fight, and the view over the bluff just outside of Mercy Point during the heart of a cold winter snowstorm.

But perhaps oddest of all, she recalled her mother speaking to her in the gods' tongue, and she could remember what the strange words meant. All this came to her as she stood in the grass of an open field inside the enormous ring wall of the citadel they'd just entered.

"Are you okay?" her brother asked.
"Yeah, why?"

"You've been standing there for like…a whole minute, just staring forward and not responding. Little worrisome."

"I…don't remember passing through the tunnel…"

"Common experience for first time transit," the stranger said. "Don't worry."

"Transit?" Arridon asked him.

"I'll explain later," he said with a smile.

"If there is a later," Gray said. "I'm Gray, their father. We're thankful for your help. Might we have your name?" he asked the stranger who'd helped them.

"Ah, of course. I am Disciple Burke, servant of The Many. I am thrilled to have met you on such an auspicious day," he said, and added a deep bow as a flourish.

"Why help us?" Arridon asked.

"Helping others is a duty, young sir. Helping you, specifically, was a spot of good fortune. I believe you might be a representation of a piece of our scripture."

"What?" Thistle asked.

"Eyes of gold are mentioned in our religious texts. I saw your eyes and decided you were to be helped. Now we let life take us where it may. I would suggest that you let life take you to the opposite side of the citadel here, where stands my order's temple."

With the moment allowing them to take

a breath, they took in the grandeur of the citadel grounds. As far across as the eye could see, and covered in a gentle bowl shaped carpet of grass and forests, the inner area of the citadel walls was a collection idyllic villages arrayed in a circle along the perimeter. At each small settlement there was a central edifice—a building for worship—standing up like the points on a king's crown. Each building was constructed in a different style, and the villages at their feet reflected that architecture.

A tall spire of white stone and glass had smaller versions circling it. A gothic cathedral of earthen stone and glass had simple, baroque huts arranged in a dozen streets around it. So on it went, each building with its followers, each occupying a segment of the citadel's massive open interior.

"Which is yours?" Thistle asked.

"Direct and beyond. Wide stone palace with columns on all sides. Did you know we have a lake?"

"I've never been here," the girl said. "It's beautiful."

"A place of welcome worship for all," Disciple Burke said. "A gift from the gods, this. Tolerance, and the ability to practice all faiths alongside one another without impediment. They were visionary. They led us out of a dark phase in our history."

"Truth," Gray agreed. "But they also dragged the hell of the Void here in their wake, so it's an argument as to the whole picture. Now, your offer to help us is received, and appreciated, but we have a destination we must make haste to. We require an exit into the city heading north and west."

"I see. I cannot speak to any exits to the west that would be safe, but the Temple of the Many is due north. You can use our gates into the Endless City, then head west. We could offer a small armed contingent to protect you, if that pleases you."

"Why?" Arridon asked him. "Why would your people protect us like that? Risk their lives for strangers?"

"As I said, I believe you might be an appearance of something from our scripture," Burke explained. "Allow me to make my case to the temple master and our congregation, and I am sure that a handful of our followers will help ensure you get to where you must go. If we leave now, we'll arrive there not long after full dark. The sun sets early when you're inside these towering structures," he said, and pointed up at the sheer cliff face of the walls encircling them.

"That'll work," Gray answered. "Lead us then, to your people."

Burke smiled and walked away into the bright green grass of the citadel's grounds.

Thistle, Arridon, and their father exchanged looks of hope with one another, and walked after the man, side by side.

"You know, my head feels much better. I think that transit thing might've helped me along," Gray said.

"Good," Arridon said. "No salve anymore…just gotta walk through walls."

As they followed the man who'd brought them through the wall, each of them tried in their own way to forget what was happening behind them in the Channel.

Sebastian's armored foot crunched apart the bone at the center of a shredded leg as he stepped over and through the carnage in the Channel. The Bleed's influence had spread amongst the soft-fleshed natives of this world like fire in a dry forest.

Thousands of them had been touched by the Bleed, and each had received the gift in a different way. Here, now, was the time to see all the colors of the horrid rainbow of mutation their master had seeped into their world.

Horns, straight, hooked, ribbed, grew from skulls as misshapen as unworked clay. Teeth—so many teeth—long, short, sharp, blunt, hooked and barbed grew in mouths far too eager to feed. Legs and arms sprouted in places that never had joints before this day, and each limb was unlike any other. Clawed, hooked, shelled like a crab or beetle, and many writhed like the tentacles on creatures from the deepest parts of the seas.

All of them murdered; all of them destroyed. All feasted upon the life that couldn't outrun them.

Their blood ran like a river down the stone street between the two walls of the close citadels, the entrance to the Endless City, where so many sought refuge from the hungry storm.

The majesty of it all made Sebastian drunk.

"Enough," Sebastian bellowed to the sea of writhing horrors.

The wet slurping of flesh sliding down throats abated, but the shuffling of a thousand feet in the strait coupled with the alien sounds of strange lungs and gills forcing air into bent and broken chests still hummed in the air. Sebastian reached down into the splayed chest of dead man and bloodied his bone-gauntleted hand. He smeared the infection on the face of his helmet and chest plate, then basked in the glory of the Bleed as the blood dried in hot summer air.

He turned his attention to the masses awaiting his voice.

"Your bellies are full. Now, assert yourself as the walking, breathing images of the master of this domain and countless others. Force fealty. Reward devotion. Harvest the fear and faith these things have within them. Break the will of those you discover and show them they have an alternative to bleeding out upon your teeth and down your throat. Teach them to worship the Bleed."

The monsters didn't respond in jubilation when Sebastian made his decree. He looked at a magnificent specimen of the Bleed standing near him. Its flesh had run like a melted candle, and the human's original decapitated head floated above the stump of its neck, tethered by the magic of the Bleed. Its lifeless eyes stared at him, unknowing and uncaring. It existed only to kill and to frighten.

Sebastian lifted his massive sword in one hand and brought it down atop the creature's levitating head, splitting that, then the entire body in half, straight through the crotch. The two halves peeled away and fell to the ground, silencing the entire horde of mutants.

"MAKE THEM WORSHIP THE BLEED!" he screamed into the Channel, and the sound of his voice ripped and tore at the walls of the city, bouncing and echoing for miles.

They were jubilant then, and they launched themselves along the path of his scream deeper into the city, where they sought out fresh slaves for the entity that bent entire realities to its will and devoured those who wouldn't comply.

Sebastian smiled inside the crowned helm made of skull and chitin atop his head. He breathed deep, soaking in the coppery air and halted when his nose tickled with a familiar scent. "Her," he whispered, and his cock throbbed inside his torn trousers, inside his armor.

Sebastian followed the tickle, sniffing the air like a dog, following the path of Thistle's scent between blood-covered market stalls, flipped merchant wagons, and corpses strewn about. The winding trail came to a fast end.

Sebastian faced the wall that rose to the clouds, covered in its spell-inscribed writing.

"Rah!" he shouted at the wall, then

punched it with a spike-encrusted fist.

The wall punched back.

Sebastian's arm nearly ripped free at the shoulder as the warding spell in the stone flashed out with defensive power. His eyes frosted over in white, then black, as a burst of agonizing white light scorched his vision. He cried out in a moment's pain as he was thrown away from the wall, repelled by an unseen force.

Their best magic holds true, the Bleed whispered in his mind. *Amusing.* "Where did the half-breed go?" Sebastian hissed. "I want her."

And you yet may have her, the Bleed assured.

"What must I do?"

They will undoubtedly wish to continue further into the city, looking for a way to escape this realm. Plunge deeper to meet them.

"A door, or gate?"

Press forward.

"And then?"

Press further forward. Sow discord, reap the souls in a grand planetary harvest. Clean this disc of a hovel and leave only those who beg me for every second of their existence.

"And she will be mine?"

All here will be under your heel, my general. Do what I tell you, and the rewards shall present themselves.

Sebastian laughed — half from excitement, half from nervousness about what it would mean to actually get what he wanted — and saw something amiss at his waist. He reached down and grabbed the handle of an old kitchen knife, and with a tug, pulled it free of the bone armor covering his flesh. A plug of blood spilled out through the hole the blade had made and trickled down his thigh.

"I am no vegetable, woman, and I shall not be pared as such," he said, and tossed the tool over his shoulder. As he strode deeper into the channel that led into the Endless City, he tasted the memory of her flesh on his tongue, and savored it.

20

London

London didn't feel like London anymore.

The streets were quiet the way they never were at this time on a Thursday evening. Some shops and restaurants were open, but many more remained closed. Several of the churches were doing a roaring trade, but equally others were desolate. She saw one that had been burnt out, just a couple of streets away from another where a glorious service was being enjoyed by a packed congregation.

Jenny walked along the bank of the Thames. The water in the river remained unnaturally still; the river itself was quiet. She hadn't realized how loud the roar of the water had always been until it wasn't there.

She didn't know where to go or what to do. She craved anonymity, and tucking herself away in a warm and secluded corner somewhere seemed like a sensible idea. She saw a pub across the street and decided alcohol would help. It usually did. The pub was a trendy, hipster place with all kinds of bullshit paraphernalia hanging off the walls, but tonight it looked like heaven. *Heaven*, Jenny said to herself, *now there's a thought.* Did it exist? Was it like paradise? She failed to see how it could be, if the god she'd spent the morning with was in charge. He'd acted like such a jerk.

"Beer," she said to the pretentious-looking bloke behind the bar. He gave her a skewed, self-satisfied grin.

"What kind of beer? We've thirty-four types here, seventeen on tap."

She'd have punched him in the face if she thought she could have actually found his chin beneath his well-oiled beard. Instead she slammed her fists on the counter and yelled at him.

"Just give me a fucking beer. I'm having a really shitty day."

He peered at her over the rims of his wire-frames and obliged.

She dug in her pocket for her debit card or phone and came up with nothing. "Shit."

"I've got it," said the guy who pulled up a stool next to her. She sighed and held her head in her hands. The very last thing she needed right now was some creep hitting on her.

"Look, that's really good of you, mate, but I...."

Her words trailed away to silence. It was Jayesh. She wrapped her arms around him and squeezed without even caring whether she should.

"A guy walks into a bar…" he said.

"It's good to see you. I thought you were—"

"Dead?"

"Well, yeah."

"Nope."

"I can see that. How did you find me? Hell of a coincidence."

"I Googled you and came up with a few possible hits. I remembered you saying you lived in a block of flats, and I found one that was surrounded. I joined the crowds then saw you escape and followed you here."

"You're not dead, then?"

"Not yet. I lost you when the buildings started coming down this morning, but I saw you and the big guy on TV so I knew you'd survived. I dodged the soldiers and just waited. I figured that if I saw anything else strange happening in London today, you'd most likely have something to do with it," Jayesh said.

Jenny took a swig of her beer, then stopped. "Am I safe with you?"

"I'm not going to try anything on."

"I don't mean safe like that. How much do you know?"

"You mean about the gods and demons? About the Bleed?"

"Yeah. Who told you? God? Thirnas?"

"No, his bosses. Thing is, Jenny, I've been sent to protect you."

She laughed into the froth sitting on the top of her beer. "Wait, didn't you almost kill me this morning?"

"I've already apologized for that. It was a ruse. A distraction to get you onside so I could make sure you got to Thirnas."

"And there was you acting like you didn't have a clue what was going on. Convincingly, I might add."

"I know, but if I'd explained you'd have called me crazy and run away."

"True. Hang on, though, you were the

one trying to get me to leave the area."

"I knew it would get messy with the blacksuits and I didn't want you getting hurt."

"I had someone else looking out for me, apparently."

"So I noticed. What's on your god's agenda exactly?" he asked.

"Saving the world."

"Nothing too heavy then. I take it the world needs saving?"

"Apparently so," Jenny said and sipped her beer.

"From what? The Bleed or big-headed gods trying to out-do each other? Doesn't matter. Listen, Thirnas didn't come here to protect people, he came here to hide behind them," he said.

"Bullshit."

"It's not. I swear. That nasty crowd who turned up at your place just now? They're a precursor to the Bleed. They're looking for you because they know you can lead them to him."

"And why do they want him?"

"Long story. Don't have time for that now."

"Why not?" she asked.

"Because if we're not careful, tonight could be the last night on Earth for all of us."

Jenny was getting used to hyperbole, but Jayesh seemed to be cranking up the bullshit levels. "Come on, please. Credit me with a little intelligence. I've been spoon-fed crap by people and gods all day. I've lost track of who I believe. Actually, the only one I really believed was Dad and he's...."

The memory of leaving him faced by the ravenous crowd overwhelmed her. She sat at the bar and bent over it, sobbing. Jayesh cautiously put his arm around her.

"I know how hard this must be. I've heard a lot of stories about your dad. He was a good man, courageous. Necessary."

She wiped her face. "So what do we do now?"

"Though plenty of others told him he was wrong, Thirnas had this idea in his head that he'd make his grand entrance and everyone would bow down to him like they used to a couple thousand years ago, but they haven't. Look."

Jayesh pulled his phone from his pocket and scrolled through various social media feeds and news sites. The reviews for God were in, and it was fair to say they were something of a mixed bag.

In some cities, people were protesting with placards proclaiming, "Not my God," and "Imposter Go Home," and the like. In a number of locations around the world, these crowds had been met by equally large, equally vociferous groups proclaiming that this was their day of salvation, the second coming. Some atheists had become believers, while some believers had abandoned their faith. There was hardly a soul who hadn't questioned their reality.

"Thing is," Jayesh said as they watched the images on the screen, "when people are told half a story, they make up the rest. The gods have been away from this place for hundreds and hundreds of years, plenty of time for people to come to their own conclusions. And with something as personal and important as faith, when something comes along that makes people question their deepest held beliefs, it leaves them questioning *everything*. But like I said, he didn't come here for them, he came here for himself. I was hoping you'd have been able to distract him, to keep him occupied until other gods could follow him through and take him back."

"And why does all this matter so much tonight?"

"He's destabilized everything. He's made it easy for the cracks to be forced open and for other things to start spilling through. He's opened the door to the Bleed.

When the Thames starts to flow again, as I've no doubt it soon will, everything will change."

"And I'm supposed to stop it?"

"You won't be able to stop it. No one will."

"Great." She drank more of her beer then turned back to Jayesh. "Remind me again, why should I believe you?"

"Because I'm telling the truth."

"The truth according to whom?"

"According to the gods. Look, I get it, you're right to be cautious. The only way I'll be able to prove myself to you is through my actions. Likewise, the only way I can convince you I'm telling the truth is by pointing out the facts. Thirnas came here this morning and reduced your life to chaos. He destroyed a part of London and now he's on the verge of causing an uprising because he's a coward and he's arrogant. He's risked the lives of every single person on this planet, including you, just to save himself. Just think on this, Jenny: Thirnas is the reason your dad is dead."

She nodded, unable to speak now, and knocked back the rest of her drink.

"I can't keep track of this. What do I have to do?"

"Stick with me. I'll keep you safe and

get you to the right place. When the time's right we'll bring the true gods through then close the rupture between this dimension and the Bleed."

"When?"

"Before the morning."

"You make it all sound so easy."

"Believe me, it's anything but. I know you can do it, though, Jen. I've got faith in you."

21

The Moon

DAY THREE / 6:36 PM

"He's going to pass out." Sam watched her boyfriend. "Shut the windows, Maddie!"

"Few more seconds."

"Shut them!"

"It's working!" Derrick said excitedly.

Once there was nothing left to use as a propellant, Maddie pressed the button to shut the doors. Juan was turning shades of blue, and Tyler's eyes were grotesquely bulging out.

"How long?" Sam cried out, watching her friends helplessly.

"The doors won't shut! It's not working." Maddie tried to find another way to get them closed. Sam furiously pulled on one door; Maddie knew she wasn't going to have enough strength to pull over the hydraulic door piston.

"Shut!" Sam was straining, putting her entire weight into it. Derrick threw his body over Tyler and Juan, pulling on the door in the back; he wasn't having any better results than his sister.

"Mom, help me!"

Sandra was slow to move; she could not help but think how much further their supplies would go with two fewer mouths to feed. Then she realized that many of those very same supplies were heading out the open doors. She pulled on her son's midsection, trying to give him the leverage he needed to shut the door. Tyler's eyes were on her in a pleading gesture. There was a whooshing sound as Maddie finally got the doors to close, then came the electronic click as they locked. She didn't know how long it would be until the cabin filled back up with enough oxygen for comfortable breathing, but it had better be soon; the two boys were an unnatural blue hue.

"Holy crap." Derrick watched as the mower now moved laterally and much closer to the towers. Sam had grabbed Tyler's hand; he was gasping, taking tiny breaths like a fish pulled from its habitat. Juan was once again unconscious.

Maddie thought him lucky. If he died, it wouldn't be in the throes of terror like the rest of them.

"Fifteen percent," Maddie read out the oxygen level. It was close to a survivable rate, though it would be extremely uncomfortable to attempt to gasp for a breath that wasn't there.

Derrick looked wildly around for the trailing winch cable that was still too far off to the right. Gonna be close," he said quietly, doing his best to gauge their trajectory.

"Sixteen percent."

"He's closed his eyes! Is he dead?" Sam was terrified. Tyler squeezed her hand briefly to let her know he was still with her.

Derrick's heart sank when they blew past the first tower, the cable nowhere near the mark.

"Seventeen percent." Maddie was intent on doing the only thing she had control over.

"Going to need to open the doors again, Maddie." Derrick could barely speak over a whisper. He did not think Tyler and Juan could survive that long without air, but none of them were going to make it if they didn't try. He cleared his throat and spoke louder. "Maddie, you need to open the doors again."

"NO!" Sam screamed.

"We're not close enough," he said weakly.

Maddie began to look around. "Shit, he's right."

"They'll die! You can't!"

Tyler again squeezed Sam's hand.

"We're at eighteen percent. Tyler, grab what air you can." Again the doors whooshed open, the air rushing out pushed them further over. Maddie waited until the readout went to zero, as soon as that happened, she closed the doors, this time without incident. The veins on Tyler's neck stood out like cables holding his head in place as he held onto the air in his lungs with all the power he could muster, even as his heart slammed into his chest, even as his lungs burned, even as his brain screamed at him to grab a breath of fucking air!

"Two percent...we have a seal

problem," Maddie said uselessly. They could hear the escape of air.

Sam took a breath of air and popped the seals on her helmet.

"What are you doing?" Derrick cried in alarm.

She shook her head, a stern look on her face. She took off her helmet and placed it over Tyler's head. Derrick knew, at best, he'd only get a couple of breaths before he was again out of oxygen, but to a starving person, a single cracker is a welcome sight.

Juan's head was lolling about as Derrick copied his sister's actions. Whether the boy took any air in was impossible to tell.

"Five percent," Maddie said as Derrick put his helmet back on. Sam was taking deep breaths in preparation to give Tyler another go. He motioned for her to give it to Juan. They whipped past another tower; this time the mower went directly over, but the cable was still too far off to the right to catch hold.

"We have three more chances," Sam said before placing her helmet on Juan.

"How does she know?" Maddie asked.

"She's got some sick fascination with the towers...I think she named them all," Derrick said. He was looking for the seal break; he planned to plug it up with the expanding foam. "Got it," he said as he filled in the crack.

"Nine percent. Coming up on try number three." The mower moved swiftly past the tower; they all turned to watch the cable. They felt, rather than heard, as the heavy hook clanged off the side of it before once again resuming its winding journey.

"Two more," Derrick whispered. There was no need to say it aloud, as they were all keenly aware.

Sam stopped getting air to Juan and Tyler as the oxygen climbed to eighteen; they were seconds from the next tower.

"This is it," Maddie said. She was fearful of what would happen if it missed and almost as fearful of if it caught. There was a better than average chance the winch would be ripped free from the mower; it could even take the entire front end with it once it snagged. There was a high-pitched whine that traveled up the entirety of the cable as it dragged against the side of the tower.

"It looped around!" Derrick said excitedly. "This is it!" His elation was lost as quickly as a ruptured balloon as the cable slipped loose. "Fuck!" He didn't even care that his mother was right next to him. "What's going on? Maddie, the cable is getting shorter."

"Reeling it in some."

"We only have one more shot," he said in alarm.

"Think about it for a second. We're traveling god knows how fast, over a hundred miles per hour, easy. That cable snags and all this weight stops short; we'll be lucky if we're not ripped in two. Best case scenario, the winch comes free, but that does nothing for us."

"Two minutes." They were all looking at the next and last approaching tower. Maddie had reeled in the cable about halfway; that was all she dared. Tyler was breathing regularly as he did his best to rouse his friend.

"Maybe let him miss this part," Sam told him.

"You always were the smart one," he told her, a waning smile upon his lips.

"Sam, will the tower hold?" Sandra asked.

"Hadn't thought of that," she replied. "They're not built for this kind of abuse, and with the gravity so much less than Earth's, they don't need to be as heavy duty. I...I honestly don't know."

"Can't tell you how sick I'm getting of new things to worry about," Maddie said.

There might as well have been no air in the mower as they got closer to the last tower, as all of them were holding their breath. The vehicle again sped past, the trailing hook directly behind them. Derrick spun to watch. Maddie had her hand on the winch controls, ready to slowly spool some out if necessary.

"Everyone buckle in, helmets on!" Maddie warned.

"Contact," Derrick said. Once again, there was the thrum of vibration shooting up the cable and shaking the entirety of the mower. "Catch," he prayed. "Catch." His hands were crushing the back of the seat as he watched. It happened so fast he wasn't even sure he was seeing it correctly. "Caught!" he shouted out at the same time the line went taut and the front end of the mower dipped down violently. There was the strained whirring of the winch as Maddie did her best to let out a measured amount, doing what she could to keep them from stopping too suddenly.

"You smell that?" Sam asked. "Smells like fire."

"Winch housing," Maddie said through pursed lips. "Not slowing down enough. Try not to brace." She said the words even as she put both of her arms in the locked position against the steering wheel.

Derrick had undone his harness quickly, moving over the seat.

"What are you doing?" Maddie asked as

she watched him go for the controls.

"Letting the cable go. We're already heading downward; that line pulls tight and we're going to nosedive into the ground at speed."

Maddie spent less than a second doing the math in her head. When she figured out just how right he was, she turned the cable-lock switch.

"Are we free of it?" He was hoping to see the cable falling away.

"Don't think so. Sit back down!"

The cable pulled tight, the front end of the car was nearly pointing straight down as the cable suddenly pulled free.

"Oh shit, now what?" Tyler asked as they were all looking at the ground rushing up to meet them.

"I'm going to reverse the magnets. It'll help. I hope," Maddie said, she could feel the belt pressing against her abdomen. "Otherwise it's going to be like tossing snowballs at a tank."

"Helpful," Sandra sneered.

"As opposed to all the wondrous things you've been doing for the last half-hour," Maddie said as she punched codes into the display.

Sam could hardly believe it had only been a half-hour since the life she knew had ended; she prayed it would return to some semblance of normality, but she didn't have high hopes, especially when she let herself dwell on the notion that her father was, in all likelihood, dead.

Now it was a waiting game; the impact could crush them like a used beer can or bounce them back into orbit, especially with the reverse polarity on the magnets. Maddie hoped she would be able to switch them back after they made contact, in a bid to prevent that. If she was knocked unconscious or the power was again cut off, there would be absolutely nothing they could do. Maddie had both her legs pressed up against the floorboard; she was doing her best to tamp down the fear that was threatening to overwhelm her.

"I don't like this!" Sam was doing her best to press herself back into her seat.

"Two hundred feet." Maddie sought comfort the only way she knew how, and that was by verbalizing the problem.

Derrick had managed to give enough slack on the seat belt to fit his mother and himself, Juan was not going to be afforded the same luxury. "Tyler, you need to put him down by the floorboards. He could kill someone if he slams forward."

Tyler knew precisely who was in the line of fire; he quickly manhandled his friend down by his legs and did his best to wedge him in there. "I'm sorry," he said softly.

"I think we're slowing!" Sam now had her legs on the dashboard.

"Get them down! You'll put your knees through your face!" Maddie slapped Sam's legs.

"I'm scared, Maddie."

The magnets had changed the pitch of the vehicle slightly, enough that they were no longer coming in head-on. The bottom of the front bumper made contact first. The hit was jarring, the entire front end bent upward at the junction between the windshield and the hood, the lights flickered but stayed lit. Maddie dislocated her index finger as she was holding it to the screen.

"Shit." She tried to get her vision to stop vibrating as the vehicle rebounded. The front end was again taking flight as the rest of the mower pounded the dirt. The squealing protests of the metal dominated all sound. Two of the skid plates were ripped free and the entire frame was twisted. Maddie moved as fast as she could, but they were already back up five feet in the air. The vehicle went dark for three seconds before coming back on; the reboot took another ten. "Come on, come on." Maddie waited to punch in the magnetic reversal.

"Do it," Sam urged.

There was a slow whir and the car dipped down at an angle. "Three are good to go, one is being a bitch," Maddie said as the rear driver's side pitched up while the rest of the car wanted to go down. They were racing just above the ground, slowly descending.

"Oh shit." Sam looked through the window. "We're heading straight for it!"

"Aitken basin," Maddie said flatly. It was a huge impact crater on the south pole of the moon. With a circumference of sixteen hundred miles and a depth of eight, it was not something they could go around, especially since they could neither steer nor stop.

Their chances of survival were already on the slim side; if they plummeted to the bottom of the crater, it would become a mass grave.

"Umm, Maddie, do something!" Derrick watched everything play out before them.

"Steering wheel is a little useless at the moment." Maddie twisted the wheel back and forth as if she needed to demonstrate.

"The air brakes, use the air brakes!" Tyler shouted out.

"You do realize that they are air-*assisted* brakes, right?"

"Assisted or not, use them. That'll work,

right?"

Sandra shook her head. "Seen sharper points on a ball. Really Samantha, is he the best you can do?"

Sam had utterly tuned out her mother as she was staring down the abyss, and she did not like that it was staring back. Derrick looked at the multitude of spider webs that had formed across every window within the vehicle. He'd been amazed it had held so far; he had no illusions that it would survive another impact.

"How far?" he asked.

"A few miles." Maddie had pulled up the GPS; she figured it was safer to watch a liquid crystal display as opposed to the real thing. More comfortable to remove yourself from reality in that way. The enormous, black, un-navigated crater was beginning to dominate the screen.

"So, does that mean we're not going to use the brakes?" Tyler seemed genuinely confused.

"What's going on?" Juan said, his voice muffled.

"Good to hear you, buddy," Tyler said enthusiastically as he helped his friend up.

"Might have been better off staying down there," Sandra told him.

"Maddie, the windows," Derrick pointed out.

"What else can go wrong? Sorry boys, those of you who can suit up, you're going to want to do it now."

"No!" Sam was angry. "I will not be safe and sound while my friends gasp for air!"

"I don't know what your definition of 'safe and sound' is, kiddo, but this ain't it," Maddie said. "And you can't help them if you're actively dying, now can you?"

"I'll be all right," Tyler told Sam tenderly. "Do it for me."

"Don't ever do anything for a man. You do it for yourself. If it just so happens to align with his wishes, then so be it," Sandra said as she clicked her helmet on.

"Was that necessary?" Maddie asked.

Sandra did not respond. Sam reached her hand back. Tyler grabbed it.

"I love you, Sam. I think I loved you that first day in kindergarten when you shared your crayons. Definitely the day you gave me your sandwich. I have a confession, though, and I hope we can work through it."

"Anything," she sniffled.

"I didn't forget my lunch like I told you. I ate it between classes." He wiped his face as tears flowed from his eyes.

Sam smiled and let out a half sob mixed with a laugh. "I'll do my best to forgive you; it'll be hard, but I'll try."

Tyler pushed Juan to the side as he leaned forward so he could give her a kiss, everyone except Sandra was doing their utmost to provide them with as much privacy as possible in the small confines.

"I'm glad this thing will be over soon," Sandra said, watching the two teenagers kiss.

Maddie turned. "What the fuck is wrong with you? You can't let them have this one moment?"

"I'm going to make sure, when this is over and we're back at a base, that you'll never do more than clear clogged toilets," Sandra told her.

"Want to know what? If we do get back, I'm perfectly content with that. Don't think I'm going to let your actions go unnoticed, though; good chance we'll be working side by side. I'd pay good money to see you wiping shit off the side of a bowl."

"I'll destroy you, Maddie."

"Really, Mom? Dad is probably gone, we've just survived going into orbit, and now we're about to drop down into the middle of the moon, and all you can think to do is be a jerk?" Derrick asked.

"It's who she is. At least she's consistent." Maddie had resumed looking at the screen, the vehicle was still canted, though it was noticeably lower. "Come on you bucket, drop down." She smacked the dashboard. If it touched down there was a chance she could stop, though what she was going to do then was unknown. It was unlikely the mower could be driven.

"Maddie, what are we going to do?" Sam asked.

"I realize praying in this day and age is an antiquated notion, but in terms of things that can be done, that's about the only one that has even a modicum of a chance."

"I've never done it before."

"Never?"

Sam shook her head. "Mom said only the deficient pray, and that if she ever caught us doing it, we'd be punished. It seemed a useless threat because, at the time, I didn't even know what it meant to pray or to whom I would even have tried."

Maddie led her in a short prayer; the whole while, Sandra glared at them.

"Amen," Maddie concluded.

"I feel better," Sam said as she raised her head and opened her eyes.

"Opiate for the masses," Sandra sneered.

"Right now, I wouldn't mind being a little numbed up." Maddie raised her head as well.

"How'd that work for you? Are we still heading for the hole?" Sandra asked, she'd no sooner finished her remark when the front passenger wheel skidded against the ground before rising slightly and tapping back down.

"Brakes now, right?" Tyler asked.

"Brakes now," Derrick responded.

Maddie kept her foot depressed on the brake. All of the wheels were frozen in the locked position, although, with only one intermittently touching the ground, it was far from a successful venture, more of a gesture.

"We're not stopping? Why aren't we stopping?" Tyler asked.

"All we're doing is turning a bit." Maddie had her full weight on the pedal.

"Maybe we'll spin, start heading the other way, maybe?" Sam intoned.

"That wouldn't be horrible…it's possible; I just wish we were turning quicker. The crater is so damned huge, but…"

Each time the wheel touched down, they held their breath, hoping this would be the time it would stay rooted and it would spin them free from the approaching nightmare and every time it rose back up, there would be an audible gasp and an inaudible formation of *dammit*.

The next time it dropped down was much longer than any of the previous times. The mower was, indeed, spinning.

"Oh, thank the Lord!" Maddie cried out as an escape route was showing its way, then, what they'd wanted to happen did so, and right now, it was unthinkable. The driver's side wheel dropped down, effectively stopping their slow, circular escape route.

"The Lord giveth and the Lord taketh away!" Sandra screamed maniacally.

"Better chance of stopping, right?" Juan had finally gained his bearings.

"Should be, but we're going too fast without enough room. I don't think I can stop it."

"Can't we jump?" Tyler asked.

"Have you lost your mind? We're traveling close to a hundred miles an hour. Odds any of us would survive that kind of leap are beyond dismal. And even if, Tyler, you somehow did manage not to break your neck, what are you planning on doing at that point? You know, without oxygen and all," Maddie asked.

"I meant more that you all should jump. At least you'll have a chance." Tyler's eyes were downcast.

"Nope, we're all in this until the end." Sam was once again facing her boyfriend; there was no sense looking the other way. And besides, she found deep solace in his features.

"You want to hold my hand?" Juan asked Derrick.

"You know I'm not gay, right?" Derrick replied.

"You knew?" Juan seemed shocked.

"We've all been friends forever, man. It would be weirder if I didn't. I'll still hold your hand, though," Derrick said as he reached over.

"Okay, since we're all being honest with each other, I thought the last year you were a huge pain in the ass. Up until today, that is. Whew. There. I said it." Tyler blew air through his cheeks.

"What? You mean when I didn't leave you alone with my sister?"

"Smart kid," Maddie said. "This is it." She grabbed the roll bar above her head as the front end dipped down the steep embankment of the crater. The darkness below was so encompassing that the headlights could not penetrate more than a few feet ahead, and none of it was anything they wanted to see; more often than not, it was a large rock followed by more blackness. The mower was getting pummeled as it careened off of boulders like a well flipped steel bearing in a pinball machine. The occupants were continually bumped from side to side.

The glass had blown out sometime during the first mile down. Tyler's grip on Sam's hand had at first intensified, then waned as he ran out of air.

"Do something!" Sam screamed.

Maddie was doing her best to steer around the more substantial obstacles, though with one of the magnets working against her, control over the vehicle was minimal. She felt for the boys, but their troubles were rapidly coming to a conclusion, and there wasn't a thing she could do for them except try and help the rest of them survive so they could get a decent burial.

"Reverse the magnets, Maddie!" Derrick offered.

"I should have thought of that." Maddie was angry; if the magnets repelled, they could push up off the ground and stop slamming into every rock on the cliff face. The mower lifted slightly, though the troubled magnet was still out of phase and was now pulling the rear end downward. Sandra had banged her head into the ceiling more than once, and she was thankful for the helmet. The front end slid up and over a sizable pointed rock, but the rear was not quite as lucky; the point lodged deep into the suspension and tore the wheel free and with it the electromagnet. The mower was now two feet off the ground and spinning like a top as it continued to head down.

"What the fuck!" Sandra had one hand on the door frame and the other the roll bar slightly behind her. Derrick closed his eyes, doing his best to hold onto his last meal. Sam was weeping, her head nearly in her lap. Maddie had finally let go of the steering wheel and was bracing herself much like Sandra. Parts were flying off the mower, some being strewn over a mile away from the centrifugal force. Maddie could not help but wonder when it would be her turn and how badly it would hurt. The terrifying descent lasted for more than eight horrific minutes. There was little left of the mower, save the frame, when they finally came to a rough but blissful stop. Maddie ripped her helmet off and summarily threw up. Her head was hanging over the side of the frame, ribbons of bile hanging down, she groaned in agony as her stomach fought to settle itself. It was more than a minute later when the importance of what was happening dawned on her.

22

A Feast Fit for Three

"It's hard to see," Arridon said. "Do they ever light these lampposts on this road?"

"Not anymore," Burke answered as they approached the fire-lit settlement around the Temple of the Many. "The temples of the citadel used to split the cost of the oil needed, but as more and more people travel away to find better opportunities, there are less and less tithes coming in. We commit to moving about in the citadel and city by day. Inside the Endless City, beyond the Channel, you'll find far more light at night in the gate cities. Not much beyond."

"Gate cities?" Thistle asked.

"There are countless thousands of towers and castles and structures in the gods' streets. Kings and queens and elected governors rule over blocks of them, or, in the case of very large buildings, they lay claim to one tower, or perhaps two. Imagine that; an entire kingdom stacked up on fifty floors of a single structure," Burke said, and then whistled in amazement. "The settlements just inside the Channel are called the gate cities. Kingdoms across the street from one another for miles and miles. Then, of course, there is less human settlement as the ruins become wilder, where they lie abandoned."

"Where are we headed?" Thistle asked her father. "Where's mother's family citadel?"

"Family citadel?" Burke asked, almost stopping as they passed the first small farmhouse on the outskirts of the village. "You descend from nobility?"

"Yes," Gray answered him. "They don't know that, though."

"Why didn't you tell us we were, what? Nobles? What does that mean?" Thistle

asked.

"Mind your volume," he advised in a whisper after looking around at the houses they neared. "Noble families were the social and economic elite of the gods' society. Some factions also recognized a...I guess you'd say divine appointment of responsibility to rule. Each of the noble families governed the territory within a citadel."

"What is your spouse's family name?" the disciple asked.

"Frost," Gray answered. "We are of House Frost."

"The Cold Wind Blows," Burke said. "As our scripture says. Masters of time and space," he added. "Knights of the Transit. House Frost is known to us."

"What's he talking about?" Arridon asked.

"Your mother's family gained its power through piercing through the layers of the realms. They pioneered the science and magic that allowed the gods to flee the Bleed and come here," he said as they entered a dark area between the outer village buildings and the better lit center area near the large column-ringed temple ahead. "House Frost was blessed with golden eyes all, great magical skill, and intellect that could harness the greatest of sciences."

"And they were rumored to have gathered their kin and run at the first sight of the demons," a resonant female voice called out from the darkness ahead. "Skill and intelligence did not imply courage, it would seem."

The family halted, but raised their weapons in defense. Disciple Burke dropped to a knee, and lowered his head in deference to the voice. A woman—tall, and broad of shoulder with a shaved head the same as Burke's—stepped into the light. She wore a spotless white robe, as he did, though hers was lined with red trim and gold lettering in a language they couldn't see well enough to recognize.

"And yet here you are, golden of eye, and at our door," she added. "Perhaps my assertion is quite wrong. You must come to the temple. We will dine in your honor, and send you away with our blessings."

"Pontifex, may I introduce you to Gray, Arridon, and Thistle," Burke said.

"You may, and well done, Disciple. Your keen eye for prophecy has led you down the right path, I suspect. I am deeply sorry if my words offended," she said. "I spoke without proper reflection. I am honored to greet the children of House Frost."

"Who are you?" Gray asked her.

"Pontifex?"

She giggled. "That is not my name, but the title I assume as the leader of the Many. Most refer to me simply as such, but if you like, you may call me Andela," she said, and added a gentle bow. "Arridon, Thistle, and Gray, it is my pleasure. Now, if you'll follow me, we have a meal in preparation for you."

"You knew we were coming?" Arridon asked her, wary.

"Portents showed us that guests were likely. You are those guests, it would seem. If we are wrong about that, then we will feed you anyway, and send you away with our blessings nonetheless."

"Please," Burke said. "Enjoy a hot meal, allow yourself a bath, rest your feet, perhaps take a short nap, then head off to Citadel Frost. If it pleases you, I'll join you on that journey. I've been that far into the city and would serve as a passable guide."

"How far is that?" Thistle asked.

"Without delays, perhaps an eight hour walk. It's only a few hours past where the last gate city is. Safe, I would say," Burke said with a shrug. "As safe as today can be."

"Let's do all of what Burke suggested," Gray said. "But quickly. Then we can get into the city proper and make the journey to arrive not long after dawn."

"What about the monsters of the Bleed? Aren't they going to be close behind? Can we afford the delay of a meal and bath?" Thistle asked.

"We've been moving since dawn without a break. We must rest, or we won't make it," Gray told her. "As I said, quickly."

"Come. You waste much of your precious time arguing about your precious time, on a day with auspicious activities," Pontifex Andela said. "And by now, the food is on the table."

There was no arguing with that.

The twin mahogany front doors of the coliseum-style Temple of the Many swung shut behind them with whoosh of air. The square passage they stood in led to a massive, open area filled with tables and people. Music lilted in on the summer night breeze, and the sound of strings and woodwinds soothed frayed nerves.

"If I hear those doors lock, I'm going to start shooting people," Gray said, hand suddenly full of his wife's pistol.

Burke held his palms up. "They have no locks."

"Good."

The Pontifex led them down the white marble passage to its end, where it opened into a massive, open-air cathedral. A carpet of stars filled the night sky above, casting down an ethereal luminance that rested atop the room lined with marble columns, each adorned with several sconces aglow with torches. At the center of the sprawling room were a dozen banquet tables, each covered with a brilliantly patterned tablecloth in every color. Atop those cloths were platters and bowls of all manner of food and drink. Nearly fifty simply clothed people stood with welcoming expressions amongst the tables. Some grinned with glee as the brother and sister entered the room with their father.

"Well shit," Arridon said, wiping saliva from his lips. "That's more food than I've seen in my entire life." He started to walk deeper into the room to feast, but his father snapped a hand around his wrist. Thistle froze as well.

"Eat only after asking them to try it first. Something could be poisoned. Drink the same way. Eat until you are full, but not stuffed. I won't have you cramping or slowed because you had five extra bites of bacon."

"Do you think they have bacon?" Thistle asked, her head snapping to the side to search for the rare, crisp treat.

"I already saw it," Gray answered. "If those of the Many are agreeable, we should take a bag or two of food with us and water. Do not leave this room without all three of us gathered. In your head, count to a hundred five times, and then meet back here. Burke, can you meet us here in that time? Then take us to a hot bath?"

"I'll stay right here," Burke offered. "I'll gather some food and water for us to bring."

"Perfect. Now, once we are refreshed, we'll head out of the temple and find a place to rest once we get into the gate cities."

"You don't want to sleep here?" Pontifex Andela asked. "Should I be offended that you do not trust us?"

Gray looked over to her and shrugged, pistol still in hand. "You do what pleases you. I'm going to protect my kids. And kids—no alcohol."

"Same goes for you," Thistle replied.

Andela smiled—a warm one—and nodded. "It pleases the Many greatly that you grace us with your presence this night. May our food and drink sustain you, and our hospitality reinvigorate you."

Arridon and Thistle leaned their weapons against the wall of the entryway, and went off to plunder. Both teens halted with their first handfuls of food and waited for their hosts to try the dishes before they jammed their own portions into their faces. Despite the bizarre and horrible day they'd endured, Gray couldn't help but smile at his children.

"A drink?" a young girl asked him. She offered him a large flagon filled with something the color of rubies.

"No," Gray said, lifting his gun-free hand to wave the wine away. "Not tonight."

She departed with a smile, and Gray drifted over to where the Pontifex stood just inside her grand coliseum of worship. She oversaw the celebrants all mingling about, trying to be the ones to give his kids some food or drink. They were giddy for the chance to feed them.

"Who are the Many?" he asked her. "And why do you serve them?"

"Who? Or where? Perhaps even 'when.' The Many are an amalgam. We are a collection of people who are aware of the gods' original home, at least in the sense that it is not of this world, or of this dimension. As a reflection of the unending number of realities in our existence, and the unending number of souls in those realities, we believe in *the Many*. The many places, many people, many cultures, many sciences, many fates and futures, and more. We venerate the magical splendor of an infinite existence, and the bounty of wonder that the gods brought to our world."

"Sounds lofty."

"It is."

"Are you going to try to kill my kids and me?"

"What? No. Why would you think that?" the Pontifex asked, startled.

"My wife taught me that faith is a good thing, but most religions are not. Too many veer into the territory of the cult. 'Have a healthy skepticism,' she used to say, so call me a trained skeptic."

The Pontifex sighed, and surveyed her domain. "We are not murderous, even though one of the facets of our faith is studying the Bleed. It is ubiquitous across a million dimensions. It is entropy, I suppose."

"I see. Do you worship the Bleed?"

"It is a piece of the multiverse. A power of the infinite cosmos. Some believe in it more than others, but all now can see that it pervades, invades, and seems to be an inevitable force that cannot be stopped. You would be absent of feeling to not recognize its importance."

"You and Burke alluded to something about predicting we were coming. Is that some kind of prophecy from your scripture?"

"It is."

"What does your prophecy say about us?"

"'Four eyes come under the midnight moon, casting a golden glow on the day the blood runs. Four eyes searching for cold and heat to wage war on that which will not be beat. Four eyes find it,' is the specific passage."

"And you think it's us. Make sense. What comes next in your prophecy?"

"Doom. Damnation. The blood flows; everyone dies," she said. "It is our lot, should those with the golden eyes arrive."

"Are there any other interpretations of the prophecy?" Gray asked as he watched his son and daughter move about the followers, both smiling and thankful for the gifts of food and drink.

"I don't follow."

"Does anyone believe in a different path for your scripture?"

"There are many paths, all creating new futures. Some do believe in divergence. A different outcome as events transpire. Some believe the prophecy is immutable. Unchangeable. We should celebrate what we have been given, and then allow what will happen, to happen. Everything is open to opinion. There are some who believe that if you were to never arrive, the end times would never come, for example. The prophecy, unfulfilled."

"Are there any that believe that if we do not find this 'cold and heat' the apocalypse will be averted? Anyone here that might mislead us, or make an attempt on our lives?"

She thought on it for a minute. "I can't say as I know of anyone who has expressed such a belief. Up until the last few days, the idea that the Bleed would come to the mainland and end the world was very much a piece of the gods' history, and worry."

Gray returned his attention to the banquet in honor of his and his children's arrival. He watched as Burke gathered several food items and wrapped them before putting them in a small leather backpack. He filled the bag as Gray watched.

"I think we'll be going. Our time is too limited for this," Gray said, and left her side. "Arridon! Thistle! One last bite and we're off."

"What? Why?" Arridon hollered back over the crowd's gentle noise.

"Eat up, drink up, we're gone," he yelled back.

"Dad!" Thistle said. "This is the best thing that's ever happened to us. Give us a minute."

"*Now*," Gray said, and judging by the looks his kids sported, they understood that now meant now. The two of them scrambled to find mouthfuls of good food before returning to their father.

"Burke," Gray said.

"Yes?" the disciple answered, returning with his backpack filled with food and drink.

"I don't trust you; please don't take that personally."

Burke chuckled. "Of course."

"I would like for you to bring us to the citadel wall, and do your thing that gets us through that wall again. Can you do that for us?"

"Of course. Will you want me to guide you through the gate cities to Citadel Frost?"

"Let's see how the wall magic goes first."

Thistle and Arridon arrived, trading eye rolls and sighs. Their bellies were larger than when they arrived just a few minutes prior, though, and for that, Gray was thankful.

"We gotta go?" Arridon asked.

"Yeah. Sorry, Andela."

She shook her head, dismissing his apology. "The prophecy gave me no expectations regarding disappointment. I am happy that a moment in our scripture came to pass in my presence, though I wish it was something of a less world-ending nature."

"We are not happy," a man's voice said from a nearby table. "It is not enough for us to observe the events as they pass. We can do something about the prophecy. We must do something."

They turned and assessed the speaker. Long and lean, similar to Arridon, and like the others gathered for the reception and meal, wearing plain clothing. He carried a large carving knife. With wide, dark eyes the color of dawn he glared at the trio, then at the two members of the clergy standing near them.

"They are going to leave," Andela said, her voice firm. "Now put down the knife, Tobin, and let us celebrate our last days before the Bleed reaches us."

"If they die, then they cannot continue with their role in the scriptures, and we will avert damnation," the man said, taking a step forward. "If the prophecy cannot move forward, the apocalypse will not happen."

Gray clenched the pistol's grip in his hand, and readied himself to kill a human being.

"We don't know that. The prophecy isn't understood well. Guards, take Tobin here into custody until our guests have departed," the Pontifex commanded.

But no guards appeared to do Andela's bidding. Two more members of the congregation stepped forward under the sky of stars, and lifted blades in their hands.

Many wept, for they did not want to murder, but knew in their hearts they must.

23

London

He led her along silent streets, heading back deeper into the heart of the city.

"Where is everyone?" she asked.

"It's late. It's been a hell of a day. Most people are at home, I guess. The authorities have been warning folks to keep out of this area since first thing."

"So what are we doing here?"

"It's the heart of power. This is where we need to be."

This was a walk Jenny had done a thousand times before, but she'd never known the place to be so quiet and still. They were on the embankment alongside the Thames. The river remained silent, the water virtually motionless; the moon and stars were being reflected as if it was a mirror.

Parliament loomed up ahead. The buildings were dark, unoccupied like everywhere else. Jenny was about to comment on how she'd never seen the place like that when a thunderous noise rang out. She stopped in her tracks, terrified. Jayesh took her hand and pulled her forward. "It's okay," he said. "It was just a sonic boom. Look."

In the skies high above Big Ben, a bright blue-white light had appeared. It was another comet like the one they'd seen Thirnas arrive in earlier. This one looked even bigger, and its plume was longer and ice white.

"That your god?" Jenny asked.

"Yes," Jayesh replied. He looked up at the falling star with an expression of pure devotion writ large on his face. The massive orb slowed down as it approached the surface and contracted in size just as Thirnas's craft had. It lit up the surrounding area, giving everything a lick of ghostly white illumination, picking out the shadows which might have preferred to remain obscured.

The craft landed with almost impossible grace in St James's Park, though it brought down trees and fences by virtue of its enormous size.

"That's a stone's throw from Buckingham Palace," Jenny said to herself. "Just a couple hundred meters from the Queen, and no one's even come out to see what's going on."

"Some things are bigger than royalty and superstars," Jayesh said. "But there's nothing bigger than the gods and the demons and the Bleed."

"I suppose."

"We need to move faster. The sooner my god is released, the sooner this will be over."

He was virtually dragging her now. Jenny dug her heels in. "Slow down."

He didn't.

Breathless, they reached the park and approached the enormous globe which still glowed brightly, turning murky night into daylight around it. Jenny tried again to pull back, and this time Jayesh's grip tightened and his manner became even more aggressive. His face, illuminated by the globe, bore an expression of dogged determination. No matter how much she protested, he wasn't listening.

"Wait. This doesn't make sense."

"It'll all become clear."

"My dad knew about Thirnas, but he didn't say anything about other gods arriving."

"Your father was a fool."

Jenny lashed out at him. "Let me go. Fuck you and your god."

"No, fuck you and *your* god."

Tired of her resistance, Jayesh punched her in the face and knocked her out cold.

Seconds later, Jenny came around. She was being pulled along by Jayesh now, her dragging heels carving lines in the grass, and though she tried again to fight, it was too late.

He hauled her up to her feet then slammed her palms against the side of the orb and threw his body against hers, pushing her hard against its surface. Rivers of light ran from her fingertips, dancing around the sphere and quickly encircling it, increasing in brightness until she could no longer bear to look, until the entire world was searing white and had lost all form and focus.

24

The Moon

DAY THREE / 6:46 PM

"I'm breathing normally." The surprise of that was enough to overcome vertigo. She undid her seatbelt. She had to pull herself through the broken-out window. "It's not freezing, either." She was looking around. It was no longer pitch black, which made about as much sense as her being able to take in oxygen without her helmet. She turned the dial on her chest to shut off the air to make sure that she wasn't somehow still benefitting from the flow. "Shit." She raced back to the other side of the mower. "Sam, Derrick, help me!" She pulled Juan out.

"What are you doing?" Sam asked through tear-streaked eyes.

"There's air—somehow there's air. We need to get them breathing!" Maddie put Juan gently down and had Tyler halfway through before Sam was next to her and helping.

Derrick was quick to join them, pulling his helmet off and getting to work. "Hasn't it been too long?" Derrick asked, though he was doing chest compressions on Juan and alternating with breaths.

Tyler was coughing before they even got him to the ground, he started to kick out with his legs and swing his arms wildly. Maddie held Sam back. "He'll be all right soon."

"Sam, help…I'm getting woozy."

Sam got down by Juan's head and was getting ready to breathe for him like they'd all been taught in their advanced first-aid classes.

"Gonna need to take off your helmet first, sis."

"Right." She couldn't keep her eyes off

of Tyler, whom Maddie was now checking over.

"Stay still, chowder-head. I need to see if you've broken anything," Maddie told him forcefully.

"Why is my girlfriend kissing my gay friend?"

"The spin down must have mixed your brains up," Maddie told him

"No, that's normal," Derrick said in between compressions. "Come on, Juan." Derrick had studied hard in his classes and still, he knew that under the best of circumstances, the success rate of CPR was below fifty percent. But Juan was young and not likely to be suffering any heart disease. His arms burned and he'd still not fully recovered from the ride down. Sam was close to passing out; there was enough oxygen to breathe but possibly not enough to share.

"Maddie, you're up," Derrick ordered.

Sam fell away as Maddie moved in. Two breaths later, Juan sputtered and coughed.

"I do all the heavy lifting, and you get the glory." Sam had her hands on her knees and was watching.

"I've got the touch. Now go, make sure your boyfriend hasn't broken anything." Maddie sat down slowly on her ass. There was not one part of her that could believe they'd all made it. She looked up and over to see Sandra standing next to the mower, her helmet still on, watching them all. "You realize we can breathe, right?" Maddie said.

"And are you sure it's safe to do so?"

"So there's fear in you that the air might not be safe, but you haven't said one word to your kids? You seem perfectly fine with letting them be test subjects. Are you sure they're yours? Even if this is poisonous," Maddie inhaled deeply, "you're going to run out of O2 soon enough. What difference does it make?" She caught sight as Sandra quickly looked to a discarded helmet. "Cold as ice, aren't you? Just gonna take all of our packs, if that's the case. Damn. Not sure how semen survived in that frozen wasteland between your legs. But I guess there's cryogenics, so what do I know." Maddie laughed. "Still, though, how are you planning on getting out of this crater? It's eight miles up and nearly vertical in some spots. I guess that's the problem we're all facing, isn't it?"

Sam was watching her mother and could only shake her head. "Fine," Sandra answered. "I don't need your condemnation." She removed her helmet. "This shouldn't be," she said after taking a few tentative breaths.

"Is it possible the air the towers are

producing settles here?" Derrick asked.

"Possible, not probable. You're fine," Maddie told Juan after she checked him out. She stood up and went over to the popping and groaning mower. "I'm going to go out on a limb and say we're not going to take this out of here."

The adrenaline of having survived the plummet was beginning to wear off, and the reality of just exactly where they were was settling in. No radio to communicate with any of the bases that survived, no chance of escaping their vast prison, and what rations they did have were scattered for miles.

"First order of business should be looking for some of the water jugs and food packets," Maddie said. Though, given the condition of the mower, she didn't think it likely that the water had survived. The food should be all right if they could find it, but without liquids, they weren't going to last long, air or no air.

"I'm the senior person here, I'll be the one that issues the orders." Sandra looked at the group.

"I have no desire to get into a pissing contest with you, especially since we're not going to want to get dehydrated. Lead away," Maddie smirked.

"Right then." Sandra was taken aback;

she'd been expecting a fight, and when it didn't materialize, she wasn't quite as sure as to the direction she should take. "All right, all of you go look for food and water."

"And you?" Maddie asked.

"Someone has to stay behind."

"For what reason? No one's going to look for us here, that's if they even think we might have escaped the blast. And in any case, they'll be dealing with any number of emergencies now that power has been cut. Help isn't coming. If we're going to get out of here, it's going to be up to us—up to all of us. I'm not sure why I'm saying this because you've already shown me your true colors and most of them are black, but when we leave to look, there's a good chance we won't be able to find our way back. It's light down here, but we still can't see more than fifty feet ahead. I mean, if you'd rather stay here on your own, it's not going to hurt my feelings. Kids…grab anything worth salvaging." Maddie bent over and grabbed her helmet. She rooted around in the skeletal frame before tossing a handful of protein bars around.

"What about the packs?" Tyler was holding up two of them.

Maddie fairly growled at the kid; he looked confused but put them down. She didn't want to take the extra weight on the scavenging raid. She'd lied to Sandra about not coming back to the mower; it was the only landmark they had and would become their base of operations, especially since she'd put a miniature transponder on it and getting back to it would be as easy as following her watch display. She couldn't leave Sandra alone with the packs—that might become too much of a temptation to the woman.

"Eat up!" She triumphantly ripped the package open and took a bite, hopefully diverting Sandra's attention. "Just like my grandma used to make," she grimaced.

"Your grandma fried plastic?" Tyler had also taken a bite; his nose wrinkled and the sides of his mouth were downturned.

Maddie again shook her head when she noticed Sandra pocket one of the bars and open another. The situation they were in was bad enough, but it seemed to her as if Sandra was determined to kill them quicker. The first mile was easy enough. The terrain was flat and the direction they needed to go was littered with shiny pieces of mower parts, but as of yet, not one was of any use to them.

"This would make a good weapon." Tyler had picked up a baton-sized piece of the frame which, because of the way it had broken off, was sharp at one end.

"Who are you planning on using that on? All the moon dragons were killed off before we landed." Derrick trudged on.

"You never know...one of them could have survived." Tyler fastened the short sword to his belt.

"A jug!" Sam cried out, from a few feet ahead. "Oh," she amended when she got close enough to realize it had been completely crushed. A split on the bottom had emptied all of its precious commodity onto the thirsty ground, which had eagerly swallowed it up. The terrain had started to elevate, and walking became more difficult as they were coming across a field of loose rocks and scree.

"Be careful; you can twist an ankle easily on this," Maddie warned.

"Yes, it would be a shame to die here with a boo-boo ankle," Sandra said sourly.

Maddie sidled up close to Sandra. "We all realize this situation is dire. How about putting on a brave face for the kids...you remember them, right?"

"Fuck off, Maddie."

"Super helpful." She walked off to be closer to Juan, who was having a difficult go of it. She'd just noticed that he was wearing foam slippers, the kind only worn before heading to bed.

"Sure wouldn't mind finding my pack; I've got boots in there," he told her when he saw her looking down at his feet. By the time they moved past the large debris field, he was walking with a pronounced limp, and when they finally came to the point where she could reach out with her arm and touch the side of the crater wall, she knew he'd never be able to climb it—not with that footwear. "Who am I kidding? Without ropes and crampons, none of us are getting up this thing." She spoke softly so as to not be overheard, but Derrick was close and astute enough to realize the predicament they were in.

"This thing has a circumference of more than fifteen hundred miles. Stands to reason that there must be a more accessible climb somewhere."

"That your attempt at humor?" Maddie asked.

"Little bit." He sat down.

Sandra grunted.

Their quest had been less than successful, having only come across four prepackaged meals and no water.

"Headaches are going to settle in soon." Derrick was referring to the first signs of dehydration. "Especially if we keep walking around."

"Not sure what choices we have. The

only chance we have is to go up and out and get to a base."

"You realize that the closest base to this crater is over a hundred miles, right?"

"I know."

"And even if we send one person up with all the O2 tanks, it won't be enough."

"I know that, too. But giving up isn't really on my agenda today."

"Then we should probably go back and collect up the packs. Then I'll climb it," he said after a moment of reflection.

"You want to be the one to play hero?" Maddie asked.

"Not really, but I'm not letting my sister go, my mom won't go, Tyler will only get lost or fall, and Juan is injured."

"And me?"

"Not to be mean, Maddie, but I'm half your age."

"I'm in my thirties, junior, not dead."

"Okay, here's a better argument."

"I'm listening."

"The workout facility has a wall that simulates rock climbing."

"We have a gym?"

"Exactly my point," he smiled at her. "But I love climbing that thing. I pretend I'm on a mountain on Earth. It's limited, but of us all, I'm the only one that has any experience climbing sheer faces."

"Derrick, this is eight miles up, not, what? Fifteen, twenty feet of handholds? Going to bet there are belaying ropes and pins on your rock wall as well as a mat at the bottom. How many times have you slipped only to be saved by that safety harness?"

Derrick let his head hang down. "You just said we're not giving up."

"We're not. But we have to be smart about this. I'm going to do it."

"Maddie, if you go, you're leaving my mother in charge."

"You and your sister are going to have to take control. You can do it."

"I don't want to be defeatist, I don't. But I would rather we were all together...you know...when it happens," he said haltingly, doing his best to hold back the tears that threatened to emerge.

"It hasn't happened until it's happened—you hear me? I've been in some pretty rough scrapes in my life, and I'm still here. This is just one more challenge. Okay?" She reached down and raised his chin. "You hear me?"

"I do." He had a tough time looking her in the eyes.

"Get up. Let's go back and get the packs. Okay, everyone!" she yelled out. "Saddle up. We're heading back!" Her voice sounded flat, like she was yelling into a dampening snowstorm.

There hadn't been an abundance of hope when they'd set out, but what little they'd been able to muster had been quelled. The walk back looked more like that of a funeral procession, except for Tyler, who either hadn't or didn't want to grasp the severity of the situation. He was parrying his sword with an unseen enemy. Maddie was impressed with his footwork, and it seemed to be at least lifting the spirits of Sam, and maybe, after all, that was really what he was actually trying to do.

Derrick had wandered a few feet off to the side and was studying the ground.

"Not too far," Maddie told him.

"You should come here." He hadn't looked up.

Maddie couldn't help but be slightly perturbed; they were running out of time, and there was none to spare to look at cool moon rocks. "It had better be a freshwater spring," she growled.

"Umm, not quite." He had gotten down on his haunches and splayed his hand out on the ground.

"What is that?" Maddie asked, looking down.

"I mean, it sort of looks like a bear paw print, smaller, maybe, and too elongated, but the toes and the claw indentations..." Derrick looked up to gauge Maddie's response.

"Nah...you're just responding to the bleak situation," Maddie responded.

"You know, at first, I would have thought the same thing, pareidolia. But umm..." He pointed behind him. There was a long line of prints that paralleled their trek. "That's a lot of random."

"What the fu...? Tyler, Sam, stop screwing around. Get over here and stay close." Juan, who had been lagging by a few feet, had caught up.

"Taking a break? I'm all for it." He sat down. "My feet hurt so bad." The bottoms of his footwear were shredded, and inside, there was a fine coating of blood and fluid from the many broken blisters.

"And me? Do you want me to stay close?" Sandra asked.

"You? No, go explore," Maddie told her.

"What's so interesting that we decided to stop?" The other woman came over. "What the hell is that!?" she screamed.

"I don't know, but if you keep yelling like that, I'm sure we'll find out soon enough."

"Something is here with us." Derrick stood and looked around. He couldn't see anything, but the hairs standing up on the back of his neck were quite explicit in letting him know that though he couldn't see anything, they were indeed being watched.

"M...moon dragon?" Tyler whispered to the group.

Derrick wanted to tell him not to be foolish, but that was a good a guess as any.

"How is that even possible? Are they... maybe just leftover relics from some other time? Like, maybe the Russians sent up a circus bear or something?" Tyler asked.

"I was hoping the same thing," Derrick said. "Then, I saw where one paw had overlaid one of our footprints."

"This is madness. Nothing can survive out here. We know there is no other life on the moon," Sandra said. "There has to be another explanation."

"Go out there and tell it that it doesn't exist; let us know how it goes." Maddie kept a watchful eye out. As if the prospect of dying from lack of water and food wasn't enough, they had another life form to contend with, and they had no idea of its intentions. Was it friendly or shy? Or was it savage...stalking its prey before it pounced?

"Maddie, if there is something out here, doesn't it stand to reason that it has to drink water? That it has to eat something?"

Derrick asked.

Maddie didn't give her first answer, which revolved around them being the something it ate, but it did stand to reason that, before they had come down here, it had to have eaten something, and it was unlikely that whatever it was, was only preying on lost people from the moon colony. If people had started going missing, news of that would have gotten around, and fast.

"Want to know what else stands to reason?" she started.

Derrick nodded. "That if there's one, then there's more."

"I didn't think of that."

"Still, though, it makes sense to follow the tracks back, see if we can get some water."

"You want to follow this thing back? Are you insane?" Sandra asked.

"I'm listening to all the wonderful options you've been throwing out there, so I hear what you're saying, but I don't care." Maddie dismissed the woman. "You can stay here and the rest of us will check it out."

"That might be for the best," Sandra replied.

"Mom, you realize that predators usually go after the easiest prey and generally, that's the ones that are alone, right?" Derrick asked.

"I suppose we should stick together. Safety in numbers, and all." Sandra looked at the group, not in the slightest apologetic that she'd once again thought of her safety over the others.

"Why does she keep looking at my feet?" Juan asked.

"She's sizing up your injury," Tyler said. "Figures if the shit goes down, you'll be the one separated and sacrificed from the herd."

"Is that true, Mrs. Morrison?" Juan asked.

Maddie was impressed at Tyler's ability to read others; it was a good chance his goofball routine was just that, a routine.

"It makes sense that if we are attacked, it will be because they smell the blood of an injured person."

"I have blisters; I'm hardly on my last legs."

"We'll see. Lead on." Sandra motioned for Maddie to go ahead.

"Maybe don't you think we should go back to the mower and get whatever we can?" Tyler was holding his weapon up.

"Yeah, that might be for the best," Maddie replied.

The group stayed close, all heads were

on swivels as they looked through the murk. More than once they stopped as someone hissed that they'd seen something moving.

"Oh, no," Sam said when they got back to the mower. There had not been much left when they'd ventured out save the frame, and in some places that had been warped by the ride down into the crater and the multiple collisions it had suffered. But what they were looking at now was a jumbled pile of scrap. The heavy aluminum had been bent and folded in numerous places. Whatever had done the damage had been more powerful than a bear, and now Tyler's weapon looked to be no more than a sharp stick to prod a wild beast with. He seemed to know it as well as he examined the frame and then frowned at his mighty sword.

Derrick, undeterred, grabbed a broken bit of metal. It wasn't sharp, but it would make a good club. Everyone rooted around until they found something that could be used, except for Sandra.

"Spill it, why aren't you looking for something to use as a weapon? You figure everyone is just going to make a human shield for you?" Maddie asked.

"I prefer weaponry from this century, as opposed to that of the caveman." Sandra produced a pistol from her uniform pocket.

Maddie was warring with punching Sandra or hugging her, instead, she nodded and followed the tracks that led into the interior of the crater.

"Maddie, you saw the mower, right?" Derrick caught up to her.

"It's wary of us." She wasn't sure of her own words. "It was a display of power, an attempt to ward us off, like a silverback gorilla destroying a camp."

"But, we're following it to its home."

"If we run, it will know we're scared. That's the worst thing we could do."

"You have no idea if that's true. We can't assume a creature we didn't even know existed an hour ago will behave like anything from Earth."

"Don't I? Whatever it is has to be from Earth originally. This is something from the Chinese or maybe the Russians — an experiment of some sort. They conducted it here because of the inherent dangers it would have posed on Earth. Shit, this could be from the States, for all we know."

"So, an experiment so dangerous that it had to be clandestinely performed on the dark side of the moon, in a virtual prison cell with walls eight miles high. Maddie, I was worried before, but I'm terrified now." Derrick grabbed her arm.

"Listen to me, Derrick, I'm not going to

tell you everything is going to be all right. I have no idea if that's the case. Right now we're in up to our necks and the water is still flowing. We have to show this thing we're in charge like animal trainers used to do with tigers, bears, and elephants, any of which could kill a person with hardly a flick. We'll use our brains."

"Not to play devil's advocate, but what if it's smarter than us? I mean, look." Derrick pointed to Tyler, who was periodically stabbing at the ground with flourish.

"Don't underestimate him; he'll defend your sister to the end."

They'd walked for over an hour, hadn't seen or heard anything out of the ordinary the entire time. The group was beginning to tire, and Juan was miserable, having a difficult time keeping up.

"Everyone good with calling it a day?" Maddie asked. "We'll make camp here."

"A fire sure would be nice." Sam picked an area to sit down. "I saw a picture of a family camping once. They were sitting on logs, had a huge fire in a stone pit...they were all laughing. Looked like they were having a great time. This ain't that," she lamented.

"But we do have s'mores-flavored protein bars." Tyler pulled one out of his pocket, which he handed over to Sam.

"It's salmon flavored, you dolt." She laughed and tossed it at his head. "No, wait, give that back, I'll eat it." Tyler sat down next to her and they shared the bar.

"We're going to need to set up a guard duty rotation," Maddie said.

"Good, you do that," Sandra said.

"I take it you're not planning on taking part?"

"Oh heavens, no. I'll delegate that to my subordinates."

"I wish you and your husband had switched spots; he and I could have worked together."

"Well, I guess it's unfortunate then that he isn't here." Sandra had lain down and was doing her best to find some semblance of comfort. Maddie was going to make sure that, during her shift, each time she walked past Sandra, she would kick up as much dust around the sleeping woman's face that it could become possible she'd suffocate.

"I don't want to stay here too long. We'll each patrol for an hour, tight circles around the group. Do not wander."

"Maddie, I have to take care of some business." Tyler looked uncomfortable.

"What is wrong with you?" she asked.

Tyler got up close to her ear. "I have to take a huge Derrick."

"A what?"

"A huge Derrick and wipe my Juan."

"I don't get it. Spit it out, boy."

"One of those bars did something to me; I have some bung juice needs to be dropped off."

"Gawd, I hate teenagers. Take Juan with you and stay close enough I can see you." She watched the boys travel out. "Sandra, I'd like to borrow the gun while I'm on watch."

"Not a chance." Sandra's eyes stayed closed as she responded.

Maddie stood, wanting to yell at the boys that they'd gone far enough. She could barely see them as it was. But she was fearful of alerting anything nearby. Tiny hairs on the back of her neck were rising, a flash of goosebumps traveled down the length of her arms. She wanted to believe she was imagining the sensation that she was being watched. "It's paranoia, Maddie, don't let it overtake you," she whispered. She looked around to be sure; when she came back to where Derrick and Juan had gone, alarm fired a hot shot of adrenaline through her system. She couldn't see them anymore. "This is the group I'm stuck with." She debated chasing them down or staying put. Derrick and Sam looked to be sleeping, and she didn't want to disturb them. Sandra was not going to help, so if she left they would be completely unguarded.

There was a loud, heavy thump and an otherworldly scream off to her right. She didn't have to worry about anyone sleeping anymore. Juan was running back toward her, he kept looking over his shoulder and was urging his friend to hurry up. For his part, Tyler was doing his best to make speed, but with his pants down around his ankles, he was not having much success.

"What's going on?" Sam was next to Maddie, her small knife-like weapon in her hand. "Why are Tyler's pants down?"

Maddie flashed back to a book she'd been reading. It was a cringe-worthy, comical scene in a zombie book. One of the characters had quite literally been caught with his pants down. *Cash something*, she thought his name was. He'd died a horrific death, but that was in the pages of a horror novel; this was real, and infinitely less humorous and more terrifying. Sandra was up and had the gun pointed directly at Tyler.

25

Divergent Paths

Arridon grabbed his axe from where it rested on the floor, leaning against the pristine marble wall. With his other hand, he grabbed and tossed his sister's pitchfork to her. She caught it and spun the tined end outward towards the small group of followers threatening them. She tried to look fierce. In the back of the large room other followers backed away, wanting nothing to do with those who had decided on violence.

Their father turned to the double doors they'd entered through and saw two burly men with swords. The guards that Pontifex Andela had summoned to protect them were now standing at their backs, preventing them from leaving. They had firm faces, set with the intention to do harm. Though, to Arridon, they seemed a bit afraid, based on how the tips of their swords wobbled, and how their eyes shifted back and forth between their potential victims. Perhaps their resolve lacked.

Gray lifted their mother's pistol slightly at the two sword-wielding men as Arridon and Thistle warded the crowd away with their axe and pitchfork. Six—no, seven—servants of the Many stepped forward, blades in hand.

"Come any closer, and I'll split you in half," Arridon threatened them. He debated threatening them with his imaginary god's magic, but discarded the idea.

"You don't understand," the man with the wild eyes said, taking another step forward. "Our stories say you are the harbingers of the end times. What else matters than stopping that prophecy? We could save the lives of everyone in the Endless City and all the towns and villages south of it. Hundreds of thousands of lives for what? In exchange for just one of you, and a few of us?"

"One of us?" Thistle asked, lifting her pitchfork a bit higher.

"Four eyes find it," he said. "Only you two have golden eyes. If one of you is killed, the prophecy cannot be fulfilled."

"Hogwash," Pontifex Andela said, stepping forward to place her body in the center of the standoff. "The wheels are already in motion. That they appeared before us is enough. The Bleed has arrived; all is over, save for the waiting. Spilling their blood will change nothing."

"Your opinion is noted, Pontifex, but your time as a leader is over, is it not? You have led us to the moment of our doom, thank you very much. The Bleed is here, and all your words are for naught. Step aside, and let us try to avert the apocalypse." He lifted the knife.

That's how they stood for what seemed an eternity.

Arridon's pulse beat so fast he couldn't tell where one thump ended and the next began. He licked his lips with a dry tongue and swallowed, waiting for the moment someone would make a move...attack, take charge, back off...anything.

The wild eyed man jumped forward,

lunging with the blade and sinking it into the chest of the robed Pontifex. She cried out in shock and pain, grabbing her attacker with both arms, but the cards had been dealt for her. She collapsed to the tiled floor of her place of worship, dragging the man down atop her.

Chaos exploded in every direction.

Gray took his chances with the guards at the door. Arridon heard and felt two blasts from the god-pistol. As two men cried out in pain and fell to the floor, the rest of the murderous followers rushed into the small passage the family occupied.

Arridon acted before he could think and allowed his instincts to guide him. He'd never be the same again.

He swung his axe down onto the back of the man who'd stabbed the poor Pontifex. Strong like a sailor, his wiry muscles gave him enough strength to bury the entire axe head into the man's spine, severing it with a wet crunch. He watched as blood sprayed, the knife-wielder's eyes went empty, and as his body went limp. The man fell over, and the weight of his undoing nearly wrenched the handle of the weapon out of Arridon's hand. It came free from the corpse with the same wet crunch.

Heart set afire, Arridon looked to his sister, who looked on in shock. Her shock evaporated as another crazed follower dove forward at her, holding his own sharp knife. He slashed the air, near her face, seeking to rend her flesh. She stumbled a step back, then two, then planted her feet and drove the pitchfork forward as one of his slashes sent him a bit off balance. She impaled the man just below the ribs with all four sharp iron tines. His forward energy deflated and he went down hard, taking the pitchfork from Thistle's hands, leaving her defenseless.

"Step away!" their father screamed. "Don't touch the blood!"

Arridon did that, and lifted the axe, placing the head of the weapon up in a threatening angle. He waved it back and forth, sending errant droplets in both directions. As he did that, Thistle rolled her victim over and yanked her pitchfork free. She brandished it, and the rush of followers who had wanted to kill them halted in their tracks.

"Numbers are different now," Arridon said. "We took four of yours. Only three of you left. Back off, or you'll die under these stars and never see your final dawn."

"Burke," Gray yelled, looking around for the disciple that had led them to the temple.

"Right here," the bald man said from his

crouch near the floor. He was hunched over the unconscious body of a zealot Arridon hadn't seen sneak in close. The disciple stood, and shook his head in disgusted sadness. "I'm sorry about this."

"I don't care about your fucking sorrow. Can you take us to the wall and transport us through? Right now?" Gray asked.

"My magic will not fail you. I'm ready to go."

With delicate steps, Gray walked over the bleeding guards and pulled open one of the mahogany doors. One of the men coughed, and sent out a spray of blood across the floor. The older man yanked his booted foot away from the red stream on the white stone and paused, watching as the man breathed his last.

"If any of you follow us, we'll kill you," Gray said. "Let's go."

Arridon and Thistle backed away from the last of their attackers, and slipped out the door into the village surrounding the Temple of the Many. Gray stepped through the door, holding it open with one hand, gun raised in the other.

"Burke," he asked.

The disciple picked up the leather backpack filled with food and water and threw it over his shoulders. He walked out the door without a word, and left his people behind.

Gray let the heavy wooden door close.

"Everyone okay?" Arridon asked as they entered the night.

"Yes," his dad answered.

"I'm okay," Thistle said.

"Burke, are you okay?" Arridon asked the robed man as he walked with a hurried pace ahead of them. Their guide stopped on the small bridge that crossed the moat-lake around the temple. He turned, and wiped tears from both cheeks. His eyes were reddened and his lips trembled. He tried to smile, but couldn't.

Arridon went to him on the bridge and gave him a hug. Thistle joined, and they stayed like that until Gray walked over the bridge past them, heading west in the direction of Citadel Frost.

The people of the Many watched them depart and readied for the approach of the end of their existence as they knew it.

"Fishbowls," Burke said as they approached the sheer cliff wall of the citadel. "The gods used to keep fish in glass bowls as pets, or decorations. The fish would swim in circles all day and night, doing their rounds against transparent walls that encompassed their entire world."

"Just like these walls, eh?" Arridon said.

"We might as well have gills. It's not as claustrophobic in the larger citadels or in the city. Walls fade into the distance, or are obscured by the massive buildings," Burke explained.

"Are there exits to this citadel?" Gray asked. "Or only by the spell?"

"There are gates to the north and west. We're in between them."

"Can the demons breach the gates?" Arridon asked.

"I don't think so. The magic of the walls is still active, and I know the gods built the city with the defense of it in mind, should the Bleed return. As long as no one opens the gate from the inside, or is hit with infected blood, the citadel will hold until the demons find a way over the wall. The people of the temples could survive inside for years."

"Good to know. Get us through please," Gray said.

"As you wish," Burke said, and the air grew thin. With intonations, and precise movements, the same as his performance in the marketplace of the Channel, he began again the spell he used to make the passage through the magical wall. Within moments, the tunnel appeared through the thick wall, revealing a street with a stone and wood building that disappeared into the sky opposite.

"Follow us," Gray said to him as they reached the portal. "I'd like you to come. We may need passage through the walls of Citadel Frost if the gates there are sealed."

Burke nodded, and Gray led them into the spell's passage.

The spell's power triggered another bout of delirium for the travelers. Time and space and their ability to comprehend it bent to the will of the magic in Burke's spell, and to the magic inherent in the god-made wall. They entered the tunnel of one mind, coherent and aware, and exited in a different way: peaceful, rested, no longer fraught with the intense sense of peril that had infected them.

Like being born again, they stood in the streets of a foreign land, the Endless City, and they looked around with the eyes of babes.

"Well shit," Arridon said under his breath as he took in the majestic splendor of the gate city region of the Endless City.

Nothing their father could've said would've properly prepared Thistle or Arridon for the visual immensity of the buildings in front of them. For a thousand yards in every direction, all they could see were square and rectangular constructions that erupted from the flat stone and grass of the city's surface and shot into the sky like teeth in the mouth of a world-sized giant. Each story marked with intricate stonework, level upon level of windows and terraces, the buildings rose thirty, forty, a hundred stories up, disappearing into the night sky, only visible by the pins of light coming from the fires of those who lived in the upper stories of the towers. Deep into the city, auras of lights in a dozen colors radiated into the sky from building peaks like wildfires made of magic.

A hundred thousand lights lit up the gargantuan structures, and together those fires illuminated the smooth city streets with a soft ember glow. As the buildings faded into the distance, shrinking away until they disappeared into the night, the lights also became less frequent, but the crushing weight of the sheer size of the city couldn't be ignored, or understated.

Scuttling about in the dim light were the citizens of the towers and buildings. They went from building to building, looking over their shoulders with each step and giving the visitors a wide berth. Demons may not be about, but fear of them coated everything and hung in the humid air.

"You can walk west for a month and not

reach the boundaries of the Endless City," Burke said as he watched the people run about, "that is," he smiled, "if you aren't eaten by whatever roams the ruins that deep."

"What's to the north?" Thistle asked.

"The Bay of Swords. About a day or two's solid walk from here. The city hugs the water the entire coast, but doesn't go out onto the peninsula. However, despite the cold, there are settlements out there, too. A large kingdom, in fact."

"Fantastic," Gray said. "Maybe we'll visit after the Bleed turns its people into demons. The streets are quiet here. Let's move while it stays that way. The Bleed could be upon us at any time."

"Truth," Burke agreed.

They paused their conversations as six riders atop four-legged beasts the likes of which the brother and sister had never seen thundered down the wide street in their direction. As tall as Arridon, and a thousand pounds apiece, the thinly coated, earthen-colored beasts of burden carried their armored, lance-wielding riders with no effort, twice as fast as a man could run. They had fierce, dark eyes and flared nostrils.

"Here, here," Gray called out to them, and they slowed. "These are horses. These are the animals the pistol is named after," he said to his kids.

"Be gone to shelter, citizen. Evil wreaks havoc this night," a female knight said to him. She flipped open her faceplate, revealing a dark and beautiful face. Her eyes reflected the faint moonlight like discs of silver. The blood of the gods ran in her veins.

Arridon thought she was perfect.

One of the animals huffed and snorted.

"We are aware. The Bleed has won the war at the world's edge against the gods. Have you seen the monsters? Are they near and close?"

The knights on the strange horse creatures circled them. Both man and animal were agitated by the state of the world. The female knight spoke again.

"Aye. Tooth and claw are near to us. No more than a ten minute walk to the south. They poured through the Channel in a river of blood at dusk and are taking the gate cities one by one. The screams are…We retreat to shut our tower kingdom's doors. We shall weather this storm."

"What's your name?" Gray asked her.

"Duchess Del'Zovo. Who asks?"

"Gray, father of Arridon and Thistle of House Frost. I wish you luck, Duchess. Avoid touching all blood, and you shall fare better than those who do not."

"Thank you, Gray, father of Arridon and Thistle Frost. Farewell," she said, then flipped down her steel visor. With a snap of the reins, the horses galloped off into the city night, heading north for a keep or tower.

"You put your pistol away?" Burke asked Gray as he stroked the fledgling stubble on his shaved head.

"Don't reveal what you possess unless you have to?" Gray supposed. "Also, don't appear threatening to people who know how to fight better than you. Kids, are you ready to run? We're going to have to run for as long as we can. If they're as close as those knights said, we have to get distance."

"I think I ate too much to run," Arridon said, rubbing his belly. When his father gave him a dirty look he laughed. "Kidding, dad."

"Drink some water, and let's get going," Gray said.

By the time the cork had been pressed back into the skin, the sounds of the screaming echoed to the canyons they stood in. Underneath that were the sounds of forced chanting and crying.

They ran for their lives.

"Do you remember being a little kid?" Arridon asked his sister as they took a break from running to walk awhile. As he spoke, he kept his head tilted upward, staring up into the forest of massive buildings that had no end. Ten paces ahead, their father and Burke walked, talking about something and sharing a laugh about it.

The day didn't seem so terrifying at the moment.

"Some. Mostly I remember being hungry and trying to steal fish from the market down at the docks."

"Oh man, I remember doing that too. What I was getting at, is do you remember being little, and walking amongst the adults? The men dad used to hang out with? Fisherman and loggers he used to be friends with?"

"They were so tall."

"I can't help but think of that now," Arridon said, pointing his axe up at the soaring, god-made buildings that dominated the world in every direction. "I feel like the tiniest child walking amongst the greatest giants right now. This place is... unbelievable. If I wasn't seeing it with my own eyes, I'd never believe anyone telling me about it."

"And you've been here before. Dad said you were born in Citadel Frost," Thistle said, shifting her pitchfork to the other hand. "That's unbelievable."

"Crazy, right?"

They kept on walking in silence through the abandoned city with its cloud scraping edifices. They listened to Burke discuss pedantic details about his belief in the Many with their father for hundreds of yards. Time enough to pass two stone buildings with stained glass windows three times as tall as Arridon. The two structures were linked by an arched stone bridge ten stories above the street.

"Wow," Arridon said, pointing ahead. "I thought that was the ground ahead, but it's a wall we're walking towards. It's getting higher."

"Oh wow," Thistle said, realizing the street ahead wasn't street surface; it was a horizon-wide wall, topped with a dull metallic rim. The faint blue light of dawn's approach in the sky gave them a tiny bit of perspective, allowing them to realize the full scale of what they saw.

"That's Citadel Frost," their dad said. "Couple miles up. If we follow this street we'll arrive at the main eastern gate. Hopefully the doors are open."

"I can pass us through the wall with my spell," Burke said. "The variant I know is a universal breach."

"A what?" Arridon asked.

"I can get us through any of the city's walls with it," Burke explained. "Unless there's a specific counter-ward incantation, in which case, we're going to have to use a physical gate or door that hasn't been barred shut with a spell."

"I didn't understand any of that," Thistle said. "But I will cross my fingers and hope your spell works."

Burke chuckled and turned back to Gray as they walked. "Does Citadel Frost house a Thaumaturgical Turbine?"

"One of three in the entire Endless City, as I was told. It is near the top of the clock tower, where we are headed," their dad answered. "Though I doubt it's powered at this point."

"Oh I don't know about that," Burke said. "God-tech and magic are a hardy mix. Explorers are always returning with functioning god-tech. I'm hopeful. If we can reach the turbine, and have your children pass through it, we'd be better off."

"Can you stop volunteering us for dangerous tasks?" Arridon said. "What the hell does a 'turgid turbine' do, anyway?"

"A *Thaumaturgical* Turbine is magical

machine that accelerates and enhances the powers someone has. All gods have some kind of latent ability, and the turbines awake those powers, and amplify them," Gray explained.

"And you think that'll…what?" Thistle asked her dad. "Give Arridon the cock-shrinking powers he's always coveted?"

"Possibly," Gray said as they passed another massive building, this one made of glass and steel, with arches like sunlight and leaves.

"This magical machine…it'll work on us because we're half-gods?" Arridon asked.

"Allegedly not without risk. They didn't use it on their half-blooded children because there was great worry their weaker half couldn't contain the powers the turbines unleashed. However, your mother maintained that they didn't use it on mixed blood children because they wanted to control who had powers. With the gifts your mother had, I suspect you both will awaken some impressive talents, especially for those with mixed blood."

The brother and sister exchanged excited looks and picked up the pace.

Behind them, something metallic fell to the ground with a hollow ring.

All four halted and spun, raising their weapons to defend against whatever made the noise. As before, Arridon felt his heartbeat explode in speed. His hands gripped the axe from their shed with ferocious strength. At his side, Thistle set her jaw, and prepared to stab anything that came near with her pitchfork.

"Run," their father said. "We're close."

"FILTHY HALFSIES!" a great and terrible voice screamed from the canyons between the buildings. The noise echoed up and down the streets of the great city, growing in power and distortion until it became a howl of anger and anguish.

"Sebastian?" Thistle said. "How?"

"MY LOVE," the voice called out in reply. "I CAME FOR MY KISS."

They ran. Thistle faster than them all, and for good reason.

"He died. I saw him get mauled," Arridon said as they ran.

"The dead may still be affected by the Bleed," Gray said, huffing and puffing.

As the four survivors sprinted as fast as they could down the street toward the insanely tall wall of Citadel Frost, the sounds of scraping claws and clopping hooves closed in behind them. Three hundred yards distant at first, then two hundred, and as they approached the three story tall arched gate into the citadel, the monsters growling and mewling at their heels were just a hundred yards away.

"WHY DO YOU RUN FROM ME, MY LOVE?" the thing that Sebastian had become bellowed. A scrape of a sword on cobblestone punctuated his question. The grind of the steel on stone sent shivers up and down their spines.

"The gate is ajar," Gray said with a grin. "Get through, and shut it from the inside!"

Arridon could see the split of light coming through the center of the doorway. There would be just enough room for them to slip through sideways, but that was it. Shutting the door after getting inside however…seemed impossible. The doors had to be thirty feet tall, and ten feet wide, and if they were made of anything durable, they'd each weigh as much as a sailboat. Arridon knew pushing them shut with brute strength would be impossible.

"Just run through," he hollered to the group. "They're too big to shut. We'll race them to the clock tower."

"It's *three miles* to the center of the citadel where the tower is!" their dad blurted, mostly out of breath. Something very close behind them skittered and laughed maniacally as it neared their feet. Gray turned and fired off a shot with the god pistol, triggering a yelp of pain.

Arridon didn't dare look back to see

what it was Gray had hit.

Perspective in the light of the rising sun, buried amongst the roots of the city as they were, was a strange thing. They ran forward until their lungs burned and ached, and when they had nothing left to give, the doors suddenly were upon them. The four ran to the gap, slowing only a small amount to approach it from the proper side and turn their bodies sideways to slip through.

The doors were as thick as Arridon's entire wingspan and took time to pass through; an eternity it seemed as the sounds of horror closed the distance at their backs. Burke was first through, then Arridon, then Thistle and finally their father. The older man had no sooner stepped into the space inside the walls when he threw a shoulder into the door, digging his heels in and pushing with all his strength. Despite the blatant futility of the task, Arridon dropped his axe on the ground and did the same, and soon after Thistle and Burke joined. The four grunted, giving their all, but moving the door was beyond them.

Burke stepped back and began to wave his hands in the air and chant at a rapid pace. The wind whipped up at their heels, and a surge of energy tore through the space, putting Arridon's short brown hair on end. The disciple pushed forward with his palms, aiming the wind at the door, adding the power of the skies to their push.

"Shove! Now!" he hollered at them.

They listened. The door moved forward —as improbable a task as Arridon could imagine—an inch, then two. He pushed harder, invigorated by the success and by the sound of Burke chanting in his strange language, stirring the wind to shove the door with them.

It began to close. The two foot gap halved, and then closed just as a pair of ten-jointed limbs burst through. The pallid, gelatinous arms swung at them like whips. The door refused to sever the wild tendrils of bone and skin, and one of the arms smashed into Gray's back, bouncing him off the door hard and sending him to the gate's hard, smooth, flagstone surface.

"Dad!" Arridon yelled. He abandoned trying to push the door and snatched his axe up. He swung it in a powerful, overhand arc at the base of the limb where it was jammed in the door. The sharp blade of the axe bit into the rubbery flesh, and cracked the spindly bone at the center. A pair of mouths on the other side of the door cried out in anguish, then laughed in glee as Arridon chopped the limb again, then again before it fell to the group, twitching and writhing. As it fell, the other limb turned on him, striking in his direction, knocking the axe from his hands.

The sound of Thistle's pitchfork hitting the door rang out as if a bell had been struck. She'd impaled the snapping, whipping limb on her weapon, holding it fast. It tried to snap and strike, but she held it firm.

"Well chop the damn thing off, idiot," she said to him as Arridon stood there.

He grabbed his axe and did just that with a single powerful swing. The door closed with the sound stone on stone.

Burke ended his incantation, and the winds whipping at the air died down, and went still. He sat on the ground hard, covered in sweat, out of breath, and spent. As he tried to gather himself, the brother and sister went to their father where he rolled on the ground, groaning. He sat up with their help, but couldn't bend easily.

"Can you walk?" Thistle asked.

"I think so. We need to get to there," he said, pointing at the center of the citadel grounds.

Although about the same size across as the Citadel of Temples, Citadel Frost's circular area was different in every way. Rather than a large open space at the center, ringed by small settlements hundreds of yards apart, the structures of House Frost began at the center of the grounds, and grew outward from there. The clock tower her father spoke of, and pointed to, was the largest building. Fifty stories tall at least, made of brown and black stone and designed in a baroque, gargoyle-covered style. It dominated over twenty or thirty similarly styled buildings of lesser height.

To the north, rather than a complete wall, the citadel instead ran into the shores of a lake, giving the massive noble palace an even larger feel, and one direction that was fully invulnerable. A village of thirty houses clustered there, tiny by comparison. The modest buildings there still reached up three to five stories, plus the sloped roofs crowning them.

"We have to move," Gray said. "Help me up."

"To the turbines in the tower? Is that the plan?" Thistle asked him.

"Yes, then to the portal in the clockworks, which should activate when you two approach it. Burke, thank you."

"Of course. I don't think I could do that again though. Or another spell. I need to eat, drink and rest."

"Eat and drink as we walk. You can rest when we're dead, or when we go through the portal, whichever happens first."

Sebastian dragged the tip of his blade across the surface of the door his small horde of mutants couldn't push open. The razor sharp tip — covered in human blood — left a gouge where it touched the door, and he haphazardly drew the shape of a single droplet of blood.

His master's signature.

At his feet and back, his retinue of monsters slithered and crawled, agitated by the door that stymied their hunt. Sebastian's malicious calm remained though, and he stepped away for a moment to plan for how to get through the doors to his prey. Inside his slit-visor helm, mounted to and a part of skull, he salivated. Where the spittle hit the blue stones of the castle's entrance, it sizzled and boiled with his rage.

He stepped away from the door, allowing his minions to rush in and press on the door, to no avail. He stalked around the street, going up and down the way, looking up and searching for a way to climb the sheer wall, but seeing nothing. Then... he saw the clearing of buildings to the north of the citadel's distant wall. The ground there was clear and flat, an opening too large to be a simple field, and too empty of trees to be a park.

"Water," Sebastian muttered, and then smiled. "I wonder, then, if that water enters the citadel? Let us swim," he said to his horde, and they issued forth from the door, streaming up the perimeter of the massive walled compound towards the lake Sebastian believed to be there.

26

London

When Jenny came around she was locked in a small, square room. She stood up and shook her head clear. There was a single barred window high on the opposite wall to a heavy-looking metal door. Daylight poured in. How long had she been unconscious? It felt like seconds, but the night had been pitch black when she'd been outside next to the second comet in St James's Park. She checked her phone. It was half-seven in the morning. The lock screen was clear: no missed calls or messages. Nothing from Dad. She leant against the wall and sobbed for him. He was dead; she knew it. She'd clung on to the vain hope he'd somehow escaped from their overrun flat, but the lack of any contact left her in no doubt he was gone forever. It didn't matter what he'd told her yesterday about her parentage, because he'd been right. He'd loved her and cared for her and provided for her since the day she'd been born. And yesterday he'd given his life to keep her safe.

Losing Dad made everything else pale into insignificance. The comets, the gods, Jayesh...the events of the last twenty-four hours seemed inconsequential in comparison to her loss.

Wait. Twenty-four hours?

She looked at the phone's lock screen again and checked herself. *Shit.* It said it was Sunday. Had she really been out of it for almost three days? It didn't seem possible. It felt like no time had passed at all. She looked down and realized that she was leaving wet footprints as she paced around the cell. Her clothes were still muddy and soaked from being dragged across St James's Park. As improbable as it seemed, the only conclusion she could reach was that the impact of touching the comet had somehow temporarily skewed her relationship with reality: three days for the rest of the world had passed in mere seconds for her. Right now, a rip in time felt like the least of her concerns; just another unwelcome complication she'd have to deal with.

She looked for somewhere to sit, but the cell was empty. She slid down into the corner opposite the door and tried to piece together everything she'd missed from news pages on her phone. And Jesus Christ, it looked like she'd missed a monumental few days. There had been so much news that most of what had happened on Friday and Saturday had already been bumped from the headlines. She had to search the individual players to join the dots.

Thirnas, it seemed, had been unilaterally vilified by the press, by world leaders, and also by the heads of every religion she could think of. She'd seen the first glimpses of that last night—no, two nights back—with the reactions in and around churches following her escape from the flat. She couldn't help thinking he'd brought it upon himself. God or no god, he was a cocky bastard. With hindsight, there'd been a certain inevitability to his rapid fall from grace after the arrogance of his very public arrival and his decision to tell the population of the planet he was their lord and savior. He'd misjudged the mood of more than seven billion people.

But the way the god had been swiftly written-off by everyone didn't ring true. Jenny thought there had to be more to it, and it didn't take her long to discover the reason. The second god she'd released (thanks to Jayesh) had appeared far more typical. A cliché. Flowing white robes, bright lights and hosts of angels. This god seemed to be the real deal (if you believed in that sort of thing, and judging from what she was reading, many billions of people clearly did). His message of peace, love and unification and his vociferous criticisms of Thirnas had clearly gone down well with the nervous masses.

She didn't get chance to look any further. She heard footsteps. They stopped outside the door. Jenny got to her feet and readied herself to fight, not that she had anything left to fight with. She braced herself as the door was pulled open, but decided immediately to comply with whatever she was ordered to do. The door opened and she saw Jayesh. There were around thirty blacksuit soldiers in the corridor behind him.

"It's time," he said.

"Time for what?" she asked. "More of your bullshit? Have you got your story figured out today?"

He shook his head. "You're a smart little bitch, I'll give you that. You've given me the run around and allowed your god to cause far too many complications. You backed the wrong one."

"I don't think so. My dad believed in Thirnas, so I believe in him too."

"Your dad's dead, remember? Anyway, none of that matters now, though. You're about to witness true divine power."

"Screw you, you dick."

He smirked. "Take her away."

The cell flooded with soldiers. They surrounded her and marched her out.

This place looked old. Steeped in history. Given where she'd been last night, it could have been anywhere—the Tower of London, Buckingham Palace, Westminster Abbey, the Houses of Parliament, St Paul's Cathedral, or any one of a hundred other historic buildings in the immediate vicinity. That, of course, was assuming she was still in London. She knew she could have been anywhere. She cursed herself for wasting time looking at the news. She could have checked where she was on Google Maps. The temptation to look now was strong, but she figured that any sudden movement would have been a mistake. The guards surrounding her were heavily armed. She wouldn't have stood a chance. Right now, doing what she was told looked like her only option.

Daylight.

She was led out into a cold and wet morning. She squinted into the sudden daylight and realized she was still in London after all. Big Ben towered above her, and despite the fact she had been held imprisoned here, the familiarity of her location was comforting. Yet that comfort was also fleeting, because the sight that greeted her when she was escorted further away from the grounds of the Houses of Parliament and towards Westminster Bridge was like nothing she'd seen before in all her years living in the capital.

It reminded her of the Nazi rallies she'd seen in history books and documentary footage. Crowds lined the banks of the Thames; thousands upon thousands of people filled the Victoria Embankment on one side and Queens Walk on the other, all of them turned back to face the bridge she was now being led towards. From her current position she could see that the bridge itself was also heavily congested with figures, all blacksuits, most of them standing to attention and in strict formation. But as she neared, she became aware of a brilliant white glow emanating from the center of the crossing. It was the same kind of divine light she'd seen previously, most recently when—either a few days or a few minutes ago depending on your frame of reference—she'd been forced to make contact with the comet that had landed in St James's Park. She looked up and saw Jayesh's god towering over everyone else.

The entire scene was deathly silent. Not one of the soldiers or the thousands of civilians alongside the river was making a sound. The lack of noise was bizarre and oppressive. Was it reverence or repression? She so wanted to shout out, but didn't dare for fear of the consequences. She was certain her time to talk would come soon enough.

The unnatural quiet extended to the river. Through the balustrades of the bridge she could see that the water of the Thames remained as inert as when she'd last seen it; frigid and barely moving, hardly even a ripple. It was so bizarre that it distracted her, and it was only when the marching stopped that the enormity of the situation hit home again. The guards turned her around. She was standing directly in front of Jayesh's god. The celestial being was even taller than she'd first assumed. He—or she or it or they—was sitting on a throne that appeared to be made of pure energy. It would have been undeniably impressive, she thought, had it not have been plonked right in the middle of Westminster Bridge. The light washed and glowed constantly, pulsating, and in the momentary fades she saw that Jayesh was standing alongside the throne. Fucking prick. She couldn't wait to get her hands on him.

"Is someone going to tell me what's going on?" she demanded, and there was an audible gasp from those nearest to her.

"Wait until Oldros addresses you before you speak," Jayesh sneered.

"Fuck you. What the hell's this all about?"

She looked up into the face of the god towering over her. He leant down to answer. "You're feisty," he said. "I like that."

"And I don't care what you like. I want my world and my life back."

"I wish I could help."

"You're supposed to be a god, aren't you? If you can't sort it, who can?"

Her arrogant tone belied the nervousness she was feeling inside, and that nervousness increased the longer she waited for the god to reply.

"Thank you for everything you've done, Jennifer," he eventually said. "My name is Oldros, and on behalf of the gods, I wish to recognize your valor and determination. In answer to your question, your world will never be the same again, but you can stand here in the knowledge that you made a difference. You facilitated my passage here. Without that, the planet and everyone living on it would have been lost already. We are all at the mercy of the Bleed."

"How can you be at the mercy of anything if you're a god?"

He shook his head. "There's a lot about the multiverse that a mere semi-mortal like you could never understand. There are movements and energies and powers the likes of which you couldn't even begin to comprehend."

"Try me. And for the record, there's nothing mere about us mortals," she said. She didn't know where these words were coming from, but she didn't feel anywhere near as confident as she sounded.

"But that's where you're wrong," Oldros continued. "You're limited by your mortal frame. Even you, a rare half-breed, can only dream of the things I've seen in other dimensions. So I say to you again, Jennifer, be thankful for the role you've played. The gods are eternally grateful for your sacrifice."

"Sacrifice?"

"Don't listen to him, Jenny."

She'd never been so relieved to hear that familiar voice before. She saw the light and felt the energy of his arrival. She didn't need to turn around to know who it was standing behind her. The way the nearest blacksuits backed away was proof positive. Thirnas had returned.

"Give it up, Thirnas," Oldros said. "Your pathetic little mercy mission failed."

Thirnas stepped in front of Jenny, gesturing for her to take cover behind him. Jayesh ran towards Thirnas, trying to get past him and get to Jenny, but his speed was no match for the god's. Thirnas grabbed his arm and swung him over his head with remarkable power, throwing him far into the distance. Jayesh landed in the Thames and the inert water swallowed him slowly like quicksand.

Thirnas squared up to Oldros. "I'm not going to let you destroy this world and these people."

Jenny pushed her way forward again. "What? I thought you were here to protect us from the Bleed?"

The god on the throne shook his head. "Believe me, child, if I could change the outcome, I would."

"You can," Thirnas said. "*We* can. There's still time. We can fight."

"At what cost? This planet and its people are inconsequential, you know that," Oldros said.

"No one is inconsequential enough for you to sacrifice them. Every person here has worth, regardless of whether they're a god like you and I, a half-breed like Jenny, or a mortal."

"You've always been overly sentimental, Thirnas," Oldros said. "There's no room for it. We are at war, don't forget. You show sentimentality where our enemy shows ruthlessness."

"But this is genocide. *Specicide*."

"I know, but there's nothing we can do to stop it. Release your hold on the tides. Bring this nightmare to an end."

"Never."

Jenny went to snatch a weapon from the blacksuit nearest to her. Before she could get anywhere close, Thirnas grabbed her and the two of them disappeared. They reappeared down river near Whitehall Gardens, far enough away to avoid being swallowed by the huge silent crowds on either side of the river. Thirnas covered her mouth with his hand to stop her speaking.

"Listen to me, Jenny," he said. "Don't argue, don't fight, just listen."

She nodded and he relaxed his grip.

"You need to get away from here. Did your father tell you about the transports?"

Confused for a moment, she nodded again when she remembered her conversation with Dad about escape routes up high.

"Good. The nearest is at the top of the spike."

"The spike? What the hell is that?"

He pointed along the river. "That building."

She immediately knew what he was referring to. "You mean the Shard?"

"Spike, shard, whatever, but yes, that pointy tallest one. Go there and climb as high as you can. There's a portal almost at the very top. A clockwork room."

"This is bullshit."

"You have to believe me. This is the only chance you have. Take it!"

"But I don't understand...."

"I came here to stop the tides and prevent the Bleed from getting through."

"So why is he trying to do the opposite?"

"Because the Bleed needs to feed, and this is such a crowded, over-populated planet that there's enough food to keep it occupied for some time. Oldros's plan is to lead the Bleed here then seal off its escape.

He thinks that sacrificing the Earth will satisfy the Bleed and stop it from growing in strength and destroying other realities, but he's wrong. The more he feeds it, the more powerful it will become."

"Can we stop him?"

"I'm going to try, but I don't know if I'll succeed. That's why you have to go."

"I can't."

"You can. You *must*. You're the only half-breed on the planet, Jenny, and Oldros will kill you to prevent further travel to and from this dimension. As long as you're alive, no matter where or when you are, there's still hope. Now go!"

Thirnas disappeared in a burst of brilliant energy. And at the exact same instant, another burst happened midway along Westminster Bridge.

The moment Thirnas reappeared he threw himself at Oldros. Where the two of them met there was an explosion of intense heat and light, strong enough to vaporize many of the nearest blacksuits. Huge crowds of them backed away from the two gods grappling. Thirnas had Oldros by the throat.

"I won't let you do this," he said,

smashing the other god's head repeatedly against the ground. Oldros soaked up the battering and then, in a move so swift Thirnas didn't see it coming, he shifted his weight and flipped their positions. Now Thirnas was the one at a disadvantage.

"If there was an alternative, I'd take it," Oldros said. "I'm sorry. I know you have an attachment to this planet and its people, but there's no other way."

"There has to be," Thirnas wheezed, barely able to breathe.

"You know there isn't. You know that sacrifices have to be made to keep our people safe. This planet is expendable, Thirnas. Accept its fate. Kill the girl!"

"Never."

Thirnas tried to attack again, but he was a minnow fighting a shark. Oldros easily overpowered him again and again. Whatever energy Thirnas threw at him, a blast with a hundred times the strength came the other way. Before long Thirnas was barely able to stay standing. A kick to the back of the legs brought him to his knees, then a punch to the side of the head from Oldros laid him out cold.

Oldros crouched down over the crumpled body of the other god. "I'm sorry, old friend." He unsheathed a curved, ornate-looking blade from his belt and plunged it deep into Thirnas's heart.

Jenny, defying orders and refusing to flee, watched from a distance. From here it was hard to make out any details, but she saw enough to know Thirnas was dead. She saw Oldros stand upright and wipe his vicious blade clean, then watched helplessly as he threw Thirnas's body into the river below.

The remaining god on the bridge raised his hands in victory and called to the noiseless crowds gathered in front of him along either side of the Thames. Blacksuits and civilians alike surged forward. Oldros's voice boomed around the city.

"My children, the false god is dead, and with him dies the unnatural hold he placed on your planet's rivers and tides. The waters will now flow again. I thank you for your devotion and urge you to join with me here to celebrate this blessed release."

The god held out his hands, then beckoned the masses on either side of the river to come closer still. And they did. At first they walked, then they ran, then they sprinted, rushing forward in huge numbers. They raced with each other to be the first to feel Oldros's hands on them, to receive his blessing.

When the fastest of them were mere meters away, almost close enough for him to touch, Oldros disappeared in another burst of unimaginably bright light. Jenny had to look away. She shielded her eyes until the incandescent light had faded, then looked up and saw that there was now a gaping hole in the middle of Westminster Bridge. The crowds were continuing to surge, oblivious. Unable to stop, hundreds of them were falling like lemmings into the waters below.

Jenny covered her ears when a noise rang out, the likes of which she'd never heard before. It was louder, even, than the din of the buildings collapsing around her when Thirnas had first arrived: a deep, guttural growl that seemed to be coming from the bowels of the Earth itself. Everything shook. It was like an endless, tireless earthquake. She walked towards the Thames, struggling to keep her balance, then peered down into the river. The water, which had been impossibly still for so long, had become a raging torrent. It crashed and bubbled and flowed, so active now that it almost appeared as if it was being boiled. And unless her eyes deceived her, the typical Thames' gray-brown had changed. The murk now had a definite crimson-red tinge, and as the churning waters mixed, the intensity of the color began to increase.

For a moment longer, Jenny remained where she was, watching as waves began to appear on the Thames. As the water writhed, the color changed again. It was like watching paint being mixed in a blender. The gray gave way to brown which gave way to blood red. Within a couple of minutes, almost the entire river had turned crimson. It looked like a ruptured vein. And the water, she realized, was flowing in both directions. Whirlpools of crisscrossing currents were carrying this noxious pollution, this awful poison, both deeper into the city and out towards Essex and Kent.

Was this the Bleed? She had no one left to ask, but she knew it couldn't be anything else.

The crowds were still dropping into the water from the bridge in huge numbers, hundreds at a time with thousands more waiting to leap. Some of them, she saw, were being washed up on the riverbank, staggering back onto dry land. They had fallen into the river as humans but emerged as something else altogether.

Near to where Jenny was standing, a short flight of stone steps led up from the splashing blood-red water. The unprecedented currents carried people along at speed, and as Jenny watched, a number of them became trapped at the bottom of the steps, caught like leaves and twigs in the mouth of a storm drain. An arm reached out of the foaming water, fingers clawing to get a grip of the slippery stone surface. Jenny expected a shoulder, head and torso to follow in that order, but what pulled itself out of the river was barely recognizable as human. In fact, it was barely recognizable as a clump of *several* humans.

The first arm—stripped to the skin, covered in boils and blisters—was growing out of someone's back, the elbow erupting from spoiled flesh between the shoulder blades. On one shoulder, the arm had been reversed: one body, two left hands. The thing's head was on sideways and its grotesque shape was truncated at the pelvis. It hauled itself up with effort, an ungainly, lop-sided climb, then stopped in front of her on all threes like a fleshy tripod.

"What the fuck...?" she said. When the monstrosity came at her like a rabid dog she snatched up a nearby rubbish bin and brought it crashing down on its back. She staggered away, aware of more ungodly shapes pulling themselves up and out of the river now.

She'd done more damage to the deformed creature with the bin than she'd thought, because she could see an ooze of red-black blood spilling out from a crack in the back of the thing's head. Another one from the silent crowds—a woman who had so far managed to stay away from the polluted river—walked towards Jenny and, as she did, she inadvertently slipped in the blood. At first it was almost comical, and Jenny laughed involuntarily, but the laughter disappeared as quickly as it had started. The very instant that the woman made contact with the blood, she began to mutate. Her skin alternately sloughed from her face then tightened elsewhere so that her expression seemed to have half-fallen from her skull. Then her right arm extended until it was long enough to reach the ground, and a fifth limb—unrecognizable as either an arm or a leg, a perverse mixture of both—burst out of the center of her chest. She moved forward, spider-like, but because of her suddenly increased size, she found her way forward blocked by trees and lampposts and an abandoned coach.

Jenny turned towards the City and could see the Bleed advancing with the reverse-flow of the Thames. Ahead of her, the Embankment stretched out and curved right. The Shard was on the other side of the water, and whether it proved to be her salvation or not, she knew it was where she had to go and that meant crossing the Thames at some point soon. She had no choice but to race the advancing crimson tide whilst avoiding all contact with the toxic waters and the foul creatures continuing to emerge from the murky depths. Waterloo Bridge, Blackfriars Bridge, Southwark Bridge or Tower Bridge—it didn't matter which: she just had to hope and pray one of them was clear. *Pray? What was the point of that?* she laughed aloud. The god she would have looked to was dead, and the only other god she'd known had been the architect of this hell. She was on her own.

She almost waited too long.

The fifth limb of the mutant woman hit the ground just to her left, and Jenny glanced back to see that the nightmarish freak had split herself in two trying to force her way past the wreck of the coach. The contents of her ruptured chest spilled out of her. Her innards writhed. Her intestines unraveled themselves and slithered along the ground towards her like snakes.

Jenny raced alongside the Thames. There was another deafening noise from way behind her and she looked back over her shoulder to see that Big Ben had been brought down, collapsing into the river and causing a tidal surge. A wall of bloody water rose up like a tsunami, all red froth and random body parts. She knew she had to beat the wave. It was that or die trying. It was clear from the sheer volume of red river water now cascading over the side of the Embankment that there would be no other escape.

Jenny sprinted faster than she ever had before. She was terrified and exhausted...adrenaline and fear were the only things keeping her moving forward. She knew that she'd be dead if she stopped or even slowed down. Behind her now the flood water was everywhere, and the situation was clearly going to get far worse, very quickly. The poison would be carried along gutters and down drains and would eventually find its way to every part of London and beyond. She hoped its toxicity would reduce the further it got from here, but she didn't hold out much hope of that being the case.

Waterloo Bridge. Was this where she took a chance and tried to get across? She already knew that was out of the question; to get onto the bridge she'd have to take a sharp left and climb the steps up then double-back on herself, wasting precious seconds. And anyway, there didn't seem to be any point. The bridge was lined with still more of Oldros's misguided worshippers standing in the path of the contagion-filled wave.

The river widened slightly, and the wave appeared to finally be reducing in power. As Jenny neared Blackfriars Bridge, she thought she just might stand a chance. A desperate glance back revealed that the height of the tide was below wall level now and the polluted waters were no longer washing over and out onto the street. She pulled up, breathing hard, doubled over with stitch. She'd covered maybe half the distance between Westminster and the Shard. Was it even worth the effort of trying to get there? What difference would it really make? If she fought her way to the very top of the tallest building in London, so what? Would she achieve anything other than delaying her inevitable death? She had an image in her head of London flooded with blood-red water, and of its entire population turning into those horrific mutated creatures she'd just escaped; the horror of what she'd seen spurred her onward.

There were dismembered limbs and mutilated people dragging themselves out of the water all the way along the Embankment now and her choice was simple: run or die. Or maybe the choice wasn't simple at all? She watched as two conjoined people—a young girl and an elderly man, fused together at the pelvis by a swollen mass of deformed flesh—tried to drag themselves (itselves?) in opposite directions at the same time. She found herself instinctively looking for their respective other halves. And then she saw another woman with a crown of fingers, and another with a pus-filled boil where their face should have been, and another centipede-like string of seventeen people—something out of that shitty horror movie years back…. And she revised her previous thought: she could run, she could die, or she could become a part of this freakish hell. She imagined the pain as her body tore itself apart then twisted and reformed. She imagined her mind, her conscious, her *everything* being absorbed as part of this toxic nightmare.

The din was unbearable. Those of them who still had mouths were wailing in agony as a result of their newly manifested mutations, whilst also yelling and screaming a chorus of battle cries: an army ready to fight. There were so many of them that from a distance they appeared to be a single unending mass. There were places where they actually *were* a single mass.

Run or die or *this*.

A bellicose roar came from the area around the Palace of Westminster. She looked back towards the broken stump of Big Ben's tower and watched as a massive creature rose up out of the crimson depths. As tall as Big Ben used to be, and from this distance the details were thankfully indistinct, but she could see that it was made up of hundreds of people welded together as one. It thumped its improvised hands down on the surface of the river, immediately causing a second tsunami of blood to rise up, this one more than twice the height of the first.

Run or die or THIS!

Jenny swerved around the foot of a creature which, by virtue of its insanely long, spider-like-legs, had stepped right over her and taken the lead. She ducked down as a spindly arm with even spindlier fingers swept through the air just above her head, then banked hard left. The creature's ungainly shape took it by surprise and as it tried to spin around to follow her, it tied itself up in knots and came crashing down, blocking the way through for countless more.

Millennium Bridge next. She was actually thankful for all the shitty tourist-related jobs she'd had over the last few years. She knew this place like the back of her hand, and she knew that, whilst she could stay down by the river, the low walls here would leave her dangerously exposed. Between the flood wall and the buildings on the other side of the narrow footpath, she wouldn't stand a chance of escaping the poisonous tide. Her best option now—maybe her only option—was to run up White Lion Hill. Sure, it would put some extra distance on the run, but a few more minutes of painful physical exertion was a small price to pay. *Better exhausted than fucked-up and mutated*, she thought.

A race up the hill and she was on Upper Thames Street now, and here, for the first time, she was aware of some of the otherwise hidden population of London beginning to emerge from the early morning shadows to try and see what was happening to their beloved city. Millions had remained in their homes until now, but the world was beginning to wake up to the nightmare unfolding along the Thames.

"Get away from here," she yelled at anyone who'd listen, but in the blood-soaked chaos of things today, no one was taking any notice of her telling them what to do.

She could hear the next wave racing the along the Thames below, catching up then overtaking her. As the roar of the water faded, it was replaced with the awful noise of human pain and suffering. Innocent people who'd strayed too close to the water's edge or who'd been touched by the impossible mutations now filling the streets had been corrupted by the Bleed. Just a glancing touch, a drop of spit, a splash of blood or a single drop of corrupted water was enough to turn human to inhuman. At this rate, Jenny thought the entire human race might be gone by the end of the day.

The gods had sacrificed this place. Her home. Her everything.

She felt an anger in her chest that made her move even faster.

At the junction of Upper Thames Street and Queen Street Place, she considered momentarily taking the right turn and trying to cross the river over Southwark Bridge. It felt too soon, too much of a risk, and instead she kept going. It was a calculated risk because she knew that every bridge she passed was another chance gone, and now only one more remained if she wanted to get to the Shard in time: London Bridge.

She had to run even farther from the river to reach the start of the bridge. When she doubled-back and started running across the road that stretched across the water, all she could see up ahead was the Shard. It was almost in touching distance. She'd hated it when it had first been built, despising its elongated pyramid-like shape and how it stood at odds with London of old. But now it was that same defiance, that utter arrogance and contempt, that gave her hope.

Halfway across the bridge, another earthquake-like growl stopped her in her tracks. The ground shook, and she thought for a second that the bridge might be about to collapse, but the danger was elsewhere. The massive mishmashed creature she'd seen forming around the ruins of parliament was now advancing along the river. It was coming towards her with terrifying speed. But was it actually coming for her, or just coming to destroy everyone and everything else? It didn't matter — the net effect would be the same. She knew she was going to die, but she wasn't ready to give up and roll over. Not yet. Not after making it so far and getting so close.

She was about to start running again when the multi-person monstrosity kicked through all the bridges she'd passed. Blackfriars, Millennium and Southwark bridges were destroyed with remarkable ease. Jenny wondered if she was going make it across this bridge or whether she'd end up in the toxic red water flowing way below her, when suddenly the creature stopped. It scanned the river and surrounding area with compound eyes made from scores of human heads welded tight together.

No question: it was definitely looking for her. A few days ago she'd been invisible, serving overpriced chips to tourists near the London Eye. Today she was the lynchpin in a desperate battle between good and evil, the lone half-breed forced to fight in a battle to the death between demons and gods. It felt like the fate of the entire world now rested in her hands, though she still didn't know what the hell she was supposed to do. It was a responsibility she'd never asked for.

The ghastly creature spotted her and reared up again, ready to strike. Jenny raced to cover the final few meters to the other side of the river and head for the Shard, but after covering more than a couple of miles, the final few steps seemed to stretch on forever. She looked back down the bloody river and saw the thing pull back a massive, engorged hand then swing it forward again as if throwing a ball. A bulbous mass disconnected from the rest of the limb and flew through the air. Jenny banked hard left into St Thomas Street to avoid it, then pressed herself up against the nearest wall when a massive conglomeration of fused people smashed into a row of terraced buildings opposite like a wrecking ball.

It must have been several meters wide. The diseased mass began to pulsate and to grow. Countless arms and legs reached out from its fleshy bulk, stretching, then gripping, then dragging forward. It was growing in size. Self-replicating. Jenny was rooted to the spot, unable to move, and those few moments of frightened hesitation were enough for the monstrosity to gain advantage and take control. It grew right across the street in front of her, forming a fleshy dam meters tall, ever-expanding. The melded flesh rippled and danced as what was left of the individual people it was formed from fought to get closer to her. Faces strained at their new skin bonds, desperately stretching towards her. Bulging eyes and gaping screams, and mouths open wider than should have been possible.

Now the grotesque form had reached the side of the Shard and was beginning to grow upwards, dripping tentacles reaching towards the pinnacle of the immense building.

A boil-like protrusion appeared in the thing directly in front of Jenny, looking like it was about to burst or to swallow her whole. She backed away, trying to find a way past the swollen mass, but not seeing any way forward. Desperate to find an escape, she raced back towards the end of St. Thomas Street, then turned left and kept going. If she couldn't go through, she'd have to go around.

Does this thing know where I'm going, or is it just trying to stop me? It was a sensible question. She raced through a maze of backstreets and alleyways, trying to lose the monstrous thing and not get lost herself. She had a decent knowledge of much of London, but here she was running blind. The Shard stood tall and proud, visible above everything else, and she used it as her marker. Jenny turned left again, running parallel with St Thomas Street and the entrance to the Shard now, then found herself right in the middle of the Guy's Hospital and Kings College London campus. She looked up at the hospital building ahead of her and saw huge numbers of terrified faces looking back. Patients and staff alike looked on in abject terror at the surreal bloodbath unfolding frighteningly close to their building. Some tried to flee, others were too scared to go anywhere. Jenny was aware of a blockage at the main entrance to the building as people fought with each other to escape. They didn't know what she knew, hadn't seen the things she'd seen. *If they had any sense*, she thought, *they'd stay put.*

Many of the faces at the windows began to react to what was behind her. She looked back and saw the fleshy blob, which had blocked the street before, had now grown and was seeping over the top of the first row of buildings, advancing slowly but with arrogant inevitability. Sticky strands of skin that once been parts of people shot out and stuck to the side of the hospital, forming a web-like mass which quickly grew and strengthened, pulling the tumorous thing along.

Jenny ran on. Through a gap between buildings she saw that the flesh was now more than a third up one side of the Shard. She kept going, energy levels flagging, then stopped when the sun was blocked from view. A huge shadow had been cast over everything, turning day into night. Behind her was the grotesque human-shaped thing she'd seen near Westminster, but now it was more than double its original size having swallowed up more and more people along the route. Its composition brought its scale into focus: all along its surface, shapes which had once been individual people bristled and swayed like the microscopic villi that line the small intestine. They were like feelers, searching for more flesh to absorb. Jenny saw a group of people break free from one part of the hospital. Disorientated, they burst out from a fire escape and ran towards the monstrosity instead of away. They became part of its foul mass as soon as they made contact. It was virtually instantaneous, and completely inescapable.

This abhorrent colossus was feeding off the population of London, growing stronger with every living creature it consumed. How long would it keep growing? Would it consume the entire world? The thought of becoming a part of it herself was almost too much for Jenny to comprehend. She couldn't imagine a worse way to die.

This was the Bleed. Evil incarnate.

She made it to the entrance to London Bridge railway station, but getting inside and through to the Shard looked like it was going to be a harder task than ever because the appearance of the towering flesh-monster had caused the thousands of people in the Shard to try and escape. She was fighting against an avalanche of terrified individuals, and it took all her remaining strength just to keep moving forward. It was like swimming against the strongest imaginable tide. She thought she should tell them to stop and go back inside, but she no longer had the words, and their panic made communication unlikely.

Eventually she'd forced her way through the bulk of them and had made it into the building. The light inside flickered, shadows filling the place from the chaos outside, darkness steadily eating away at the remaining brightness coming through the glass cladding. Skittering shapes crawled away in all directions like overactive slugs, smearing the windows with sticky blood trails. It was a surreal and mesmerizing sight, and Jenny was distracted by the bizarreness of it all. She stood in the middle of a vast atrium, watching with her hands on her hips, sucking in desperate gulps of air and doing everything she could to contain her mounting panic. All around her, people continued to go the other way, desperate to get out of the building and away from whatever it was that had attached itself to the outside, knowing nothing of the awful fate which awaited them.

Jenny's dangerous malaise was abruptly truncated when part of the flesh-beast formed itself into a rudimentary fist and began to hammer at the side of the building. Suddenly, for all the Shard's size and strength and its crisp, geometric beauty, it now felt fragile and precarious.

Where do I go?

The lights in the building flickered, and Jenny's heart skipped a beat because she knew that if the power failed, she'd fail too. Her legs were heavy as lead and climbing the best part of eighty floors up with any speed was going to be an impossible task on foot. She'd been here once before as a tourist herself, but that day had ended in a booze-fueled bender with a Japanese couple she'd met, and though she remembered being up high, she couldn't remember how she'd got up there or back down. Another flood of people came towards her from one side of the atrium as an elevator emptied. She remembered there being offices in here, and a huge hotel spanning many of the mid-section floors, but she'd originally come for the viewing platform. Instinct told her to take the elevator and she slipped inside just as the door slid shut. It was no surprise that she was the only one going up. Everyone else was doing everything they could to get down.

The lift climbed quickly, almost too quickly, leaving her stomach on the ground floor, and it juddered and shook as the creature outside continued to batter the building. It could only have been a minute, two at most, but it felt like she was trapped in that small metal space for hours. Part of her felt claustrophobic and wanted the doors to open; part of her wanted to stay in there forever.

By the time she made it out onto the viewing platform and the lift she'd used had filled with the last remaining people and was on its way back down, she was the only one left up on the seventy-second floor. She ran to the window and looked down over a scene of apocalyptic impossibility. She'd never seen anything like it, not even in films or on TV. She was looking back along the Thames towards the Palace of Westminster and the horrible gap where Big Ben and the clock tower had always stood. Given that the river itself had been dyed red by the Bleed, it should have been easy to follow its meandering route through the city, and yet it was all but impossible. The mighty Thames had burst its banks in too many places to count, and virtually the entire swathe of London she could see from this side of the Shard was now submerged under toxic, poisonous, crimson waves.

Although she was high above street level, she could still make out more detail than was comfortable. She could see individual people running to escape from the Bleed but being outpaced, outmaneuvered, and swallowed up. She saw people being torn in two and others being welded together. She saw people trying to help one other get away but failing miserably. As she watched, a woman tried to pull an injured man away from where the bloody water lapped against a curb. In turn, another man tried to help the woman, while his partner tried to drag him away, painfully aware of the futility of what they were trying to do. The furthest back of the group tripped and fell, and immediately the water was washing up and over his legs as if it had a will of its own. Almost instantaneously, the first man melded with the woman who, in turn, melded with the other man and his partner. In the time it took her to blink, four people had become one foul creature.

Where would this end? Would it end at all? For miles around, the blood-red water was flowing across the land, corrupting every scrap of flesh it came into contact with. The enormity of what was happening was impossible for Jenny to comprehend, because she couldn't imagine anything being able to stop this awful, ungodly scourge. The blood in the water wasn't being diluted—if anything it seemed to be getting stronger. It was becoming brighter and more vivid, increasingly thick and viscous. No longer lapping, rippling and flowing, it appeared to be moving with intent.

How had this happened? How had her world changed so much so quickly? She'd lost everything she cared about, and all she wanted now was to stop. Being stuck up here seemed like the final cruelty. Not only had she been unable to prevent this from happening, she was now forced to face her failure head-on. It was impossible to look away from up here. Everywhere she turned she saw more: nothing but glass. Endless, panoramic views of hell.

A grotesque, corpulent protrusion whipped through the air outside and smacked against the window in front of her. Formed from what looked to be around fifty conjoined people, as it made contact with the glass, the individuals gripped any available edge and held on. Some fixed their engorged mouths to the glass like the suckers on octopus tentacles, others dug their elongated fingers into any gaps they could find. Once secure, the smaller creature she'd escaped at ground level dragged itself up in front of her, blocking out what was left of the sun, smearing huge swathes of the view outside with saliva and blood and pus and Christ alone knew what else.

The monster hauled itself higher up the side of the Shard, bringing the bulk of its deformed mass level with the viewing platform. And then something which was unmistakably a head swung into view. There was no doubt it was looking for her and that gave her some perverse reassurance: *If I'm that important, maybe I really can do something to save the world?* That lone, baseless thought felt as clichéd and desperate as it sounded.

The eyes of the beast were like those of the creature which had destroyed Big Ben — fly-like compound eyes formed from tightly packed human heads. They shouldn't have been able to see anything, but the way they moved from side to side, staring and searching, was an uncanny approximation of human sight.

And then the aberration saw her.

In a split-second it focused all of its attention on her, and she had nowhere to go. In fact, though she wasn't aware of her actions, she found herself moving towards the glass, keen to get a clearer view of the monstrosity that was about to kill her. *You won't absorb me so easy,* she wanted to tell it. *I'll give you gut rot, motherfucker.*

The beast was now hanging from the side of the building, a number of distended limbs and sticky, web-like strands holding it firmly in position. It had two main arms, broader than all its other appendages, and as she watched, it extended those arms from lop-sided shoulders and pushed itself back. Close up, the aberration was an unruly conglomeration of things that used to be people, but from more of a distance the individuals became less defined and the whole instead came into focus. She estimated that the horrific face she was now staring into must have been as high as several houses. Not only could she now clearly make out its features, she could also read its expression. And with that, she started to anticipate its intent. It was going to come for her, of that there was no doubt, but there was something else that shocked her more. She thought she recognized the face she was looking into.

Thirnas.

He'd fallen into the bloody Thames, but had he somehow survived in there? Was he here to save or to kill her? Was he here at all, or was this just a shadow sent to haunt her? She heard his voice in her head as he spoke to her, but didn't know if she was imagining it.

"I can't stop this, but I can buy you a little time. Keep climbing, Jenny. Get out of here."

She hammered on the glass with frustration. "I can't do this on my own," she screamed.

"You can," he told her.

And then he was gone.

The part of the Bleed in which Thirnas still existed was torn from the side of the Shard by the other, much larger creature, then thrown to the ground like discarded litter. Another recognizable face formed from the mass of writhing deformities. Jayesh.

"Motherfucker!" she screamed, and Jayesh grinned at her, feeding off her fury. He pulled his head back and butted the window, the force of impact sending her flying back across the viewing platform. Then again, and this time Jenny heard the glass crack. Then again. And again. And again and again and again—and Jenny knew that at any second the strengthened glass would give way and she'd be killed, either sucked out by pressure and sent spiraling to the ground, or swallowed up by the foul monsters that had, one way or another, been trying to kill her since this nightmare had begun.

She went to run deeper into the building, determined to prolong the chase and make it as difficult as possible for the thing that used to be Jayesh to get to her, but she stopped when his head rocked back again but didn't strike. For an instant she thought she saw a familiar green-glow where everything else so far today had been blood red.

Thirnas was fighting back. He'd regained control of the fleshy mass he'd become a part of and, while Jayesh had been focused on Jenny, had climbed back up until now the two of them were almost level. Thirnas—or what used to be Thirnas—had a size disadvantage which he fought to negate with ferocity. He grabbed the other beast by the shoulders and tried to pull Jayesh away from the building. He was less than bothered. He morphed and changed his shape, not letting go of the side of the Shard, but at the same time turning himself inside out so that he now faced Thirnas, even though his arms were stretched backwards and were still clinging on. More arms and fists and tentacles and spears appeared from his endless gut and took hold of the god. The two of them grappled furiously as Thirnas kicked and punched and ripped and pulled at all the fleshy strands anchoring Jayesh in place. For a moment it looked like he was going to fall. Thirnas continued battering him wildly, refusing to stop until his grip was broken. Jayesh started to drop, the center of gravity of his unwieldy bulk having shifted. Jenny rushed forward again, convinced the two monsters were about to drop down into the blood-filled streets of the capital below, but one of the Jayesh creature's tentacles uncurled on the way down and whipped back up, grabbing hold and almost snapping the top off the Shard. Windows shattered, and up here on the seventy-second floor it was like the door had been opened on a jet flying at forty-thousand feet. Jenny managed to reach a staircase and wrap her arm around the metal banister before being she could be sucked outside. She pulled herself back up to her feet and fought to keep moving forward against the ferocious wind.

Then, as quickly as it had begun, the howling gale stopped.

Jenny saw that the thing which had been Jayesh had started to ooze into the gaps. Gelatinous flesh was flooding in through the broken windows, like a turgid river formed from virtually liquified people. All she could do was run.

Jenny was the last whole human left in the Shard, and she was able to use staircases and the metal interior framework of the building itself to climb higher and higher. As she ascended, it began to feel more precarious. Was it because she was running out of energy, or was it because the Shard itself was now unstable? She paused and looked down, and though her increased height and the oceans of blood now made it harder than ever to see what was happening at street-level, she could make out enough to know that Thirnas's battle with the Jayesh-monster had been lost. She watched helpless as two more arms grew from out from Jayesh's bulk and tore what was left of Thirnas in half before dropping the two bloody chunks like discarded litter. Jenny was distracted by more noise as a door below her flew open and the narrow space through which she was climbing began to rapidly fill with molten flesh.

The thought of drowning in human remains was enough to keep her moving at a frantic pace, but she questioned whether there was there any point. Was she just giving herself farther to fall when the Shard inevitably collapsed into rubble?

But she couldn't stop. She had to keep going.

She pushed through another set of doors and found herself at the bottom of what she knew had to be the final staircase. She started to climb, using her arms more than her legs now to drag herself upwards; every fiber, muscle, sinew and nerve now felt impossibly heavy.

She couldn't see the Jayesh-demon anymore, but she could feel its presence. The Shard was rocking. Shockwaves ran through every surface as the evil creature now focused on the lower levels of the building, trying to bring the whole structure down. And it was working, because she could already feel a definite swaying, as if she were at sea. The noise was deafening; the silence of her isolation long gone and replaced with the groans, cracks, bangs and pops of the building beginning to die.

On the other side of the Shard now, and she could see the monster in its entirety again. It had positioned the bulk of its ever-expanding mass a short distance away, anchored in the bloody Thames, using a myriad of gore-soaked appendages to pull the building over. It was starting to list to one side. It wouldn't be long before it came crashing down.

There was a single door at the top of the staircase. Jenny burst through without thinking, and found herself in small, windowless room with a machine in the center. It looked like nothing she'd ever seen before, but she knew that this was exactly where she was supposed to be. A clockwork room. The machine looked impossibly complex to operate, yet she knew what to do. Had she always had this knowledge? Had Dad taught her? Or Thirnas? Or her mother or the father she'd never met?

The floor was at a forty-five-degree tilt now and it was a struggle to stay standing upright. Jenny adjusted her balance and continued to do what she had to. Her hands moved over ancient-looking dials and levers with furious speed, but it wasn't fast enough.

The building collapsed, and as Jenny fell, the room was filled with unbearably bright light.

27

The Moon

DAY THREE / 6:56 PM

"Shoot it!" Juan demanded.

"Not me, not me!" Tyler was duck running, exaggerated side to side movements hindering his forward progress.

Maddie was a horror movie and book fan; she couldn't help but wonder if this was something like *the Thing* and Tyler was now the monster, as if he'd been tagged and was It.

"Juan!" Maddie had to stop him from running past and out into the wilderness, so to speak. The boy was wide-eyed and pale.

"Saw something, was close. I...we saw it!"

"What was it?" Sandra never took her eyes off of Tyler as he finally got into their makeshift camp. He was hastily pulling up and buckling his pants. Derrick was doing slow revolutions, peering into the darkness as best he could, making sure nothing was coming up from their blindsides.

"It was gray, huge..." Tyler was out of breath. "Threw a boulder at me, missed by a couple of feet."

"Look out!" Derrick screamed. Maddie turned just in time to see a rock the size of a small engine materialize out of the murk. It crashed less than ten feet from their location. If it had been on target, there wouldn't have been enough time to move.

Sandra fired from where the rock had come from. There was another scream. To Maddie, it sounded more like rage than pain.

"I think I got it." Sandra kept the pistol aimed.

"I think you should save your bullets," Maddie told her, the chance she'd hit something in the dark was about as good as them happening upon a Starbucks, although given the propensity for that company to expand, that was a possibility.

Another rock was hurtled, this one off to their side. It was closer, but Maddie thought it more of a warning than a desire to kill. She could be wrong, though, and the consequences were entirely too dire to chance it. How could they possibly get any rest with an enemy that could rain down five hundred pound missiles seemingly at will?

"We have to get moving," Maddie expressed to the group.

"Are you insane? That thing is out there."

"What good is staying here? It knows exactly where we are and we can't defend this position. For all we know, it's looking for more rocks to crush us with," Maddie told the other woman.

"Should we vote?" Sam was looking to keep the peace.

"This isn't a democracy," Sandra told her.

Maddie couldn't help but notice Sandra's gun was now pointed at her midsection. "Do you mind?"

"Not at all," Sandra replied.

"I'll take that gun from you and beat

you senseless if you don't stop pointing it at me."

Sandra slowly moved it away, but her direct gaze implied she was doing so in protest.

"Are you sure we still want to follow it?" Tyler was nervously looking around.

"Nothing's changed, we find out how it's surviving or we die." Maddie gathered their minimal provisions.

"I think we die either way. I saw that thing, Maddie; it's not going to share." Juan was staying close to her side like a toddler clings to its mother in a busy department store.

"Stay close, but not too close. If it tosses another rock, we don't want to get all tangled up." Maddie's heart was laboring, she was scared for herself, scared for all of them. It was bad enough when you had to keep yourself safe, but she felt personally responsible for the four teens, especially since Sandra had shown that the only one that mattered to her was her. The group was moving slowly, continually scanning the area ahead and around in addition to above.

It was subtle, and Maddie wasn't entirely sure, but it seemed the further they traveled the lighter it was getting; she felt she could see nearly a hundred yards out.

None of it made sense. They could not see the sun, and there was absolutely no light source she could discern, nor imagine. Perhaps by getting further away from the crater walls, ambient light was leaking down.

"Is it possible to digest your heart?" Tyler gulped.

Maddie thought the boy was attempting to inject some humor into the moment but there was nothing funny in his expression; he looked in distress. "Are you hurt?"

He shook his head. "This might be the first and the last time I ever say this." He had the attention of the entire group. "I wish I was in calculus class right now."

Sam groaned. "I thought you were going to tell me you loved me."

"Are you crazy? This wouldn't be the last time," he told her, they reached out and joined hands.

Maddie almost said, "You don't know that…you might want to tell her," but instead, she said, "Anyone else notice it's getting lighter?"

"I thought I was seeing things." Derrick looked around. It had gone from a candle in the middle of a cave to sunlight filtering through dense, soupy fog. It was far from perfect, but being able to see did wonders for alleviating their fear. Whatever they'd been following had made sure to not be in their field of vision.

"Maddie, we need to stop." Sam gently touched her arm. She pointed to Juan, who was a few feet behind and limping. He was hurting so badly he was no longer looking around, but rather where his footfalls were going to land. He winced with each step.

"How are you doing?" she asked as he nearly rolled up on her.

"I'm with Tyler, I'd rather be in calculus."

"That bad, huh?" Sam asked.

"Worse," he told her.

"Is stopping wise?" Sandra asked.

"You late for a spin class?" Maddie had got down to get a better look at the boy's feet. He had collapsed, sitting with them outstretched. The group had been antsy at first, but the longer they stood still, the more fatigue began to settle in. One by one they sat down. Derrick, Sam and Tyler were with Juan.

"Holy shit, bud...your feet are busted," Tyler told his friend.

"That's helpful," Maddie chided. Juan's left foot was the worst of the two, a massive blister on his heel had burst and was bleeding, dust and coarse dirt had caked in and around the open sore. She wished she had some water to clean the wound out.

The best she could offer was a field dressing. She had Tyler and Derrick help her get the top part of her suit down, rolling it to her hips, then she began to take her shirt off, before suddenly feeling self-conscious. "Turn around."

"Damn, Maddie! You're ripped," Tyler said.

"Why are you looking?" Sam asked.

"I'm just saying. I didn't know old people could be ripped."

"Old?" Maddie pulled her suit back up. "Fuck. I hate the feel of rubber on my skin." She jumped around a bit, getting used to the new tactile feeling.

"I don't think you're old," Derrick told her; she noticed his cheeks were red.

"Oh, for fuck's sake, boy, I'm twice your age, and we're here." She tore her shirt into strips.

"So you're saying…."

"No, I'm not implying that if we weren't here…I'm not having this discussion. Not now, not ever. Get your little teenage hormones under control." Maddie did her best to wipe the worst of the grime from Juan's feet while trying not to further tear the skin away. "I'm sorry I can't do any better than this," she told him.

"Just to not be walking is fine with me," he told her. His head was thrown back and his bottom lip clenched in his teeth as he fought back tears that threatened to spill forward from the pain.

"It's all right bro; you can cry. I won't tell anyone. I mean, not until we get back anyway."

Maddie knew Tyler was just trying to make Juan feel better, but it wasn't working. To think on it was to realize that there was nothing to go back to. All of their friends and families, they were gone, wiped clean from the surface like a stain upon a countertop from an aggressive housekeeper with rampant OCD. She wrapped up his right foot, much like she had the left, gingerly got his slippers back on and told him to get a little rest. They couldn't stay long; there were so many different doomsday clocks ticking over their heads, and the only solution was to keep moving. Sandra was racked out, her arms crossed over her chest with the pistol laying against her stomach.

Maddie was exhausted and wanted to lay down with the rest of the group. Instead, she did a lazy circle around them, not as vigilant as she wished, but enough to hopefully give pause to anything that might want to advance upon them. She was on her tenth circuit, her vision blurry, her steps halting, she wasn't focused on anything in particular, and took just that moment to look down. "Impossible." She stopped mid-step, placing her foot down to the side of what she was looking at. It wasn't much thicker than a needle and leaning heavily to the side. "What am I looking at?" She got down low, feeling rejuvenated. She gently touched the top of the small plant. "This is a hallucination. I'm so tired and stressed out that I'm seeing things." She had an urge to pull it out of the ground so she could get a better look. No matter how much she wanted to, she could not justify that action. Under seemingly impossible odds, there was life. Where there was one, there had to be more. "How is this getting water? Does it need water?" She vaguely remembered something from one of her childhood classes about some varieties of desert plants that could get all of the moisture they needed from the air. "I have so many questions…are you cultivated? How are you propagated? Who or what brought you here?" She leaned over to see if there was a scent to the offshoot, some other sense she could use to verify that the plant existed, when Tyler called out. A tiny tendril, no more significant than an eyelash, protruded from the top before slowly withdrawing.

"Maddie, something's coming!"

She stood and looked around, not seeing anything. She thought perhaps he'd been dreaming until she followed where he was pointing. The gray looked darker, like dust was being kicked up.

"Everyone up! Look alive!" She quickly got back to the rest of the group. For the moment, the plant-based alien life form was forgotten for what she figured was the dangerous, animal-based one. Whatever it was, was still far off.

"Run?" Sam asked, although, "To where?" was the better question.

"Don't think so," Maddie told her.

Sandra got angry when Sam clasped the other woman's hand.

"I'm your mother! Shouldn't you be coming to me when you're scared?"

Sam did not reply. Maddie let out a sigh when the cloud appeared to be veering away from them. She finally took a deep breath as it passed by their location. "Shit," was all she could manage as it once again turned, this time heading straight at them.

"You think this is the rock-throwing thingy?" Tyler asked.

Maddie wanted to ask him how many entities did he think were out here, but she suspected there was a good chance that there was a whole, extraordinary ecosphere. It made sense. Now was what was coming their way: prey or predator? She felt she'd answered the question, as animals that were generally eaten did not willingly rush into the unknown.

"Time to get to work." Tyler slashed his weapon back and forth and had moved out in front of the group.

"Told you," Maddie mouthed to Derrick, who was watching in amazement. Sandra, per her now typical persona, was moving to the back.

"You have the gun, Sandra. Either hand it over so it can be used or get out in front," Maddie said.

"No," was all she said in return.

"Seriously, mom?" Sam was moving to get closer to Tyler.

"You should get back here with me," Sandra told her, but when her daughter didn't move, she didn't push it. Derrick and Juan made a line up front.

"Pull back. We create a phalanx, easier to defend our sides." Maddie was getting them into position. It wasn't enough, but it was all they had. At a hundred yards, the entity stopped; a swirl of haze and dust obscured the thing.

"Can't see anything." Derrick leaned forward, as if that would help.

"It's like camouflage," Tyler said. Maddie wasn't so sure. Why would anything try to hide itself with a concealment that could be seen from great distances? There was a better than good chance it didn't care; that didn't bode well for the group. The airborne dirt was slowly beginning to settle, and still, it was not moving. Maddie had the distinct impression that it was sizing them up, weighing its odds of success versus injury. Eating was paramount, not getting injured while procuring food, a close second.

"That's right, we're badass. Keep that in mind! Start yelling! Make it scared!" Maddie was screaming, waving her arms in the air.

"I'm scared too!" Juan yelled. "Don't make me any scareder!"

"Dude," Tyler said.

"What? It's not like it understands English."

"Not that. Scareder isn't a word."

"Are you shitting me? Yell!" Maddie urged.

"Fish protein tacos are horrible!" this from Derrick.

"What the hell is wrong with you kids?" Maddie made sure to yell her question.

"I love Samantha Morrison," Tyler shouted, stamping his feet, "and if you come any closer or try and hurt her, I will cut off your head and stick it up your ass!"

"Aww." Sam yelled as she stood on her tiptoes and kissed his cheek.

Juan felt the need to join in the reveal. "I have a crush on Derrick!" he screamed, his voice cracking.

Maddie couldn't help but look around to see the boy's reaction; he was turning a bright shade of red.

"Um, thanks?" Derrick called, uncertainly.

"I just thought you should know, in case I die!"

"Um, okay!"

It was surreal to Maddie—to them all, really—to see this playing out at this moment and in this way. Nervous giggles followed non-verbal screaming until Tyler spoke.

"I can see it!" He was pointing vigorously with his weapon.

"What is it?" Sandra had backed up further.

"Looks like a giant tick," Maddie said.

"*A what?*" Sam asked.

Insects weren't a problem on the moon; the only ones they'd brought with them were the kind that could help, like bees and butterflies. None of the kids had ever seen, or just as likely even heard about, the parasite. How lucky for them.

"It's a bug from earth. It attaches to

people, buries its mouthparts under the skin, and drinks your blood. They tend to carry a lot of diseases which can be passed to humans if attached for too long. Don't remember them being able to run, though." Maddie was looking at the beast; it really was very similar to the creature she knew. Razor-sharp mandibles formed pincers alongside a small mouth. Eight legs attached to a squat, round body, but for every similarity, there was a difference. For one, it was covered with fur, and what she figured were eyes were sitting atop two antennae rising high up on its back. And where ticks were tiny, some as small as the head of a pin, this one was on par with a baby elephant. Some of that could be attributed to the lighter gravity on the moon, but not all of it.

"*That* attaches to people? Wouldn't it suck them dry?" Tyler asked.

"They're not that big, not close, not ever."

Even with the distance between them, they could hear the click-clacking of its mouth opening and closing in anticipation of a meal. The beast moved much slower now, coming in a few steps then moving to the side, its eyes always swiveling to keep them in view no matter which way its body was pointed.

"Sandra, feel free to put a bullet in that thing." Maddie had her stick held high in case it charged.

"Don't want to waste the bullets."

"And yet you fired one into the dark? Now that you can see the thing, you're getting miserly?"

"I have six left. I think it would be best if I hit it squarely, don't you think?"

Maddie couldn't argue with that. The creature kept circling, coming in closer with each loop.

"What's it doing?" Tyler asked.

"Probing," Derrick said. "Looking for a weakness, seeing if we attack. We don't know it, and it doesn't know us."

"I think I like that it's afraid of us," Sam said.

"For now," Maddie replied. "Eventually, hunger or desire will force its hand."

Tyler screamed out and lunged forward twenty feet. The tick-beast, incredibly, backed up a few feet, in what looked like a fearful retreat. None of them suspected that it was merely getting into position to launch. It did. Twenty-five feet in a single jump, pouncing down dangerously close to where Tyler had stood before he wisely backed up. There was an explosion then a loud, grating, screeching noise as Sandra fired her gun. A small hole appeared in the monster's side and a brackish black fluid leaked out. It scrambled backward at a pace Maddie didn't think it was capable.

"It's so fast," Sam shivered.

"It can be hurt. If it can be hurt, it can be killed." Maddie said the words, but they weren't brimming with confidence. Sam was right; the animal moved much faster than they did. If it charged straight at them, some of them would be hurt or killed. It was the size of a cow, now Maddie was left wondering if it weighed as much. If it decided to jump and land on them, they'd suffer broken limbs at best…crushed to death at worst. Now that the animal had been wounded, it appeared more wary, but not completely sold on the idea of leaving its catch behind. It was once again circling. Blood still dripped from the wound, but it was not the cascade of life-giving fluid Maddie had hoped for.

She knew instinctually that aiming for the eyes was the best bet, but with them sitting high up and mobile, it would be a difficult shot, and if missed, the bullet would harmlessly whine off into the distance instead of slamming into the face or head, where it could potentially cause some severe damage. The animal charged in halfway before veering off at a sharp angle.

"Shit," Tyler said.

"I know," Maddie said. "It's trying to get us to run, to break apart so we'll be easier to hunt."

"No, I mean, I think I shit." Tyler had turned to look at the back of his pants.

"Smells like it," Juan said in all seriousness.

"Eww."

"Can we maybe worry about that later?" Maddie was having a hard time believing she needed to even say that.

"Teenagers, right?" Derrick voiced.

"Just because you say it like that doesn't make you not one," Sam told him. "She's still not going to date you."

"Wh…? That's not what I'm saying."

"Kids! The monster, remember?"

"We're not adults, we can multi-task," Tyler told her.

"Don't make me stab you and leave you as an offering."

The tick-beast was on its third trip around. It feinted an attack at least once every revolution.

"It's trying to lull us." Maddie was determined to kill it.

"Lull? Every time it moves forward, adrenaline rushes through me," Derrick said.

"And I bet it knows that. You can't

indefinitely produce adrenaline, and at some point, you'll crash."

"It can't be that smart, can it? It's a bug," Tyler said. "Earthworms seem pretty stupid to me. Bees are all right, I guess, but then they're not trying to eat me."

"Mosquitoes used to have hunting tactics. The male would make a loud buzzing sound with its wings near your head to keep you distracted while the female got its blood meal to fertilize its eggs."

"What's a mosquito?" Derrick asked.

The tick lunged again; this time it did not stop. Maddie braced for impact. She wished she'd taken a long enough piece of metal that she could have planted the end into the dirt and used it as a skewer. Her legs were shaking, her mind was screaming at her to run; she swung her blade as the beast crashed into her shoulder. The mandible missed ripping the side of her face open by mere inches. She flew into Sandra, and they both went sprawling to the ground. Tyler had jammed half of his makeshift sword into its body; he'd been dragged for thirty feet before the blade had come free.

Maddie was shaking off the effects of the collision and trying to get her bearings as stars swirled around her head. Juan was on the ground, unmoving; Sam was kneeling next to him while Derrick stood guard, and Tyler raced back to them.

"Get off me, you oaf!" Sandra shoved hard.

Maddie's whole side ached from where the thing had hit; her arm was pins and needles, and she could not feel her hand. She pushed up with her good one. "Where'd it go?" she asked, alarm in her voice. She stood slowly, favoring her left side.

"Underground, Maddie! It dove underground somehow!" Derrick was looking around wildly. If it had disappeared that quickly, it was very likely it could appear just as fast. Maddie felt the ground tremble, which was impressive, since her legs were still shaking.

"Sam, Derrick, move!" She knew it was going for Juan. "It's coming!"

Instead of running away, Sam grabbed Juan's arm and began to pull. Derrick, realizing what was happening, grabbed the other. Tyler was still too far away, and Maddie was restricted to using one side of her body. Small stones around her began to shake then roll as an earthen mound arose and grew as it moved closer to their location. The mouth and head of the beast sprouted from the ground where Juan had just lain, the mandibles closed quickly and dove back down. When it realized it had captured nothing but dirt, it once again rose up, this time using its eyes as a periscope, surveying the area around it. It took everything in before submerging.

Maddie's pain was immense, and she was convinced her shoulder was dislocated—that was something she could live with, but if it was broken, she didn't imagine a sling and bedrest was going to be a viable means of recovery. She couldn't shake the dead stump feeling of her left leg; it was as if she'd slept on it for four nights straight. She was dragging it behind her as she half-hoped to get to Sam and Derrick. Tyler had grabbed Juan and was propping him up.

"Move!" she urged, watching the shark fin-like dirt mound up and swim towards them.

The tick surfaced again, its mandibles making a loud popping sound. It missed again, but this time, it rose higher, looking around to see just how very close it was. Sandra had moved out in front and fired. A muffled, warbling cry could be heard emanating from the surface, like a giant buried alive, full of pain, terror, anguish and dirt. One of the antennas had been hit, the bullet ripping through the tissue and folding it over so that the thing's eye now rested uselessly against its body. Blood spouted from the wound like a high-pressure hose. Maddie wanted to celebrate, but while the injury was gruesome, she didn't think it was fatal. Either it died or they would; there was no chance they could outrun it, and nowhere to hide.

Juan had finally come to. He was in worse shape than Maddie, and she barely had control over half her body. Tyler was dragging his friend, not in any particular direction, just keeping him moving so that the all-seeing eye of the beast couldn't get a fix on them underground. It was after the fourth miss that the animal knew it was expending too much energy on the underground hunt and when it came up again, it stayed there, adjusted its line of sight right for the weakest of the group and charged. Still holding Juan, Tyler turned to face the monster, his sword arm raised, his teeth gritted, his face a mask of anger.

"No!" Sam yelled out as Derrick wheeled around to do what he could. It was a balsa wood covered window against a category five hurricane; the outcome was predetermined. Sandra, for all her narcissism, was advancing on the monster, arm extended, she hadn't fired yet as she tracked her target, wanting to make sure that every shot counted.

"Shoot!" Maddie begged as the thing thundered toward the kids. Even if she were to kill it now, it was traveling fast enough that its momentum would bowl straight through them. Sandra aimed, three quick shots, two were close to the head and one in the body. The animal lurched with each hit but had not stopped nor even seemed to slow, though the one remaining good eye turned toward Sandra before lolling backward. Tyler was tossed some ten feet in the air; Derrick had been winged and sent to the ground as well. Only Sam had gotten away clean; it was Juan that suffered the brunt of the attack. Maddie felt bile rise in her throat as she saw his broken body crumple to the ground. The tick thing had begun to dig down into the ground, but the injuries suffered had been too severe. It was halfway in before it stopped, its legs spasming wildly in its death throes.

"Fuck," Maddie hissed as she shuffled over to Juan. His entire side had been ripped open by the mandibles. Blood poured forth, pulsing through her hands as she tried to apply pressure, but the wound was larger than both of them. "Tyler, I need a shirt!" Juan was trying to cough, but all that came forth was a blood choked "*ungh*," sound. She didn't see any way he could survive this, but that wasn't going to prevent her from trying. Tyler ran over and tore his shirt off, sliding down next to his friend. His face was grim as he looked upon him.

He grabbed the other boy's hand. Juan's breath was hitching, his eyes wild with panic as his lungs filled with blood and he could not get enough air to breathe. He gripped Tyler's hand hard and pulled him close. Tyler buried his head next to Juan's and began to sob, his back heaving. Sam was crying as well. Derrick was taking out his frustration and grief on the beast's body as he repeatedly stabbed and beat it until he collapsed from exhaustion, tears cut channels through the grime on his face. Maddie's hands were bathed in Juan's rapidly cooling blood. The boy had passed some minutes before, but she could not bring herself to stop trying, as ineffectual as her actions were. She finally stood and wobbled away, unsure of what to do or where to go. She felt guilty for not protecting them well enough, and now one of her charges was dead. Tyler had not moved away from his friend. Sam had her head resting on his back and was crying with him as he rocked back and forth.

28

The Clock Tower

With the beating Gray took at the Citadel's massive doors, and the drain Burke had suffered so they could shut those doors, they couldn't sustain anything more than a jog, and that only lasted a minute at a time.

Through the outer ring of House Frost structures they ran, then they walked through a series of small forests and fields divided by a pond with bright water that rippled in the early dawn sun. They ran through the next section of taller towers, with their arched windows and stained glass, all connected by the same smooth blue flagstone thoroughfares. After almost an hour, they reached the soaring central clock tower.

Erupting from a large courtyard and ringed with twenty four water fountains all still shooting their jets without witness, feebly, into the air, the clock tower seemed more like an oversized headstone than a place of science, magic and wonder. A cyclopean headstone with a single, giant white eye, ringed by numbers in the center of its face. It wasn't the mile their father said it was, but still; the tower scraped at the sky.

At the tower's foot on each side was a replica door of the one that they'd entered through to get into the citadel, though the doors on the tower were a tenth the size. Beyond the tower to the north was the village on the shore of the lake that split the citadel wall open. Fog rolled in on the lower ground, seeping into the waterfront hamlet, and creeping up towards them.

The four beleaguered survivors stood in the courtyard, listening to the water bubble, taking the spectacle in.

"What's inside?" Arridon asked his dad.

"First floor is a big open room. Glass elevator going up in the center of the building, surrounded by the winding staircase. On the outer walls are the labs and research facilities. Very big...feels giant."

"What's an elevator?" Arridon asked.

"Anything to worry about?" Thistle added.

"You'll see what an elevator is. And on a normal day, no, nothing to worry about. Today...I can't say," he said with a small chuckle. "Could be sea monsters in there, for all I know."

"I can take a sea monster," Arridon said. "Poke 'em in the eyes and they all turn tail."

"I love your confidence, son," Gray said. "Now, we get in, and get to the highest floor the elevator goes. That'll put us right where the turbines are, and near the portals."

"Then we leave this world for another?" Thistle asked, her tone dreadful.

"Yes. We leave this world for one with a future," Gray answered. "And let's do that. Arridon, get the door."

"What's that down by the town? Near the water," Thistle said, pointing across the grassy expanse between the clock tower and the collection of dwellings on the shore of the lake that split the citadel's wall.

They all looked, squinting in the morning light.

"I see movement," Gray said.

"Oh shit," Arridon said. "They fucking swam around the wall. The demons…and that big armored bastard."

"They're right. I see them too," Burke said.

"Arridon, the door please," Gray said.

Arridon and Thistle shot to the door of the clock tower and each grabbed one of the large brass handles. With a lean and a twist, the handles rotated down, and the twin doors acquiesced to the brother and sister. As they parted, white light spilled outward, far brighter than the inner sanctum had any normal right to be.

Gray and Burke burst into the central chamber of the tower and the two who opened the doors pulled them shut. Just above the twin handles, set into the door, was an enormously complex lock. Gears upon gears interlaced into both doors, and when cranked…

Arridon grabbed the handle on the lock and spun the gear it connected to. Each of the army of mechanical pieces twirled and spun, sliding two bars out from inside the door itself to lock into the door opposite. He let go, and each of the connected gears flashed with a burning, golden glow. He grabbed the handles of the door for a yank. Nothing moved.

"Strong. Wow," he said.

"Try the elevator," Gray said, heading across the open tiled floor towards a column of glass that disappeared up into the open center of the tall structure.

"Well shit," Arridon said as he went slack-jawed at the sight of the translucent tower his father limped to the foot of. Surrounding that tower of glass was a spiraled set of stairs that wrapped around it like a snake, following it all the way to the ceiling where both disappeared. Beams of light came diagonally down from white rectangles mounted against the walls, creating the illusion that the central room was open to the outside sun. Despite that, the interior was as cool as their root cellar back in Mercy Point.

"Lock the other doors," Thistle said, pointing to the other three walls of the first floor.

Arridon saw that each side of the room they stood in had the same double doors, lockable with the same mechanical device. Thistle went to the door she was closest to, and Arridon did the same. Gears spun, light released, the doors sealed shut. He ran to the fourth and final door, and repeated the process as he heard his father belt out a string of curses.

"Damned elevator isn't working," Gray said as he slapped a metal panel on the single-story stone base of the column of glass.

"Still don't know what an elevator is, Dad," Arridon said.

"Stairs. Just go," he barked at his son.

The group of four ran to the wide staircase that wrapped around the tube of glass running from floor to very high ceiling and began their ascension to the upper floors. One step turned into ten, ten turned into thirty, and as the sweat poured down their backs, they had ascended nearly ten stories above the smooth stone floor. They paused their urgent climb to chug water from the skins Burke had filled for them at the temple. Arridon leaned upon the railing of a bridge that led to the side of the tower where an exposed walkway followed the perimeter of the building. Many doors were on the outside of the space, leading to rooms filled with who-knew-what.

A thunderous boom echoed up the hall, shaking the dust free.

"They're at the doors," Thistle said.

Another boom came. Then another, and then a rain of attacks as hundreds of smaller hands and feet or tentacles and claws smashed into the wood and iron. The cacophony of noise grew and grew until the lower, deeper sound of wood cracking and breaking joined in.

Without a word, their climb restarted. Frantic, hand over hand, foot after foot they stepped and pulled themselves up landing after landing, exposed and open to the drop to the first floor. Breathless, entirely soaked in sweat, they pushed and pushed upward as one of the doors below finally gave its all. With a crushing smash, the massive doors blew in off their hinges and fell, exposing the tender innards of House Frost's clock tower to the rampaging infection of the Bleed.

Scores of demons flooded in, searching for them.

Their cries of pain and hunger mixed and spilled up into the tower, echoing and invading the calm of the already terrified people trying their best to escape.

"WHERE ARE YOU, MY DEAR?" the thing that used to be Sebastian bellowed.

"Walk off the edge, you prick!" Thistle yelled over the railing down to it.

"I AM MADE OF WHAT IS BELOW THE EDGE…WOULDN'T YOU LIKE TO TASTE THE VOID?"

"He's going to make me throw up,"

Thistle muttered as they moved upward further. She looked over her shoulder at Burke, who trailed them. "Hurry up, Burke!"

"I'm trying."

The stairs started to vibrate as the demons began to float and claw their way up to them. With each step they passed, the stairs shook a bit more. In between the thousands of footfalls and claw-clicks, the booted stomps of the demon-knight Sebastian rang out, counting down the seconds until the servants of the Bleed reached them and ended their lives.

Arridon stopped, and when Burke got to his step, he slipped a long arm around the struggling man and gave him help. Arridon strained against the task, but he could not leave Burke to fall behind. He would not. He wouldn't leave a stranger behind to suffer the demons, and he certainly wouldn't leave Burke. Not after what he'd done for Arridon's family.

"Ten stories," Gray managed with too little air. "Then there are more doors."

"Dad, they fucking smashed those magical doors downstairs like you used to crush wine bottles. I don't think it's enough," Arridon said, helping Burke.

"We just need it to last until you both get through the turbine, or we get to the portal. Seconds. We need seconds," he said, rubbing his pistol-wielding hand across his burning chest.

No one had any spare lung power to say anything else. All they could bear was to climb, hands and feet at the same time, and try to ignore the hideous laughter of Sebastian as he and his army of infected marched upward and onward. They closed the gap at a frenetic pace.

"Six stories," Gray managed. "Two more," he said a minute later.

By now they crawled. Legs made of stove coals, lungs filled with sour mucus, unable to give precious air fast enough. The things climbing had no such issues. With mutated anatomies made for hunting and killing, they pressed upward without abatement, starving for flesh and souls, eager to feed their master.

"Here," Gray said as they reached the final landing. To their side, the glass tube they'd been ascending beside disappeared into the ceiling, but the stairwell they climbed reached a lower entryway. A thick door made of steel blocked the way, but with a crank on the handle by Thistle, it opened inward.

More stairs lay beyond, leading up into a dark room.

"Up one," Gray said.

Arridon pushed Burke through the narrow opening and ushered his sister behind him. His father followed, and when all three were up the stairs to the level above, he stepped through and yanked the heavy iron door shut. He slid the locking bolt closed and took a second to steady his breathing. He went up the steps two at a time, emerging into a small room with a steel door mounted right where the glass cylinder would've surfaced. Opposite that were two more doors, also both made of metal. One was plain; the other was adorned with runes and etchings of gears, levels, and other mechanical shapes.

"That one," Gray said, pointing towards the special-looking door.

As they went to it, the sound of flesh and claws on metal rang out down the stairs.

The demons were just yards behind them.

Thistle wrenched the ornate door open, setting free a deep and low vibration emanating from something inside the room. Along with the sound came a chest-churning vibration and a powerful front of warm air. Blue and red light flickered in the space beyond.

"Go ahead," their father directed.

The four entered the large room beyond,

and after Arridon fastened the same mechanical lock, he turned and stopped.

A massive machine — larger than anything built by man he'd ever seen, save for the ships that sailed the sea — took up the entirety of the wide room, twice his height and shaped like a cylinder tipped on its side. Rotating discs of translucent red and blue light orbited the round length of the device, moving in concert with mechanical rings. The inner core of the cylinder was hollow, large enough for a person to walk through. The device thrummed and vibrated with power as the room glowed with surreal light.

Their father spoke. "All you need to do is walk through the turbine. Go through this end; the magic will awaken any talents you might have by the time you exit. One at a time."

"Will it hurt?" Thistle asked.

"I think a little," Gray said. "But my girl is so strong."

"Want me to go first?" Arridon offered her.

"No. If anyone in this family is getting cock-shrinking power, it's going to be me first," she said, and strode over to the nearest end of the whirling tube of god-tech. She stopped at the threshold, took a deep breath, and walked into the guts of the tunnel of light.

Arridon held his breath.

Through the walls, and through the floor, he felt and heard a thumping. A groan of metal protesting force shrieked through the upper levels, and Arridon flinched.

"They're at the first door," he said over the vibration of the turbine. As he spoke, the metallic rings running in concert with the spools of light spun faster and faster. The noise grew to match.

"Go," his dad said, pointing to the machine.

Arridon sprang up and ran to the place his sister had entered. When he reached the spot, the interior of the tunnel transfixed his eyes. The lights inside were a hundred times more intense. The colors were far more varied, and somehow transcended crisp definition. They glowed beyond what was visual. He felt their power through sight, and something else; a sense he'd never used before. A sense that told him his sister was walking around the outside of the machine back towards the room's entrance, safe and sound.

He stepped forward into the thaumaturgical turbine and let the lights cascade onto him, and into him. Two steps later, he exited the opposite side of the turbine, heart calm, mind settled, and body refreshed. Arridon felt like he's just awakened from the best night of sleep he'd ever had, but with no memory of walking the fifty steps of the tunnel.

Resounding booms of something hitting the door of the room brought him into the moment, and he ran back to the other side of the machine where his father, sister, and Burke stood. Thistle stood with fists clenched at her side, jaw set, staring at the door as it shook in the frame. Arridon joined them, acutely aware of the movement of air on his skin, and the strong, imposing presence of the walls nearby. Somehow, he imagined them as one in the same, and built a wall out of air in his mind's eye, just inches from his body.

"Whatever powers you had latent are now awakened," Gray said. "You might already have some idea what they are. Your mother said it was intrinsic, like knowing how to walk or talk."

"I think I know," Arridon said, thinking of his walls of air.

"Me too," Thistle said, fists still clenched.

"I can sense them," Burke said. "Like... feeling the sun on your face, even when your eyes are closed."

"Good. Now, we need to ascend one more level to the clockworks. Your mother said the portals are there. The stairs to go up one more level are back in that hall, through whatever is trying to beat down that door."

"Open it," Thistle said, but they didn't have to. The gears and their spell-seal failed under the assault, and the door they'd held shut burst inward, setting loose a wave of mutated flesh, hungry for their destruction.

Thistle was the stone the wave broke upon.

The teenage girl stood firm and lifted her fists up as if she were going to fight them barehanded. Then she did. Sort of.

She swung at them from several yards distant, and her punches landed with invisible, concussive force. From afar, she pulverized them with magical force, each blow mimicking her movements, each blow savagely powerful. Thistle smashed one after another into the walls and floor, breaking skulls, ribcages, and entire bodies apart. She grunted in anger with each strike, building into a scream as she laid waste to everything that came through the doorway.

Then nothing more appeared, and she ended her wrath. Thistle turned and faced the three men, each standing with mouths agape.

"Now would be a good time to go find

those stairs," she said.

29

London

It was dark. And hot. Really bloody hot.

Jenny didn't know how she'd survived the fall, or if she'd even survived at all. It was pitch black, but she sensed that everything was back upright and in the right place: the machine, the walls of this small room, the door through which she'd entered. The floor was level again. *Perhaps I've found some kind of protected bunker?* she wondered, though quite why a bunker would have been built at the top of the tallest building in London was anyone's guess. It made about as little sense as everything else that had happened to her over the last few days.

She had to get out.

She felt around in the darkness for the door, ready to fight through the remains of London. Maybe she'd just set off a bomb? Perhaps she'd unleashed a weapon that had neutralized the Bleed and eradicated the demon threat? Wishful thinking, she knew, but that was all she had left.

Jenny let herself out and found herself in a long gray corridor. It was too long and too old to be where she was. Her only option was to follow it, so she walked with her back pressed up against the wall, ready to face more demons around the next corner.

But there were no demons here.

Was this an office block? A hospital or prison?

Christ, it was so bloody hot.

An elevator. She got in and pressed the button for the ground floor. She braced for carnage, but instead found herself in an opulent, marble-floored hotel reception.

Jenny had never been to Australia before, but she was there now.

She left the hotel and walked out into

bright sunlight and stifling summer heat. She crossed a main road, weaving between cars, then stepped out onto golden sand. A beach. Exhausted, she walked down to the ocean, and there she saw only blue-green water, no trace of red.

When Jenny turned back, she recognized the city from images she'd seen on TV and online. This was the Gold Coast. Surfer's Paradise on the east coast of Oz. *But why here?* It must have had something to do with the collapse of the Shard, she decided. It didn't feel like this was where she was supposed to have ended up, though it could have been worse.

Dressed for the London weather, she stuck out like a sore thumb. She discarded her dust and grime covered jacket and jumper and kicked off her boots, then walked aimlessly back across the sand and into a café.

"What'll it be?" the guy serving asked her.

"Coffee. Black. Strong."

She took her drink without acknowledgement or payment and wandered through the café towards the large screen TV fixed to the opposite wall.

THE UNITED KINGDOM DEAD.

THE BLEED CONTINUING TO ADVANCE ACROSS EUROPE.

IT'S ONLY A MATTER OF TIME: AUSTRALIA, AND THE WORLD, HAS LESS THAN A MONTH.

The date on the TV was wrong. It was three weeks ahead of where it should have been…unless she just lost the best part of a month traveling several thousand miles in what seemed a heartbeat. It didn't make a difference.

By luck or design, she had a matter of days left to stop the Bleed.

30

The Moon

DAY THREE / 7:07 PM

Derrick was sitting down, facing the other way, his head in his hands. Sandra–while not completely unaffected–displayed no outward signs of her feelings, which were predictably more concern for her well-being than for that of the deceased boy. As far as she was concerned, his troubles were over, and there was not much sense in wasting any more time on him. She wasn't entirely without compassion; there would perhaps be a time to feel sadness in the future, but right now they needed to move on. It had already been proven there were monsters around here, and the scent of fresh blood could attract predators for miles.

Tyler gently moved Sam away as he stood. He wiped his face with his arm and began to dig at the dirt with his stick. Sam stood and helped.

Sandra walked over to Maddie and voiced her concerns.

"For once, we agree, but I don't think they're going to listen. We might as well help so we can get out of here faster."

Sandra didn't move, not that she'd expected her to. The pins and needles' effect in Maddie's arm and leg were beginning to wear off and was being replaced with pain, fortunately not the all-encompassing pain of a dislocated joint. She figured if she lived, she'd be all right. The big question was: would she live? She wordlessly began to dig next to a determined Tyler. Derrick reluctantly joined in. In under an hour, they had a big enough hole to lay their friend to rest. Once he was under a mound of dirt and stone, they joined hands while Sam led a small prayer.

Much to Maddie's surprise, Sandra hadn't said one disparaging word to them the whole time.

They left the area with no set destination in mind, each knowing that they could not stay there. Tyler continually broke down as Sam did her best to comfort him. Derrick was in close to a state of shock, Maddie's thoughts were so jumbled she couldn't do much beyond plod along. Sandra, by default, was leading the downtrodden group.

"We'll stop here for a rest," she told them as she leaned against a large rock. She bent over and rubbed her calves and thighs. Not a word was spoken as the rest of the group sought out a spot to sit. The ten minute respite turned into twenty-four hours. They hadn't set up guards; on some level they cared about being attacked, but fatigue, hunger and extreme thirst can sap the will out of the hardiest of people. Coupled with the loss of their friend, most in the group were already losing hope and desire.

Maddie woke up to what she figured was the next morning, though the light had in no way changed. She had a coughing fit that induced panic within her when she had difficulty breathing. "I need water so bad," she managed to rasp out. "We have to get moving."

"What's the point?" Tyler was lying face up, looking into the sky. "We're all going to die here. I'd rather it be by thirst than what…" He broke down and began to cry again. Maddie noticed no tears were forthcoming; he had no moisture within him to release.

"We have to. We're still alive. Juan…" Sam choked up. "Juan would want us to."

"Would he? He's not here to tell us what he wants, is he?" Tyler was angry and lashing out.

"It's not her fault." Derrick stuck up for his sister, but the fight was already out of the other boy.

"Up, let's go." Maddie tapped his shoulder. He got up and they started moving. "We're not dead until we're dead."

"As good a morale-boosting speech as any." Sandra was by Maddie's side. She wasn't sure if it was sarcasm or not, and right that very moment, she didn't care. Of all her problems, Sandra was the least of them.

After a few more miles of walking, Maddie wanted to recant her statement. She was having difficulty moving her joints as she became even more dehydrated. Her steps were halting and every movement caused pain. Maybe Tyler was right; what was the point? She could just as easily die here as wherever she ended up dropping, and she'd suffer less discomfort.

"There's something up ahead." Sam wanted to be excited, but she couldn't find it in her. Maddie was on the verge of saying screw it and sitting down, when she managed to look to where the girl had pointed. There was indeed something ahead, but what it was, she did not know.

"I...I think that's water!" Derrick lurched forward. "No, it is!" He began to run with a sideways gate, unable to orient himself correctly.

"Mirage," Maddie wanted to yell, but her throat was closing. "Fuck it. A water-filled mirage is better than what I'm living." She followed; Tyler was last, and begrudgingly so.

By the time Maddie got there, Derrick was up to his waist in the illusion, splashing it around like a toddler their first time in a kiddie pool. He dipped his head down and drank heavily.

"Is it poisonous?" Maddie could hardly believe she'd asked the ridiculous question.

"I'm not dead yet!" Derrick was smiling.

Maddie joined him, unable to contain the joyous feelings that exploded within and without her as she stepped into the cool liquid. Sandra had fallen face-first at the shore and was slurping noisily, Sam dived in like a swan and came up laughing like a loon. Tyler had to be coaxed but eventually joined.

Maddie had a bellyache from swallowing so much of the water, but other than that, after fifteen minutes, she'd yet to feel any ill-effects, if it indeed was poisonous. She'd dragged her waterlogged self to shore and was contentedly looking up. When she finally sat up, she saw the source of the unlikely oasis; there was a ribbon of water leading away from a small waterfall some few hundred yards away, yet another peculiarity on a surface that should have been devoid of all features.

"Get your fill, we need to get out of here!" She doubled over, as now that thirst was sated, hunger forged its way to the front.

"We could stay here, at least for a little while," Sam argued.

Maddie shook her head. "No can do. We know there are other things out here, and this here's the local watering hole."

"Oh." Sam stood up straight and looked around as that thought settled home.

"Besides, something is weird about that waterfall; I think we should check it out."

"Go then." Sandra was lying back.

"Sure thing. Say hello to whatever giant

crocodile-thing might live around here," Maddie told her, now wishing she'd taken a few moments to, perhaps not strip, but at the minimum have taken her boots off. She was completely soaked and walking was going to get uncomfortable real soon. Tyler was better for the water, though it only served to put aside his grief for the moment.

"I hate you," Sandra grunted as she got up.

"Are you seeing this?" Sam was pointing to the waterfall. It appeared to be moving in slow motion, presumably due to the lack of gravity. But that wasn't what she was referring to. Behind the water there was a line of brightness. "It's a cave—it has to be!"

Maddie wasn't so sure, and besides, caves were darker, not brighter. If it was lit, then there was a bizarre natural phenomenon happening or something in there had the capability to produce light. Maybe they could get help; maybe somehow they could make it out of this mess. She was excited at the prospect as they approached, but she felt anxious once she reached the opening; she did not know what to expect as she walked through the falling water.

31

The Great Goodbye

"Be careful, son," Gray said to him. The fear audible in his father's voice was as palpable as the look on his face.

Arridon walked past his sister and over the carnage she'd created. His boots slipped, and crunched on the gore, but he ignored the unpleasantness. She'd given them an opening to move, and he wasn't going to waste it. The feeling inside him — whatever the turbine had done to him —

grew with each step and he *knew* he had the ability to face whatever came. The realization made him smile.

In the room with the metal door, where the thing called an elevator had an exit, stood several hesitant demons of the Bleed. They swung their multi-jointed, sharp arms as Arridon entered the room. He watched as rivers of saliva fell from their misshapen, fang-filled mouths. Their hazy, cancerous eyes narrowed into evil slits, and the young man returned the expression. As the stalemate broke and they leapt at him, Arridon set free a power within him.

With a casual wave of his hand, a gust of heat and power flowed from his body, solidifying the air just a few feet in front of the closest monster. The naked humanoid with errant, spiky tufts of fur on its body, hit the invisible barrier with its head, and with a crack broke its neck on the conjured wall. As its body fell to the floor, twisted, clawed hands clacking on the stone, the next mutant did the same, smashing its chitinous, insectoid body on the steely surface of hardened air.

"Move now," Arridon said, keeping his hand in the air, angled to match the location of the wall. As he moved the hand slightly, he felt the wall's position change to align. He watched as the group of monsters hit the wall over and over, pushed back or forward as he moved it.

Behind him, the other three moved into the room and towards the back.

"You two are amazing," Gray said. "Your mother would be so proud."

Thistle and Arridon both remained silent.

Gray went to a smooth part of the wall and examined it, looking for something on the surface. After several seconds of running his shaking fingers along the wooden bottom border, he found a switch, and depressed it.

A section of the wall recessed then slid to the side, revealing yet another stairway. Over his shoulder, Arridon saw lights flicker to life wherever the stairwell led. More magic of the gods.

"Dispatch them, and follow," Gray said as Burke and Thistle disappeared up the stairs.

Arridon returned his attention to the wall of force he'd created. He thought about how exactly to use his awakened powers to destroy the monsters and came up with a solution. He waved his other hand and allowed the magic to create another wall behind the monsters smashing into the first. He turned to face the creatures—mindful to keep his hands oriented properly so the wall didn't change angles—then brought his two hands together with a mighty clap.

The two walls of force came together with a thunderous boom, obliterating the assaulting demons into slabs of bloody pulp. What remained of them slid down his wall to the floor, leaving hanging streaks of bone and blood in the air. Arridon closed his hand and interrupted the flow of power from his body, ending his rule over the nearby air. Warmth rushed back into his body, and he felt lightheaded for a second. The floating blood lost its grip on his wall and fell to the tile with a wet slap.

He ran to the stairs and pulled the sliding door closed. It locked into its place with a hiss and a click. Arridon scrambled up to join his family and Burke. He stopped when he saw the back of the clock.

"Whoa," he whispered.

Walking on the flagstone streets far below, the white clock face on the tower's peak looked huge. The numbers had seemed tiny from so far below, but here, in the cavernous space of the clock and its machinery, the numbers looked to be the size of trees, and the clock face itself was larger than most of the buildings inside Citadel Frost. Behind it all, moving as if in a timeless, well-rehearsed dance, a dozen giant gears spun in all manner of angles and speeds. They ticked off the seconds and managed the process of time here in Citadel Frost.

Below the enormous machinery hanging in the air of the massive room stood a bizarre contraption of ornately arranged rings. Each golden circle grew out of a raised steel and gold platform, arranged one inside another, though tilted at crazy-making angles. The etched rings were as tall as Thistle and as thick as a man's thigh. The odd looking piece of god-tech could've been a sculpture in the garden of a wealthy and eccentric king, but in this room…it had to have great purpose.

They gathered at the base of the short platform the idle rings were atop.

"Is this the portal you spoke of?" Burke asked.

"I think so," Gray said. "Based on how they were described to me, I believe this is it."

"What do we do?" Thistle asked. "You said it'd work for us. How do we make it work for us?"

"I don't know. She said it would activate when you approached. Maybe there's something you need to touch? An activation rune, a button?"

"What's a button?" Arridon asked.

"You touch it to summon an elevator,"

his dad replied as he searched the perimeter of the platform for something that might activate the device.

"That's not funny," Arridon said. "You're keeping me in the dark on purpose."

"It's pretty funny," Thistle said, mirroring her father's search on the opposite side of the apparatus.

"At a time like this, I can't believe my own family would mock me," Arridon said with a sigh. He turned his attention to the remainder of the room below the massive clock face and suspended machinery powering the movements of the tree-trunk hands and walked to the brick wall that ascended the four or five stories up the vaulted ceiling above and searched the shelves and desks there for clues. He found piles of tantalizing evidence of magic and madness, but nothing directly helpful.

"I wish I could read the gods' tongue," he said while flipping through a massive tome filled with drawings of clockwork parts and constructions. "They knew so much."

"And you'll know it too, in good time," Gray said, still searching. "Just need to get you through this portal."

Banging erupted at the door below.

"What?" Arridon blurted, setting the

book down. "That door was hidden. How'd they find it?"

"Scent," Burke guessed. "I imagine the Bleed gives its hunters better senses than ours."

The banging continued and grew in volume as the pursuers at the door became frustrated by its resistance. This door wasn't the equal to the others, and within seconds they could hear the groan of the metal's failure. The monsters would be through it and into the room long before they had the portal to safety opened.

"I'll hold them off," the young half-god said, trotting to the opening in the tile floor that led to the door being smashed open. He had complete confidence. He had magic now. "Keep searching."

"Dad," Thistle said. "What are we looking for?"

"A switch, a button, a rune. Something that your mother might've had put here when we only had Arridon as a little baby. Something I would recognize."

Thistle returned her attention to the discs standing on their edge atop the raised dais of the device. She stepped up as the banging below intensified, and dared to touch the precious-seeming metal. Her warm fingers ran along the etched words on the cold metal. Thistle followed the words from the tops of the circles all the way around to the bottoms, and then switched to another of the many rings. She flinched when the sound of metal bending erupted up the stairs near where her brother stood. She looked over at him and took a deep breath. The rings captured her attention again.

"Do you see anything?" her dad asked.

"No, but...I just got this weird sense that the words on these rings contain the answer. Can you read them?"

"I can," Gray said, and hopped up on the central circular platform with a wince. As the metal door groaned further, straining from the tidal wave of murder pressing through it, he produced the pistol then started to examine the markings. "Magical gibberish, magical gibberish... names of places I've never heard."

"Look for something special, right? Something that would have meaning to only you," Thistle said.

Gray continued as the smashing at the door built to a crescendo. He switched to the back side of the first ring, and skimmed the words there. He then went to the second ring, and its back, and then the third ring.

"Come on," Thistle said. "There's got to be something."

"I'm not getting anything that's making sense. Lots of numbers, more places. Names I don't recognize," he said, then leaned on one of the rings. The empty disc shifted, moving forward away from his weight on a smooth trajectory. It glided around, carried forward by his momentum until it came to rest angled slightly askew now. "Wait. The letters align across the discs differently... and...shit, the etchings are different too. The metal has changed. I think we just need to spin these rings until we get the right combination."

The door gave way. Arridon lifted his hand into the flat shape of a blade, as he'd done before, and he felt the power rush out of his limb, creating the invisible barrier again. This time, he angled his hand to be flat, putting a lid on the floor where the stairs would enter the clockwork room.

The fury of the monsters smashed into his magical ceiling, and his hand lifted as if they'd punched up at it physically. He forced his hand downward, pressing the horizontal wall of energy he'd summoned against the floor, sealing the creatures inside the cramped stairwell. They slathered and hissed, screaming half obscenities at him as they scratched and clawed at his barrier.

His palm itched.

"Something's different," Arridon called out. "My wall isn't as strong."

Burke appeared at his side. "Your reservoir is lower. Magic is no different from physical stamina. You can expend it. The more you use it, though, like a muscle, the stronger it gets."

"At this rate I'll be able to lift boulders by nightfall," Arridon said, pressing his hand down with increased pressure.

"Best hurry," Burke hollered to Gray and Thistle. "Our gentleman sorcerer is nearing his magical sunset for the day."

"Spin that one there," Gray said to Thistle who responded by pushing on one of the rings. It spun around, realigning in a new way, creating new words and combinations. Gray read the creation, looking for a solution but finding none.

Thistle searched too, searching for words that she could recognize. Nothing came out to her; it was all god-gibberish. But then...near the floor..."What's this?" she asked her father. "These images, they're...flickering. I can see them, then I cannot."

Gray leaned over and looked where she pointed. He laughed. "It says, 'home,' in the god-tongue. Try touching it, and speaking the word aloud." He said the word in the gods' tongue for her to hear, and stepped back out of the ring.

Thistle knelt to the floor, placed her fingertips on the cold metal, then repeated the word.

The machine she stood atop flashed to life, sending a pulse of warm, fire-like light around the circles on the floor then across the rings in the air. The floor beneath her started to vibrate, and she stood and exited the platform's center. As she did, the rings began to spin opposite one another, faster and faster until they shown with a golden light from within and became invisible. Their eyes saw form a translucent, golden globe of light.

"IT WILL BE SO LONELY WITHOUT YOU," a dark and familiar voice said from the stairwell.

Arridon looked from the portal to the stairs and saw the hulking, armored form of the thing that was Sebastian striding up the now-empty stairwell. In his right hand he held a two-handed greatsword. He lifted the tip with great care, and aimed its point at the center of Arridon's barrier. He pressed the sword into it, and Arridon felt a sharp stick of pain in the center of his palm.

"Ouch, shit!" the young man said. "I can feel that."

"YOUR MAGIC WAS MADE TO FAIL," Sebastian said to him, pushing his sword higher and higher, piercing the magical wall with minimal effort. "AND LO, WATCH AS IT DOES, HALFBREED." Sebastian drew the sword back out of the wall, and returned it with an upwards slash. Arridon knew what that blow was going to feel like before it landed, and he gritted his teeth.

The blade slashed upward, ripping through the hardened, invisible air, tearing into Arridon's hand at the same time, splitting skin and muscle and nearly severing the hand in half. He screamed out in pain and clutched at his ruined left hand. His barrier disappeared, and Sebastian strode up into the room with nothing between them but the time it took to cross the distance. Sebastian and Burke backpedaled away from the Bleed's giant avatar and his blood-soaked sword.

The god-cannon in Gray's hand thundered, and Sebastian reeled back, his armor pierced easily by the impact of the weapon's fire. The giant staggered, forced to take a knee by the shot, then as a second and third shot smashed into his chest, the knight-demon bent over, slapping a bone-mailed gauntlet to the floor. Black and green ichor spilled from his chest, spreading like lava upon the smooth tile surface. He coughed, and laughed.

"Is this funny?" Gray screamed at him, pulling the trigger, sending another projectile into his armor at the shoulder. "Laugh now, you piece of shit!" he fired again, puncturing a hole into Sebastian's neck.

"HA HA HA," the monster encased in bone laughed. In a fluid movement, the general of the Bleed scraped his hand through the puddle of his own blood, and flung it at Burke, who had been watching, shocked.

The swamp-colored blood hit Burke in the face, and he cried out. His hands shot up to his face to wipe the offensive substance away, but when his fingers touched the blood, all they did was smear it around. He looked to Gray then Arridon, and by then, his eyes had already undergone the change. The glowing pip of hellish light had taken root in the black center. Tears of defeat ran down his cheek, and then he snarled in rage at Arridon.

Gray's pistol thundered twice rapidly, tearing a hole in Burke's chest then his head. He went to the hard stone floor, dead before his face bounced off of it. His body twitched several times and Arridon saw the man's lifeless hand metamorphose into a canine-like claw.

"Got any left for me?" Sebastian said,

his bellow gone.

Gray spun, and pulled the trigger on the pistol. It clicked and did nothing. He looked to Arridon. "Jump into the portal," he whispered. "Live good lives."

Sebastian's blade carved Gray in half across the waist, nearly severing his torso from his hips and legs. Gray doubled over at the spine, spilling his guts to the floor before toppling onto his back in a spreading pool of his own blood.

Thistle let free a scream that frightened Arridon. Full of rage, and sorrow, and *menace*, she leapt through the air, higher than possible, cocking a fist back. Arridon felt the tremendous, incredible power blossom inside her, and when she punched that fist downward at Sebastian in his armor, it hit him with the power of a battering ram. He crumpled into a crushed ball of bone and rotten flesh, and was shoved down the stairwell like garbage into a compost heap.

Thistle landed on the floor and immediately went to her knees, her body and magic drained by the godlike strike she'd released.

Arridon wasted no time and went to her. He scooped her up and walked her towards her father's dying body and the portal. She had no strength left, and the burden of moving her taxed him. When they reached their dad, he was stiff, and his breathing shallow and ragged. He looked over to his children with tears in his eyes. He smiled.

"I did it," he whispered. "I got you to the door. You'll be safe."

"Yeah, dad, you did," Arridon said, his voice shaking and his eyes erupting with hot tears.

"I'm sorry," he added. "For failing you for so long."

"It's okay," Thistle said, dropping down to embrace him. "We didn't know."

"No, no," he said, holding up a hand weakly. "Don't touch my blood. Just go. Let me have this victory. Step into the portal, go to wherever your mother wanted you sent."

The rejection sent Thistle into a fit of sobbing, and Gray's face of pure sadness soured at it even worse. Seeing his daughter cry felt like he'd been cut in half again.

"We'll be back. We'll avenge you," Arridon said, trying to say something fierce, trying to feel brave and strong.

"I'll take my vengeance in the form of grandchildren," Gray said, crying. "Never return. Flee, and keep our family alive. You could be the sole survivors of House Frost, and all of this world, so do not let our legacy perish. I'm so damned proud of you. Go. Take your mother's pistol and this magazine of bullets and go before they return."

Arridon grabbed the pistol and the rectangular thing his father called a magazine with his good hand. He tucked the weapon into his waistband, and the magazine into his pocket. He and Thistle — both sobbing with body-wracking anguish now — stood, and ascended the step to the portal's level. The spinning rings of light had now coalesced into a seamless sphere of perfect golden illumination. As they gazed into the center, their vision became hazy, and the sights that could be seen inside, and beyond, shifted and changed. They saw a white room with a round table, then a forest glen. Images of a cold and desolate tundra appeared, then a sterile, square room filled with tables made of steel. The longer they looked, the more the visions changed.

"Promise me we'll always stick together," Arridon said to her.

She gripped his uninjured hand tight — tighter than ever — and she nodded at him. "Always. You and me. Always."

He kept crying, but he nodded, and the two of them stepped into the portal, disappearing from the world.

Gray died alone, but in victory.

The sound of blood dripping filled the clockwork room for some time.

"They'll be back. They always come back," the crushed Sebastian said. "They always think they can win."

Epilogue 1

Nowhere We Know

Jenny was completely alone on the wrong side of the world. With no money, no friends, no phone, and no way of getting anywhere fast, she didn't know what to do. The enormity of everything that had happened over the last few days was a weight that was almost impossible to bear. After walking the red-hot streets of Surfer's Paradise for hours, going around in circles, she just needed to rest.

The clockwork room was the only place that offered her any kind of comfort and familiarity. She worked her way back to the hotel and slipped into the lift in the middle of a pack of tourists, feeling as conspicuous as she knew she looked. It was a relief when she made it back to the top floor and she was alone again. She found the door to the room and let herself inside.

She'd barely taken a step into the shadows when she was attacked. Someone grabbed her from behind and wrapped an arm around her neck. They viciously pulled her head back and hissed into her ear, "Who the fuck are you?"

"I'm Jenny."

"Where's your damn suit?"

"What suit?"

"Don't get smart. How have you survived out here just wearing that?"

Jenny elbowed her assailant in the ribs and pushed her away.

The woman looked out through the open door, then ran along the corridor outside. Jenny chased after her, figuring whoever this was, she'd likely had as little control over her arrival in Australia as she herself had. "So where exactly did you come from?" Jenny asked. "Where do you think you are?"

"The fucking moon, where else?"

Epilogue 2

No One We Know

Thistle thought she could hear her brother's voice, but it was lost in the roar of churning water. *Water?* She'd been holding Arridon's hand, but when she looked he wasn't there. Her head was spinning, and nothing made sense. She knew she was no longer where she'd been, but where she'd ended up was anyone's guess.

She felt drunk, but she hadn't been drinking. Breathless, but she hadn't been running. She stumbled forward, moving from light towards darkness, using the water noise to guide her. She fell through the water flow and ended up on her hands and knees, head spinning.

Other voices now. Not Arridon.

"Derrick, do you see what I see?'

"I see a girl, sis, but I don't know who the hell she is.

Arridon thought he must have blacked out. He felt sick and could barely walk in a straight line. When he left the clockwork room his eyes were hit by more light than he could stand. He staggered towards the nearest window and stood there in disbelief.

Where the hell was he? No longer in any citadel he recognized, that was for sure.

He looked around for Thistle, but she wasn't there.

Maybe she'd gone on ahead of him?

There was the outline of a metal door in a metal wall. Another elevator? There was a small arrow pointing down. He pressed it, and moments later the door slid open. Still not thinking straight, he walked in. The doors closed, and he dropped so far and so fast it felt like he'd left his stomach at the top.

Arridon walked out into a place filled with more people than he'd ever seen in his life before. They were dressed in the strangest clothes, and no two were the same. They spoke in a multitude of tongues and used words the likes of which he'd never heard before. They walked around him and into him, cursed him and laughed at him. More of them went past at speed, packed together in metal boxes on wheels.

This world was filled with bright lights and noise. He turned around to look for Thistle and to try and get back to the clockwork room.

The building from which he'd just emerged seemed to stretch up into the gray sky forever. It was tapered and pointed, like a shard of glass.

Someone grabbed his arm. He turned around fast, ready to fight.

"Take it easy, halfsie," the man said. "I'm on your side."

"Who are you?"

"My name's Phil. I work in insurance—that's what I let the rest of them think, anyway. Who are you?"

"Arridon."

"Nice to meet you, Arridon. I got wind that someone was coming in via the clockwork room and thought I'd come to meet you."

"What is this place?"

"London, and if I'm honest, you picked a particularly crappy place to end up. The world's on edge, Arridon. War is on the horizon."

About David Moody

DAVID MOODY first self-published **HATER** in 2006, and without an agent, succeeded in selling the film rights for the novel to Mark Johnson (producer, Breaking Bad) and Guillermo Del Toro (director, The Shape of Water, Pan's Labyrinth). His seminal zombie novel **AUTUMN** was made into an (admittedly terrible) movie starring Dexter Fletcher and David Carradine. Moody has an unhealthy fascination with the end of the world and writes books about ordinary folks going through absolute hell. Find out more at *www.davidmoody.net*.

RUPTURE; THE BLEED: BOOK ONE

Contact: david@davidmoody.net
Web: www.davidmoody.net
Facebook: facebook.com/davidmoodyauthor
Twitter: @davidjmoody
Instagram: davidmoodyauthor

About Chris Philbrook

Chris Philbrook is the Amazon and Audible best-selling author of the **Adrian's Undead Diary** series, **The Reemergence** series, **COLONY LOST**, and the fantasy world of **Elmoryn**. Chris has several years of experience working in game development and editing as well as writing fiction for several major game design companies.

Chris has authored ten novels in the horror/post-apocalyptic series **Adrian's Undead Diary**, plus five urban fantasy novels in **The Reemergence** series and three dark fantasy novels in **The Kinless Trilogy**. His first science fiction novel; **COLONY LOST** has received stellar reviews. He writes young adult sci-fi under the pen name W.J. Orion.

Chris calls the wonderful state of New Hampshire his home. He is an avid reader, writer, role player, miniatures game player, video game player, husband, and father to two little girls.

Contact: Chris@thechrisphilbrook.com
Web: www.thechrisphilbrook.com
Facebook: facebook.com/PhilbrookAuthor
Twitter: @PhilbrookAuthor
Instagram: @PhilbrookAuthor

About Mark Tufo

Mark Tufo is an International Best Selling author of Horror, Science Fiction, Apocalyptic Survivalist Fiction, Young Adult Dystopian and Paranormal fiction. He has penned over forty books, sold over a million copies, and been translated into five languages. His books have won numerous awards and have spent weeks in the number one slot on the Amazon charts.

All of his titles are available on iTunes, Audible and Barnes and Noble through Devil Dog Press LLC.

His longest running series, **Zombie Fallout**, now in its thirteenth instalment, is currently being adapted for television at the anticipation of his fans. See the book trailer here: *https://www.youtube.com/watch?v=FUQEUWy-v5o&feature=youtu.be*

Contact: mark@marktufo.com
Web: www.marktufo.com
Facebook: https://www.facebook.com/Mark-Tufo-133954330009843/
Twitter: @zombiefallout
Instagram: @mark_tufo

Printed in Great Britain
by Amazon